KRYSALIS

David Lescombe, one of Whitehall's top civil servants, believes he has a happy marriage to Anna,
a successful barrister. But when Anna disappears
and, at the same time, Krysalis, a unique NATO
file, is removed from David's safe at their home,
security services on both sides of the Atlantic are
quick to accuse Anna of treason. David deter-
mines to find his wife and clear her name. But
every step takes him further into danger . . . and
the evidence against Anna mounts up.

As David uncovers more and more about the
woman he married and thought he knew, he also
begins to catch glimpses of another tantalizingly
vague figure: Gerhard Kleist, the psychoanalyst
first consulted by Anna some years previously. Is
their relationship merely that of doctor–patient?
Are they lovers? Or is Kleist's role something
more sinister?

John Trenhaile has written a compelling novel
about an ordinary relationship plunged into the
world of murder, chase and double-cross that his
growing readership has come to expect. It is also a
remarkable and sensitive portrait of a vulnerable
woman which will remain vividly in the memory
long after the last page has been turned.

JOHN TRENHAILE

KRYSALIS

The extract from an article by Lord Chalfont
from *The Times* of 8 August 1977 is used
with the kind permission of
Lord Chalfont and Times Newspapers Ltd.

This edition specially produced for
The Leisure Circle Partnership
by William Collins Sons & Co. Ltd.

Photoset in Linotron Meridien by
Rowland Phototypesetting Ltd
Bury St Edmunds, Suffolk
Printed and bound in Great Britain by
William Collins Sons & Co. Ltd, Glasgow

'Beware the fury of a patient man'

JOHN DRYDEN
Absalom and Achitophel

AUTHOR'S NOTE

The quotation on page 326 is taken from Thigpen & Cleckley, *The Three Faces of Eve*, Chivers Press (Library Association of Great Britain), 1985, page 165, where the authors ascribe it simply to 'Bernheim', without further elucidation.

Anna Lescombe, one of the characters in this novel, is a barrister of some standing. I practised at the Chancery Bar for thirteen years. Past professional colleagues (and, I hope, present friends) who think to find themselves within these pages will be committing the crime of deceit, albeit only of self-deceit.

Anna Lescombe was adopted shortly after her birth, as indeed was I. But members of my immediate family who likewise imagine that I have represented them here will fare even worse than my former colleagues, for they will be making a mistake.

Before . . .

ONE

David Lescombe did not look like a man about to face a make or break interrogation. Only the churning in his stomach gave the game away; and only to him.

He walked up and down the corridor with measured pace, hands clasped behind his back. At one end was a high window overlooking London's Whitehall; whenever he reached it he would pause for a few moments to examine the busy scene before resuming his steady progress to and fro.

On every sweep of the corridor he passed a leather-padded door above which hung a sign: Committee Room Twelve. Soon he would have to pass through it. Whenever David thought of that, his stomach knotted and he walked on a little more quickly, as if by doing so he might escape what lay on the other side of the innocent-looking door. He glanced at his watch. Did he have time to run to the lavatory? No, don't risk it, this morning of all mornings, don't risk *anything*.

He was about to be subjected to the process known as positive vetting.

He came to a halt by the window. Outside it was a cold, bright winter morning, but David no longer saw it. His subconscious, eager to find a means of escape from the present, had taken him back to his childhood: to another corridor not unlike this one, with busts of former statesmen on pedestals, and heavy-framed oil portraits hanging from the walls. His public school, the headmaster's study, waiting for judgement.

He had been seventeen, then. A prefect, someone in authority. Someone *liked*. In his class was another boy whom nobody liked. David took a good-natured interest in him, protecting him from the worst excesses of bullying. Hamilton, that was his name.

David folded his arms and leant against the window embrasure. Why think of Hamilton, a quarter of a century later? Ah, yes, of course. They were shortly going to vet him as a precaution against betrayal . . .

The class were waiting for a maths lesson to start. Their master, 'Beaky' Tozer, had come in, taken one look at the floor beside David's desk and barked: 'What's *that*?' 'That' was a pool of black ink, flowing in glossy abundance over the classroom's parquet floor.

David didn't know who had spilled it. His desk was next to Hamilton's, however, and he deduced immediately that one of Hamilton's enemies (they were legion) must have sluiced the ink as a frame-up: not the first time that had happened. For a moment there was silence. Then, from somewhere at the back, had come the drawl: 'Oh, Hamilton, what *have* you done *now*?'

'It wasn't me!' Hamilton's pale, freckled face grew taut with fear. A brawl developed, with accusations and counter-charges flying. David couldn't believe the stupid childishness of it all. He and several others ended up in front of the headmaster, part of a long drawn out inquiry as to who had spilled the ink.

David weighed up the pros and cons, assessed the risks and embarked on his first amateur attempt at crisis-management. He knew the headmaster would expect him to name the guilty party. Instead, he'd confessed to the crime himself, pleading carelessness.

'Why?' the headmaster had asked; 'I mean, why own up to something we both knew you didn't do?'

David wasn't sure even then. Standing by the window overlooking Whitehall, he still couldn't be certain to this day. Part of it was a feeling that Hamilton had suffered

12

enough and should be protected from false incrimination at the hands of his enemies; more, perhaps, had to do with David's pragmatic sense of how best to deal with the ridiculous. If he confessed, there would be a swift end to an incident that was sapping House morale to an extent he regarded as nonsensical beyond words . . .

The adult David laughed out loud. He was remembering how, after he'd taken his punishment, a fine as he recalled, the headmaster had said to him, 'There's something I want you to know, Lescombe. It may affect how you handle this kind of thing in future. Hamilton claimed that it *was* you who spilled the ink.'

David had stared at him, uncomprehending.

'He shopped you,' the headmaster said impatiently. 'Because he's a coward and a sneak, and he knew that as you were sitting next to him he had some pathetic chance of making it stick. But you've tied my hands, Lescombe. You and your silly, quixotic confession . . .'

David moved away from the window, still smiling at the memory of the daft things one did in adolescence. Then the leather-padded door swung open, bringing him fully back to the present with a lurch. 'Mr Lescombe?' he heard a voice say.

'Yes.'

A man stood on the threshold of Committee Room Twelve, holding open the door. He was wearing an old, thick tweed jacket over flannel trousers, very large in the bottom, and brogues that had been polished almost red. Two jowls hung suspended from either side of his ruddy face, ending in little pockets of dead-looking flesh. He succeeded admirably in his aim of not looking like anyone's idea of a member of the British intelligence fraternity. He could have passed for an altogether different kind of vet. 'Would you come in now, please?' he said.

As David followed him his mind was busy making connections. Because he'd done his homework, deliberately seeking out others who had undergone this process and survived, he knew that this man was Jeremy Shorrocks, assistant director of MI6. Genial, that's what they said about him. A pushover. Brewster, he's the one you've got to watch . . .

There were three people in the Committee Room Twelve: Brewster, a deputy permanent secretary within the cabinet office's security hierarchy; Shorrocks; and a woman wearing a police commander's uniform whom David guessed must be from Special Branch. There were no introductions. David swiftly identified the chair he was meant to occupy and sat in it without waiting to be asked.

During the silence that followed he tried to still the beating of his heart and concentrate on working out how they would see him: a tall, lean man in his early forties wearing a good suit and a calm expression. Yes, fine; stay with that.

'Mr Lescombe . . .' It was Brewster, the chairman sitting at the centre of a long oak dining-table, who spoke. 'Thank you so much for agreeing to make yourself available this morning.' His smile turned conspiratorial. 'I know how these things interrupt schedules.'

'Not at all.'

David crossed his legs at the ankles and languidly rested his hands on the arms of his chair, the fingers unclenched. He prayed that any connoisseurs of body-language who might be present would notice and approve.

'You know why we're here: to consider whether there are any security objections to your admission as a member of the Krysalis Committee.' Brewster combined a slight stutter with a liking for mid-word stress.

David cleared his throat, and instantly wished he hadn't. 'Yes indeed.'

'You appear to be clean,' Brewster said, but reluctantly, as if a man without blemish was unique in his experience.

Shorrocks pushed back his chair and removed a pair of heavy spectacles. 'Boringly so,' he agreed with a smile. 'First vetted in 1985, no-shows on all subsequent re-runs, nice wife, nice boat down at Brighton, no other hobbies, no vices . . .' He closed his spectacles with a snap and tossed them onto his papers. 'Glad I'm not married to you.'

'I'm glad you're not,' David said. 'They'd have to sack us both.'

Shorrocks guffawed.

'There's just this *one* thing,' Brewster continued; it was clear to David that any attempt at humour would be lost on him and he resolved to keep a tighter grip on himself. 'Just one query.'

'Hardly worth raising, really,' Shorrocks put in.

'This is Krysalis.' Brewster's voice had turned acid. 'It's not just your common or garden positive vet, now is it?'

'Sorry.'

But Brewster's irritation was unappeased. 'Lescombe will understand, I'm sure, that we don't want to overlook anything. With the Vancouver summit less than three months away, and Washington breathing down our necks.'

'Quite,' David said. 'Please ask me anything you like.'

His polite smile signalled that he did not anticipate any disasters, but inside him the fear was gathering swiftly now. If he could but pass this vet he would become a member of the elite Krysalis Committee, that select band of Englishmen and Americans whose job it was to prepare ground plans for the next European war. It would mean more money, more prestige, but above all it would mean that he belonged. That in his chosen career he had, at the impossibly early age of forty-two, become a major power-player. For a second he let himself imagine that moment of bliss when he would say to Anna: 'I've done it!' Next second he had levered himself back to reality to hear Shorrocks say, 'Your wife, Anna.'

With a Herculean effort David somehow managed to keep his face under control.

'At one time she seemed to be rather friendly with a German chappie.'

'Indeed?' David forced himself to produce an unruffled smile. *Say something!* 'Am I allowed to ask, what does "friendly" mean, in this context?'

15

'Just that. Our informant . . . let me see . . .' Brewster flipped through several pages. ' . . . Ah, yes, this is a couple of years back, although it only surfaced recently . . . a Treasury man, went to his favourite restaurant, there was your wife at the next table, didn't seem to notice him although they'd met before . . . her companion talked fluent German to a passing acquaintance, óbviously his native language . . .'

'So it's linguistics in the Treasury now, is it? I often wondered what they did.'

Idiot! They don't like fun and games. But Shorrocks laughed; and this time even Brewster permitted himself a smile. Only the female commander continued to sit there, flintlike, unimpressed. Shorrocks wrote something on a scrap of paper and slid it in front of Brewster, who affected not to see it. David would have given three years' pension to know what it was.

'I think that must be Duggy Atkinson,' he said quickly. 'Your source.'

'I'm afraid we're not allowed to disclose – '

'Oh quite. Do excuse me.'

Brewster cleared his throat. 'Then it would appear that the same thing happened next week and the week after that.'

'I see. Two years ago, you say?'

'Yes.'

David looked up at the ceiling, as if pursuing some elusive memory. In truth, he was trying to quell the feeling of apprehension that had begun to undermine his performance. What on earth had Anna been up to? No, don't think about that, just *deal with it*. 'But not since then . . . however, the restaurant sounds all right.' David was seized with a sudden inspiration. He took out his diary. 'What's it called?'

Shorrocks chuckled. He produced the restaurant's name and even, after further research, a phone number. 'According to our source, you should try the salade Niçoise.'

'I see.' David's forehead creased in a frown. 'I'm sorry, I feel I'm missing something terribly obvious but . . . it hasn't

16

been made a crime to have lunch with Germans, has it?'
Wonderful! Keep going!

'Do you know which Germany?' the woman commander asked; and David turned to her. 'I think we can safely assume West Germany,' he said.

'Why?' she asked. David raised his eyebrows. 'East Germans having lunch with lady barristers, well . . . ha-ha. That *would* be in the file, now wouldn't it?'

'Ha-ha,' Brewster agreed. 'But you can see our problem, I'm sure. Do you recognize this man, from our informant's description?'

David shook his head. 'Anna's circle of friends doesn't totally overlap with mine. Possibly a client? She's always had quite an extensive Euro-practice.'

'Possibly.' Brewster made a note. 'Now you *know* the next question, and it's a frightful bore, I realize that, but – '

'How's the marriage?'

'Ah . . .'

'Sound as a bell, I'm happy to say.'

'You're surprised by this information but not perturbed by it; would that be a correct summary?'

Damn right! David thought; but what he actually said was: 'As to the second part of your analysis, yes; the first part gives me pause. I don't find it surprising that my wife should lunch several times with the same man. What were they discussing, do we know?'

'We don't.'

David shrugged. 'She's a barrister, very successful. Quite a lot of wining and dining goes on at the bar, from what I hear.'

'When you next see your wife, will you put this to her?' Shorrocks asked.

'Something that happened two years ago? I suppose I might. If I remember, which I probably won't. Why, would you like me to?'

'Noo . . .' Shorrocks shook his head with a smile. 'And for the record, let me just say that Lescombe does have a point:

17

the Germans – half of 'em – are on our side now, you know. Not like last time.'

Big Ben struck the quarter, affording Brewster an excuse to crush his ebullient colleague with magisterial silence. 'Can I take it, then,' he said at last, 'that you have no objections to the admission of Mr Lescombe to the Krysalis Committee?'

'You can.'

Brewster opened a plastic-backed folder at the last page. David drew a deep breath. Brewster was uncapping his fountain pen, was actually on the point of appending his signature, when Shorrocks cleared his throat and David's chest tightened. Surely there could be nothing else, *surely*? But Shorrocks merely nodded towards the far end of the table.

'Commander?' Brewster's face was flushed.

'No objections from Branch, sir.'

Brewster signed.

David sprinted through the arch into Whitehall as if competing for a place on the Olympic team. He did not pause until he came to a phone booth on the fringe of Trafalgar Square. It seemed like an eternity before Anna answered, but then there was that wonderful, musical voice: 'Darling! How did it go? Did they . . . ?'

'*Yes!*'

'Oh *David*!'

'It's all right. It's all right.' Memories of his wife having lunch with mysterious Germans fled from his mind, leaving only a heady mixture of love and exultation: Let Anna have lunch with everyone and anyone, who cared . . . ?

'I knew it,' she cried. 'The champagne's in the fridge; damn it, I'll put another bottle in to chill.'

David was shaking, he could scarcely hold the receiver steady, but one thing he must say and the words came rushing out, 'I'm too ill to drink – '

'Ill! What's wrong?'

18

'Nothing that a few hours in bed with you won't cure.'

He ran out of the booth, leaving the receiver to swing at the end of its cord. When the next surprised caller picked up the phone he was astonished to hear a woman's joyous laughter still echoing down the line.

TWO

The woman kissed him in a long, drawn-out farewell before turning to make her way down the path. As she did so, however, she caught sight of her lover's brass plate, 'Gerhard Kleist, MA, ABPsS, Consultant Psychologist'. She leaned close to it and breathed out slowly, misting the metal. When Kleist eased her aside and bent to lick away the moisture, the woman giggled.

He kissed her one last time, pulling her so that she could feel all of his body through the skimpy black dress she wore beneath her coat; he stroked her hair, relishing its thick feel, allowed one hand to stray to her behind . . . *'Ciao.'*

'Ciao.'

Kleist watched her swing down the path, those long legs covering the ground with the same self-willed assurance that had characterized her love-making, and wondered if he would see her again. Probably not; she wasn't the kind to be interested in revivals. Besides, her husband would be coming home from the Middle East next week: a far from ideal situation. So, let the first time be the last time.

Kleist rested his back against the doorframe for a moment. It should have been a wonderful evening, but . . . He shrugged, victim of a momentary unhappiness beyond his art to cure, and with an effort of will obliterated it. He lingered a moment longer, scanning the night sky, then closed the front door behind him and turned off the porch light.

As he made his way across the hall to the foot of the wide

oak staircase that was the house's best feature, he caught sight of a strip of colour beneath the telephone table and paused. A scarf, her scarf, God damn all women, why couldn't they be more careful? He picked it up and held it to his nostrils. Joy. How appropriate. The Hermès silk flowed through his hands: rich, precious . . . and damning.

He glanced at his watch. Two o'clock. She had been gone a quarter of an hour now and that meant she wouldn't be coming back; which in turn meant that the scarf was no longer merely a personal adornment, it had become evidence.

He walked upstairs to his first-floor consulting room, where he opened a cupboard beneath one of the bookshelves. It contained nothing but a white metal case with a carrying handle. He turned it upside down to reveal a pilot light and two switches.

Kleist put the scarf inside, set one of the switches and upended the case. He went to collect a wadge of toilet paper from the lavatory next door. By the time he came back the pilot light no longer glowed. He opened the lid and tipped a tiny residue of ash onto the paper. Seconds later, the last traces of his visitor's presence were being flushed into the sewers of NW3.

As he set the room to rights the doorbell rang. Kleist threw up his hands in exasperation: she had come back after all. Women!

He ran down the stairs two at a time, remembering to turn on the outside light. But then his hand froze on the latch; for despite his having pressed the switch, the glass between the diamond mullions next to the front door stayed black. A duff light-bulb . . . ?

Kleist quickly stepped away from the door and to one side.

'Gerhard,' he heard a voice say; the tone was imperative, urgent. *'Gerhard, lass mich rein!'*

Kleist started, unwilling to believe his ears. Folly, such catastrophic stupidity . . . 'Vogel?' he rasped.

'Ja. Mach schnell!'

21

Kleist turned off the hall lights. Only then did he slip the latch.

'What the – '

'Ssh!'

His caller held the door open half an inch while he surveyed the driveway. 'Clear,' he said at last. 'Here, you'll want your light-bulb back . . .'

'You're mad! To visit this house – '

'If I had a choice, believe me, I wouldn't come within a mile of you. Let's get out of sight, for the love of God!'

The two men spoke rapid German. They kept their voices low from habit, but their fear showed through. It showed in every syllable of every word.

Kleist escorted Vogel into his living room. He made sure that the curtains were fully drawn before switching on the desk-lamp, then poured two large whiskies. Vogel dropped into a leather armchair with its back to the windows. He was breathing fast, and for the moment showed no inclination to do other than calm down.

Kleist sat at one end of a sofa, first pulling it around so that his face could not be seen by anyone who might somehow find the means to look through curtains as well as glass. 'You haven't changed,' he said, a touch of envy in his voice.

Vogel must have been in his late forties, but he maintained the face and figure of a younger man. His sandy coloured hair had kept its original youthful texture, like his moustache. With his cultivated German accent and understated manner, he might have passed for a well-to-do member of one of the modern professions: publisher, perhaps, or financial consultant. Certainly no one taking a casual glance would have been likely to fasten on his real job, any more than they could have guessed Jeremy Shorrocks', and for the same reason. Vogel was senior London resident of the *Hauptverwaltung Aufklärung*, or HVA: East Germany's secret service.

'You're not quite the same, I think,' Vogel remarked at last. 'Fatter – a little. More lines in the face.' He drank a generous slug of whisky. 'You should try a few early nights. Take a book to bed, instead of a woman.'

Kleist said nothing.

'I have to be out of here *fast*, so listen to me. You once had a patient, Anna Lescombe.'

'Haven't seen her for years. If you came here just to say that – '

'Shut up. I'm here to give orders, not listen to a dissertation. You pointed the Lescombe woman in the direction of her husband, David.'

'So?'

'So when did you last see her?'

'Two years ago.'

'Professionally?'

'No.'

'When did you last treat her, then?'

Kleist thought. 'Five years ago, I suppose. Minor counselling, nothing serious. A booster, if you like.'

'No other contact?'

'I phone her every other month, to chat: one friend calling another. What's the point of all this?'

'You know about the Vancouver summit, perhaps?'

'Who doesn't?' Kleist scoffed. 'Zero-option conventional arms reduction in Europe, my God! They'll put you out of a job, my friend.'

'No, they won't. You're going to see to that. David Lescombe, the husband of your patient, has just been appointed to a committee called Krysalis.'

'To what?'

Vogel shook his head impatiently. '*Listen!* Never mind what it is, just take it from me, this is urgent, urgent like in *panic*! If we can lay hands on Krysalis before Vancouver gets under way, we are going to *win*. So heads are on lines, Gerhard. Careers hang in the balance, mine, yours . . .'

'I do as I'm told.' Kleist had turned sulky. 'You've no complaints.'

'If we don't get Krysalis, we shan't complain, we shall

dismiss. *Sack.'* Vogel glanced around the room. 'We both know that this oh-so-pleasant lifestyle requires more than professional fees to keep it going.'

'Just tell me what you want and get out.'

'You have to contact the wife, Anna. Bring her back under control, before the summit meeting.'

'But Vancouver's slated to start in two months' time, isn't it? I can't help you.'

'Kleist, I am telling you – '

'You don't understand. I haven't seen her for two years or more. I can't just force her into psychotherapy she doesn't want or need! There's professional ethics to consider.'

Vogel tipped his head back and laughed at the ceiling. 'Ethics!' he said, suddenly bringing his head forward again. 'You wouldn't know an ethic if it got up and spat at you!'

Kleist flushed. 'How the hell do you think I manage to – '

'I don't know and I don't give a shit. Now listen. David Lescombe is going to be away for the coming weekend and for some days after that, too.'

'How do you know that?'

'How do I know anything? Just accept that he *won't be home*. You will use that opportunity to contact Anna Lescombe – you said you phoned her sometimes?'

'Yes, but – '

'So she won't be surprised to hear from you. Good. You will reduce her into your control, just as before. You will programme her to open her husband's safe and bring us what she finds inside, after which she will take the material back and replace it. You will ensure she remembers nothing of what she has done. Then, Gerhard, and only then, you can relax.'

'Vogel, allow me to tell you something.' Kleist's voice was restrained, even polite. 'You must understand that I am talking purely in a professional capacity now, and what I have to tell you is that you are insane. Just that. Insane.' He stood up. 'If that's all you – '

Vogel's hands moved with such dazzling speed that for an

24

instant Kleist's mind told him he must have drawn a gun: he actually 'saw' a weapon lying cupped in his visitor's hands. Once the slipping cog re-engaged, however, he realized it was only a photograph. He looked down at the image Vogel was holding out to him and his face turned white.

'Sit down.' When Kleist hesitated, Vogel shouted, *'Sit down!'*

Kleist obeyed, very slowly. 'Please . . . My housekeeper, you'll wake her . . .'

'To hell with your . . . your *servant*! You seem to forget how things are. There aren't many servants in East Germany.' Vogel's voice had turned sour. 'Your sister, Ilsa, for example.' He jiggled the photograph. 'She does all her own housework. Cooks for the kids. And for Walther, that layabout husband of hers.'

Kleist could not take his eyes off the photo, which showed a blonde woman, her middle-aged face lined and unremarkable, standing beside a man a full head shorter than herself, with her hands resting on the shoulders of a small boy. The man was holding a baby. Kleist knew these four people well. He was, in a number of very real senses, attached to them.

'The hospital has given her a raise.' Vogel flipped the photo over so that he could look at it. 'They are considering taking a bigger apartment. Four rooms instead of three, think of that!' He let his eyes roam around Kleist's richly furnished lounge. 'You have money. This house. Women. Reflect, Gerhard: those are all things that can *change*.'

'I'm a naturalized citizen. No one can throw me out of England.'

'Naturalized, yes . . . on the strength of Institute 631's forgeries. One phone call, that's all it takes.'

'You wouldn't risk sacrificing me.' Kleist felt a degree of confidence return. 'I've run too many of your people.'

'My orders are to procure Krysalis forthwith. For that purpose I am both authorized and prepared to make *any* sacrifice.'

Kleist stared at Vogel, knowing he was beaten. 'I'll need

time,' he said at last. 'It could take months to re-establish that kind of trust, the necessary degree of dependence . . . why can't you just burgle the house, steal this Krysalis thing, and have done with it?'

'Because we can't risk leaving the slightest trace, that's why. When the General Secretary leaves Moscow to go to Vancouver he wants Krysalis in his pocket and no finger-prints on it.'

'All right, suppose I get the combination out of the wife. Then you can send somebody around to – '

'To get caught in the act, as usual! Shut up for long enough to hear what I'm saying, Kleist. If anything goes wrong, Anna Lescombe takes all the blame. She opens the safe, no one else goes anywhere near it. *No traces*. We want it done clean, we want it done professionally, but above all we want it done yesterday. Get me?'

'I keep telling you, that's impossible. I need at least three months.'

'I know. And I feel sorry for you.' Vogel studied the photo one last time, flicked it, put it back in his pocket. 'Sorry, too, for Ilsa.'

'Why?'

'Because you have a fortnight.'

The First Weekend

THREE

Mr Justice Scott began delivering his judgement immediately after lunch, and by three o'clock it was obvious to everyone in court, especially Anna herself, that she had lost. Scott J. was a nice man, at least there was that. He skated over her failure to call evidence as to the state of the reinsured cargo not only when it was offloaded at Kaohsiung but also when it reached the roads three days beforehand. Anna quietly thumbed through her brief until she found her Advice on Evidence. Paragraph 43: she remembered it well. 'I can see little point,' she read to herself, 'in calling additional evidence as to the state of the goods in the interim period.' Right at the end. An addendum. A not-thinking kind of afterthought. On one construction of the contract, her advice had been right. On one construction.

And so now here they all were, clients, solicitors and barrister, two years older and, as far as the client was concerned, £400,000 worth of damages and costs the wiser (she pulled a notebook over the figure marked on her own brief, £5000, ridiculous). In the red and in the wrong. And it was her fault.

Afterwards, outside court, the atmosphere was correct but cool. Should we appeal? her instructing solicitor inquired. 'I'll think about it,' she said. 'I want to sleep on it.' She wondered if it sounded as worldly wise in her mouth as it always seemed to her when coming from others.

Her feet hurt, she was drenched in sweat, she felt utterly

29

exhausted, but somehow she summoned up the energy to trudge back to chambers.

'How did you do?' Duncan Broadway QC inquired in the clerks' room.

'Oh, lost.'

'Bad luck. Scotty got it wrong, did he . . . ?'

'Bless you, darling; you're better than a large Scotch any day. Roger . . .'

The senior clerk looked up inquiringly.

'Roger, am I still okay to take the first three days of next week off?'

'Yes, I've kept the diary clear.'

'Thanks.' Anna skimmed through the messages waiting for her. 'Who's this, Roger?'

'A Mr Christ phoned.'

'I knew things were bad, but – '

The clerk was too busy sorting out next week's schedules to acknowledge her attempt at humour. 'Said would you ring him back, not urgent, social.'

Then it clicked. 'Did he leave a first name? It wasn't Gerhard by any chance?'

She looked at the number Roger had scribbled down on the yellow Post-It slip. *Yes!* Anna felt a marvellous upsurge of energy. She went to her room, where she paused only to fling wig and gown onto a chair before snatching up the phone. Thank God it was Friday, the two men who shared an office with her had already gone home for the weekend . . .

'Gerhard? Anna. I can't be-*lieve* it!'

'Hello.'

He sounded a touch bored, she thought; no, don't think like that, snap out of it, something's going right today. 'God, you pick your times to call! I wasn't expecting you to ring till next month, at the earliest.'

'Am I early? I can always ring off.'

'Don't you dare!'

'Something wrong, luvvy?'

30

'Oh, Gerhard!' She perched on the desk. 'It's years since you called me that.'

'Mm, two. How's tricks?'

'Shitty. More shitty than usual. Juliet's being a pain.' She paused. 'I've just lost a case.'

'You should know how difficult children can be, by now. And as for the case: you have to lose some. At least, I thought you did.'

'My fault, this time.'

He laughed, a rich blend of mellow sounds that still had the power to loosen all the muscles in her stomach, his roller-coaster laugh ... 'Always your fault, yes? Anna Lescombe, the big failure.'

'Oh, you . . . !'

'Sorry. Look, I've got some time off at last and so I took my courage in both hands and thought – '

'That you'd phone. I'm so glad you did.' Anna simultaneously took a deep breath and a momentous decision. 'What are you doing this weekend?'

'I'm free most of tomorrow. But it's a Saturday, aren't you and David – '

'He's off on one of his seminars, bless him. He often is, these days. He won't be back until the end of next week, I shouldn't think.'

The pause was a long one. 'Gerhard? Hullo, are you there?'

'I'm here. You sound . . . I'm concerned.'

Another jagged pause. Anna stared out of the window. 'Things have been better,' she said at last. 'You know . . . ?' And she laughed, trying to pass it off as nothing.

'We can talk tomorrow. Come to the house. Come early. Lunch. At the usual place.'

'Oh, *Gerhard*.' How had he guessed what was going through her mind? 'Will you phone Seppy or shall I?'

Again that wonderful laugh, pulsating down the line. 'Leave everything to me. Until tomorrow, then . . .'

As Anna replaced the receiver she gleefully told herself that as well as a much needed holiday she had tomorrow to look forward to now. One whole day in the presence of Gerhard, without distractions, or worries.

No, there would be worries. As she guided the BMW through London's rush-hour traffic, so her mind weaved its way through a maze of potentially disastrous conversations that might happen when she met him. But by the time she reached Islington she had the thing under control. Going to spend the day with him might be a mistake: if they hadn't met for two years, that was for a reason. Each moment she spent away from him represented a tiny moral victory, further proof that she could do without his therapy, and without him, too. But by going to his house tomorrow, and remaining untouched, at least she would prove to herself just how far she had come.

Anna liked to remind herself how far she had come, and grown. She regarded it as a matter for quiet pride.

As she went up the steps to the front door she savoured an anticipation that had nothing to do with Gerhard Kleist. The first thing she did on entering was flick through the post. Circulars. No Cornish postmark, no familiar hand. Nothing, in other words, from her daughter Juliet. Anna made a face. There was something unpleasant about the power mail had over people. It got to the point where you were afraid to look.

She had sent her daughter a sweater. That was a month ago now.

Anna checked the answering machine, then made herself a large gin and tonic before deciding to have a bath. As she lay in the foam, glass conveniently nearby, she again found herself dwelling on the day's events. She had lost a case and she was to blame. This year, she'd lost more than she'd won. Not all of them were her fault. This one was, though. How was it likely to affect her career? *How could she have been so stupid not to see that point on the construction of the contract?*

No. This is wrong. Think positive. Tomorrow is another day. Everybody makes mistakes. You can only do your best. Look forward to the next *good* thing: three whole days off . . .

Gerhard had taught her the verbal tricks, how to cope, when all of life had been one long cope. By the time she'd finished dressing there was a smile on her face again. She looked at her watch. David had promised to ring at eight: forty minutes away. I'll put the time to good use, Anna thought; Juliet's my daughter, by God, and if she doesn't much care about me I love her, and she's only sixteen, and if I want to phone her I will.

But it was such a rigmarole. That dreadful girl who ran the commune in Cornwall, and always answered the phone, put up so many barriers. At last, after much negotiation and some old-fashioned pleading, Anna heard the familiar snuffly voice at the other end of the line.

''Lo.'

'Hullo, darling. Mummy. How are you?'

''Mall right.'

Pause.

'I hadn't heard from you for such a long time, I just thought I'd ring to see how you were getting on.'

Silence.

'I sent you a sweater a few . . .' (she was about to exaggerate and say months, mentally altered it to days, then compromised) ' . . . weeks ago. Did you get it?'

'Mm.'

'Is that "mm yes" or "mm no", darling?'

'Yes.'

'Is it all right?'

'Mm.'

Sometimes Anna wanted to scream at her daughter when she was like this, but tonight she just felt very, very sad. She was trying to think up a way of cutting things short when Juliet said, 'Dad came down.'

Anna heard a note of accusation in the adolescent voice and for the second time today knew herself to be on trial; this time, not as a barrister, but as a mother. As the ex-wife of Juliet's father.

'Oh, yes? How is Eddy, then?'

''Sall right.'

'Good.'

'Why don't you phone him?'

'Did he say that, darling?'

Silence. Then: 'You never phone him. Never. Why don't you?'

'There's not much I really want to say to Eddy, I'm afraid.' Anna gritted her teeth, but before she could stop herself the words were out: 'Why don't you phone me, darling, you know how much I worry?' She swapped the phone from one hand to the other, wiped her forehead. 'Couldn't you just once – '

'The sweater's too small. I gave it to Fergie. Look, I can't talk any more now.'

'Juliet, please don't – '

But the purr on the line meant that her daughter must have hung up. I will not cry, Anna told herself bravely. And I must not drink any more, either, because that will . . . *not* . . . *help*.

She kept to her resolve until eight-thirty. When by that time dependable David still had not rung, she poured another double, to give herself Dutch courage, and called him.

It seemed ages before he came to the phone. Anna was aware of a comfortable buzz of conversation in the background; something about it told her that David wasn't going to be pleased and the longer she waited the more chance her heart had to sink.

A clunk; then a brisk voice said, 'Hello.'

'David? Anna.'

'Hello, love. Yes?'

'Have I interrupted anything? Are you busy?'

'I am, rather. Sorry. Can you make it quick?'

'You promised to ring me, that's all. When you didn't, I was worried.'

A long pause. 'Oh, damn.' He sounded dispirited. 'I am sorry. I forgot.'

'Not going well?'

34

'So-so.'

'Me too.'

'What's up?'

'Oh, I lost a case today, that's all.'

'I'm sorry.'

'It doesn't matter. Not important.'

'I see. Look, Anna . . .'

'Yes?'

'Can you do something for me? I've made a hash of things, rather.'

'Yes, of course.' She picked up a pen. 'Shoot.'

'It's the marina. They're expecting us tomorrow. I ordered fuel and one or two other things before I knew about this blasted weekend. Can you phone in the morning after nine-thirty and cancel? Only I don't want them to charge us.'

'I understand. Anything else?'

'No, that's it. I'm really sorry I forgot I was supposed to phone you.' His voice seemed softer, the tension in it had faded somewhat. 'But . . . well, it's a bit embarrassing to be called out of committee by one's wife, actually.'

'Mustn't keep you, then. I love you, David.'

'I love you too, darling.'

'Bye.' Anna quickly put down the phone, even though she knew he had started to say something else. She was worried that it might take away from the power of 'I love you too, darling', and she couldn't bear that, not tonight of all nights, so she cut him off.

Afterwards, there didn't seem to be anything to do except make herself a cup of soup and crawl into bed, hoping that sleep would cure her headache. The last thing she did was appropriate Juliet's pyjama case, the one in the shape of a pussycat with a zip up its stomach, and lie down hugging it to her. She liked its smell. Juliet's smell.

On Saturday she got up earlier than planned and agonized over what dress to wear. In the end she chose a dark blue suit and – an impulse, this – a rather bold hat, hoping that the contrast in styles would end up transmitting only safe messages.

She felt virtuous about her early start, but she soon discovered that virtue, as well as being its own reward, can also exact a special kind of price. She parked the car and was just stepping onto the pavement when she glanced up in time to see a girl who looked scarcely older than Juliet walk out of Gerhard's front gate, shouldering a tote bag as she did so.

Anna folded herself back inside the BMW and watched the teenager slouch off down the road. God, he likes them young now, she thought. *God . . .*

She waited quite a while before getting out of the car again and going up the path. When she rang the bell, to her surprise June opened the door: loyal, efficient June who had been Gerhard's receptionist ever since he put up his brass plate, but whose hair sadly no longer matched the plate's sheen. June, untrue to her name, had turned autumnal.

'Hello, my dear,' she said.

'How lovely to see you again. I wasn't expecting that, at the weekend.' Suddenly a great light dawned across Anna's horizon. 'Does he work Saturdays now?'

'Not often. There's this kid he's been assigned by the court, you know, one of *those.*'

So Gerhard wasn't into teenagers yet, then . . . Anna felt pleased about that without knowing why, or wanting to. 'Oh, yes. Those . . . Can I go up?'

'Of course.'

She knew her way; she had visited this aggressively red-bricked house off Keats Grove many times before. Gerhard refused to be separated from his beloved Hampstead; even when he was young, and comparatively poor, he had found an attic somewhere under the eaves of Fitzjohn's Avenue wherein to practise as a psychotherapist. She had known her way there, too. Sometimes she felt as though she had always known where to find Gerhard Kleist.

Anna climbed the oak stairs, relishing their dull gleam as

36

the first sign of homecoming, and pushed open the door to his room.

It was like entering the portrayed studio of a seven-teenth-century master: Pieter de Hooch, perhaps, or Francken the Younger. Anna knew those names because Gerhard had used them to describe the effect he was after. When he'd bought this house ten years previously they had been going through a good patch: friends, rather than doctor–patient. She had even helped him choose some of the fabrics. Gerhard was ignorant about material, he cared only for wood. Light poured into this south-facing room through high windows, onto a herringbone parquet floor the colour of honey. Beneath the windows stood a long table of pale oak, on which were the half-finished model of a Spanish galleon and the canvas-backed plans for it, weighed down by a lump of abura, Gerhard's favourite carving wood. Gauge, pinchuck, callipers and glue were neatly aligned, as always. The priceless Laux Maler lute rested in its usual place, against the side of the floor-to-ceiling bookcase that ran the length of one whole wall. Yes, everything was just so; she had time to absorb that comforting knowledge before his voice coiled out to caress her.

'Hello.'

Anna walked towards him, her shoes tap-tapping across the varnished wooden floor. He was all in white today: linen shirt open at the collar, white shoes, even the belt holding up his white slacks was white. As she approached he rose from his seat and stood with legs slightly apart, hands in pockets, watching her. Although he was only forty-six years old, his stance somehow epitomized the stern authority of a patriarch.

'You look like Coco Chanel,' he said. 'In those photos of her when she was young. Chic personified, only softer.'

All the breath went out of her and then she laughed. 'You really know how to lay it on, don't you!'

'Yes.' He wasn't at all abashed. 'But it takes practice.'

And oh, but he was so lovely, so gorgeous. So fine, still.

37

'It's been rather a long time,' she said, and her voice sounded artificially bright, like that of a widow preparing to say, 'Won't you come back after the service . . . ?'

'I've been terribly busy. And – '

'No apologies. Not today. But June said you'd been working, are you sure I'm not in the way?'

'Of course not. Relax.'

'Oh dear. Now you'll be categorizing my insecurities again.' She raised a hand in the solemn gesture of one who intends to take an oath. 'Freud said . . . or are you Jung, I never could remember?'

'I'm Pisces, actually.'

'Two fish swimming in opposite directions, how appropriate.'

And they laughed, glad to find the spell broken, although, yes, of course he was Pisces, his birthday fell on 3 March: there were some things you inevitably transferred from one year's diary to the next, no matter how redundant they might seem.

'What's been happening?' He sounded, to use his own word of yesterday, concerned. 'When we spoke, I sensed a regression. We seem to have lost some ground.'

'Ah, *we* do, do we?' Anna made a rueful face. 'Yes. You're right. Give me, us, give *we* a drink, will you?'

'Good idea. Wait a moment . . .'

While he disappeared into the lavatory Anna meandered over to look at his model galleon. 'What's the hold-up, you're still stuck on the rigging?' she called.

'Time. The enemy of everything.'

Kleist carried in a tray on which stood two flute glasses and a bottle of Laurent-Perrier's Ultra Brut champagne. He poured two frothy glasses of the matchlessly dry wine, allowing them to settle a moment before he touched Anna on the shoulder. 'Here . . .'

'You're like an elephant, you know that? You never forget . . .'

'Of course not.'

'I hardly ever drink Laurent-Perrier now.'

Kleist smiled, raised his glass. 'Here's to you.'

'And to you. To your perfect taste. As always.'

She sat on the special posture chair he used, the one with no back. For a moment he watched her rock to and fro while he read the evidence and tried to analyse it. Then he said, 'How far down have we gone?'

'What do you think?'

'A long way.'

'No.' Anna tossed her head, sweeping strands of hair out of her eyes, and knocked back the drink. '*We*, as you put it . . . have come up since last time. Things have been getting on top of me, that's all.'

'At work?'

'At work, yes. And . . .' She heaved a long sigh. 'Juliet's being tiresome.'

'In the usual way?'

'Yes.'

'How many times do I have to tell you? The fact that someone happens to be your child – '

'Doesn't guarantee they'll turn into a wonderful human being. I know. She's just so difficult.'

'Some people are. It's almost certainly just a phase she's going through. Adolescence is such a bore, especially for the adolescent.'

'Especially for those around her, you mean.'

'She'll grow out of it.'

When Anna said nothing he went on, 'So what else is wrong?'

'Oh . . . David's never *there*, somehow. Not like he used to be.'

Kleist refreshed her drink without having to be asked.

'He got this wonderful promotion last month. There's some standing committee, ultra hush-hush, you get onto it and you're like God. The trouble is, he has to fit it in with all his other work, and the committee meets every day. Or it seems like every day. Some weekends they troop off to

39

the country, and . . . oh, I don't know. I love him so much.'

'Still?'

'Yes, still.' She paused; then, as the sense of his remark filtered through to her, said, 'Why the surprise?'

When he did not respond immediately she looked up from the depths of her glass to find an indecipherable look on his face. 'You understood what you were getting when you married him,' he said quickly.

'You warned me, yes.'

'Subtly, I hope.'

'You never really approved of David, did you?'

Kleist hesitated. 'I thought you could have done better.'

'I could have, then. Before I got to know David properly.' She smiled affectionately at him. 'But you weren't the marrying type.'

She had wanted to pass it off lightly, but his refusal to meet her eyes told Anna that it was up to her to rescue them from the discomfiting situation she had inspired. 'What did Seppy say when you rang?'

'He was thrilled. Usual table, usual time.'

'You're an angel.' It was true, today he really did look like a suntanned angel, replete with power . . . 'I need to talk to you, Gerhard. I hope I'm not using you – I've kept my distance over the past two years, haven't I?'

'I always assumed you had a valid reason.'

'In a way. I never told David I'd been in therapy. You advised me not to and so I never did, even though I often wanted to. And somehow keeping my life in watertight compartments just became . . . well, too difficult. Can you understand that?'

'Easily.'

'I think that really the only reason I've come to see you is that David's gone away, you see. And I feel a bit cheap. As if I'm carrying on behind his back.'

She waited for him to prompt her, but he said nothing. At last she took her courage in both hands and said, 'I need help.'

40

'My dear, whatever is the trouble?'
'I'm worried. No, not worried. Frightened.'
'Of?'
'Losing the man I love.'

FOUR

David Lescombe let the phone ring twenty-seven times before terminating the call, which he did by replacing the receiver on its rest with almost excessively gentle respect, as if anxious to preserve British Telecom's equipment for as long as possible. Behind him, people were emerging from the refectory in ones and twos, their chatter an irritating distraction from the problem confronting him: what to make of his wife's extraordinary behaviour? When a hand descended on his arm he turned away from the phone booth, remembering just in time to fashion a neutral smile.

'I suppose I really ought to ring mine up. You romantic types give the rest of us a bad name.'

The speaker was a fat Welshman in his upper fifties who derived obvious satisfaction from being obliged to spend most weekends away from the demands of family and garden. While David was trying to think of something to say they were joined by a woman, much younger than either of them.

'Leave him alone,' she said tartly. 'I think it's beautiful. We need more like him. Come on, you.' She put one hand through David's elbow and clasped it with the other. 'I want to hear all about NOCC.'

'Thanks, Sylvia,' he murmured, as she shepherded him away.

'No problem. I rode to the rescue because he's right: you *are* romantic, and I love it.'

David flushed.

'Is everything okay, though? You look a bit peaky.'

'I'm fine. My wife forgot an errand I asked her to run, that's all.' His voice was tight. 'Well, here goes . . .'

'Good luck. I envy you, incidentally.'

'Heavens, why?'

'No one offered me a shot at Vancouver.'

'Nor me.'

'Don't be too sure. Your specialism is exactly what they need. Pull out all the stops today, and who knows – a place on the touring eleven could well be yours. See you.'

David laughed, but his heart was beating unpleasantly. His third Krysalis weekend, his first paper. He did not relish the thought of facing the high powered mid-Atlantic men and women who awaited him in the lecture room, especially since the predominant thought in his mind wasn't the 1983 Montebello Council and its long-term effects on NATO's Nuclear Operations Command and Control (the subject matter of his coming dissertation), but where Anna might be.

As he queued at the electronic door, waiting his turn for the guard to scrutinize his pass and check him off the list, he ran through the more obvious possibilities. A girlfriend. A shopping expedition. An urgent case, necessitating her presence in chambers.

On a Saturday? And why hadn't she telephoned the marina, as he'd asked her to?

During the coffee break he'd dithered over whether to call Anna. On the one hand, she might think he was phoning to check whether she'd remembered to contact the marina, which could be interpreted as a vote of no confidence. On the other, she had sounded rather low the previous evening and perhaps she needed cheering up. In the end he dialled the Islington number. When he got no reply, he decided to waste even more precious time by phoning Brighton himself. No, they told him; we were still expecting you . . . Mrs Lescombe hasn't been in touch.

He remembered her saying quite specifically that she would be working at home all weekend.

Last night, on the phone, he had unexpectedly found himself repeating how much he loved her, the kind of declaration that did not come easily to him. But Anna had put the receiver down before he could finish, as if there was something more important on her mind. Her conduct seemed irresponsible and irrational.

David felt let down, he was angry and he could do without this hassle. Here, he was on probation: attached to Krysalis yet not quite part of it. The Politburo had 'candidate members', which struck him as a useful phrase. The paper he was about to deliver could change his own status from candidate to full voting committeeman. He knew how these things worked. If he performed well, there would be a subtle change in the atmosphere. Suddenly he would belong. And although he had demurred, he felt sure that Sylvia's words were true: he might even find himself going to Vancouver as an observer of the most crucial superpower summit this decade. But for the moment he was still a spectator of the game.

His wandering eyes came to rest on the pistol in the holster strapped around the guard's waist. No game. This was real.

The man examined David's pass, compared it with the face, and handed it back. David entered what had once been a large classroom, in those days when the house was a boarding school, and made his way to the rostrum. As he placed his notes upon the lectern, he hoped that the audience saw him as he projected himself: a calm, professional, hard-working civil servant, accelerating quickly through the fast lane. *The Krysalis Committee . . . and he, David Lescombe, was on it!*

Nearly.

Where could Anna have gone?

He cleared his throat. 'Ladies and Gentlemen . . .'

As the buzz of conversation died away David found himself the cynosure of some very hard eyes. He hesitated a moment, then began.

'The purpose of this paper is to examine several implications of the Montebello Council's decision to cut stockpiled warheads, having regard to recent developments in the so-called "bottom-up" command structure. My intention is three-fold . . .'

Were they listening? Would he be able to answer their questions afterwards?

' . . . First, to examine what has happened to the AirLand Battle concept in the light of the so-called Gorbachev revolution . . .'

What was the matter with Anna?

David ruthlessly ejected her from his mind.

FIVE

After lunch the weather turned cold, making them hurry back to Hampstead, eager for a log fire. When Kleist dug out a bottle of Rioja the colour of black plums Anna at first protested, but he overruled her: 'on medical grounds', as he jocularly put it.

While they drank, she rounded off the story of the past two years. Because of the Rioja's strong, oaky taste she failed to notice the mild sedative with which he had adulterated her glass.

'I can see why you're feeling low,' he said when she had finished.

'But pulling myself out of it . . .'

'Ah, yes, that's another thing. Have you considered becoming a patient again, for a short while?'

She smiled into his eyes, wanting to soften a rejection that she sensed would hurt him. 'I really don't think it's a good idea. Just chatting with you is enough.'

'Didn't you find therapy helpful?'

'*Helpful!*' She couldn't be sure if he was joking or not. 'When you first met me, I was a wreck. A total wreck. And look at me now: successful barrister, married, going to work every day like any normal person.' She stifled a yawn. 'You did that.'

'No. You did it.'

'Oh, come on! You saved me, Gerhard. And you ask if therapy was helpful!'

'Then surely just a few sessions wouldn't hurt. After all,

you've been back for refreshers in the past. Most patients feel a need for that, there's no stigma attached.'

'No, Gerhard.'

'Look, you've got three days' holiday next week, that's more than long enough for me to – '

'I was planning to go away, actually. Paris, I thought Paris. Or I might get around to the chores I've been neglecting. The car needs a service, my wardrobe's at an all-time low, I . . .'

'You sound frightened of therapy. Are you?'

She shook her head, without meeting his gaze.

'You do remember, don't you, that it's impossible for a hypnotherapist to make his patient act out of character?'

'I know.'

'If I told you to kill or rob, you'd refuse whether you were in a trance or not.'

She smiled, but held her peace. He studied her face for several moments before speaking again. 'How are the relaxation exercises going?'

'Not well.' She sighed. 'I do miss them.'

'Oh, why? I taught you how to self-hypnotize.'

'Yes, you did. It was so refreshing. That more than anything else was what transformed me, you know. Whenever I was feeling down, knowing I could retreat into a beautiful world all of my own . . . but . . .'

'But what?'

'It faded.' She yawned again. 'Sorry. Tired all of a sudden.'

He allowed the silence to continue, wanting her to make the running. But when she did not speak, he was at last forced to say, 'I suppose I could . . . ginger it up for you again? Only the self-hypnosis, I mean: the relaxation exercises.'

Her face lengthened. 'I don't know.'

'Think of one good reason why not.'

'I'm just giving self-reliance a chance, that's all. Though to be honest . . .'

47

'Yes?'

'It's the trances I do miss the most.' She half turned towards him, refusing to cover that final inch which would have caused their eyes to meet. 'If I did say yes, could you pep it up for me in just one session? No repeats?'

Kleist's smile was broad. 'No repeats; you can still go to Paris on Monday. I'll come with you, if you like.'

'Part of the therapy?' Her smile was arch.

'Definitely.' When still she hesitated he said, 'We'd better go upstairs,' and rose.

This sounded like an invitation to bed and so it was, after a fashion. In his consulting room Kleist had a Z-shaped Corbusier chair, perfect for inducing the relaxation which constituted the first step down the road to forgetfulness. Anna needed a moment of courage to sit down in that painfully familiar couch, with all its attendant memories, but then the routine came back to her without conscious thought or effort, like riding a bike again after years of driving a car. She settled back and arranged her limbs until they were comfortable. Once she was at her ease she looked around, taking pleasure in each little detail. She had never expected to see this place again.

The room was beautiful; not just because she had helped create it but because he lived here and it was him. Wood, everywhere. He had become an expert carver early in life; she remembered how he could carve a perfectly straight line without the help of an edge, his eye was that good and his hand, of course, obeyed him, because everyone, everything in the world, obeyed Gerhard.

Kleist pulled a chair up close beside her. 'Look at me.'

Anna did so. Within seconds she had no limbs, no body, no head; just eyes. She was floating, no, that was the wrong word, she was suspended in amniotic fluid, weightless, and she, meaning this pair of eyes, she was being pulled into another pair of eyes the colour of pale blue curaçao.

He began the soft, lilting incantation that had fallen on

her like the summer rain of evening, poignant and sad, a threnody; apart from David, the one constant in her tired existence since he had first taken her by the hand nearly sixteen years before and said, 'It will be all right. It will.'

'You are falling deeper and deeper into a refreshing, restful trance, deeper, lower, falling, until your eyelids are so heavy that you cannot raise them, cannot open your eyes, and when you reach that point of heaviness I want you to indicate it to me by raising the middle finger of your right hand . . . yes, good . . . and when I say so I want you to open those heavy, heavy eyelids in a blink, just one, now . . . and again . . . now . . .'

So long since she had felt herself falling, falling, Alice in the White Rabbit's burrow, the fantasy amused her, soon he would begin to count . . . so normal. So reassuring. It had not been a mistake to come back, after all . . .

'You can open your eyes, Anna.'

She lay still, staring into the liqueur-rich pools, which now were lit from within. When at last he stood up quietly and moved out of her vision she remained immobile.

Her head was placed in such a way that she could see another of his lutes, in a glass-fronted press beside the door. He had made it; for Gerhard, as well as being a lutenist, was also a luthier. She knew this instrument. He had explained it all to her, long ago. Spruce for the body, sycamore for the neck; a sound-board of cedar and fingerboard of rose; for the bridge, pearwood, and plum for the pegs; strings of gut; assembled with pearls of skin glue, a jewellers' piercing-saw, dedication and love. The beautiful lute expanded to fill her vision until she was aware of nothing else.

Sometimes, as now, he used the instrument to focus a patient's attention, but he'd also played it to soothe her, in the old days, before her perceptions of him changed. Anna wondered dreamily if Gerhard guessed how much she'd come to loathe this lute, which had sent her dear friend Robyn into such ecstasy . . .

49

Solid bars of golden light angled through the windows, telling her that the sun was out. Suddenly the rays were blocked and she heard Gerhard say, 'Can you see my wrist-watch, Anna?'

She looked. 'Yes.'

'It's an Omega.'

For an instant nothing happened. Then all her limbs seemed to relax, as a body settles after losing its struggle with death.

Kleist slowly let out a sigh. The worst hurdle, the fear that had kept him awake every night since Vogel's visit, was behind him. Two years' absence notwithstanding, she remained his creature.

'Anna,' he said quietly, settling himself at her head. 'Can you hear me?'

A long pause. 'Yes.'

' "Omega" is the same now as always. When you awake, you will not remember anything of what happens between my having spoken the word Omega and my speaking the other word known only to you. Do you understand?'

Half a minute passed. During that time Anna neither moved nor uttered a word. Eventually Kleist rose and took a few steps around the room. 'Anna,' he murmured. When still she failed to respond, he removed a handkerchief from his pocket and wiped his hands with it. This had to work. *It had to!*

'Yes.'

He stopped in mid-stride and wheeled around, not sure what he had heard. Anna's eyes remained shut, her lips were parted. Kleist hesitated no longer, but again took his place at her head.

'Everything I say now you will record, deep inside your mind, and you will obey the instructions I shall give you, answer the questions I shall put. Do you understand?'

Her brow slowly furrowed into a frown; she opened her mouth, closed it again. 'Yes.' A whisper.

'David has a safe in the house. It was delivered three weeks ago. Do you know how to open that safe?'

After another of those nerve-wracking waits she shook her head.

'There is a problem. A serious one. For some reason, no one can now open the safe. David says there is a mechanical fault with the lock. But the Foreign and Commonwealth Office believe that he must have forgotten the combination. We both know that is ridiculous, don't we? David would never do a thing like that.'

He paused while studying her face, but could not say how she was taking it.

'David's employers desperately need to open the safe, right now. National security depends on it. You are our last hope. Have you watched David open the safe?'

Eventually she nodded.

'Then it is possible that, under hypnosis, you can throw some light on what has gone wrong. There is a square keyboard on the door: the nine digits and a nought, plus two other electronic keys. Go back to the day when you are watching your husband open the safe. Describe to me what his fingers are doing to the keyboard.'

Anna said nothing.

'Let me assure you, I would not ask you to do this if it were not urgent. Outside the room, civil servants are waiting anxiously to find out if you can help.'

Still she did not respond. Kleist lowered his voice.

'I'm not supposed to tell you this, Anna, but David's career is in the balance. His superiors are very angry with him. They blame him for forgetting the combination. We both know that they are wrong, and that David is right. So you can save him. But between us we *must* somehow find a way to open that safe.'

'Yes.'

Her voice was low, although this time it sounded firmer. Kleist, hearing a note of acquiescence there, wiped his forehead in relief. He could keep this house. His sister, Ilsa, still had a future. All he had to do was keep calm, stay on track.

While he waited for the memories to surface from Anna's subconscious, he opened a notepad and drew squares to represent the keyboard he had described earlier, ready to record the combination to the Krysalis safe.

SIX

As Anna opened the front door the phone began to ring and she rushed to answer it. 'Yes?'

'Anna? Is that you?'

'David! Oh, I – '

'Where've you been?'

'Out. Why, what's the – '

'I've been ringing you all day. You didn't phone the marina, you forgot to put the answering machine on, I've been worried sick. Darling, what is it . . . ?'

Anna leaned against the wall, trying to clear her aching head.

' . . . Only you told me you'd be working at home this weekend.'

'Okay,' she said. 'Keep calm.'

'I am calm.'

'I've got a headache.'

'Well, don't drink too much this evening, then.'

'Why not?' she flared. 'It is Saturday, you know. Are you going to tell me you don't drink, you and the rest of them down at bloody Midhurst.'

'Anna! Don't *ever* say things like that on the phone. This isn't a secure line.'

'Sorry. Wasn't thinking. No, I didn't phone the marina, I forgot.' *Damn, damn, damn!* 'Sorry. Is there anything else?'

'Hey, listen, it's me. Remember me – David, your husband? What's got into you?'

'Nothing. I need a break, that's all.' She paused. 'I might

53

go to Paris on Monday.' When David did not respond at once she hurried on, 'What's got into you, come to that?'

'I don't – '

'You talk as if forgetting one phone call's the end of the world. Well, listen, I've got news for you. I've got problems of my own. I lost a case on Friday. Juliet's being a total little bitch.' The tears were flowing freely now. 'You're drifting away from me, you pick on my failings . . .'

'Darling, that's just not true.'

'Well, why did you phone me tonight then? It was because I forgot to phone the marina, wasn't it, you wanted to carp on – '

'Listen. I've had a lousy day. I – '

'I , I, *I*! David, I'm telling you: there are two "I"'s in this house! I'm miserable. And I can't make you care.'

'You're miserable! Successful barrister, good-looking, rich, a husband who loves you . . . what else do you want?'

'*Time!* Time to be with you now and then, like in the old days.'

'Next weekend. I promise. Assuming you're back from . . . Paris, or wherever it was you – '

'You promised this weekend.'

'Oh . . . Oh, look, just try and pull yourself together, will you? And when I ask you to do something, would – '

Anna slammed down the phone. The instrument fell to the floor. She stepped over it on her way to the kitchen, where she made herself an almost fatally anaemic Bloody Mary. Part of her knew that it would make her feel worse, but another part craved the kick. She'd have just one drink, then she could attend to whatever it was that seemed so important. Oh, yes: the safe . . .

Anna had a second drink without noticing. Damn David. What possessed him to talk to her like that? She had been cradling her head in her arms, but now she raised it and shouted at the ceiling, 'How *could* you?' before dissolving into tears.

'How could *you*?' a voice murmured inside her brain. 'You've been drinking too much, you're feeling rotten . . . but it won't mend matters if you snap at David, will it?'

Strange. There wasn't only this one voice inside her head, there were others, too, all speaking at once . . .

Anna sat up, dried her eyes. She knew she had to do something. But she couldn't remember the whole of today, and now it happened again – another of those fearsome blanks. One moment she was in the kitchen, the next she found herself entering the study, without any recollection of going there. Of course, the important thing. The safe.

She could not understand why the safe was so important. David's safe. Surely she ought not to touch it without his permission?

Anna was swaying. She raised a hand to her forehead. Sleep. What she needed was sleep. Forget the safe. To-morrow.

Bed.

The safe.

Her hands knotted themselves into fists, she raised them to her temples in an attempt to drown out the monotonous drum beat that was driving her insane.

David, where are you?

Why aren't you here?

Another blank. Anna came to upstairs, sitting on her bed. While she was 'out' she had made herself coffee, apparently. She took the cup back to the kitchen, washed up, dried her hands, folded the tea towel neatly. She replaced the Delft cup in its usual place on the stripped-pine dresser, mending an ugly gap in the row. Her ability to go on functioning after the day's intake of alcohol strained even her belief. 'One thing you learn at the bar,' she used to tell her friends, 'is how to drink.' Typical Anna quip, they would say admiringly. Smart. Witty. *Such good value.*

She had knocked over the phone when David rang. It was suddenly very important that she replace it on the hook. For a long time she sat on the lowest stair, gazing at the telephone and vainly trying to work out why it meant so much to her.

Then she was in her bedroom again, putting on her night-dress. But it was all wrong, because she ought to be dealing with the safe, for David's sake, only she didn't much care for David, right now. Tomorrow. Everything could wait for tomorrow.

Once she got into bed and settled down, however, her mind remained active. Outside in the darkened square a passer-by, or perhaps it was an animal, knocked over some empty milk bottles. Anna briefly raised her head to listen, but the sound was not repeated. London seemed strangely silent, although she could just hear the sigh of mingled traffic and voices that always hovered on the edge of consciousness in any metropolis.

Her vision blurred. She squeezed her eyes tightly shut, then opened them and strove to focus on her surroundings. She must be sickening for something, she vaguely supposed; this wasn't just the after-effects of alcohol. Flu . . . just when she was planning a few days off.

Her mind strayed again, along with her eyes. The room was largely white. David had encouraged her to do with the house as she pleased, and a white bedroom had most certainly pleased her, but what had he thought of it? Did it ever feel to him like a prison? The orange street lamps made bars of shadow out of the window-frame, gridding her bed with black, so that for an instant even she felt herself to be inside a cell.

She was so tired. Why, then, couldn't she sleep? If only her head would stop *pounding*!

Take a sleeping tablet.

The pills were in the top drawer of her bedside table. She took the top off the tub and tipped its contents onto the sheet. David's words re-echoed in her brain. *Successful barrister, good-looking, rich, a husband who loves you . . . what else do you want?* Anna picked up one of the tablets and chewed it, unable to face the thought of getting out of bed and going to fetch a glass of water.

She couldn't hold her head upright. It kept falling forward. But still her brain wouldn't let her rest.

She ought to take a sleeping tablet.

Tomorrow, very first thing, she must attend to the safe. If only her headache would go, perhaps she could do what was necessary tonight, before she slept.

No. Too tired.

Her fingers made contact with something small and round lying on the sheet. Perhaps a pill would help her sleep . . .

The phone rang.

Anna hung suspended in another world, a realm of utter darkness. She wanted to stay there. Ringing phones were nothing to do with her. Yet she felt acute pain; she could hear and her brain was commanding her return.

The phone rang.

The same call? Or was it later?

The bed racked her with its hardness. She changed position and for the first time identified the pain as a headache: throbbing, blinding, productive of extreme nausea.

The phone rang.

She awoke with a single word at the forefront of her mind and that word was 'safe'.

Her right hand grasped the telephone receiver, lifted it off its rest. She didn't want to do that, but already she was back in the world of natural reactions, where phones got answered because that's what one did.

'Anna! Anna, for Christ's sake, is that you?'

She knew this voice. It belonged to her husband.

'Anna . . . why don't you answer?'

'Hello.'

'Oh, thank God, thank God. Anna, what the hell's going on? Are you all right? Anna? *Anna!*'

'All righ . . .'

'What?'

'Must have . . . overslept.'

57

'Darling, do you know what time it is?'

Anna had not yet opened her eyes but through the gauze of pain she knew it was daylight outside. She must speak. 'Sunday morning . . .'

'*Sunday!* It's Monday! Monday morning, seven o'clock. Anna, what is *wrong* with you?'

She sat up in bed and opened her eyes. Nothing. She was blind. Just whiteness. She'd tried to do something terrible, and ended up blind instead. Justice. Retribution.

The whiteness softened into pastels. Anna stared at the face of her alarm clock until it reconstituted itself. She had slept for over thirty hours.

'I'm sorry . . . Monday, how silly. I was working till all hours last night.'

She couldn't understand her need to lie, and it frightened her. She desperately wanted to tell David the truth. But something stronger than her will prevented it.

'I phoned the house, no answer . . . Anna? Darling, please *talk to me*!'

'Tired, that's all. Just very tired.'

'I'm coming home.'

Sharpness, focus; Anna instantly became functional. The pain was expanding and contracting inside her skull like a monstrous heart, and soon she would be sick, but only soon, not yet, not yet . . . 'Where are you?' she asked quickly.

'Still at the seminar. Anna, you're ill. I'll be back inside two hours.'

'No. I don't want – '

'I love you.'

'*David!* You mustn't – ' But she was talking across the purr of an empty line.

Anna put down the phone. For a few seconds she sat there, feeling dreadful. Then she threw back the duvet and jumped out of bed.

Her chin hit the floor with a bang. For terrifying seconds she couldn't work out what had happened. She became aware of another pain, in her legs this time. Her muscles had gone to sleep along with the rest of her, only they needed longer to wake up. She couldn't move.

Don't panic.

She sat upright, with great difficulty, and rested her back against the bed. She had to go to the bathroom. Crawl.

The indignity of it struck her with great force: on her hands and knees, like an animal. Once in the bathroom she began to retch and then she did panic, because her stomach was empty and she seemed to be sicking up endless amounts of bile, acid, something that tasted terrible and made her teeth rough, and she couldn't stop. The pain was like a monster that possessed her utterly. She managed to turn on the bidet's cold water tap and slurp a drink. After she'd brought that up and drunk some more the spasms slowly began to abate.

Aspirin. No, Alka-Seltzer: she found a sachet in the medicine chest and mixed it into a glass of water. Down it went; up it came. She tried again. This time the clear, fizzy liquid stayed in her stomach.

David would be home soon. That was the thought, the one cogent, coherent thought, which kept her going. So she had time, but not much.

Time for what? *For what?*

Anna looked at herself in the mirror. Her long blonde hair tumbled in rats' tails to frame a narrow oval face whose principal features were black circles around eyes that opened but a slit. She stared at this apparition, expecting it to assume a life, a will of its own. For this was another Anna, not her: a person who suffered from weird, ugly dreams. Gerhard would certainly be interested in those.

The safe! In her nightmare she was opening David's safe and removing some papers; she, a barrister, turned thief.

Anna gripped the wash basin in an attempt to steady herself. Perhaps it hadn't been a nightmare. *What if she had really done it?* She somehow made her way to the study and sat down in David's swivel chair. She could not take her eyes off the safe, but neither did she dare approach it.

She was in the wrong place.

It did not strike her as odd that this conviction should suddenly overwhelm her, or that she knew exactly where to go next. At the top of the house was a little room she'd kept all to herself. My sewing room, my boudoir, she'd say to friends; where I entertain my lovers from *cinq* until *sept* (how they laughed!), the place where I keep my secrets, my own, my very, very own.

All her life, ever since her mother had given her away, she had wanted something to call her own.

Nothing matched in this cramped, untidy room. The chaise-longue was faded, the curtains too new-looking, the Singer sewing machine almost antique, the old, jumble-sale desk . . .

She snatched open the desk's bottom drawer. A splinter lodged in her wrist, but she scarcely felt it. Anna reached down and it was there, the bulky comb-bound file in its grey plastic cover, exactly as she had seen it in her dreams of the night before.

She pulled it out. The rubric in the upper right hand corner caught her eye, 'Top Secret'; then, opposite, the type-written formula 'This is copy number . . . of seven copies' and somebody had written '5' in the blank space. And halfway down the page was the single word, 'Krysalis'. Just that.

Someone had opened the safe. But instead of stealing whatever was inside, they had put it here, in her worm-eaten old desk. Why do that? How had they known about her 'precious' drawer, the one where she kept all Juliet's letters?

She put the file back with the thin bundle of childishly addressed envelopes, knowing that she must phone . . . whom must she phone?

Gerhard.

'Hello.' He said it in an odd, high-pitched tone which made the greeting sound like a threat. Was he nervous? Why be nervous about speaking to her? 'Anna, I've been very worried, I've been ringing the house for ages, you didn't answer, I – '

'You've got to help me. I've broken into David's safe. I've got the papers. I stole them. I stole David's file.'

'*You* stole . . . ?'

'It must have been me. Help me.'

Even as she spoke she realized that she was going to have to explain, but he seemed to grasp the situation with miraculous speed. 'Don't move it. Don't talk to anyone before I get there, not *anyone*, you hear?'

'When will you . . . ?' But the line had gone dead.

Anna hung up. She drifted into the living room and sat down to wait. Time passed. How long would it take Gerhard to come from Hampstead to Islington? She looked at her watch over and over again. Whenever she heard a car slow as it drove past the house she rose to her feet, meaning to go to the window and look, but she could not manage that. For it had suddenly become critically important that Gerhard arrive before David; she dreaded the thought of peering through the net curtains at the wrong face there on the pavement.

Anna had almost given up hope when she heard someone run up the steps to the front door. The bell rang. She crept into the hall. 'Who is it?'

'Gerhard.'

She opened the door. 'Show me,' he said, pushing past her.

Anna took him to the safe in David's study. Kleist stared at it. 'You said someone had broken in.'

'Yes. Me.'

'But the door . . .'

'That's how I found it. Locked.'

'And the papers . . . ?'

Without another word she conducted him to her room on the top floor and opened the desk-drawer.

'I was afraid of something like this,' he muttered. 'On Saturday, you were deeply, deeply distressed.'

'Was I?'

'You don't remember?'

61

Anna shook her head.

'It only came out during the trance. I told you to forget everything, but I was very worried. The resentment you'd built up towards David . . .'

'Gerhard, why did I do this?' She was obviously frightened. 'I've been cured for years, haven't I? *How* did I do it? Tell me. I don't even know the combination to the safe.'

'Why do you say it was you who opened it, then?'

She spread her hands helplessly. 'Who else could it have been?'

'Burglars. Spies.'

'They wouldn't have put the papers here, they'd have taken them.'

'Anna, if you're going to keep on saying you stole – '

'But I must have done. I dreamed it all. I can see myself now.' Even as she spoke it was coming back to her. 'I heard this voice inside my head . . .'

'Voice? Are you seriously telling me you've been hearing voices?'

The face she turned to him betrayed growing wonderment. 'Yes.'

'My God, you're such a fool!' His own face was white; Anna could see how angry he was and it shocked her, because he'd never let her see raw hostility before. She looked at him for a moment, unable to comprehend. Then – 'Gerhard . . . I think I'm going to be sick.'

She ran to the lavatory. By the time she came back his mood had altered. He was studying the file, going through it page by page. The minute flicker of his eyes told her that he was reading it, really reading it. He sat with one leg crossed over the other and his back arched. Now, as he came to the bottom of the last page, he allowed his right hand, the one holding the file, to fall onto his thigh, while he rested his chin in his left palm. His eyes were nearly closed. He resembled a man who has heard Mozart for the first time, and recognized the voice of God, and known that life has changed.

It struck her how incongruous he looked still wearing his gloves in a centrally heated room.

'Do you understand what this is?' He spoke to the floor, but Anna heard.

'No.'

'Oh, Anna, my Anna . . .' He lifted his head and gazed into her eyes. 'What have you done?'

'But how *could* I have done it? I don't even know the combination to the safe!'

'The only possible explanation is that it's in your subconscious. Dreams, voices . . . does anyone know, suspect, that you might have this?'

'Of course not!' His expression terrified her.

'When will David be coming home? My Christ, why didn't I think of that before — *when*?'

She darted a look at her watch. 'Soon. He'll have left the seminar . . . Gerhard, I think it might be best if I went away for a while, what do you think?'

Kleist stared at her. That was so exactly what he wanted her to do, and so much the very opposite of what he'd expected her to say, that for a moment he could only sit in silence. 'It's a . . . a little difficult to just, well, run away from something like this,' he temporized.

'Running away is the last thing I mean to do. But listen. I'm a barrister, I've done enough cases to know how these things work. People panic, because they talk first and think later. I've got a solicitor and tomorrow we'll call him, I'll make a statement, but the first, only thing I need is *time*!'

'But . . . but wouldn't that seem like running? To the police, I mean?'

'You don't understand. Look at me.'

'Anna, I — '

'No, just look at me.' She laid both palms against his chest. 'I'm calm, yes?'

Reluctantly he nodded. There was something terribly wrong with Anna but he couldn't put his finger on it yet.

'I'm a trained lawyer. You can't tell me how things appear

63

and don't appear to the outside world, because I understand better than you do. Now. The first thing to face up to is that David doesn't know anything about you. He doesn't realize I've been in therapy, or why I went into therapy in the first place or anything about my problems. Right? *Right*?'

He nodded again. At last he was beginning to understand. She was scared out of her wits, but determined not to show it. She wanted to run away, she *had* to run away . . . but first someone, an outsider, must provide her with corroboration of *rational* reasons for flight. Somebody had to give approval. Someone like Kleist . . .

'Maybe it was a mistake not to tell David,' she went on. 'None of that matters. All that counts is that *David doesn't know*!'

He could not but admire her. She was talking it through rationally, calmly, like a true professional. All she needed now was the right kind of gentle encouragement.

' . . . If I'm going to save my marriage, we need to prepare David. The trauma of hearing everything at once could knock him out.'

Kleist knew the time had come to test his theory. Oppose her. Force her to step up the argument. He drew a deep breath: 'But if you let me talk to David . . .'

'After nine years of marriage? Suddenly tell him I've been in therapy before and after I met him and he never knew about that, about *you*!'

'He'd understand.'

'*No!*' She clenched her fists and began to pound his chest. 'He *wouldn't*! Gerhard, I live with that man and I'm telling you: he would not. So I have to go. Just for a day, maybe two, while we sort out what to do.'

'But you'll be incriminating yourself!'

'You *must* keep a sense of proportion. This is a serious situation; it isn't a major crisis. The file hasn't disappeared, it's *there*, on the desk. David knows that I was thinking of taking a few days abroad, he won't be wholly surprised to come back and find me gone.'

Kleist could see it was working. Don't stop, he told himself; go on. 'But Anna, he's bound to call the police when he finds the file out of the safe.'

'Of course.'

'They'll discover your fingerprints on it, they'll assume you've taken a copy.'

All the while his brain kept leaping two, three moves ahead, anticipating how to meet his own objections and overcome them; but she didn't need him. She was perfectly capable of working it out for herself.

'Gerhard . . . Gerhard, do just think for a moment. *Think!* All these things are true whether we call the police ourselves, now, or David does it later. They've only got my word for it that I opened the safe last night, not weeks ago. Forty-eight hours won't make the slightest difference to either the file or my chances in a criminal court. But they *could* just save my marriage.'

He hesitated, pretending to consider. He stayed silent for so long that Anna suddenly surprised him by saying, 'I know what you're thinking.'

He raised his head and stared at her, almost persuaded that it was true.

'You want me to wipe my fingerprints off the file and the safe, don't you? Then there'd be nothing to connect me with either of them. I could just say I came down to find the file lying on top of the safe.'

Kleist swallowed. It was perfect; so perfect that he couldn't think of a way to knock it down. But Anna was still equal to the occasion.

'No.' She shook her head with a smile. 'I couldn't do it.'

'Why?'

'Two reasons. First, I'd trip myself up. I'm not a good liar. And secondly, if they believed me, it would mean that David had been almost unbelievably careless. Mean the end of his career. Do you think I could live with him for the rest of my life, knowing he'd been unfairly dismissed and it was my fault?'

For a moment he was tempted to tell her he already knew the safe's combination, that they could put the file back and no one would know; but he wanted that file. Besides, she might yet end up talking to the police and he could not risk it.

'There's another reason why I have to come clean, eventually,' Anna said; and he looked at her with as much apprehension as if she really had acquired the power to read his mind.

'What?'

'You're assuming this file was the only thing in the safe. I don't know what David kept in there. Suppose there were other papers, I've taken those as well, hidden them somewhere else?'

'I have to think.' Kleist began to stride around the room, keeping his gaze fixed on the floor. At last he came to rest by the window and stood there looking out over the square. Muscles twitched beneath the skin of his face, turning it into a restless sea of anger. Now it came down to it, he genuinely did not know what to do for the best.

Anna was right, in one way: here were the papers, nothing was missing. In another sense, however, she was dead wrong, because from her point of view there was only one course of action worth considering: anyone with her best interests at heart would see it as his duty to persuade her to stay, be utterly frank, and face the music. But Kleist had started to see everything from quite a different point of view: his own.

How would Anna respond to interrogation? First, she would tell them about nigh on sixteen years of episodic psychotherapy. Tell them, in other words, about *him*. Then, suppose she admitted to hearing voices, *a* voice, that's what she'd said. What if, under someone else's hypnosis, perhaps, she got around to identifying that voice as Gerhard Kleist's . . . ?

She wanted, needed to run away. She had persuaded herself that that was the only course. Kleist knew it was pointless to try and influence her further. When he'd first set foot inside the house a few moments ago he felt he was facing disaster. But the more he thought the more convinced he became that fortune might be presenting him with the kind of once-in-a-lifetime prize that leaves a man breathless. He possessed the file, he controlled the woman. Between them, they amounted to treasure beyond price. If he could only stay cool enough to plan the next move . . .

Kleist became aware that Anna had stopped speaking and was looking at him expectantly. He dithered a moment longer, aware that the risks matched the likely rewards: both were astronomical.

It was the need in her eyes that decided him.

'You're right,' he said. 'It's best if you get away for a while. But I'm not taking you to Hampstead.'

'Why not?'

'Because if they find you there — and my God! but they'll be looking hard — they can take you on the spot, won't even need a warrant.'

They. She knew who he meant: spooks, David called them; MI5 and Special Branch and the other crowd who were like Jehovah, they couldn't ever be named.

'Abroad's different,' Kleist said. 'And didn't you say you were planning a trip to . . . where was it, Paris? So that would be the first place he'd think you'd gone . . . I have a villa, in Greece. They won't find you there, not easily.' His voice had grown steadily more decisive, until now he was issuing orders. 'And I can treat you, while I prepare a report on your mental condition.'

'That makes sense to me. If you set everything out, the . . . the history . . .'

'Give David time to adjust, without pressure . . .'

She smiled at him. For the first time he noticed a tic at the corner of her mouth. 'I knew you'd understand.'

'I want you to think back.' Kleist sat down again. 'Who knows about us? Who could trace you, through me?'

'No one.'

'I said to *think*. Of course there's someone – who first referred you to me?'

'My doctor. But that was years ago, he's dead . . .'

'There'd be no official evidence of your consulting me since that time, because you never had another referral . . . Is there anything unofficial, even a diary entry, a – '

'Nothing. I never told anyone about us.'

'Except Robyn.'

'She's in America. I haven't seen her for two years.'

'All right. Now listen. I want you to get your things together . . .'

It seemed like only a few minutes before Anna returned, carrying a suitcase.

'Do you have your passport?' he asked her.

'In the study.'

'Let's get it.'

'The file . . .'

'I'll leave it on top of the safe.' Wonderful, he thought, how convincingly a man can lie when he has to. 'Here, give me that case. And for God's sake, hurry!'

He hauled her as far as the first-floor study and was thrusting her inside, when down below they heard keys jangle on the pavement, followed by the sound of one being inserted in the lock.

'Darling,' a voice cried. 'I'm home.'

Kleist eased the study door shut and held a finger to his lips. As Anna looked at him she felt a moment's uncertainty. She could risk telling David everything, throw herself on his mercy; it was not too late. Tell him that she had been in and out of therapy for sixteen years without letting him know, describe the horrors that had led her to being treated by Gerhard Kleist, *no, she couldn't do that, couldn't confess to the business with Juliet, no, no, no . . .*

Kleist put his mouth close to her ear. 'Get the passport,' he whispered; and Anna obeyed. When she returned from the desk, Kleist held her close. 'Wait until he goes upstairs,' he breathed. 'Then, you go out. Here are my car keys . . . wait for me *inside* the car, where he won't see you.'

'What will you be — '

His face contorted into a scowl. *'Ssh!'*

Footsteps were approaching. David tramped past the study on his way upstairs. Kleist waited until he could no longer hear his progress, then opened the door and looked out. The landing was empty. 'Ready?' he mouthed.

Anna nodded, then dug the nails of her left hand into her palm, trying to make sure she stayed alert, before sliding from the room. A quick look up the bannisters, and she was running.

David called: 'Anna! Is that you?'

She had nearly reached the front door. But if she went out that way, David might see her, and follow.

Hide. *The cellar.*

She raced on through the hallway, passport clutched to her breast, until she reached the stairs to the basement. At the bottom of the last flight she stopped and raised her head, listening. Above, all was quiet. What could David be up to? When he came home, what did he like to do first . . . ?

She did not know. *Oh God, how couldn't she know?* Gerhard would expect her to have reached the car by now. *'Don't leave me,'* she heard herself say. *'Oh, God, please don't leave me!'*

Meanwhile, Gerhard had folded up the Krysalis file and stuffed it into an inside pocket of his overcoat. Now he moved silently across to the windows to position himself behind one of the wall-length drapes. From there he could keep an eye on both the study door and the street below. Still no sign of Anna.

From another pocket of his overcoat he took a Colt .45 and silently checked the magazine. Seven rounds. This gun had not been fired for a long time, there were traces of rust on the breach. Kleist stared at it, conscious that sweat had broken out on his forehead. The shot would make a noise. A lot of noise.

He had never had to use a gun before.

Where the hell was Anna?

He'd deliberately chosen to send her on ahead, almost as a decoy, because if either of them was going to be caught he wanted it to be Anna and if the worst came to the worst he might be able to use her interception as cover for his own escape. But she hadn't run into David and she hadn't left the house. He stared down into the street. Empty.

What would Lescombe do next? Where would he go?

Kleist wiped away the sweat with the back of his gunhand. The Colt weighed heavily in his palm; the jerky movement all but caused him to drop it. He was shaking.

Footsteps overhead.

Kleist stared up at the ceiling, trying to map David Lescombe's movements. A door closed. That meant . . . *what did that mean?*

Someone was coming downstairs. Kleist swallowed. His throat ached as if with tonsillitis. Now the steps had almost reached the study door. Now they were outside, on the landing.

Now they had stopped, and silence filled the house.

Kleist tried to release the safety catch. It was stiff from disuse. He jabbed at the lever, accidentally knocking the gun barrel against the wall. The noise of metal meeting plaster sounded impossibly loud; breath forced itself between his teeth in a gasp.

'Anna,' he heard David shout. 'Anna, where are you, love? Come on, darling, stop playing games!'

The safety catch was off, the Colt ready to fire. Kleist raised the gun until it was pointing at the door. He squeezed even further into the embrasure, and held his breath. A hand rattled the door knob. Movement in the street simultaneously dragged Kleist's gaze downwards. Anna had emerged onto the pavement and was running towards the car. Then the study door opened, and Kleist refocused all his attention on the room.

'Anna!' Very loud . . . *'Anna!'*

70

A long pause. From where he was standing, Kleist could not see whether David had actually entered the room. What if he crossed to the window? *Suppose he looked out and saw Anna in the street?*

Kleist closed his eyes. By now he was shaking so badly he'd become terrified of dropping the gun; the floor was parquet, no carpet to deaden the sound, David couldn't fail to hear *that*. But if he tried to move . . .

The study door closed. More footsteps . . . but outside, on the landing. Kleist let out all the breath in his lungs. *Move!*

He tiptoed to the door, opened it a crack and listened. David was upstairs again. Gently, gently . . . out the door, close it . . . onto the landing, listen, wait . . . silence.

Kleist pocketed the Colt and bent to take off his shoes. Next second he was running. He had almost reached the hallway when, to his horror, someone rang the front door-bell.

For a second he went rigid. Then hasty footsteps sounded overhead and almost without realizing what he was doing he sped to the back of the house.

The cellar.

Kleist slithered down the back stairs and made his silent way through the utility room, past the boiler, and so into the scullery. Beyond that was an area from where a flight of steps led up to the pavement. First the bolts on the outside door, then the key . . . but no, the bolts were already drawn, the key turned; of course, Anna must have come this way too . . .

What was happening up above? Kleist slipped the door open and listened. A delivery man; David having to sign; the front door slammed . . . *Go!*

Anna was in the driver's seat; she had the engine started by the time he reached the top of the steps. Kleist flung himself into the car beside her. Then they were being borne along by the tide of traffic and there was no going back.

Monday

SEVEN

As David threw his raincoat onto the bed he heard a noise downstairs. 'Anna?' he shouted.

There was no reply. He called his wife's name again: 'Anna? Is that you?' The sound of a door closing somewhere below caused his tense expression to soften a little; that meant she was at home. Sounded like the study . . . but when he went down to find no one there, relief turned to vexation. The least she could have done was wait in for him.

His deliberations were interrupted by a delivery of wine. He signed the chit with a mind only half on the job, while his eyes scanned the square. There was Anna's red BMW; wherever she'd gone, she hadn't taken the car.

David went back upstairs to shower and change. As he knotted his tie in front of the mirror something about the room's reflection seemed not quite right and he turned with a frown. Anna's suitcase no longer sat in its usual place on top of the wardrobe and her nightdress had gone from under the pillow.

As he turned away from the bed his eyes lighted on two images of himself, making him start.

A black and white photograph of a much younger David stood on the stripped-pine chest of drawers between the bedroom windows; it showed his face three-quarters towards the camera, with a narrow tie and white shirt just visible. In those days his hair had been lighter – the photo was fifteen years old – and there was more of it, but the preoccupied smile was the same. No, not quite . . . above the chest of drawers hung a mirror, disclosing David's contemporary face, and he was startled to see how extensive a network of lines had eaten into his skin. He was forty-two, but looked five years older; a curious reversal of the state of affairs disclosed by the photograph, which was of a man in fact aged twenty-seven who appeared to be scarcely out of his teens. The new-style David was sallow, etched with the tension that comes from long, midnight oil-soaked hours of labour in the service of his country.

He had never liked either the photograph or its silver frame, which was too extravagant for his taste, but Anna clung to both with the passion that characterized her enthusiasms.

He wondered what he ought to do next. Phone somebody, perhaps. But he'd raced away from Midhurst before breakfast, he was hungry, there would be more chance of reaching the right decisions if his blood-sugar level was high.

The refrigerator yielded enough to make a sandwich. He sat alone in the kitchen, munching stolidly and staring at the dresser which occupied nearly the whole of one wall.

He felt rattled. Usually he kept his imagination well in check, but today it seemed that the rooms were smirking at him, as if they'd witnessed some scene which had left behind this, its own, extraordinarily unpleasant atmosphere.

It suddenly occurred to him that Anna might have collapsed and be incapable of speech, a stroke . . . He cursed himself for his stupidity in not thinking of that before. It took less than five minutes to hunt through every room, look under beds, check closets. But then he knew for certain that she was not in the house.

He went to sit at her desk in the first-floor study, feeling guilty because her behaviour made him cross and a husband ought not to feel cross when his wife acted out of character, he ought to be concerned. He was concerned, of course, but he was offended also.

He found it hard to take seriously her passing mention of going to Paris. Too unlike her. But why had she left just as he arrived home, and without saying a word? He felt sure he'd heard a door close somewhere in the house while he was upstairs earlier and that must have been her, it couldn't have been anyone else.

He drew up a list of names on Anna's scratch-pad, pulled the phone towards him and started to dial.

'Hello . . . David Lescombe here, I'd like to speak to my wife, please . . . She's not in? Yes, I know she was due to take a few days off, I just wondered if she'd been into chambers this morning, or contacted you . . . no, I see. Thank you.'

Next: Ferring, and Anna's parents.

Lydia Elwell answered the phone with her usual note of querulous aggression. 'Hello . . . hello, who is this?'

'Uh . . . me, David. I'm so glad to find you in, Lydia.'

'*We* never go anywhere.'

David recognized this formula as the prelude to a mildly critical resumé of his and Anna's most recent holidays, with overtones of extravagance and want of application, and he had no time for it. 'I was wondering if Anna had been in touch,' he said, more loudly than was necessary.

'We haven't heard from her in ages.'

'She's not with you, then?'

'Certainly not. Why – don't you know where your own wife is?'

David's heart gave a thump, for he knew he had gone too far too fast and now would have to give some explanation for his mistake, but he couldn't think how to do it without complicating a situation that was already labyrinthine. 'You may dig a hole for your minister,' they used to teach, tongue in cheek, at Civil Service College, 'as long as you cart away enough soil to ensure that nobody can bury him.' David had no idea of his hole's dimensions, and the realization was enough to make his shoulders sweat.

'David? David, are you still there?'

'Yes, oh Lord, I see what's happened. I got onto the junior clerk at Anna's chambers and he must have scrambled two messages, it looked as though she was going to her mother's, he said. I'm so sorry.'

'I don't know how Anna copes with her staff. They'd never have put up with it in my day. How is she?'

'Fine, thank you. Look, someone's pushing a message under my nose and I've got to rush . . .'

'Oh, mustn't hold up running the country.'

Sometimes when David talked to Lydia Elwell his head wanted to explode with self-righteous wrath, but now was not the moment. 'No, well, nice to talk to you.' He put down the receiver while she was still in the middle of the string of codes you were supposed to use when terminating a conversation, telephonic, son-in-law, day.

Where was she? *Where had Anna gone?*

He looked at the scratch-pad, wondering who to phone next. He wanted very much to make another call, because his efficient civil servant's brain was ordering the known evidence and presenting options in a way from which he urgently needed to be distracted. One, Anna knew he was going to be at a residential seminar for a long weekend; two, she had sounded distraught on the phone; three, she had been drinking; four, her suitcase was gone; five, she was gone . . .

The evidence, he coldly reminded himself, remained ambiguous. He consulted his list. Cornwall.

For what seemed like a long time he listened to the peculiar rasping tone generated by the St Mary Abbott exchange. At last he reluctantly abandoned the call. They were probably feeding the pigs, or weaving, or doing whatever communal types did with their days. Besides, Anna had never got on with her daughter by that disastrous first marriage, so she would hardly have fled to Juliet.

The options were narrowing now. David added another name to the list, writing it at the foot of the page, to indicate that it was a last resort and that there might be alternatives which he had not yet considered. Then he rang the police and two local hospitals, drawing a blank in each case.

Perhaps she really *had* gone to Paris?

The final entry on his list appeared to have been written in darker ink than the rest. He could not take his eyes off it. He imagined himself already talking to the person whose name it was, trying to anticipate the questions . . .

There had to be a simple explanation. But every time he tried to pin one down, he encountered only this hole where perceptions of his own wife ought to reside and did not. Something that another, perhaps more sensitive husband might have noticed had passed him by, leaving not the longed-for easy answer, just this ridiculous void.

They had tickets for the South Bank at the coming week-end. Brahms, the second symphony. It enraged David to think that at this crucial juncture the thing he remembered about his wife was that she shared his liking for Brahms. Unless, of course, she really didn't like Brahms at all . . . Oh, don't be stupid, she wouldn't walk out on you just to avoid going to a concert! No, but – how had her voice sounded when he proposed the outing and she'd agreed? David could not remember. He was starting to experience an eerie kind of nausea allied to *mal de mer*: the deck wasn't stable, nothing could be taken for granted any more.

By now he was angry: angry enough to search Anna's desk. Her diary. He hesitated only a moment before opening it. There were few daily entries, but the last section of the book overflowed with names, addresses, phone numbers, none of which meant anything to him. He skimmed through with a frown. Who were these people? Professional colleagues? Friends? More than friends . . . ?

The memory of his interview for the Krysalis Committee surfaced and refused to go away. But none of the names in Anna's diary sounded the least bit Germanic.

He slammed the diary shut and tossed it back inside the drawer, now angry with himself as much as with Anna. He was reacting like a fool.

David clasped his hands on the lip of the desk in front of him and rested his weight against them. He had only one number left to ring now. Before he telephoned, however, there was something he must check. He rose to his feet and went across to open the safe.

For a long moment he stared into the cavity without moving. This, then, was how knowledge of betrayal began; he had often wondered. He allowed himself a moment more of peace, not knowing when he would have another one, and went to pick up the phone.

The man he was calling answered on the second ring. 'Yes?'

'My name's David Lescombe. I'm deputy head of department, defence department, FCO.'

'Yes?'

'My copy of the New Testament's disappeared.'

This time there was a long pause before the inevitable 'Yes?'

'Unfortunately, my wife appears to have gone as well.'

He felt pleased with his performance: professional, businesslike, untheatrical and underplayed. But the voice at the other end merely said, 'Are you at home?'

'Yes, I'm at — '

'I know. Stay there.'

And the line went dead.

EIGHT

Albert had just finished washing up after lunch when he heard the phone. He let it ring several times while he dried his hands and folded the tea towel before going through to the bedroom to take the call.

'Hi,' said the voice at the other end. 'Guess who this is?' And they laughed, so that anyone listening in would think that they were just a couple of high-spirited men enjoying a joke, instead of two extremely professional people covering their tracks.

'How are you?'

'Fine, fine,' said Albert. 'What's up?'

'Sorry to bother you, but your father's been trying to get hold of you.'

Albert, whose father had been dead for five years, examined his fingernails critically and said, 'Oh yes?'

'I explained you'd been out of town.'

The adjutant was enjoying this little charade; Albert could tell from his voice. 'Ah.'

'So he might want to ring you later. I said I didn't know if you'd be going out or not.'

'No, not. Did he leave a number?'

'Sorry.'

'Never mind.' A pause. 'Anything else?'

'No, except it looks as though we'll have to cancel tonight.'

Albert's thin mouth extended slightly in a smile that came nowhere near his eyes. 'So it does, yes. 'Bye, then.'

He replaced the receiver and stood in thought for a moment. Then he went over to his bag and unpacked it again, knowing he wouldn't be going back to the regiment for a while. When the phone stayed silent, he embarked on his fifteen-minute routine for cleaning the flat: not the full 'churn-over', as he called it, but a real dust-killer, all the same. Albert had a horror of dirt.

Still no call.

He straightened his tie, turning his head first to the right, then to the left. His suntan from a recent ski-ing holiday had already begun to fade, but in the mirror he still looked every inch the taut, fit army officer that he was. His hair needed cutting – Albert liked to keep it unfashionably short – but that would take up too much time and he didn't want to miss the call. There were some shirts to iron. The wine-cellar was seriously depleted. He could take a chance, sprint to the delicatessen and buy olive oil, they'd sworn the first pressing would be in by Monday and that was today. The deli people were fairly reliable, for Eyeties; which meant little enough, of course. On the other hand, if he spent more time adjusting his neck-wear . . .

The phone rang.

This time he didn't give it a second chance, the receiver was in his hand and up to his ear in a trice.

'Hello, son,' said the familiar voice.

'Isn't it a bit early for me?'

Albert's miraculously resurrected 'father', an MI5 officer whose name was Fox, rested his arm on the car's windowsill and blew a cloud of smoke at the windscreen while he considered this. 'Not exactly *early*,' he said at last. 'At least . . .' he took another drag on the cigarette and added one more line to the several which already disfigured his forehead. 'Not so much early as . . . um, what's the word I want now, prophylactic, no that's something else, isn't it, something to do with that horrible disease . . .'

'Preventive?'

'Ah, preventive.' Happiness reigned, but only temporarily. 'Not *exactly*, no.'

Albert sighed and leaned back, stretching his arms as far as the car's interior would allow.

'What I think you must understand, what I would like to convey to you . . .' Fox leaned forward to stub out his cigarette, spilling a light shower of ash over his suit ' . . . is that this is probably nothing at all. Trivia.' He nodded his head in an attempt to give his statement weight. 'But on the other hand, it could be *the* big one. In which case, the woman has definitely got to be stopped. Anyway . . .'

As Albert got out he studied the square with interest. The impression he had was of a pleasantly middle-class oasis in a difficult part of north London: the word ghetto sprang into his mind and refused to go away. The tall, terraced houses had a well-kept air about them, and if there was money to splash on the exterior it followed that there would be more inside, where wind and rain could do no damage.

'What's the timescale?'

'Very tight.' Fox pushed on the Lescombes' front door, which he had left ajar when coming down to greet Albert. 'Vancouver's so close, that's the problem. So I want you to pick it up as we go along. You have to realize – '

He was interrupted by a loud crash from some upper region. Fox grimaced.

'You're doing a search?'

'Category one.'

'Looking for?'

'Whatever it is that we find.'

They climbed the stairs. At the top of the first flight Fox turned left into a drawing room. Albert had a fleeting impression of Liberty fabrics and large bookcases. Then a man was rising to his feet and he concentrated on him.

'Mr Lescombe, can we resume where we left off . . . ?'

It was clear that Fox did not mean to introduce the newcomer, so Albert held out his hand and murmured, 'I'm

Albert,' with that quiet amusement which both forgives and covers up for an absent-minded host. David shook hands; then his eyes connected with Albert's face and instantly narrowed as if in recognition. Albert found that intriguing. He was sure they had never met.

'Shall we sit down?'

Albert felt glad to hear Fox take charge, because he knew that a moment more and David would have asked him what his function was in all this, and Albert was blessed if he knew.

Loud banging sounds echoed through the house. Two sets of footsteps thundered down the stairs. As they passed by on the landing there was a burst of crackle, followed by a quick exchange on a walkie-talkie.

Fox sat in the dead centre of a Chesterfield and twitched the wings of his waistcoat before resting his hands on his knees. His suit was as near black as made no difference, he wore a white shirt and dark crested tie, a signet ring squeezed the flesh of his right little finger. The sartorial image of a churchwarden was belied by a suspiciously dark head of hair that had plainly been bouffed with the help of a dryer. The bottom-line impression was of a successful if rather close-to-the-wind nightclub owner.

'Mr Lescombe.' Fox paused for long enough to give his waistcoat another little jerk. 'As I was saying earlier, we have considered your preliminary statement. It is very clear and we thank you for that, but we find certain aspects of it unsettling.'

'Oh?' David said. His tone sounded impatient, a trifle supercilious perhaps, implying that Fox only found the statement unsettling because he was too thick to understand it. Albert wandered over to the window-embrasure and rested one elbow on the top of his other hand, holding his palm to his cheek. Somewhere above him he could hear floorboards being prized up.

'Yes.' Fox was not to be deterred. 'The seminar you were attending was important, was it not? Yet you departed in a

84

precipitous hurry, leaving behind an impression of considerable agitation?'

Before the last word was out of his mouth David had leapt
to his own defence. 'What I can't seem to get you people to
understand is that that is the perfectly normal reaction of a
husband who's fond of his wife.'

Albert flicked a fingernail against his upper teeth while he
thought about the word 'fond'.

'All right, we'll move on for the moment. Mr Lescombe,
your wife is a busy, professional woman. She has a career of
her own and it is a distinguished one. She is, if you'll forgive
the phrase, free, white and over twenty-one.'

'She's thirty-nine.' David's voice matched his stare; both
were glacial.

'Leaving aside precise numbers, she's an adult. She mentioned the possibility of going to Paris, I believe?'

'Yes, although she sounded so tentative I didn't give it
another thought.'

'Nevertheless, her passport's missing and she may have
gone abroad, mm? I take it she's not done anything like this
before?'

'No.'

'No history of mental instability?'

'Of course not. She's a barrister.'

'She is a barrister. Not the sort of person who goes off the
rails. Furthermore, we have your categorical assurance that
she does not know the combination of your safe. Yet when
she drops out of sight for a while, your first reaction is to
connect her disappearance with the missing file. Why?'

'I've told you, we'd had a tiff. I was worried for her. I still
am, worried out of my skin, and nobody seems to care.'

'When you quarrelled, did she mention the possibility of
her going away?'

'No. And I said tiff, not quarrel.'

'In any case, what you're giving us is merely your interpretation, is that it?'

'If you like.'

'What do you think has happened to her?'

'How the hell should I know? Kidnap, murder, anything's possible. Perhaps she came in while whoever it was burgled my safe was on the job and they made off with her, to make sure she didn't talk.'

'Oh, come, come. In broad daylight, with neighbours watching? Taking her passport for good measure?'

'It happens!'

'If you say *that*, I have to tell you that your experience of these matters is greatly superior to mine.'

'That wouldn't surprise me in the least. You've got a bloody nerve, coming in here – '

'Mr Lescombe.'

'Accusing me of lying.'

'Nobody's – '

'What I want to know is, what are you doing about finding her?'

'Her? Nothing. Krysalis is another thing. Your stewardship of that file appears to have been rather less than perfect, does it not?'

Fox tilted his head, awaiting an answer; but David had begun to eye Albert sideways, as if trying to fathom who he was and what he was doing. 'Mr Lescombe?'

'I . . . you're referring to . . .' David lowered his eyes. 'Am I allowed to name it? I mean, I don't know who this – '

'You may speak freely in front of this gentleman; indeed, I hope you will do so. I beg you to do so.'

Somewhere up above, glass shattered. Everyone froze into silent, embarrassed immobility. Then a distant voice shouted, *'Fuck!'*

'So, Krysalis, yes.' Fox spoke as if nothing had happened. 'For the benefit of my colleague, perhaps you would be so good as to outline what Krysalis is.'

David half turned so that his gaze could embrace Albert, still tapping his teeth, over by the window as well as Fox.

'Krysalis is a file that's updated once a quarter. It contains a lot of things, but what's troubling your excitable colleague here is that at the moment it's got in it the entire NATO General Situation Plan, plus the formulae for identifying S and T SPs on time-spans one, two and three . . .' He shook his head, angry with himself. 'I'm sorry. It gets to be a habit, after a while. It sets out current NATO thinking on strategic and tactical sacrificial pawns in West Germany in the twenty-four hour period following a Soviet conventional attack.'

Fox produced a mumble in which the word 'pawns' could be heard to end on a high note.

'They're the places we'd be prepared to see go before using nuclear weapons against the enemy.'

'This is . . . shall we say, sensitive material?'

David snorted. 'Top secret, sensitive . . . enough to bring down more than one government if it got out. Krysalis actually uses the phrase "sacrificial pawn", can you imagine what the *Mirror* would do with that?'

'And the list of sacrificial pawns is quite specific,' Fox said to the room at large, before reverting to David. 'You brought it home,' he said; and Albert stopped molesting his teeth.

'Yes.'

'Why?'

'I had permission. Once the safe was installed.'

'We'll come back to the safe in a minute; can we for now just establish why you had it at home?'

'All members of the Krysalis Committee keep a current version of the file with them at all times.'

'Why?'

'Convention. Discussions frequently take place out of working hours in members' private homes.'

Until this point Fox had been allowing the conversation to proceed at a brisk trot. Now he dropped the reins and sat back. There was a long silence. David fidgeted; his legs seemed to be too long for his liking. Albert continued to stare out of the window.

'I have to tell you frankly,' said Fox, 'that we were not aware of the cavalier attitude which the London end of

87

Krysalis has displayed. We hope to God that Washington will never find out.'

'Washington's exactly the same as London.' David heaved an impatient sigh. 'We ring up our American opposite numbers at home. You can do that now, you know; it's called International Direct Dialling.'

Upstairs, the banging, which had ceased since the accident with the glass, resumed with double intensity. When the doorbell rang Albert murmured, 'Shall I . . . ?'

'If you wouldn't mind.' Fox looked at his watch. 'It'll be Leadbetter.'

A few moments later Albert escorted a man of about his own age, say thirty-five, into the drawing room. Fox again took charge. 'What have you got?'

'Well, we've oiled the wheels and put them in motion.' Leadbetter, a thoughtful man, obviously liked to set his own pace. He opened a notebook and tugged a couple of times at his undernourished moustache, as if a little pain might stimulate thought. 'Usual alert at all ports and so on. So far, we can't find anyone who remembers seeing her after tea-time Friday.'

Fox turned his head a fraction. 'Did you see your wife on Friday before leaving for Midhurst?'

'No. She was off at the crack, before I woke up. I left later than usual, because I wanted to go to Albemarle Street, to pick up a compass. I'd ordered it specially. They don't open till nine-thirty.'

'Ah yes, you sail . . . Where was Krysalis when you left?'

'In the safe.'

'Yet your wife doesn't have access to it?'

'Of course not. It was installed by your department.'

'Has she ever been present while you've opened the safe?'

'Possibly. I can't remember.'

'But she might have seen you open it?'

'Yes.'

'And remembered the combination?'

'Oh, *really*!' David stood up and began to pace around the

room, while Albert looked on with a sympathetic smile.

'Mr Lescombe, all I'm doing is pointing out that your wife could have had access to the safe without your knowledge.'

'She could.' That was what made David so angry; being compelled to face what could not be endured.

'Did your wife know you were in the habit of bringing home confidential papers?'

'I didn't tell her, if that's what you mean.'

'But did she *know*?'

'She might have guessed, I suppose.'

As David stalked up and down the room he kept meeting Albert's eyes. There was something pleasant about the man's smile. Why did his face seem so familiar . . . ?

'Mr Lescombe . . .' Fox was speaking again. 'Tell us about your wife, please. What's she like?'

David wilfully chose to misunderstand. 'Like that,' he said, pointing. 'It's recent.'

His finger indicated a framed photo standing on an ebony Steinway grand piano. Albert examined it with interest, while Fox made a production number of apology for not having expressed himself with sufficient clarity and what he had really meant to ask . . .

So that was Anna Lescombe. She looked younger than thirty-nine, Albert thought, and the blonde hair pulled back tightly into a bun would equally well have suited a girl half her age. Lovely, outdoor colouring: the kind of face you saw bobbing behind a horse's head mid-week, on a by-day, when most of the men were at the office and the hounds were working double-time because it was a treat for them . . . Albert forced himself to concentrate. Rounded features. A firm chin that stopped just the right distance short of aggression. Cheeky smile. Twinkling eyes that spoke before the mouth opened, giving it all away. Eyes like those could never keep a secret; Anna Lescombe was bursting to tell. And this inquiry, Albert realized, is a waste of time. God, though, she'd look fabulous in pink . . .

Anna grew on you. It wasn't until you'd been studying

her face for a few moments that it suddenly dawned how beautiful she was. Those luminous eyes . . .

Albert had just one fantasy and it was only mildly sexual: a woman on a horse, galloping, with her hair pulled back like Anna Lescombe's. And here she was. Living with — Albert glanced at David — the kind of prat Whitehall seemed to favour these days, who nevertheless was nobody's fool and wasn't sure how much he trusted his wife.

Yet he was *fond* of her. Again that odd expression came back into his mind. Did it represent Lescombe's attempt to distance himself from Anna and so save his career?

'She's the usual sort of professional woman, I suppose.' David was speaking again. 'She had to work twice as hard as the next man, who because he was just that, a man, would always get on, you know what I mean? Conventional, middle-class upbringing.'

Ah, that's interesting, Albert thought, because you're not conventionally middle-class upbrought, are you, my man; in the army we can spot that a mile off . . .

'Won a scholarship to Somerville, commercial chambers, top-flight. Goddammit, she makes six times what I do every year, why on earth would she want to spy . . . ?'

He stopped with a strange look on his face, the kind the hero wears when he's been slugged from behind by his best friend.

'As an adult, however, her life was *not* entirely conventional.' Fox deliberately chose to ignore the word 'spy', but his voice hardened. 'There was an unfortunate first marriage, I believe? A child?'

'Oh, so you know about Eddy, do you? What else do you know?'

Before Fox could respond, someone rapped on the door and entered without waiting for an invitation. 'Sorry, chief, can you come?'

David glared at this tousle-haired slob: part of the crew that had blundered into his domain and was busily taking it apart.

90

Fox rose. 'What is it?'

'Empty bottle of sleeping pills under the bed, with a clean set of prints matching them on the safe.'

'All right.' Fox's earlier relaxed air had evaporated. This was business, this was urgent. 'Mr Lescombe, do you know anything about these sleeping tablets?'

'No.' David's voice trembled slightly. 'Nothing,' he added, as if to cover up the momentary weakness.

'You'll come in straightaway,' Fox said. 'You can tell a neighbour that the house may be empty for a while, if you like, but keep it general.'

David was so astonished, he scarcely noticed when Leadbetter's hand descended on his forearm.

NINE

The hell-for-leather journey from London to Greece took up all of Monday, but Anna retained little impression of it because for most of that time Kleist kept her well drugged. She did not really begin to come to herself until their speed-boat entered a tiny harbour. Suddenly the water parting at its prow turned transparent green, marbled by many rounded pebbles clearly visible two fathoms or more below. Hills came down to enfold the bay, one side in cold shadow and the other still flooded with golden evening light. A dozen houses lined the unevenly paved quay; the last of them must have been a *taverna*, for Anna could see crude wooden tables covered with flower-patterned plastic, and rickety chairs.

An old man was waiting for them, along with a boy in his late teens who turned out to be his son. The youngster helped Anna down on to dry land. She wobbled a little, steadied, stood fully upright. When she took a deep breath it was rich with the smell of some pungent herb, rosemary perhaps, that sluiced through her mind, cleansing it of im-purities.

While the boy went to collect the car, Gerhard spoke Greek to the old man, who stood nervously twisting his faded straw hat and putting it on his head for a few seconds before jerking it off again to give it another few turns. His soft, sad eyes were contradicted by a thin moustache, which, together with his beaky nose, gave his face the severe look of an old soldier. She realized dully that this must be Yorgos. Caretaker, factotum, agent, he was all these things. He could be trusted, Gerhard said; and when Anna looked into the elderly Greek's eyes, she believed that.

The sound of an engine intruded on the peaceful evening, heralding the approach of Yorgos' red Fiat, driven by his son Iannis. From the sea this island looked small, but the journey to the other side was a long one. Anna absorbed contrasting impressions of many trees, a dusty road fringed with convolvulus that glowed pinky-white in the dying sun, olive groves, a gearbox whose synchromesh had gone, glimpses of the sea, now royal blue, the smell of Papastratos cigarettes overflowing from the car's broken ashtray . . . then they were jolting down a rough stone track towards a white, single-storey villa.

Yorgos gave her case into the charge of his son. He produced a scratched and dented tin from which he took a cigarette, hesitantly offering it to Anna. She shook her head, but the sight of that tin was enough to lure her thoughts away to another place, another time.

Her father had always kept his smokes in a tin. She could see his podgy fingers struggling with the air-tight lid and her nose wrinkled at the vision of those nasty stains, the colour of ginger biscuits, which had polluted her nostrils whenever he kissed her . . . How strange that the acrid smell of spent nicotine could become the odour of love to a child.

While Yorgos and Gerhard talked, she drifted through the spacious house. Her bedroom (Iannis had put her case there, so presumably it was hers) gave onto a terrace, from which a flight of wooden steps descended towards a cove. Anna sank down into a wicker chair, not comprehending why she felt so ill.

For the second day running, she couldn't remember certain things that must have happened. Such amnesia terrified her.

After a while she lifted her head. The house nestled half hidden in a grove of dark conifers. On a patio below the terrace where she was sitting she could see a brick barbecue, by an old well; below that the land sloped away steeply as an overgrown garden, littered with spiky, straw-like grass and several huge ribbed pots, still full of last season's dead flowers. Gerhard's property ended with a wall and a metal-rod gate. From there, she could just make out the beginning of a path which, she guessed, must wind down to the bay, some fifty feet below where she sat.

The bay was wedge-shaped, with the house perched half-way up the bluff to one side of it. She craned forward, trying to see if there was a beach. But the bay's landward end, at the point of the wedge, was lost to sight around the left side of the house and she lacked the strength to rise.

Gerhard's domain faced a densely-wooded hill on the other side of the wedge, rather than the open sea. As her gaze swept the bay's far shore she found her attention caught by a small, unexpected building. A chapel! Its white cupola gleamed in the fading light, a bell hung outside in the tower at one end, and to her surprise Anna found herself hoping it would ring. She could imagine nothing more beautiful than its clean, clear note summoning to prayer.

Gerhard and Yorgos seemed to have a lot to discuss. She could hear a typewriter clacking now. Was this the first stage in sorting out her mess, she wondered? Oh God, please let it not take long.

Somewhere behind and above her, the avalanche waited. And there were voices inside her head, telling her such strange things . . .

Anna did not hear Kleist come out to the terrace. She had fallen into an uneasy doze when a hand descended on her shoulder and she quivered.

'How are you?'

'Wretched.'

'Yorgos has gone now. Hungry?'

'I don't want anything.' She rubbed her upper right arm. 'Gerhard, did you give me one injection, or two? It aches so much, but I can't remember . . .'

'One mild sedative, that's all.' Kleist had given her two shots of narcotic, but the lie slotted seamlessly into their

94

conversation. 'You were looking green and I thought you could probably use some sleep.'

She rummaged in her handbag, looking for a tissue. Something bristly grazed against her hand; she pulled it out with a wan smile. 'Miss Cuppidge.'

'What?'

She held up a tatty corn dolly, some three inches long. 'Juliet's. Do you know, I put this in my bag six years ago, she'd left it somewhere and I meant to take it to her . . . but somehow I never managed to part with Miss Cuppidge.'

'What a funny name.'

'A raspy name for a raspy toy, that's what I used to say.' Again the tired smile. 'Pathetic, aren't I?'

He perched on the balustrade wall and studied her. The ravages of flight had done much to conceal her underlying beauty, but pathetic was certainly not a word he would have used to describe Anna Lescombe, not now, not ever. Normally there was something helpless, a little wistful about her childlike face that brought men to her side at parties, bearing tacit promises of protection and lavish love, although as far as he could tell she never appreciated their purpose, never even saw them through those round eyes of green-grey-blue. Radiance coupled with lack of vanity, unwitting loveliness, was, he felt, one of the most attractive human qualities.

Looking at her now, he remembered why he had fallen in love with Anna, but he could not recall why he had tired of her. A mistake, that. One of so many.

He followed her gaze to the middle distance, where two elfin boats progressed calmly towards the yellow horizon, tiny puffs of foam at the stern. 'Sailing . . .' he murmured.

'Do you remember that weekend at Yarmouth?' Anna grimaced. 'Our one and only sailing trip.'

'A disaster.'

'You'd never *been* sailing before, you told me afterwards.'

'I'm a believer in trying out new things. And at least you did meet David. He's a real sailor, if you like!'

95

Memories of wet week-ends spent with David at Brighton Marina, Itchenor, Shanklin, came crashing into Anna's mind, but she refused to let them overwhelm her. What she chose to remember instead was how at Gerhard's suggestion she'd reluctantly consented to be one of a party aboard a boat that moored for the night off Great Yarmouth, while the crew went into town to get drunk. A nice man from the Nicholson 38 in the next berth gave them milk, and she had smiled her gratitude at him, not knowing then that they would marry . . .

'Where are we?'

'This place?' Kleist seemed surprised she didn't know. He mentioned the name and Anna said, 'It's so peaceful here.'

'I don't even have a phone. The nearest one's in the port.'

'But I thought I saw wires . . .'

'Electricity. There's no tourist trade yet. I hope there never will be.'

'Too hard to get to.'

Gerhard pulled up another wicker chair beside her own and sat down. 'Like you?'

Anna nodded.

'If we use the time wisely, perhaps we can do something about that.'

She allowed her head to loll around until she could see him properly. 'I'm cured, that's what you told me. Often.'

'I believed you were.'

'Even though I kept coming back to you?'

'I've told you many times: patients frequently come back to their therapists to discuss problems and progress. There was nothing unusual in it.'

'We became lovers, didn't we? That was unusual. Sometimes I wonder if maybe you cured me of depression but not of Gerhard Kleist.'

He smiled. 'You know that's not true. You love David now, not me. But professionally, you've become a major challenge. So what about it, Anna? A spell of intensive, one-on-one therapy, here, while I arrange things in London?'

'No time.' She felt confused. 'First I must sort out what I'm going to say, then get back to London. Start putting things right.'

'Get back?' His expression showed how puzzled he was. 'But why? Are you changing your mind?'

'Changing . . . ?'

'You asked to come. And when David agreed it was a good idea, that was obviously the logical – '

Anna felt a great shock run through her. She gaped at him. 'David . . . *knows* where I am?'

'Of course. When I explained what had happened, about your breakdown and so on, he agreed . . . look, Anna, just how much *do* you remember?'

But she continued to stare at him as if he were a phantom. 'No. Wait. Please wait. You . . . you've *met* David? Actually talked to him?'

'Yes.'

'When?' she wailed.

'He found me in the house, after you'd left to go and sit in my car. Of course, I had no choice but to come clean. The three of us sat in the car and talked; don't you remember?'

She shook her head violently.

'You got very upset at one point. That's when I gave you the sedative. David held your hand while I did the injection, you must remember that, surely?'

Her face was bloodless. 'No,' she whispered.

'Well, you went out like a light, so perhaps that's not so surprising.'

'Gerhard.' Her voice was suddenly hoarse, as if all her saliva had dried up. 'Tell me the truth. Please. Am I going insane?'

He laughed. 'Good God, no. Whatever gave you that idea?'

'I can't remember anything about today. You . . . you really talked to David?'

97

'Yes. There was no choice. It's utterly inconceivable that I should bring you here without his consent.'

'What did you . . . I mean, did you tell him anything?'

'Only what was necessary for professional purposes. Your taking the file, of course.'

Anna made a strange sound, halfway between a groan and a croak.

'I had to tell him that, when I gave it back to him. I didn't attempt to cover all the ground, but I'm satisfied he understood what you need in order to be cured.'

She felt so muddled. The voices inside her head . . . yes, one of them was David's: 'Successful, good-looking, what else do you want?' No, no, that didn't sound right. As she listened to Gerhard speaking, it seemed to her that perhaps David *had* said that what she needed was a holiday . . .

She banged the arms of her chair and cried: 'Why can't I remember? *Why?*'

David knew. *He knew.*

'How did he take it?' she asked. Funny that she hadn't thought to ask that before.

'Very well. I'd say that, of the three of us, he was the keenest on the idea of your going abroad while he and I sort things out.'

'I must phone him. Talk to him.'

'Certainly you must; it's essential. But now it's far too late for anything of the kind.'

Kleist watched her narrowly, eager to learn if the suggestions that he had implanted hypnotically in the course of their journey had taken root. He could not afford to let her go, now; could not allow her the least leeway. 'How much of today can you actually remember?' he asked casually.

Anna made a great effort. 'I remember . . . oh, I don't know . . . a ship?'

'That's it. We drove out through Dover.' Anna asleep on the back seat, lax passport officers, harassed by thousands of tourists passing through every day, yes, Dover had been an inspiration. 'And the flight here?'

'No.'

He'd chartered a plane, which had cost him the earth, although almost from the moment he opened the Krysalis file Kleist had seen a way of doing far more than just cover his expenses. His plan was so ambitious that at times it made his stomach churn, but he'd committed himself to it and when he thought of how much, of how *everything* depended on keeping this woman quiet . . .

'Gerhard, did you say . . . I'd had a breakdown?'

He nodded heavily. 'I'm afraid so. A very serious one. As David was quick to appreciate, what you need now, more than anything, is rest.'

'But . . . my work.'

'You'd already arranged to take a few days off, remember? David will see to that side of things. And he'll be coming out here at the weekend.'

'He will?' She eyed him anxiously, wanting to believe his reassurances.

'Yes. It's Monday now, so it sounds a long time, but if you rest and don't worry, it'll pass quickly, you'll see.'

'Is he angry with me?'

'Not at all. Just concerned for your welfare.'

'I always wanted to tell him about you,' she said, after a pause. 'Right from the start.' Some of the lines had been soothed away from her face; she looked less troubled. 'If only you hadn't – '

'Ah, yes, well, plenty of time for that tomorrow. Now, shall we go in? Only I can't hypnotize you out here, and I think that would do you good, don't you?'

She was glad to agree. The air was full of flying insects, and her skin had already begun to itch. A fire of olive logs crackled in the hearth of the largest room, filling the air with incense. There was a lute here, too; she had noticed it earlier, as they arrived. Now Gerhard picked it up and sat by the fire, tuning it. She wondered what he would choose to play. Ah, yes, Dowland's 'Forlorne Hope' . . .

The music, coupled with the realization that David at last

knew everything, gave her a much needed lift. After a while, when she was peaceful, Gerhard laid aside the lute and brushed the top of each hand in the gesture she had come to know so well. 'Close your eyes, why don't you?' he murmured. It seemed like no time at all before he was counting her down to oblivion, 'Deeper and deeper, more and more tired,' then she was under.

She could hear his voice, the stirring of the curtains in the cool breeze, the murmur of the sea as it endlessly sifted the shingle.

'Tonight, I want us to go back to the beginning.'

Hesitation. Fear. 'No. Please . . .'

But Kleist could not afford to let his patient dictate the choice of topic. When she was under he likened their link to elastic: one day it must lose its tension, its effectiveness, and then his power would be gone. If that happened now, he was finished. He urgently needed to test how far she had built up resistance to his techniques, so it had to be the event she dreaded most, the adoption. If he could take her back and hold her *there*, he could do anything.

'We must take a fresh look at the moment when the pain began,' he emphasized. 'So that we can make yet another attempt to heal it. Then later, on other evenings, we shall come forward until we arrive in the present.'

She stirred uneasily.

'How old are you, Anna?' He sensed her unwillingness to answer, so he prompted her gently. 'How old . . . ?'

'Six months.' A childlike voice, unnaturally high.

'What are you doing?'

'I'm lying in my pram.'

'What can you hear?'

'Voices.'

'Do you know the voices, who they belong to?'

Another long pause. 'One.'

'Yes. And that one belongs to . . . ?'

'My . . .'

'Yes?'

100

'Mother.'

'And the other voice?'

'Another woman.'

'They're talking about . . . ?'

'Me.'

They had been here many times before. The scene had no surprises for Kleist the skilled physician, although Kleist the man sometimes found it a touch fey, this easy backwards transference almost to the gate of the womb.

'And so, Anna . . . what are they saying? About you?'

'My . . . mother. She says . . . "She's adopted, you know." '

The pause was again a long one, but Gerhard said nothing.

'Then . . . then the other woman, she just walks away, I can hear her footsteps.'

The last word came out on a rising tone, halfway to a gulp. Anna chewed her lower lip to stop it trembling. He watched her face carefully, waiting for the crying to begin. But today there were just two tears: she was letting him look inside so far and no further, so as to give him the most meagre satisfaction, barely enough to ensure he did not delve any deeper.

He knew then that his instincts had been right: she would be difficult to control, and the knowledge frightened him.

'Why did the woman walk away, do you think?'

'Because I'm illegitimate. A bastard. No good.'

'And do you think of yourself as no good?'

'No. Then I was a baby. But now I'm strong. The woman who spoke to my mother has no power over me. She was bigoted, repressed, perhaps deliberately unkind, but above all she was jealous.'

'Wait a moment . . .'

'Because no one had ever loved her enough to pick her up and say, "Even though your own mother doesn't want you, even though she's thrown you away like – " '

'Anna.'

' "Though she's betrayed you, I won't betray you. I won't

101

leave you." ' Suddenly the monotonous child's voice changed. It began to fall, become mellow, adult. ' "I won't . . . *ever* . . . let you go." '

'Rest. Peace . . .'

He waited until she had once again become calm. 'Deeper and deeper now. Into the cool, dark depths, where all is stillness, down and down, further down, you can feel your shoulders becoming lighter, all that weight, all that burden, falling, falling . . .'

At last she was on the verge of sleep. Everything seemed to take twice as long as usual, and that too disturbed him.

'Anna,' he said softly. 'Can you hear me?'

She was breathing very deeply and slowly; Gerhard had to repeat the question before her lips moved. 'Yes.'

'Omega.'

One long, mute exhalation . . . now she resembled a corpse for tranquillity.

'I want you to remember certain things. It's dangerous for you to be seen by anyone. No one must know where you are. All right?'

After a long wait, to his immense relief, she nodded.

'Do not go out unless I am with you, to look after you.'

She did not react at all, but he hurried on. 'Remember, David wants you to be here. He cannot find the time to come to you. His job is important. But he wants you to be here. He is happy that you are here. You should stay in this house for your own protection, and for his.'

She was frowning in her trance; Kleist did not know how to interpret that. 'Forget your troubles. Trust me.'

'I trust you.'

He had already risen to his feet, not expecting her to speak. Her words startled him. After a few moments he regained enough assurance to leave her and do the rounds of the villa, ensuring every door was locked, before going to his bedroom.

On a table next to the window stood a telephone.

Kleist unplugged the instrument. Anna's noticing the overhead wires leading to the house had unnerved him, one

102

more sign that, despite the injections he had administered, she was neither as sick nor as subservient to his will as he needed her to be. He could not afford to take any chances, not now, when he was engaged on nothing less than the sale of Krysalis and Anna Lescombe as one job lot.

He looked at his watch. Iannis, Yorgos' son, was already on his way to Athens. Tomorrow, first thing, the boy would send the fax Kleist had typed out for him; then it became just a matter of time. By the weekend, it wouldn't matter a damn what Anna thought or believed. *But he must have those four days!*

There was scarcely room for the telephone in the special cavity behind his bed, along with the hypodermic, ampoules, and Luger that were already there, but at last, after a struggle, he made it fit.

Tuesday

TEN

Tuesday's council of war, like most such meetings, achieved results in inverse proportion to the amount of time needed to prepare for it, which was enormous.

The protagonists assembled at a pleasant farmhouse near Crowborough that overlooked two thousand acres of land owned by the Ministry of Defence. Because the house was small it could be swept for electronic bugging devices with comparative ease, whereas its location ensured that no one might approach without being challenged. None of this would later prevent the American representatives from making their usual snide comments about the backwardness of the natives.

There was an informal formality about these occasions that the British contingent relished. Lukewarm coffee arrived in thick china cups with a gold band around the inside of the top, and chocolate wholemeal biscuits were served on paper doilies. At one end of the room stood a flip-chart on an easel that also supported a box of coloured crayons; at the other there was a TV-cum-video. Louis Redman set the scene nicely. He came in, took a quick look around and said, 'Hi, Dick, so how many Fords are we going to sell in Surrey this quarter?'

Richard Brewster affected amusement as he guided his guest to the coffee table. 'You and I may end up doing just that,' he said quietly, 'if we can't nail this one soon. Good journey?'

'Fine, fine.'

'And how is friend Bill?' Brewster turned to the man standing behind Redman, who contented himself with a curt nod.

'Ah, I'd forgotten you knew Bill Hayes . . .' Redman smiled at his deputy, anxious to bring him into the fold, but Hayes was patently no sheep. He stirred his coffee as if trying to beat a little more warmth into it. Everything he did was jerky and vigorous, like in the old silent comedies.

The two newcomers had little in common, on the surface. Redman was an untypical, anglophile American, of quietly efficient appearance: a transatlantic Jeeves with that gentle-man's gentleman's tendency to 'shimmer'. His clothes were reasonably priced but always looked immaculate: here was a man who brushed cloth and shined leather. He also kept his manners polished.

Hayes wore price tags and let them go to pot. His curly black hair straggled over his cranium in an attempt to cover the ground as best it could, but it had long ago become the texture of light bulb filaments and there was not enough of it to go round. He wore immense rectangular spectacles with lenses so thick that he had to have the frames specially made. When he sported a bow-tie, as he did this morning, he resembled a student in some amateur play, dressed up for the part of Mr Boffin the Scientist. Or Mr Golliwog, as Brewster mentally called him; for Hayes had accelerated into the fast lane from a New York public housing project, and he was black.

'I think that's everybody,' Brewster said, gently calling attention to his chairmanship of the meeting. The minutes would refer to him simply as 'coordinator'. His position within the cabinet office's security hierarchy made him well suited to hold the ring whenever departmental rivalries must not be allowed to impede operational efficiency.

He took his place at the head of the green-baize-covered table, with Hayes down at the far end. Fox and Inspector Leadbetter, representing the home team, sat on Brewster's left. Shorrocks, captain of the touring eleven, was on his right, next to Redman, his opposite number from the CIA.

Albert kept the minutes.

'Right,' said Brewster. 'An overview. The purpose of this meeting is to establish how we're going to set about retrieving the lost Krysalis file and clear up the mess generally in time for the Vancouver summit. In particular, how are we going to do this without falling over one another's feet? Jeremy here . . .' a nod at Shorrocks '. . . will handle things for Six. He has to clear himself with Five in the person of Fox, and Special Branch, which is to say Leadbetter. And also, Louis, with you. Because this one can't be classified as exclusively domestic or foreign, it's not as easy as that.'

'I'll go along with you,' Redman said. 'As long as it gets quick results, it's okay with us.'

'You agree about the importance of this?'

'Shit, *yes!*'

The interjection came stinging down the table. Everybody turned in astonishment; everybody, that is, except Redman, who raised his eyebrows and smiled at no one in particular.

Hayes' face was hard. 'I've read Krysalis. It's deadly for us. That file contains Pentagon-originated vote-sensitive material, some of it highly critical of our pro-Europe, pro-NATO lobbies. This is all about damage containment, right? I will be frank with you, gentlemen, I do not know how you contain the damage from a megatonner like this one.' He rested one elbow on the table and jabbed his forefinger at Brewster. '*You* . . . are going to have to be pretty damn quick on your feet.'

Well, Brewster thought, the coon is in a good mood today. 'You sound a mite worried, Bill,' he said.

'Bet your ass. You know why as well as I do. In a couple of months' time or less, Bush and Gorbachev are going to face each other across that table at Vancouver. What's on the agenda? *Everything!* Reduction of nuclear weapons across the board, reduction of conventional armour and artillery, reductions in manpower, money, depots, divisions. You name it, they'll cut it. *If* NATO can manage to keep its

General Situation Plan to itself, that is. But if Krysalis goes over the wire, our President will be playing poker with a mirror behind him and that is *out*.'

'Oh yes, indeed. Especially since Krysalis makes it clear that if D-Day was tomorrow, West Germany in particular would be left to its own devices. Its own . . .' Brewster caught Shorrocks' eye, cuing him for the laugh '. . . non-nuclear devices.'

Shorrocks obliged with a deep, booming chuckle.

'Look.' Redman spread his hands, palms upward, like a priest invoking the Holy Ghost. 'Bill and I don't make policy around here. So please . . .'

'I think,' said Brewster, 'that if we could keep things on a more even keel . . .'

'Sure.' Hayes spoke the word perfectly normally, but Brewster heard *'Sho'*. 'Just as long as you realize that fuses are short.'

'Oh, I don't think we're in any doubt about that, Bill.' Shorrocks beamed across the table at Leadbetter, whose face remained expressionless. 'I don't think we've missed that one.'

'But we on our side,' Brewster put in, 'did not pursue a policy of briefing the President to endorse NATO publicly while at the same time making it clear at operational level that in the event of a Soviet attack on western Europe our so-called allies would be left defenceless. I am right, aren't I, Jeremy, that isn't our current policy at present?'

'No, no,' Shorrocks said cheerfully. 'Not as far as I'm aware, Richard.'

Hayes looked down the table at Brewster and his expression was vitriolic. They had told him before he left the States that colour prejudice was alive and well and living in Britain but he hadn't wanted to know, because he'd been raised to think of Britain as a civilized country where the inhabitants kept their feelings to themselves. It was true, they did. The Brits, however, could converse in code like no other nation. Hayes knew that these two despised him

110

because of his colour and that they had just told each other so, but he could not understand how they'd done it.

'We want that file back, safe, intact,' he said. 'We're going to use any means we have to. We'll shoot your woman on sight. I mean that.'

Shorrocks and Brewster had been smiling at each other. Now they turned faces of stone down the table and stared at Mr Golliwog.

'Also – ' Hayes respected bullets, but facial expressions left him cold – 'we need to know you're going to freeze Lescombe. We say he's the moving light here. Husband and wife together, the old team, look at the Rosenbergs.'

'There's no proof – '

'Do you *believe* him when he says his wife didn't know how to open the safe? When her fingerprints were on the keys, actually *on* them! A hundred gets you five, she kept her pearls in there along with their code-books.'

'Given our present state of knowledge, that's outrageous,' Brewster said stiffly.

'Why? It happens, goddammit. And we're not about to pull any punches just because you and Jeremy happen to be the ones who signed Lescombe onto the Krysalis list.'

'That's scarcely a relevant consideration.'

'I am *very* glad to hear it, Richard. Now. We want to be there when you grill Lescombe. What've you got in mind?'

Brewster interrogated Redman with a look, to see how far this had been prearranged, but encountered only a pleasant smile. 'Our intention,' he said, resentful at being forced to acknowledge Hayes' question, 'is to let Mr Lescombe run.'

'*What?*'

'Now, Bill.' Brewster raised one hand; he might have been a traffic policeman, or Hitler saluting. 'Let's hold it there for one moment, shall we? There's no evidence against Lescombe at this time. Assume, however, for one moment, that you're right in your theories,' (he somehow managed

111

to insert oral quotes around that word and Hayes wondered how he did it) 'even so, would it not make sense, do you not think there might be merit, in letting him lead us up the line, so to speak? See where he goes? Who he talks to?'

'That's your risk,' Redman put in mildly. 'None of ours.'

'Well, of course, he's our man!'

'Was, you mean,' Hayes yapped. 'Not any longer.'

'How can you be sure?' Fox was angry, it showed in his face as well as his voice. 'You're pointing the finger at someone who isn't here to defend himself, who has an impeccable record – '

'Oh, I don't believe this!' Hayes rolled his head around in an exaggerated gesture of despair. 'Great spies I have known . . . look, please look, we know that Krysalis hasn't made it back through the Iron Curtain yet, right?'

Brewster eyed Shorrocks, who rolled out his lower lip and nodded. 'No squeaks behind the wainscot. Not yet.'

'So she's gone into hiding, right?'

'She might have been kidnapped,' Leadbetter said.

'C'mon, who by? Just tell me, who by? Whaddas he want? Where's the demand? The threat?'

Leadbetter put up shutters of offended silence and retired behind them.

'Who's this woman working for, someone tell me?'

'Bill, if only we knew . . .' Be reasonable, that's what Brewster was trying to say, although it obviously wasn't working. 'She's an amateur. Anyone can employ an amateur. A "grey mouse", isn't that what they're called in Bonn?'

'That's more of an older, secretary-type, actually.' Shorrocks' smile was full of reassurance, backing Brewster all the way because, although on this occasion he had erred, he was at least the right colour and one of us . . .

'Well, whatever. She was clumsy, unprofessional. Prints everywhere . . . And the empty pill bottle Five found points up someone under strain, possibly terminal strain.'

'Medical records,' said Hayes. 'What do they tell us?'

'Inspector?'

'Working on it.' Leadbetter kept his face to the front.

'Good, well then, that's . . . good.'

'It doesn't mean shit. What are you planning to do about her, anyway?' Hayes' voice was barely controlled.

'We are having the airports and so forth watched around the clock. All our embassies and consulates have been briefed to look out for her, particularly Paris.'

'She's not in Paris. She *told* the world she was going to Paris, so Paris is where she's *not*. Suppose she left England before Lescombe called you, had you thought of that?'

'Certainly.' It was Fox who spoke. 'But because Mrs Lescombe has a British passport, immigration won't be holding any record of her departure.'

'She didn't have to fill out some card?'

'No.'

Hayes shook his head from side to side as if trying to dislodge it from his shoulders. 'Jee-*zuss*! What about foreign immigration services, have you alerted them?'

Albert leaned forward and spoke for the first time. 'If she went to Europe, she probably wouldn't even have to show her passport. Especially if she travelled by train and boat. We Europeans are, you may recall, one big happy family.'

'So what *are* you going to do?'

Albert shrugged. 'We shall be checking all airlines, passenger lists. It'll take a little time, but — '

'Time is exactly what we do not have,' Redman interjected. It seemed he had at last had enough of his assistant. 'Richard, there is a question I would like to ask and it bears on what Bill was saying about the foreign immigration people. You haven't alerted any European intelligence service about this, have you?'

Brewster exchanged glances with Shorrocks. Another Englishman might have seen the triumph in their eyes, but Hayes detected only the usual fish-like stares. 'Well, no,' Shorrocks said, resting a hand on the table and leaning

113

towards Redman, treating him like the confidential ally he was. 'We wanted to ask you first, you see, Louis. Having regard to what's in Krysalis, we thought it best to soft-pedal a bit.'

Redman blew out through rounded lips. It took him a long time to empty all the air from his lungs. 'Great,' he said at last.

'I hope we did the right thing?' Brewster was at his magnificent, solicitous best. 'But I don't know how much longer we can go on handling this alone.'

'You're not going to be alone, Richard.' Hayes' smile afforded Brewster a good view of his teeth, showing so white against all that black, and the inside of his lips, colour of an old cricket ball, same as Shorrocks' brogues . . .

'Good,' said Brewster. 'Yes, well, that's good, then. But going back to something you said earlier, we really wouldn't like anything to happen to Mrs Lescombe before we've had a chance to talk to her. That would be dis*tinct*ly . . .' Brewster stared at Fox, as if seeking inspiration. 'Unfortunate.'

Redman cleared his throat. 'It's difficult to go all the way with you. The way we see it is this. The lady gets one chance to surrender – '

'Then we cool her,' snapped Hayes, 'hell, we *refrigerate* her. Go tell them in Bonn, if you think it helps. And Paris. And Rome.' He shrugged. 'Doesn't change a thing. When Mrs Lescombe shows, she can say yes first time around or we're going to blow her away.'

'Louis, I really do feel we should talk it through some more. Am I to understand that you don't want to co*op*erate on this?' Brewster was genuinely astonished.

Redman smiled at him. 'On our terms, Richard. Strictly our terms. You see, I endorse every word Bill said about the Vancouver summit. If the Russians get their hands on Krysalis, Bush might as well stay home. There simply can't *be* a summit under those circumstances, and we'd be left with the task of explaining to the world, Europe in particular, why we were the ones to back away from peace talks.' He looked down the table at Hayes. 'Bill, unless you've anything else . . .'

But before Hayes could respond someone knocked at the door and put his head around it.

'Yes, Major?' Brewster said, glad of the interruption.

'This fax came through here one minute ago. Addressed to MI6 Liaison via the generic blue line. The duty clerk thought Mr Shorrocks had better see it at once. I'm sorry about the quality: it originated in Athens.'

Shorrocks looked at the document's header. 'Sent this morning?'

'Yes. It's recent.'

Shorrocks studied the fax. His eyebrows rose in astonishment. 'Good God . . . I'd better read it out. "The document, a sample of which is sent herewith, was brought to the author by a lady who is suffering considerable distress. Arrangements can be made to return both it and her, intact, and without copies of the document having been taken, provided the author is rewarded for his trouble to the tune of one million sterling. What do you propose, please? Fax your reply to the agency named below, where it will be collected. Any attempt to trace the author via that agency must inevitably result in the termination of these negotiations as well as the permanent disappearance of the document; and the shock . . ."' Shorrocks' voice slowed. ' " . . . And the shock would be such as to give rise to fears for the lady's health. For the same reason, maximize security concerning this fax. Deadline for close of negotiations, Saturday noon."'

When he fell silent, Redman asked: 'What was that at the beginning, about a sample?'

Shorrocks turned over. 'It's one page of the Krysalis glossary. The Krysalis Committee don't use NATO-speak, they define their own terms. Richard, is this authentic, in your view?'

Brewster examined the last page of the fax. 'The quality's

piss-poor, but . . . yes. I'd say so. How the hell did whoever wrote it know the liaison number?'

Shorrocks started to speak, then thought better of it. His eyes shifted a millimetre in the direction of Hayes and Brewster manfully rode to his rescue. 'I assume no one else has seen this yet?' he said quickly.

'Right.'

'Thank God for that!' Brewster turned to Redman. 'Do you want us to involve the Greeks at this stage or keep them out of it?'

'We need to trace the author of that fax.' Redman's reluctance showed on his face. 'I guess we better had involve them. But for God's sake, limit what you tell them. Bare essentials only, please.'

'Do you intend to negotiate with whoever sent this?'

'No,' put in Hayes. 'And Mrs Lescombe sent it, so give "the lady" her right name.'

'But her life may be in danger!'

'Crap. A blind. Who else knows about this fax?'

'You heard: no one.'

'What about the clerk who took it off the machine? What about the major, here?'

'Well apart from them, of course. Look, if you're implying – '

'See it stays that way. If we want to trace her, so will the other side. She's got Krysalis and it's up for sale. We're not buying. With Vancouver seven weeks off, plenty of others may, given the chance. We'll take one photocopy away with us. Oh, and Jeremy, if I was you I'd get myself a new fax number. Louis?'

Redman rose. 'Yes. On our way.'

'But surely – ' Brewster was aghast ' – surely, you want to discuss this? I mean, what the next step should – '

Redman paused by the door. 'We'll be in touch,' was all he said.

The Americans' departure provoked deep silence in the room, followed by a general loosening up as people stretched,

116

pushed back their chairs, and exchanged those ironic, mean-
ingful glances Hayes knew so well. This time the looks said:
'How tiresome our teenage children are getting, but what
can one do . . . ?'

'What can one do?' Shorrocks said to the ceiling.

'Fix that ruddy man Lescombe,' Brewster replied as he
reached for the telephone.

ELEVEN

In 1968 the Duncan Committee reported that moving the Foreign and Commonwealth Office from its Florentine museum off Downing Street to a new building would save five hundred people and a million pounds a year. Nobody can now remember who the eponymous Duncan was, but over twenty years later the FCO stands where it always did and is not likely ever to move.

David Lescombe was a dedicated professional with a lower middle-class family background, a degree from a northern redbrick university and an impatience with flummery. He disliked the pile where he did his daily grind, not on account of its antiquity but because it struck him as wastefully inefficient.

It was two-thirty on the day after Anna's disappearance when he walked through the arch opposite Number Ten Downing Street, into the grand square courtyard, and made for the tower in the north-west corner. He had been out to lunch. Not at the Travellers' Club, still laughingly referred to as the Foreign Office works canteen, but to the Institute of Strategic Studies in Tavistock Street, where he had sipped coffee and munched on a bar of chocolate while listening to a talk given by a member of the King's College Department of War Studies on the nuclear balance in Europe. Apart from an overlooked reference to an article in *Voyennaya Mysl'* by Major General Zemskov, the seminar had yielded little of interest. It did, however, enable him to have a quiet quarter of an hour with an old friend from the Brookings Institution, in the UK on a research visit, and that had paid dividends. As David bounded up the marble staircase, flanked by ancient statues of the Earl of Clarendon and the third Marquess of Salisbury, he was already framing a terse memorandum for the Superintending Under-Secretary on the crassness of the Washington intelligence-gathering corps in believing all that they were told by their hosts.

The break had also done something to distract him from worrying about Anna. Her absence was like a toothache, always there in the background, coming between him and efficiency.

His office – large without being magnificent – commanded a side view of St James's Park. Arched bookshelves flanked the oak fireplace. Above the mantel hung a portrait of an unremarkable eighteenth-century bureaucrat in a dirty dull frame, an adornment drawn from stock by the Property Services Agency. David's portable computer sat on a table beneath the huge window, along with a printer and three telephones. His leather-topped desk, also from stock, supported an old-fashioned bronze lamp standard that might have been more at home on the revamped Orient-Express, with a semi-naked goddess entwining herself up towards the bulb. The only other objects on the desk were a folding leather blotter and a framed newspaper cutting.

The frame stood upright at forty-five degrees to David's chair. The cutting it contained, now yellowed with age, was taken from a review by Lord Chalfont of the Berrill Report on Britain's Diplomatic Representation Overseas that had appeared in *The Times*, and it read as follows:

Why do something superlatively well, when, by adopting the contemporary standards of 'relevance' and egalitarianism you can turn in a really third-rate performance?

Conventional wisdom had it that as long as Lescombe left this cutting visible he could kiss goodbye to a Superintending Under-Secretaryship and its inevitably attendant CMG.

David sat down in his revolving captain's chair and pulled himself up to the desk. He had hoped to lose himself in the anaesthesia of work straightaway, but his secretary had placed several yellow Post-It slips on the outside of his blotter. One caught his eye immediately: Anna's chambers had rung; could Mr Lescombe meet Duncan Broadway QC this evening at six? His hand was reaching for the telephone while he read. Only when he had confirmed the appointment with Broadway's clerk did he sift through the remaining messages. The Swedish military attaché: that was social and could wait, as could his opposite number at Defence. But the Superintending Under-Secretary could not.

He left his office and walked along the passage until he came to the end, where he did a right wheel into the longest stretch of linoleumed floor the civil service could boast. Here the gloom was only slightly alleviated by sunshine pouring – dribbling would perhaps be a better word – through the tiny windows in the European corridor, each stationed exactly halfway between the bevel-panelled doors opposite, as if to avoid any risk that someone emerging from an office with all of England's diplomacy in his head might conceivably be blinded by a ray of light.

At the far end he came to a grand door, surmounted by a florid representation of two angels. He knocked just above the gothic-lettered name panel – Superintending Under-Secretary Sir Anthony Forbes-Anderton CMG – and went in.

'I understand the SUS would like a word,' David said to the middle-aged woman sitting at the nearer of the two desks. She nodded; and David went straight through.

'This is a bugger. This *is* a bugger. And a half.'

David had entered a larger version of his own office, which had two windows instead of one but somehow managed to appear more gloomy, as if light had less of a chance in here. The shelves behind the man who had spoken were blue with Hansards, his desk was cluttered with wooden trays, not just

120

In, Out, and Pending, but Eur(Acol), MinDef, PUS, ComSec; there was no end to them. Sir Anthony's fondness for trays had become legendary; he might have been gathering containers in which to plant seedlings. Only the minutest space was left on the desk for writing, which he had to do hunched up, his elbows into his sides and the hand held at an awkward angle.

'Sit down, do.'

'The old man', as subordinates called him, sat well back in his swivel chair, keeping his elbows on its arms. Two fingers of his left hand fidgeted with the lower pocket of his waistcoat, while his chin rested on his right fist. The Harold Macmillan moustache bobbed up and down whenever its owner wrinkled his nose, which he did often, like a distracted mouse. The SUS looked thoroughly fed up.

Now Sir Anthony's right hand lowered itself to one of the trays for long enough to pick up a few sheets of paper stapled together. Still keeping his elbow on the arm of his chair he held them up to the light, staring at them through his spectacles. His lips parted to reveal the teeth clenched, heightening his resemblance to an agitated rodent. 'This,' he repeated slowly, 'is a bugger. Isn't it?'

The last two words were addressed to a third man who had been standing with his back to the window. David recognized Croxley, who performed functions that in a commercial organization would have been assigned to the personnel director.

'Do you two know each other, what?'

David nodded. Croxley smiled, but said nothing.

'David, this is a *real* bugger, and I'm sorry for you.'

'I'm afraid I . . .' David spread his hands helplessly.

'Well, it's this business with Anna, you see.'

Sir Anthony regarded him hopefully over the tops of his glasses, seeking rescue from a predicament known only to him. David remained silent.

'I'm afraid I've been given the job of suspending you.'

David's heart thumped, but he said nothing. Ever since

121

his interview with Fox the day before he'd been expecting this.

The SUS shook his head a great many times. 'Blessed if I know why. Blessed if I know. Perhaps if we weren't faced with this Vancouver thing . . . But it's come down from on high, with much sounding of drums and trumpets, and Croxley says we're to have a rigmarole. Now where is it . . . ?'

Croxley rescued Sir Anthony by reverently laying a blue plastic-covered ring-binder in front of him, much as a treaty is laid before a Head of State ready for signing. Sir Anthony cleared his throat a number of times, adjusted his glasses, then took them off altogether, gave them a polish, held them up to the light. David remembered the last scene in Kafka's *The Trial*, where the executioners are passing the knife to and fro between themselves, perhaps in the hope that their prisoner will seize it and stab himself, thereby saving them the trouble.

'David Emmanuel Lescombe.' Sir Anthony had found the place and was following the text with his finger. 'I have been directed by Her Majesty's Principal Secretary of State for Foreign Affairs to notify you as follows. Item the first.'

Surely (this was David's inconsequential thought), surely they had not really written *item the first*?

'You have been suspended from your duties pending the outcome of an official inquiry into your recent conduct as specified in the appendix to this notification. Item the second. During the period of your suspension, you will continue to receive your salary, without deduction, and, depending on the outcome of the inquiry, the said period will either count or not count, as the case may be, toward the calculation of your final pension in accordance with paragraph four of the schedule to . . .'

Sir Anthony went on reading, but most of what he said passed over David's head. He was out for something he had not done, that's what it came down to; and he felt the by now familiar tide of anger with Anna flood through him, obliterating anxiety, eradicating fear for her safety, overriding even love, until all that remained was an impotent desire to take his wife by the neck and throttle her.

'Why?' he asked redundantly, when Sir Anthony came to the end of 'the rigmarole'.

'You took a file home,' Croxley replied. 'And it disappeared.' He did not sound judicial, or superior; not even mildly cross. Events, neutral in themselves, had determined this outcome. Fault was not an issue.

As David stood up he staggered and had to reach out to support himself on the back of his chair. His heart was overworking, the room rippled. He was out. *Out, by God!*

'Would you be good enough to give us a signature . . . ?' Croxley made a little space among the trays. First Sir Anthony signed what he had just read aloud, then David, and finally Croxley himself.

'What happens now?' David heard himself say.

'You have to leave the building. At once, I'm afraid.' Croxley sounded apologetic. 'If you've left anything behind, it'll be sent on to you. Please be available; don't leave London without telling me.'

They watched him go. As the door closed behind David, the Superintending Under-Secretary glanced up at Croxley and said, 'Have you ever had to do this before?'

'Twice.'

'What happened?'

'One of them was . . .' He mentioned a name and Sir Anthony rolled his eyes. 'Him! Still inside, is he?'

'Yes.'

'Messy. Don't want a trial, any of that nonsense. Not this time. What about the other one. Trial, was there?'

Croxley hesitated. 'Not exactly.'

'Don't get you.'

'There was an inquest.' Another pause. 'Suicide.'

'Really?' Sir Anthony's voice was hushed, appalled. He

123

took off his spectacles and threw them into one of the trays. 'What . . . a . . . *bugger.*'

As David left the anteroom he saw someone by the nearest window, resting both arms on the sill. Hearing the door close, this man now came upright and turned a smiling face in his direction.

'Hello again,' said Albert.

'Oh, it's you. I . . .' There was something about this stranger, something so familiar it was driving him mad. When Albert turned sideways on to the light it suddenly clicked. Gustav Mahler: the high forehead, gold-rimmed spectacles, studious face; an overall impression of neatness extending even to the well-turned shirt collar, and probably to the mind as well . . .

'What are you doing here?'

'Hoping I'd run across you. Your secretary told me where you'd be.' A look of sympathy unexpectedly softened his intense expression. 'You've been suspended. Bad luck.'

'Yes.' David stared at him. 'How did you know? They've only just – '

'I think it's time we had a talk. Look, it's a nice day, we could go for a stroll . . . ?'

They walked across Horse Guards into St James's Park under a watery sky, half grey and half blue. It was just warm enough to enable them to sit in deckchairs, not far from the bandstand, where David could enjoy an outsider's view of his former domain. Something about 'The Palazzo's' rock-solid façade suggested that they might be able to manage without him. He wrenched his gaze away and said, 'Who are you exactly?'

'Yes, you must be wondering about my role in all this . . . It's tough for you chaps when security marches in wearing hobnail boots.' Albert spoke with apologetic concern, as if it were all his fault.

'So you're with security?'

'No, I'm an army officer. Well, yes *and* no's the answer to your question: military intelligence. My regiment would be first in the firing-line if your file surfaced in the east. We'd have to hold the fort – literally.'

'I see,' said David, who didn't. 'What are you actually . . . doing?'

Albert interlaced his fingers and extended both hands in front of him, palms outward. 'Blowed if I know. Bloody waste of time, if you ask me.' He cast a sideways look at David. 'You're worried to hell about your wife, aren't you?'

'I'm worried, yes.' David stared at the ground. 'And I'm angry, too.'

'Why?'

'Is that meant to be a serious question?' David burst out. 'She goes off, the file's missing, my career's ruined, wouldn't it make you angry if all that happened to you?'

'You're assuming she took the file, then.'

'I don't know what to assume. My wife, my file, they're both missing, that's all I know. What kind of a woman steals her husband's top secret papers and goes off into the wide blue yonder? I can't believe . . .'

Spoken like a man who doesn't *want* to believe, Albert told himself. 'Aaah . . .' He made a scornful face. 'None of it hangs together.'

'But she's gone, hasn't she?' David's voice was bitter. 'So's the bloody file.'

'Mm. Incidentally, about that file . . . did you not think that Krysalis, wasn't it just a little, well . . . odd?'

'I'm sorry?'

'So much information written down in one document. Outside the normal run of expectations. Risky, one would have thought, perhaps?'

'It hadn't occurred to me.'

'No, well, nothing in that, then.'

There was a long pause.

'What do you want to talk to me about?' David asked at last. 'I mean, shouldn't I wait for this inquiry . . . ?'

'You can if you want.'

'Yes, but . . . who *are* you?'

'I'm muscle.' Albert smiled bleakly. 'Not-very-chief cook and bottle-washer. Typical, of course. Undergraduate cadet-ship to Oxford, a First in English, posting to Northern Ireland, and now here I am. You've no idea how these things work, have you?'

'Not much.'

'MoD have a policy of putting square pegs in round holes and calling it "flexible response", also known as shambles. When a file goes missing, when a key bod goes over the wire, all sorts of people are affected. So everyone wants a finger in the pie, to check their interests don't get overlooked. That's where I come in. Because there isn't much for me to do at present, they're using me to run around and do odd jobs.'

David stared at him. 'It's so different from what I would have expected,' he said at last.

'It always is. Look, David . . . may I call you David, inciden-tally?'

'If you like.'

'I know what you're thinking. You watch the telly, you read the posher spy books, and you think: "So that's what it's like, on the inside, really like . . ." But the truth is, the people who work for MI5 are civil servants. Which means they're fully stretched at the best of times, and when there's a panic, there's one bod for every ten jobs. So they bring in part-timers.'

'And your job is to talk to me.' David heard his voice become defensive and winced. 'They *sent* you.'

'Of course.' Albert's smile detracted from the hostile glint of late afternoon sun as it bounced off his spectacles. David noticed them properly for the first time: they were shallow, shaped like a double sycamore seed flattened across the top, and tinted with just the merest tinge of pink.

126

Cellophane-thin, they looked more of a protection against the light than an aid to vision.

'If I talk to you, will it help them to find my wife? Or only the file?'

'Both, I hope. I'm more concerned about Anna than the other.' And which are you most concerned about I wonder, Albert mentally added: your wife, or your career?

'What do you want to know?'

'The personal things, I'm afraid. The difficult bits.'

'Personal?'

'Love and death and sex. The Woody Allen things. You a fan of his?'

David shook his head.

'They're kind of tricky. The problem is that at some point you're going to have to provide the answers to certain very embarrassing questions about your life with Anna. You can wait for the board of inquiry, if you like. But you just might find it easier to talk about them to me, sitting here, in the fresh air. I'll pass on the answers, and then there's a good chance you won't have to cover the same ground again.'

David hesitated. 'Go on,' he said at last.

'Let's start with a real googly. Do you love your wife?'

'Of course.'

'No.' Albert was infinitely patient and understanding. 'No, I'm sorry, you haven't quite got the flavour of this yet. I'm going to ask you some serious questions and you're going to answer them in the same way. It's not Trivial Pursuit.'

'But of course I love my wife!'

'How long have you been married?'

'Eight, nine years.' *How can you love her if you don't even know how long you've been married?* 'Nine and a quarter years.'

'No children.'

'No. We couldn't. The doctors never found out why.'

'Yet she had a child by her first husband. The dreaded Eddy.'

David laughed in spite of himself. 'Yes. Juliet.'

127

'So perhaps you didn't really want children?' Seeing David open his mouth Albert sharply interjected, *'Think.'*

A pause. 'There were six of us kids in my family. It put me off.'

'Did she know you weren't keen?'

'I was careful never to let her know.'

When Albert did not speak for a long time, David raised his head and found the other man staring at him. These questions had begun to give off a sickly aroma . . . children, impotency, his sex life, Anna's sex life, that's what Albert was really after, the antics they got up to in bed . . .

Such antics, too. Before he met Anna, if he'd read about them in a book he'd have been fascinated, perhaps even a little repelled, thinking anyway that they were nothing to do with him. Anna had changed all that. It wasn't just her loving personality and warm smile he missed at night.

'What's the point of this?' he rasped.

Albert did not reply immediately. He continued to stare at David, who in the end was forced to drop his own gaze. Now the park seemed colder. Blustery wind sent a blue plastic bag rolling across the grass. There weren't many people about: two young lovers, the man lying with his head in the girl's lap; a woman in a suede coat walking her Borzoi . . . *Who are you?* David wanted to ask again. *Why are we both here?*

'You see, David, we need to build up a profile of your wife, then use it to project her probable actions.' Albert spoke softly, using his voice to massage David's ruffled feathers flat again. 'One thing that could affect her is how she sees you. With me?'

David nodded unwillingly.

'I warned you the water would be a bit choppy. Now. Does she love you?'

'I'm sure she does.'

'Does she ever tell you?'

'Yes.'

'When was the last time?'

'Last weekend, on the phone. Saturday.'

'Three days ago . . . so you expressed your affection to each other often, is that right?'

'To an extent.'

'To what extent?'

'We'd been married nine years, we were neither of us teenagers when we met. Life may begin at forty; romance doesn't. We knew we loved each other, dammit.'

'She didn't have anyone else?'

'A lover, you mean?'

'That's right.'

'Don't be ridiculous.'

'You can answer me straight, or you can have it wrung out of you, under oath.'

David breathed in and out sharply, once. 'No lover that I'm aware of.'

'There may have been, in other words?'

'That's not what I said.'

'But it was a cagey answer, "no lover that I'm – " '

'Oh, this is insane! Not in the least relevant. The things you're asking about are purely personal.'

'In a case like this, nothing is purely personal.'

David teetered on the lip of the precipice. Then – 'I've got nothing to say.' His voice was stony, matching his expression.

'At the inquiry – '

'I'll cope with questions then.'

He told himself that the trembling of his limbs was due to righteous anger with this army officer, whose curiosity exceeded the bounds of decency, but deep inside he knew that wasn't true. Albert had brought him face to face with something he would rather not dwell on: Anna's sexuality. At the back of his mind there lurked the fear that perhaps he did not satisfy her, not all the time. And if that was so . . .

No. No, he did not believe his wife had a lover. He would not, could not believe such a thing of the woman he adored. David suddenly stood up and moved a few steps away from

Albert, keeping his back to him. When he turned around again, the water was clearly visible in his eyes.

'Sorry.' His voice came out uneven. 'Not the emotional type, usually.'

'It's understandable.'

'Yes.' A shiver interrupted the next words; after a pause, David tried again. 'If you want the truth, I . . . I miss her.'

'Naturally.' Albert allowed the sympathetic pause to go on a little longer. Then he said, 'I think you've answered my question but, just for the record . . . did you or do you have a mistress?'

'Certainly not. To *both* questions.'

'So.' Albert tilted his head backward until he was staring at the sky. 'Whatever she was running away from, it wasn't an unhappy marriage.'

'I don't get that.' David had recovered from the weakness of a moment ago, his tone was harsh. 'What makes you so sure she ran away?'

Albert brought his head forward again. 'You seemed to be saying that yourself.'

'Oh look, I'm sick of this. My wife's gone missing, the police don't want to know, your people don't care, it's like a nightmare.' David's voice cracked. 'What has to happen before someone does something? Eh? You just tell me, *what*?'

He was shaking. Albert looked up at him with detached professional interest. 'What are you going to do?' he said.

'I'm going to find her. In my way, and without any help from you.'

'I think that's an excellent idea.'

David had already stalked off, but on hearing those words he stopped. 'What?'

'One of the things I had in the back of my mind was to encourage you to do that. You know a lot more people it might be worth talking to than we do.' Albert stood up. 'Eddy, for example.'

'Eddy.' *Of course, Eddy. But how in hell's name was he ever going to be able to talk to Anna's first husband?*

130

'Unless, of course . . .' Albert appeared struck with his own flash of brilliance. 'Unless you felt like letting me share the labour . . .' He already had a hand through David's elbow and was guiding him towards the Mall. 'We should talk about that, there's still time before your appointment with Broadway.'

TWELVE

By lunchtime on the day after their flight the BBC World Service still had nothing to say about Anna Lescombe's disappearance. Because Kleist was in a peevish mood he turned off the radio with undue vehemence, toppling it over.

Iannis must have sent the fax by now. How much did London want their file? How important to them was this woman? *Would they buy either? Both?*

Neither?

Anna had found something to intrigue her in the rocks clustered at the foot of the cliff beneath the church. From his vantage point on the terrace, Gerhard could sometimes see her, sometimes not, as she swam in and out of his vision. It was ever so: she had always presented herself to him in fits and starts, revealing only enough to be going on with.

He remembered the first time he'd met her as if it were yesterday.

Sixteen years ago she had come into his consulting room, dragging her steps, and she had looked around with a bored look on her face, as if to say, 'Go on, then, show me.' When her eyes did at last become still he had smiled into them, acknowledging her as a person who commanded his full attention, but she had not returned the greeting. He recognized straightaway that, no matter how far she might let herself go (and it was very far, then), she appealed to his sense of all that was superb in a young woman. Nothing could contain such a spirit, once it began to soar. That was his task: to set her free.

She had borne with him listlessly while he went through the opening formalities, name, address, age – she was twenty-three, then – but after he fell silent she offered nothing of herself, waiting instead for him to point the way.

'I want to talk about some myths,' he had said. 'Myths surrounding psychoanalysis and psychotherapy; what they are and what they are not.'

She said nothing, nor did she nod.

'You are not mad. I'm not a psychiatrist. It's important you understand that. Your post-natal depression, however severe, means only that you are functioning at less than your best.'

He paused, but she continued to stare into space as if he were not present.

'Our sessions together will occur at the same time each week and will last exactly one hour. This is because the patient after you wants me to be punctual and I must respect that wish, just as I respect your wish that I should always be on time for you. It is one way of saying that I can be relied upon.'

'I see. Thank you.'

He noted 'relied = trigger' on his pad and continued, 'It is unlikely that you will still be in therapy six months from now. If, after that, you still have not conquered the hostility you feel towards your child, if you're not enjoying your life more, there will be little point in our continuing.'

He had said something that mattered. Her eyes were wide open and she was looking at him properly. 'I thought . . . I'm sorry, I thought it would take years. Always took years.'

'No. Myth number one.'

'How will we know when it's over?'

'Therapist and patient know when the time has come to part. Always. Next, myth number two: that therapy is pleasurable. Therapy is hard work. Unpalatable, unpleasant things will come out; things you would rather not know. It is grinding, painful labour and I have no magic to change that.'

'I didn't expect so much honesty.' She hesitated. 'Am I allowed to ask questions?'

'Anything.'

'When it's over . . . after six months, or whenever . . . is there a rule that says we can't see each other again?'

'No.'

There followed a long silence, during which Anna's eyes roamed around the cluttered room. 'Only I would like one day to ask you about yourself. Where you live.'

He was startled. She struck him as a quick study, already initiating the games people used to delay him on his *via dolorosa* towards Truth, but more awesomely she had used the phrase 'where you live' as if she understood the central place it occupied in his world. For that, ultimately, was all of his work: showing people where they lived, instead of where they imagined they were camping.

He had known in that instant that she was dangerous to him. There were well established procedures for ridding oneself of patients who might be thought unsuitable. Gerhard ignored the signs until they were no longer warnings, they were realities that came between him and his sleep . . .

'Gerhard?'

He came out of his reverie to find Anna in the garden below him with a towel around her shoulders, shivering slightly. It was too early in the season for protracted bathes. He thought about encouraging her to change, then decided not to. A day's rest had restored most of the natural beauty to her face, and the plain black swimsuit did wonders for her lightly-tanned body, still firm and devoid of stretch marks. It was hard to believe that she was thirty-nine.

'You seemed miles away,' she said, as she climbed up the path to join him. 'What were you thinking?'

'I was remembering something.' He laughed and resumed his seat. 'Unimportant.'

She gave herself a few brisk rubs and sat down opposite

him, keeping the towel in place as if for warmth. 'Go on, tell me.'

'Oh . . . there was a time when I used to dream about you. Often.'

'I bet you say that to all the girls. But I'm willing to be flattered; don't stop.'

'One night I woke up calling your name.'

Kleist had not meant to reveal himself, but Anna's instincts were always quick. 'What did the woman say?'

He laughed again, although this time with none of his usual assurance.

'You're too transparent.' Anna's smile was arch. 'I bet she was cross. Did you try to seduce all your female patients?'

'I never slept with a patient. Never.' It was true; such a course would have been perilous in the extreme and Kleist habitually avoided any kind of risk. 'I always waited until after the therapy was over.'

'Ah, I remember. Friends, you said. Once the therapy's over, a therapist can be friends with his former patient. I loved the way you emphasized "former", you made me sound cured.' Her face darkened. 'Was I ever cured?'

'You're a successful barrister, married, quite rich, I should imagine.'

'Yes, but was I cured?'

'What, in your book, is a cure, then?'

'Not being on the run. Not hearing voices in my head. Not doing bad things I can't remember doing.'

'Such as?'

'Treason. Taking the file.'

'So it's back to betrayals, is it?'

'Your theme, not mine. When you were treating me you had this thing about treachery. Mine and other peoples'. You used to harp on a lot about it and I never quite understood why.'

'Well, honestly!' He was exasperated now. 'I'm sorry if I failed to give satisfaction. Is this really an interesting topic?'

'I think so.'

135

'You know perfectly well that at the root of all your problems was a deep sense of betrayal; first by your mother, then by others. And you felt guilty about what you regarded as your own betrayals, particularly of Juliet.'

'So you told me.'

'I got rid of the guilt, that's all. I allowed you to see that having fun wasn't always so terrible. You remember Oscar Wilde: "The only way – " '

' "To get rid of a temptation is to yield to it"?'

'That's right.'

'I'm sure.' She waited, as if expecting him to speak again. When he remained silent she sighed, stood up and walked off the terrace without looking at him.

Kleist only slowly mastered his anger. Today she seemed detached, in reasonable health . . . and fey. There was something missing. He wanted to analyse it, but his mind kept straying to London. *Would they do a deal? How much was Krysalis worth to them?*

How much was Anna herself worth?

He was startled out of these dark speculations by the discovery that she had again come to stand in front of him. She was fully clothed. Her suitcase sat on the terrace beside her.

'Gerhard, I'm going home.'

'I think that's a very silly thing to say,' he said smoothly, coming out of his chair.

'This isn't right. The sooner I go back and face whatever's coming to me, the better.'

'Now, look – '

'Please, let's not argue. I appreciate what you've done, but I can face things by myself.'

Throughout her speech Kleist's head had slowly been turning to one side, until now he was examining her out of the corner of his left eye, his brows meeting in a frown. 'What's brought this on?'

But he knew. As her self-reliance grew, so his grip on her weakened. God knows, the signs had been obvious enough.

He'd programmed Anna to open the safe, bring him the file, wait while he copied it, take it back, put it in the safe and reseal it, then forget all that had happened. But nothing had gone as it should. She had not brought him the file. She'd relocked the safe with the papers on the outside, rather than inside.

What was infinitely worse, she could remember a lot of what had happened. She recalled hearing 'voices'. One voice in particular. And now this . . .

'David is going to be very surprised if you just turn up, after arranging for him to come out at the weekend.'

'He's missing me, Gerhard, he's worried sick about me. Can't you see that?'

Despite her words, Kleist thought he detected a hint of irresolution when he mentioned David and decided to press home his advantage. 'He's already been through rather a lot on your account.'

She said nothing.

'I don't think he's quite prepared for your arrest at Heathrow. The photographers. The TV cameras and so on. It will all come as rather a shock to him.'

'I'm sorry about that. I just know that he needs me and that what I'm doing is right. I have to go.'

He studied her face for a long time. Her eyes were never still. Sometimes they lighted on him, but for the most part they seemed hardly to focus at all.

'Anna. Are you sure?'

'Sure.'

He examined her a moment longer while he sorted through the alternatives, which turned out to be few. 'Very well,' he said slowly.

These words seemed to take her by surprise. 'You'll let me go?'

He laughed. 'Why, do you think you're some kind of prisoner, or something?'

Now there was a longer pause. 'I know I've got no right to ask you this, but . . . will you come with me?'

137

'All right. I didn't bring a suitcase so there's nothing to pack. Do you mind walking to the village? It isn't very far, and I'll have to persuade Yorgos to drive us down to the port.'

'I'd love a walk.'

'Good. There's only one ferry a day, it doesn't leave until five, but if we go early at least you'll be able to say you saw the sights of one Greek harbour. Now if you'll excuse me . . .'

Kleist went to his room, shut the door behind him and leaned against it with his eyes closed. So this was how it felt between the rock and the hard place, at last he knew.

He opened his eyes again and strode over to pull the bed away from the wall. The Luger lay in its usual place. He tested the mechanism a couple of times, checked the magazine, then stood up, kneeing the bed back into place. He was shaking, his hand had become so weak it could scarcely hold the gun. Although Kleist had manipulated many minds, he had never yet been compelled to resort to violence. Physical brutality sickened him. But last night he'd implanted the idea that she should stay on the island, and that wasn't working, so he had no choice . . .

If London played, he would win a fortune and a one-way ticket out of a life that had become impossible, thanks to Anna.

If London played, HVA might want revenge, but they would never find him in Peru or Paraguay: both places where Kleist had many friends and life, for the rich, was congenial.

If London played, his sister, Ilsa, would be destroyed . . . *don't think about that!*

If, on the other hand, London did not want to buy back Anna, or Krysalis, he would contact Berlin and the machine would simply take over, wafting him to safety, together with the file. It was a one-way bet. But everything depended on Anna's not surfacing. Once she began to talk, Kleist knew he was finished. He could not possibly let her go.

138

He put on a jacket and dropped the Luger into his pocket. There was one chance left. When he'd mentioned David earlier, her face had changed. Give her a few more moments . . .

Anna had begun to wander around, wishing she had time to explore this beautiful island, and the house in its perfect setting. The insidious thought made her angry, because a moment ago she had known only a fierce desire to go home.

Her headache was back with a vengeance, she felt nauseous. The attack had come on at about the time she'd made up her mind to leave. Don't fuss, she told herself. Find something to do.

Beside the fireplace stood a bookshelf. She leafed through the few quartos of sheet music lying on top, then her attention was snared by something on the next shelf down. It contained a dozen paperbacks. One of them looked unaccountably familiar. She picked it up and to her surprise realized that it belonged to her.

The first grown-up novel Anna could remember having read was O'Hara's *From The Terrace*. To that day she could close her eyes and visualize one scene, just one, and it came at the end of the book when Alfred Eaton, the principal character, had been very ill. While he convalesced he would sit in the Californian sun on the terrace of the title, and look back over a life that had promised at every turn to be successful, yet never quite delivered. And he did not know why.

Anna had once lent this book to Gerhard, who forgot to return it. She was surprised to find her old paperback in the villa, a little the worse for suntan oil and salt water, but still intact.

Gerhard showed no signs of emerging from his bedroom. Anna carried the book out to the terrace, her own terrace, and sat down facing the sea. The sun made the water look like freshly applied blue paint, glossy and fierce. She closed her eyes, trying, like Alfred Eaton, to pinpoint the moment when she had known the promises would never be fulfilled.

139

Yes. That dinner party. Barristers. All talking law. Poor David.

Robyn, her best friend, had just gone back to the States, leaving her angry and desolate. Everyone at the table was talking, talking, talking, laughing, laughing, laughing, drinking, drinking, drinking, talking, drinking, laughing, and nobody in the room (apart from David) loved Anna at all.

The food was rotten.

She'd been busy, it wasn't her fault. She couldn't be everywhere at once. Only because she was a woman, that's exactly what she had to be: omnipresent, able to expand the frontiers of existence to cope with everyone and everything. But her cook for the evening, recommended by a friend, turned out to be a disaster: the duck was dry and the mousse separated. Fortunately, David had chosen some marvellous wines, so while the others forced themselves to eat she'd planted both elbows on the table and held a glass close to her face, concealing the tears; and to make sure that no one saw *through* the glass she kept it full, only that was difficult, because she was drinking so much, slopping some, too . . .

Anna, unlike David, spilled things. You could always tell where she had been sitting.

They were so sleek, so self-satisfied, all these guests. They talked easily and well, scarcely even aware of their power to enthral. She had devoted a lifetime of mind-bending hard work to the task of joining their ranks, but as she looked along the lines of Hogarthian features, the sharp, pointed noses, fat bellies, podgy hands, greasy foreheads, now she realized for the first time that they were parasites and she indeed was one of them. They, she, we were scavengers of human misery, battening on loss of liberty or of property; on pain, despair, and the love of combat. How David must have hated it all.

How she hated it, she suddenly realized.

Next day they had dropped by her room to thank her for the evening; which almost to a man they characterized as 'wonderful'. So mundane an adjective, she thought. Only

Guy Samuelson, one of her room-mates, smiled the rather secret smile which was his speciality, as if to say, 'Yes, the food *did* taste ghastly, didn't it?'; and to him she felt she perhaps ought to apologize (her speciality?), but instead she heard herself say aggressively, 'You should be bloody grateful for a meal your wife didn't have to cook and wash up for a change,' enjoying the way Guy's smile slipped, as if he'd unexpectedly found himself dealing with someone quite *outrée* . . .

She was going to need them when she got back to London. These were the people who would help her fight the massive negligence claim she so dreaded. They would defend her at the Old Bailey.

'Are you ready?'

Gerhard's voice brought her back to reality. She stood up, mechanically stuffing the book into her handbag, but then felt unsure whether she wanted it. It seemed too much like one of those magic artifacts which had the knack of focusing unwelcome visions from the past and, who knows, the future as well.

'Yes.'

He picked up her case and held the front door open for her. When she did not pass through it at once he went ahead, striding down the white, dusty path, almost as if relieved that he would shortly be shot of this tiresome houseguest.

'Anna?'

Kleist reached the gate. He laid a hand on the signboard, the one in the photograph of Robyn that Anna loathed so much, and turned. From the doorway she watched him, so tall and powerful and fine, so untypical of everything left behind in England.

Suddenly she heard herself say, 'I think I'd like to sit here and read. Just for a bit longer.'

THIRTEEN

As David walked through the Temple on his way to Anna's chambers the last of the sun provoked angry amber glints in numerous windows. They made him feel as though he was being watched; but then of course he was. Albert had known about his appointment with Broadway this Tuesday evening. How? There could be only one answer. They were tapping his phone. The knowledge made him angry. He also felt a little sick.

Anna worked in a four-storey Georgian building, strangely isolated from the other eighteenth- and nineteenth-century sets of chambers at the hub of London's legal universe. There was a waterless fountain outside and a lift that did not work within. As David climbed the shallow flights of stairs to the top floor he reflected wearily on the strange love affair with the past that imbued both their lives; the civil service and the bar both overflowed from Dickensian offices tacked onto one another in an ungodly, pre-town-planning jumble, as if a child, presented with a collection of building sets from different eras, had flung them together in temper.

Yet the accoutrements of a more modern age were not lacking, either here or in Whitehall. The first thing to meet his eyes as he entered the clerks' room was a fax machine humming away. There was a photocopier, one of the larger models that could collate as well as reproduce, a telex terminal, a laser printer. If the hull was Dickensian, the engine room was twenty-first century.

David approached the clerk's desk. 'Good evening, Roger.'

'Hello, Mr Lescombe.' The young man called Roger deftly cleared his screen of outstanding fees and stood up.

'I've come to see Mr Broadway.'

'He's in con. Shouldn't be long.'

The phrase 'in con' was short for 'in conference', or, more accessibly, 'in a meeting'; it usually reminded David of 'in labour,' and made him want to laugh, although not today.

'I'll wait. Is my wife's room empty?'

'Should be.' At the end of all Roger's sentences was a minuscule pause, as if he were leaving space for the unarticulated 'sir'. David thanked him and walked down a corridor.

Anna's office overlooked Temple embankment. It was cramped, part of what had once been one enormous room, now partitioned, but she had to share it with two others who tonight, mercifully, were absent.

Three reproduction desks, all the worse for wear, took up most of the available space. Beneath the window was a table, covered with briefs wrapped in pink tape, some of them thick, some thin, some consisting of half a dozen box-files with miscellaneous papers bundled on top and nothing brief about them. The whole of one longer wall was taken up with bookcases, filled with Law Reports. On the mantelpiece opposite stood a clock; next to it, the bottom half of a green wine bottle cram-full of dried out Biros and pencil stubs.

It was clear that three very different characters subsisted here. One desk was covered with books spread higgledy-piggledy. Those that were shut had their owner's name printed in sprawling black letters across the top page-edges; the open ones revealed tracts of yellow highlighter ink, and dense marginal notes written in prescription handwriting.

The second desk, facing inwards, boasted nothing except one thin brief laid out in the exact centre of a clean white blotter. David guessed that this desk's burgundy inlay had recently been renewed.

The third one belonged to his wife. Ranged along it were several blue counsels' notebooks, a paper rack containing notepaper and envelopes overprinted with chambers' address, a shiny, perpetual-motion executive toy, and a telephone. Three textbooks stood on end, their spines facing Anna's seat: a typist's swivel chair, stark, simple, good for the back. David picked up one of the books. *Scrutton on Charterparties*. He grimaced, then quickly replaced it.

Because he knew he had to, he sat down at Anna's desk and began to open drawers.

At first, nothing very remarkable came to light. Old circulars, still sealed; fee notes; bills; a few handwritten envelopes marked 'Personal'; the usual flotsam shed by a professional person too busy to keep up with daily life. Then he came to the bottom right-hand drawer, of double-depth, and as he pulled on its handle something clinked inside.

A vodka bottle, nearly empty. David stared down at it, trying to put the right interpretation on what he saw. All kinds of people kept alcohol at their place of work; it meant nothing by itself. If you were going to query a quick, companionable drink at six o'clock you'd end up pointing the finger at most of the cabinet and their outer offices.

There was no sign of any tonic water. Or of a glass, come to that.

Anna drank. Often she drank quite a lot. But once he acknowledged that she might have a drink *problem*, he had to go a step further and admit that he didn't really know her very well, perhaps hadn't wanted to, because confronting her predicaments or, worse, trying to resolve them, would have needed more time than he was prepared to give.

He had to concede that love, for him, had been pitifully blind . . .

It was the absence of a glass that bothered him most. 'What have you done?' he said aloud; and the harshness in his own voice shocked him, until he realized that it was, after all, directed principally against himself.

He had discovered earlier that the top left hand drawer would not open. The lock appeared flimsy. David, suddenly irate, picked up a paper knife and used it to break in. The 'crack' seemed to linger for ages afterward.

The drawer contained several paying-in books, cheque stubs and, right at the back, a small leather case: one of those folding albums with space for two photographs. As David picked it up the feel of the bright red leather, tooled with a gold strip, told him it was sumptuous; the sort of thing you wouldn't buy for yourself but might give a favoured friend.

He opened it. One side was empty. The other contained a colour snapshot, somewhat overexposed, of a woman standing in front of a white background. David looked closer: the whiteness belonged to the wall of a house, with a garish pine doorway just visible over the woman's shoulder. Italy, maybe. Or Spain. Continental, anyhow.

The woman was positioned slightly to the left of centre, her narrow face tilted away from the camera. Her right hand lay on top of a rugged wooden board, bearing letters. David peered closer and saw they were Greek letters, which solved the earlier problem of location. The edge of the photo excised the bottoms of the words, but the first two looked like *'i oikia'*, the house. The last word was obscure. David took a stab at it: *mikra*. The Little House.

The woman had dark hair, cut in a fashionable bob. She was wearing a large, loose jacket over a plain tee-shirt. The outfit struck David as somewhat formal in such a setting; maybe she'd been travelling and this snapshot had been taken to celebrate her arrival. He tried to examine her features, but the focusing wasn't perfect and too much light flooded the foreground. Attractive, in a cosmopolitan kind of way. She wasn't Greek, he decided.

David took the photograph out of the album and stuck it in his pocket. Then he looked at his watch. Duncan Broadway was in no hurry to meet him. Damn them, a senior barrister went missing, and now the head of chambers couldn't even be bothered to see her husband on time.

When David went back to the clerk's room, Roger glanced up without evident sympathy. 'He's still in con,' he said, as if to forestall any protest.

145

'How much longer will he be?'

'Couldn't say. Sorry.' Roger went back to his screen, holding a ledger open with his left hand and inputting figures with one finger of his right.

David's face tightened. He began to pace about the room, nine steps up, nine steps down, every so often jerking his wrist from its sleeve to see how many seconds had ticked by since he'd last looked. As he completed one of these time checks his eyes met Roger's. 'Don't do that,' the clerk's expression said; 'you're putting me off and I'm late for the wife and the telly as it is.'

David did a smart left wheel, all but ran down another passage leading out of the front office and threw open the door at the end.

Duncan Broadway stopped in mid-sentence. Startled seemed too mild a word to describe his face; he looked shocked. The world did not intrude into barristerial meetings. The world had no place there. David represented the world and it therefore fell to him to take the brunt of Broadway's mute but nevertheless wholly effective outrage.

'I'm busy,' he said frigidly. 'Can't you see that?'

The room held a lot of people. David vaguely registered men with briefcases and pads resting on their knees, a girl in a red sweater and long grey skirt. Everyone was staring at him, this representative of the world which they wished would go away so that they could resume communion with the man behind the desk, the leader. *Their* leader.

'I can see you're holding forth,' David said shortly. 'Which may or may not amount to being busy.'

There was utter silence, followed by a nervous rustle. The acolytes feared lest the leader's reaction might be of such stupendous proportions that the fallout would affect them, the innocent suffering alongside the guilty. But Broadway only smiled and said, in a lower voice, 'I'll see you in a moment, David.' He followed this up with a nod of the chin and a narrowing of the eyes, a conspirator's look: You and I are professional men, we realize that *hoi polloi* must be

humoured, but as soon as I have finished with these distasteful people we can move onto our higher plane of consciousness . . .

'You'll see me now, Duncan.'

Roger had silently materialized at David's shoulder. 'Is
everything all right, Mr Broadway?'

David turned through a half-circle. 'Shove it.' He put his
hand in the centre of Roger's Marks and Spencer's tie and
pushed with all his might. The clerk went sprawling backwards against the opposite wall of the corridor, hands splayed
in an attempt to keep upright. He might have protested, or
even fought back, except for the disabling psychological
difficulty that such things did not happen in chambers,
therefore this was not happening, *ergo* there was nothing to
be done.

'This is a monstrous intrusion . . .'

Broadway was standing ramrod straight behind his desk.
But perhaps this opening struck even him as likely to be
ineffectual, for he tailed off, and when he spoke again his
voice was its usual conversational self. 'Well, we were just
finishing, anyway.'

David stood to one side while the acolytes filed out, careful
to avoid looking at him. As tail-end Charlie shut the door,
Broadway snapped: 'What the *hell* do you think you're
doing, bursting in here like that? What do you think those
solicitors thought, have you any idea? Three of those men,
three of them, are partners in the finest firm of commercial
solicitors the City has to show, and you come thrusting
yourself in here like some thug off the streets . . .' He paused,
and stuck both thumbs in his waistcoat pockets. 'Sit down,'
he commanded.

But David ignored him, going instead to stand by the
window. 'You rang me,' he said to the glass. 'You gave me
an appointment, fixed the time. I came. You were late. When
your lateness crossed the line into downright bad manners
I decided to play the same game. What's wrong with that?'

'My God, you've got a nerve!' Broadway was swelling up

147

like a frog, his rounded stomach pressed against the black cloth of his waistcoat in a desperate fight for freedom. 'And your rudeness to me, your personal rudeness, it defied all bounds of decency . . . of . . .'

'Duncan.' David turned away from the window. 'My wife has run away and no one can tell me where she's gone. They think it's possible she may have taken an overdose of sleeping tablets before she went. People I don't know are trying to convince me of things concerning Anna that I utterly reject. If you found yourself in my place, don't you think you might behave badly too?'

Broadway lowered himself into his chair, continuing to survey David with coldness. His eyes were large, so large that they sometimes reminded people of a horse's eyes. The centre of his head was bald, but two neat manes of black hair still clung to the sides of his skull where his barrister's wig did not prevent the air from circulating. His face was round, like the eyes, and he suffered from a surfeit of chins, but the feature that stayed with people meeting him for the first time was stubble. Broadway's beard grew at a remarkably rapid rate. No matter what the time of day, the lower part of his face looked as if it had recently been dipped in soot.

David sat down opposite Broadway. The chair was still warm from one of the finest commercial bottoms the City had to show. As he stared at the barrister an impish thought invaded his mind: what would Broadway say if he called him by his nickname? Did he know that behind his back he was 'Ealing' Broadway to his colleagues, clerks, even to some of the judges? Looking at those horse-like eyes, David felt sure he hadn't the slightest notion.

'In the circumstances,' the barrister said, 'I suggest we leave the topic of your disgraceful entrance and move on.'

David said nothing. I must keep up the pressure, he told himself. This man wears a suit but he's a street fighter. Don't yield.

'I asked you to come and see me, David, because the police

have been here asking all kind of damn fool questions about Anna and I can't trace her.'

David felt angry, a little afraid. The police . . .

'Do you know where she is?'

'No.'

'So you're as much in the dark as we are?'

David nodded.

'Have you any idea how risky it was for us when we took her on? We'd never had a woman in these chambers before. But she came in and she did wonderfully well: worked all hours, charmed the clients, charmed *me*, I may say, got on famously with the bench. She had this gift of making people want to do things for her . . . then suddenly it begins to go to hell and I want to know why.'

'I don't understand. Anna's been working normally.'

'On and off.'

'She was up for a judgeship, you told me so yourself, at that party.'

'You're talking about last Christmas. It was true, then. She'd been going through one of her good phases. She'd put in for an Assistant Recordership and at that time I saw no reason why she shouldn't have got it. Right age, ample court experience, no skeletons in the cupboard.' A shiver of distaste ran through Broadway's body. 'God knows, you can't say any of that for half the High Court bench.'

'Then why – '

'Because she wasn't concentrating, that's why!' Broadway's voice had turned snappy and shrill. 'There were times when she couldn't keep her mind on the ball from one moment to the next. You're her husband, surely you must have seen that?'

David seemed to hear the clink of glass on wood again and his gaze slipped from the accusing face opposite. 'I knew she . . . she could be a little absent-minded. It's a human enough trait, who isn't?'

'Generalizations are dangerous, David.' Broadway had obviously decided to give his patronizing side an airing. 'Particularly in the case of people close to one, where habitual assumptions frequently take the place of accurate observation.'

David wanted so much to think of a response to this pompous man, but he was suddenly tired. 'If you say so.'

'I began to hear murmurings from other tenants of these chambers, from people who'd always liked her. Her behaviour was so out of character.'

'Just a minute. When are we talking about?'

'Different times, different tenants. Some of these complaints go back a good many years. Some are recent. Some people never had anything bad to say against her at all. She was moody. Unpredictable.'

'How did you deal with these . . . murmurings?'

'I played them down. On the whole, they related to minor matters. Anna's always had her tetchy side and I don't blame her for that.'

David stared at him. 'Anna? Tetchy?'

'You have to be aggressive if you're a woman and you want to get on at the bar. You have no alternative.'

'But – '

'It was if she became snappish with colleagues that tempers rose. There were times when she seemed to lose all sense of humour. Why, only a few months ago our best typist left because she couldn't stand Anna's complaints.'

'Mrs Mayhew?'

'That's right. I was surprised, Anna had seemed to be performing at her best, then suddenly – '

'Anna said . . .'

'What did Anna say?'

That Mrs Mayhew had suffered a mental breakdown, they'd had to let her go . . .

'I . . . I can't exactly remember. I didn't get the impression that her leaving was to do with Anna.'

'I see. Well, you mustn't think your wife didn't get any sympathy. She was popular, you know; people were prepared to give her masses of leeway. Everyone knew she was working under the most tremendous strain. She'd put in for the judgeship, she was probably going to get silk next time round, and then that writ landed on her desk. It's enough to make anyone – '

'Writ?'

'The damages claim.' Broadway shunted some papers around his desktop, irritated by the interruption. 'Three million pounds is a pretty big claim in professional negligence terms. We carry insurance up to twenty-five million, but even so.' He glanced up at David and then his face changed. 'You didn't know?'

David shook his head. 'Can you explain? Please?'

Broadway celebrated that 'please' by making David wait. 'It's rather an ugly story,' he said at last. 'Anna drafted an agreement, some years ago. It involved the sale of a thriving business, with a number of subsidiaries, to a rather well-known public conglomerate, actually. She was asked to include warranties as to the state of the company's accounts, and so on. She appears to have . . .' He snapped his fingers, angry with himself. 'It is *alleged* that she left out certain vital clauses, I won't burden you with the details.'

'But . . . I mean, what's the position?'

'Position?'

'Well, will she win? Will they win? How much . . . ?'

'I think it's unlikely the plaintiff will recover. But there are . . . factors. About which I'm not happy. Evidential considerations.'

'Explain that.'

Broadway's face betrayed deep dissatisfaction. 'It's irregular. But you are her husband . . .' His voice hardened. 'Dammit, you ought to know at least something about this . . .'

'I agree. Please can you tell me what the problems are?'

The barrister unlocked a desk-drawer, using one of the keys on the end of his watch chain, and took out a tome; David saw '1987' embossed in gold on the back.

'Two years ago?' he inquired.

'Yes.'

'Haven't they waited rather a long time to make a fuss about whatever it is?'

'The problems only surfaced recently.' Broadway opened this office diary at one of many bookmarks and pushed it across the desk. 'You see that entry, there?'

'Ten-thirty in court, a conference in the afternoon . . . something's been rubbed out.'

'That's the point. She had a lunch engagement that day. The date's significant.'

'Why?'

'Because that afternoon conference related to the mess she's got herself into, the one she's being sued for. The other side are going to say she arrived late and appeared . . . "distraught" 's how they tactfully put it, as if her mind wasn't on the case at all.'

David stared at him. 'That's the whole of their case?'

'Would that it were! *All* the slips mark up days when Anna went out to lunch, stayed out a long time, and then erased the entries afterwards.'

David flicked through several pages. 'These markers, they're from about May to . . . October?'

'Yes. Sometimes she juggled appointments to make those lunches; once she even asked another member of chambers to do a summons for her so that she could keep the date. Look at July the thirty-first.'

The summer of 1987; two years ago now, but David remembered it easily. He and Anna quarrelled, then somehow failed to make it up. Ostensibly the fracas concerned Juliet, what they ought to do about her. But there had been something deeper, something that could not be explained simply in terms of concern for a difficult teenager's future.

He turned back to the end of July. 'Someone's written a number . . . telephone?'

'The police seemed to think so.'

'You mentioned them earlier. Did they say what they thought might have happened to Anna?'

'No. Neither of them brought it up.'

152

'Neither?'

'There were two. The older man just sat there, keeping mum. The other fellow asked all the questions but wasn't about to supply any answers.'

Broadway's gaze no longer quite met David's. It was easy, even pleasurable, to imagine that scene: haughty QC worked over by the Bill. Broadway had a nice line in splutters.

'The talker, the young one in glasses, he was very interested in those entries. He took the diary away, we only got it back this afternoon, in fact.'

'What kind of glasses did he wear?'

'What do you mean, what kind of glasses? Does it matter?'

'I wondered if . . . no, too much of a coincidence.'

'Know him, do you? Tall, thin, sandy hair, very weak specs; I'm surprised he needed them at all, really. Those dreadful tinted things.'

'What colour tint?'

'Pink.' Broadway sniffed. 'Bloody little pansy.'

'Albert a pansy?'

'Albert?'

'Didn't he introduce himself?'

'No.'

There was a long silence, which David interpreted as meaning that until this moment Broadway hadn't noticed the omission. There was something about Albert . . . 'Albert's cagey.'

'He is that!' Broadway stared at David. 'Do you mind telling me what's going on?'

'Anna's disappeared. It looks as though she took one of my files with her. It's a file a lot of people would like to get their hands on. I'm sorry if I'm not more specific, but at least you lawyers understand what confidentiality's all about.'

'Good God.' By now Broadway was almost whispering.

'No one knows where she's gone, who she's with, or anything. I can't get any cooperation.'

'My dear chap.' Broadway's voice sounded less than warm, but there was a change in it. 'What an appalling thing.'

'Yes. And I . . . Duncan, you know what they say, about not realizing what you've got until you've lost it . . .' David laughed in an attempt to cover his embarrassment. 'Well, it's true.'

Broadway could not think of an apposite response. He was hardened to the sight of emotions being stripped raw in court, indeed, he did his fair share of that; but emotions were only all right in people you didn't know socially.

'Look, Duncan, I'm sorry . . . is there anyone else in chambers she was close to, anyone who might know where she is?'

'No. I've already asked.' He grunted. 'I suppose Robyn might just conceivably know something.'

'Who is Robyn?'

'An American lawyer.'

'He's here? In England?'

'I shouldn't think so for one minute. It's a she, incidentally, not a he. A woman attorney from New York. She spent a year here, researching for some thesis she was doing, comparative law as I recall.'

'Oh yes, that rings a sort of bell. Anna mentioned her. But why do you think she might know something?'

'Because they were like two peas in a pod. Robyn shared her room, you see. After she went back to the States, Anna was always getting letters from her. She used to read out bits to us at chambers' tea.'

David gawked at him. 'What was that again – letters?'

'Yes.'

'Anna shared a room with this woman for one whole year, a friend, you say?'

'Yes. You find that astonishing?'

'It's just that I . . . I hadn't realized they were quite so close.'

'She never told you about Robyn?'

'She mentioned her a couple of times. But as a professional acquaintance, not . . .' A thought struck David. 'What does she look like . . . here, is this her?'

154

He pushed the photograph he had found in Anna's desk across to Broadway, who nodded confirmation. He went on to say more about Robyn's work in chambers, but David was no longer listening. Again his mind had leapt to the interview before the Krysalis vetting committee, with him airily confessing that Anna's circle of friends did not overlap with his. The words had meant nothing to him at the time; now they were starting to assume a frightful reality. He might not be close to Anna's friends, but at least he knew their names!

He'd thought he knew their names . . . until he'd looked in her diary at home.

'Did you tell Albert about Robyn?' he asked Broadway. 'And these letters, did you mention them?'

'No. I wasn't asked.'

'Do you know if the clerks said anything about them?'

'I know they didn't.'

'How?'

'The police questioned me with the clerks at the same time and I jolly well saw them off the premises as soon as the interview ended.'

David felt that was good, without knowing why; but he had precious little else to comfort him. 'I just don't understand any of this. The writ, this woman lawyer . . . why should Anna have personal post sent here, and not the house?'

He stared at Broadway, as if the QC might have an answer to that question, but it was so obviously his own department that no one else could help. If the husband didn't know . . .

What other things didn't the husband know?

'I shall tell chambers that Anna's ill.' Broadway pursed his lips and looked up at the ceiling. 'Hepatitis, say. Contaminated food. Been ordered to rest.'

'Thanks,' David mumbled.

Neither man spoke for a long while. David realized that he had come to the end of this road; and with the knowledge there intruded for the first time a sense of shame. 'Look, I'm . . . I'm sorry about barging in. I shouldn't have done that.'

155

'Forgotten. Ah . . .' Broadway again seemed to be having trouble with his throat. He coughed, blew his nose, all the while looking everywhere but at David. 'I really don't know how to say it, but . . . well, it's annoying, Anna going off like this. Downright annoying. But . . . I can't find words to tell you how much I hope you find her and that everything's all right.'

'Thank you.'

'Because . . . we had our little differences, but we were all immensely fond of her. Are immensely fond of her. She's a wonderful woman, a fine lawyer. And if anything bad were to happen . . .'

He tailed off, staring at the blotter on top of his desk.

'Thank you,' David repeated quietly. 'But . . . please don't say any more.'

The two men shook hands. Then David was going down the corridor, passing through the clerks' room, making his way into the deserted Temple. A busy road. Cars hooting, the squeal of brakes, another world, nothing to do with him. He found himself sitting beside the river, staring at the Embankment wall, while he struggled to refocus his picture of Anna. He sat there for a long time; so long that dusk came quietly down on London, obliging Albert to move one bench closer in order to keep his quarry in view.

FOURTEEN

The things that tourists hated most about Athens – pollution, traffic, noise, heat – were some of the city's greatest attractions in the eyes of Iannis. He had just turned eighteen, having spent his entire life on a minute Ionian island where few foreigners ever ventured; the most significant event in the calendar was the olive harvest; and even that only came along every other year.

So as the young man sauntered along Aghiou Konstantinou heading for Omonia Square, he had every reason to feel grateful to the generous Mr Kleist, whose money filled his wallet and whose orders were simple enough to understand. Each day from now on, Iannis had to go to a telex-and-fax bureau down an alley off Zinonos Street and ask if there was any answer to the document they had transmitted for him this morning. If there was, his instructions were to contact Kleist by phone (always a different phone) and spell the document to him. (Iannis could not read any English, although he knew the alphabet. He had been worried at first that this might disqualify him for the job Kleist had in mind, not realizing that such lack of linguistic skill was a vital requirement.) He must sleep in a different hotel each night, and keep moving around during the day, until Sunday morning. Then he could come home.

But Iannis did not intend to go home. Unknown to his father and Kleist, he spent his days hunting for work. Jobs were few and far between in Athens; Iannis, however, was not deterred. He knew that the season had only just begun.

Hotels and restaurants would soon need more staff. All he had to do was stick around; and, thanks to Kleist's generous idea of expenses, that was something he could do almost indefinitely.

Darkness had fallen, but Athens still sweltered. As Iannis crossed the road and took the moving stairway down to the second level beneath Omonia Square he was busy making plans for Tuesday evening. A meal, then he would drift along to the King George Hotel and hang around there in the hope of picking up an unattached American woman. So far he hadn't had any luck, but Iannis had a good feeling about tonight.

He made his way over to the bank of phone boxes next to the newsstand and waited for one to become vacant. He looked around several times, as Kleist had taught him, making sure that no one was watching. His heart had begun to beat faster, the nerves at the pit of his stomach tingled. He had no idea what Kleist intended to do, but his instincts told him that it was nothing legal. The money he had in his wallet confirmed the message: no one paid that well for legitimate errands.

All clear. Iannis ducked into the box and produced a black silk bag from his hip pocket. His face flushed hot. He felt stupid using this bag to cover his hands while he dialled, knowing that people would look at him and laugh, but Kleist was paying and Kleist was obviously up to no good, so that meant Iannis had to watch out for himself. This way, snoopers couldn't see what number he was calling.

The instant Kleist answered, Iannis said, 'I sent it; no reply yet,' put down the phone and walked off.

His day's work now over, he could relax, but as he went on his way he wondered, not for the first time, just what Kleist was about. Iannis shook his head impatiently at the memory of his father's blind trust in the German. Anyone could see he was a crook. Not that Iannis cared. Kleist paid up front, no promises, no cheques.

The King George was off Constitution Square, a few blocks

to the south-east. On his way there he would have a meal, nothing heavy (Iannis was weight-conscious), and no beer (let the lucky tourist girl pay for that later). He crossed over to Stadiou and began thrusting his way through the crowds.

As he came to the intersection with Santaroza he bumped into a gang of students speaking some foreign language. There was a moment of confusion while the various parties sorted themselves out. Iannis never even felt the needle penetrate his arm. Only when he had crossed the road did the strangeness begin. He hadn't touched alcohol that day, but he felt drunk. His head was going round and round, his legs wouldn't obey him. He was going to be sick. All his saliva had dried up.

Iannis clutched his stomach and reached out to lean against the wall of a bank. He tried to cry out, but the words couldn't force their way past the blockage that had suddenly materialized in his throat. By the time an ambulance screeched to a halt beside him and two men were helping him into it, he was nearly unconscious. His last waking thought was how lucky he'd been to be rescued in a city where ambulances ranked as an endangered species.

Wednesday

FIFTEEN

At eight-fifteen on Wednesday morning, Whitehall Place contained only a handful of early-bird civil servants on their way to work. Jeremy Shorrocks trotted into the National Liberal Club with a nod to the porter and made his way up the curving staircase. On the first landing he turned left, as if the members' dining room was his destination, but while still well short of it he made another sharp turn, this time ascending a narrow stairway that doubled inconveniently back on itself. At the top he passed through a door marked 'Gentlemen' and, that label notwithstanding, found himself in the presence of an American; a non-member, to boot.

'Morning, Louis. Rain later, I think.'

'Thunderstorms, more like.' Louis Redman was sitting on the chair of a weighing-machine, playing absent-mindedly with the weights. Now he heaved a sigh. 'I'm going cold turkey on chocolate and gin. I've decided.'

'Shall we?'

Redman nodded and stood up. The two men went into the inner sanctum, where they rapidly inspected each of the cubicles. The place was empty.

'You sure pick your times to call favours,' Redman said as he once again lowered himself onto the padded scale-pan. 'Couldn't it have waited?'

'It could not.' Shorrocks rested his back against the wall opposite Redman. 'The brown stuff's rising over my knees. I don't know why, or where it's coming from, but I'm in deep and since no one else will help it has to be you.'

'So what's the problem?'

'The problem is, Louis, that I've not been allowed to read Krysalis.'

The American slowly raised his eyes to the other man's face. 'Joke, right?'

Shorrocks vehemently shook his head.

'But when we met up at Crowborough, you seemed to know all about it.'

'Bluff. We were still fighting to get hold of a copy, then. I'd been shown a page of briefing notes, giving me the rough idea. Do you realize – no one in Six has ever read Krysalis? Not the Director, not me, *no one at all.*'

'But we never put that kind of embargo on it.'

'If you didn't, then who did?'

Redman puckered his lips and thought. 'State, I guess. It's their cookie.'

'That's what the Foreign Secretary told me. Last night, my director went one better: he got as far as Number Ten. The answer's still no: we're not allowed to see it. On the other hand . . .' Shorrocks came off the wall and began to pace around the anteroom. 'On the other hand, we have to break our backs to see it comes home yesterday. And since this circus is being mounted to please you people, you were right, what you said a minute ago, Louis: I'm calling in a favour.'

Redman made a wry face. 'Shoot.'

'Have you read this benighted file?'

'I've read it.'

'Then what's in Krysalis? What *exactly* is the fuss about?'

Redman closed his eyes and allowed a long breath to escape from between his teeth. 'I really would rather you made a formal request through channels – '

'God damn it, why the hell d'you think we're here?' Shorrocks waved his arms around. 'A club toilet at half past bloody eight in the morning! Do I *look* like a man who's able to go through channels?'

In the silence that followed, they heard footsteps on the narrow staircase.

' . . . Three o'clock at Newbury,' Shorrocks said smoothly. 'What price?'

'Ten. Mind you, the going was firm.'

The door opened. An elderly gentleman shuffled in and, when halfway across the anteroom, registered with surprise that he wasn't alone. Shorrocks nodded pleasantly. 'Morning, Sebastian.'

The old gentleman grunted and half raised a hand. 'She ran second to Prince's Harness,' Shorrocks said.

'Oh, I saw her on the gallops up by Lambourn, once. Great little filly.'

Sebastian entered the lavatory. While he attended to the call of nature, Shorrocks and Redman continued a desultory discussion about prospects for the flat-racing season. At last Sebastian shuffled back into the anteroom, still buttoning his fly, in time to hear Redman say, ' . . . but Mike had insisted on a treble; I cried all the way to the tote.'

'Oh, bad luck!'

Their elderly companion won his battle with the heavy swing door to the outer corridor. They waited until they could no longer hear his footsteps on the stairway; then – 'Let me make one thing clear,' Shorrocks said; 'I'm not going to stick my neck out any further for Krysalis until I know what it is, what it says, and what it does.'

'Okay,' Redman muttered. 'Here's Krysalis. But you didn't get it from me, understand?'

'Oh, for God's – '

'Krysalis . . . is in two parts. The Gospels and the Epistles; it's known as the New Testament.'

Shorrocks leaned back against the wall. 'Go on.'

'The Gospels don't change too much, they're pretty well fixed. Four sections . . .'

'Hence gospels?'

'Right. Basically, it's the NATO General Situation Plan: where the forces are, in what strengths, able to call on what reserves. Inventories, lists, capacities . . .'

Shorrocks stared. 'Our careers are at risk for *that*? For

information that Russian satellites trawl every day, telling them in Moscow what's happening before we know ourselves?'

Redman shook his head. 'The gospels aren't so important. What matters is the epistles.'

'Which say?'

'Which say what the generals are to do with their lists, if war breaks out in the next twenty-four hours. Orders. Updated quarterly in the light of changing circumstances. *Strategic* orders, Jeremy.'

Shorrocks regarded him in silence. 'Strategic?' he said at last. 'You mean that sacrificial pawns business? The parts of Germany we're prepared to fling away . . . ?'

'That's right. And a whole lot more. Targetings for warheads. Counter-strikes. Counter-strikes to counter-strikes. Deployments.' Redman slid off the scales and stood up. 'Think of the gospels as the chess men. The epistles are the games people play with them.'

'And the Krysalis Committee – '

'Are the games players, yes.'

Shorrocks' mouth became slack, his gaze unfocused. 'So . . . so Lescombe and the rest of them, they . . .'

'Their duty is to plan the first phase of the next land war in Europe. Yes. By refining and analysing intelligence data, keeping the New Testament at maximum usefulness and efficiency.'

'I see.' Shorrocks spoke in hardly more than a whisper. After a while he gathered himself together enough to ask, 'How come you've been allowed to read this thing and I haven't?'

Redman's lips twitched in an embarrassed smile, but he couldn't answer that one. Shorrocks made certain deductions and faced some unpalatable truths. 'Vancouver,' he said at last. 'With that up his sleeve, Gorbachev would know what we planned to do in any eventuality.'

'Yes.'

'So when negotiating with Bush . . .'

'To use Bill's phrase, our President would be playing poker with a mirror at his back.'

'But surely . . .' Shorrocks brightened. 'Surely the, what do you call 'em, the epistles, they could be changed!'

'Not as simple as that.'

'But sometimes they're updated, you said so yourself.'

'Much of the stuff in there enshrines assumptions, basic Pentagon thinking that won't ever change. Their attitudes to allies, for instance.'

'Which are what?'

'Contempt. Mistrust. A deep-rooted feeling that Europe's a minor military theatre of scant importance, whose tinpot armies can be relied on to do the wrong thing at the wrong time and in the wrong way. The epistles tend toward frankness.' When Shorrocks said nothing, Redman looked at his watch. 'I have to go now.'

'Of course,' Shorrocks replied mechanically, after a pause. 'Thank you.'

At the door, Redman hesitated, turned back. For a moment it looked as if he might decide to keep his thoughts to himself. But then . . . 'Jeremy,' he said, 'the epistles tell the enemy who is fighting the next war and what those people really think.' He laid a land on Shorrocks' arm, as if afraid the Englishman might not be paying full attention. 'Anna Lescombe didn't just betray her country,' he said quietly. 'She betrayed its state of mind.'

SIXTEEN

Wednesday began with one of those peerless Greek mornings which normally only find their season in May or June: a brilliant perspective of long horizons and lofty cloud, of crystalline water and warm breezes. The view from Anna's bedroom brightened her up. When Gerhard suggested a picnic as the only way to spend such a magnificent day, she acquiesced at once, even though she knew she ought to go home.

'You've changed your mind,' he said. 'Good.'

'Nothing's changed. Not in the real world. At Heathrow they'll be waiting to arrest me, won't they?'

'If you go back now, without waiting for the results of my preliminary overtures, then yes, I'm afraid they will.'

She smiled wanly, trying to put a brave face on things. *'Embarrasse des riches.'*

'Come again?'

'Not one court case but two. First the trial for treason, then, when I've got a moment, there's that claim for three million pounds to fight, the one I told you about, remember?'

'Yes.'

'Oh . . . the thought of going back to chambers and facing them all . . .'

'*Out*facing them. You can do it.'

'Mm. I didn't behave very well towards them. Not always.'

'Such an awkward cuss.'

168

She laughed, then turned serious again. 'The longer I stay away, the worse it will get. Won't it?' His quizzical expression told her what he was thinking, so she decided to pre-empt him: 'Then why stay? Oh . . . a few more hours' freedom aren't going to change anything, are they? And perhaps your . . .' She made a face. ' . . . overtures will come to something.'

Kleist borrowed Yorgos' car and drove them across to the west coast, where he kept a boat moored in one of the coastal hamlets. Anna enjoyed the drive. She was starting to fall in love with this isolated place, still undiscovered by tourists. The peach trees were a mass of white flowers, irises and marguerites were everywhere in full bloom, orange and lemon trees stood laden with young fruit. It was to be an olive year, and already buds were blooming on their twigs as they strove up towards the spring sky. Everything she saw appealed to her: geraniums, poppies, roses in tubs, peeling walls in need of paint; terraced, overgrown gardens; cocks crowing in the middle of the day . . . how swiftly these things beguiled: haunting and remote as the scent of salt, and oil, and tobacco, and rosemary, which was the quintessence of every Mediterranean island

They took his boat, the *Medina*, to a smaller, uninhabited islet that lay to the south. There they swam in a deep place where you could see the bottom three fathoms down. It reminded Anna of a cathedral, with broad shafts of light pouring through limpid water straight onto the sand. They laughed a lot; and once, when she playfully grabbed Gerhard's shoulders, he first ducked her, then held her tightly around the waist. Anna threw back her head and laughed while she fought, until she had no breath left and he had to carry her ashore.

'Tell me what you're going to do,' she demanded after towelling herself dry.

'Have lunch.'

'Do about me, I mean.' She had turned serious. 'It's all such a mess. When will David be here?'

169

'Saturday. I've already got in touch with London. We can't do anything until my people reply, so you might as well relax and forget about things for a while.'

'I must ring David, make sure he's all right.'

'I've been thinking about that. Your Islington phone is almost certainly being monitored. If you try to make contact, you could put him on the spot in a very big way, you know.'

'But – '

'No buts. Try to think of it as a holiday. Now. Help me by uncorking that bottle . . .'

They lunched simply on fresh fruit, cheese and luscious 'black' wine before sunbathing a while, scents of jasmine and resin deep in their nostrils and the drone of nearby bees soothing them to the verge of sleep.

'Holidays,' Anna murmured drowsily. 'When I was a child, I never liked them.'

'Why do you say that?'

'It always seemed like water behind a dam, a holiday. You'd think about it for ages, savouring every minute before it happened . . .' She carved out a ball of sand and squeezed it hard. For many years she had regarded it as nothing but a tiresome substance that forced its way between your toes and wouldn't wash off. This sand, however, was child-wonderful, reminding her of how much Juliet loved the beach . . .

' . . . Then on the first day there was a trickle of water through the dam, just a few drops that first day, because there were still thirteen more left, weren't there? And tomorrow was going to be the same as today . . . but the trickle became a flood . . . and suddenly all that was left of the water was tears on your face . . . and you'd lost it.'

'Lost what?'

'The magic moment. When you're a child, on holiday, life is perfect. It's what tells you life *can* be perfect, that it's all there to be had if only you can find the way . . . but then you have to go home, don't you, to a world where nothing

170

works. On holiday you can somehow make yourself believe that it will happen this time, there'll be no going back to the old life, the holiday will go on . . .'

Anna, struck by a thought, raised her head. 'Therapy's a grown-up holiday, isn't it? You have sessions, life becomes perfect, but then it fades. It fades. Only this time, here, I had this ridiculous feeling, just for a moment . . . it wouldn't, needn't fade . . . ever.'

She laughed sleepily and lowered her head back onto the towel.

After their siesta she swam again, investigating strange channels carved in the rock by the currents of a luminously turquoise sea. Kleist fetched the boat and they ventured further out, following the line of a reef, until the waters changed to sapphire syrup.

He sat in the stern, watching Anna alternately swim and dive. The current took her gently away from him, but in-shore, so he did not worry. The rocking motion, the sucking of the waves beneath the boat, together with the wine he had drunk, made him feel queasy. His thoughts kept straying to what Anna had said after lunch.

She had never taken proper holidays, even when he first met her. *Especially* then, for she had come to him weighed down by the twin burdens of caring for Juliet and trying to make a career at the bar. At that time she wanted more than anything to make up for what she had endured in her own childhood by being a perfect mother; everything she did, attempted, touched, had to be so, so perfect. Anna used to arrive looking terrible, as if she had been up all night, which she had, working on papers, because she needed time with her daughter, without the nanny, without her parents, without whichever stopgap she was using at the time; and she used to say to him, 'I'm so unhappy, why am I so unhappy . . . ?'

Often he felt like answering, 'Because this is the twentieth century and you are a woman of your time.'

The memory made him glad that soon he would be done

171

with psychotherapy for ever. London must deal. Their proposal was on its way to Athens, might even have arrived already. Tonight, when Iannis phoned . . .

He was so far gone in time and space that he did not hear Anna's first scream. Only when she yelled a second time did he jolt upright, his heart thumping. A scream filled with salt water and terror. It fired him to instinctive action. He gunned the Johnson 50 and put the *Medina* hard about.

Kleist grasped everything in less than a second. Fifty yards of sea separated him from the beach. Anna was racing for the shore. Close behind and swiftly gaining water he could make out a long, sinuous shadow.

There were two empty wine bottles left over from their picnic. As the *Medina* sped off in pursuit, Kleist flung them one after the other, timing each to fall ahead of the shadow. Then he picked up an oar and began to beat the water with it.

The engine was howling. He dropped the oar, grabbed the spare petrol can and threw it at the shadow as hard as he could before again starting to thrash the sea. At the moment when Anna hauled herself onto the sand, the world wrenched sideways; there was a sudden crack, and Kleist was falling backwards.

He pulled himself up with the aid of a thwart. Not ten feet away from him, the remains of his oar were floating in two pieces. Something had bitten through one and a half inches of seasoned wood as though it were a gris stick.

He scanned the water for yards around, but it was empty: the black shadow had gone. As the pounding in his ears died away he heard Anna start to sob.

He waded inshore. She ran to him, knocking him over, so that they collapsed in a tangle of arms and legs on the sand.

'I was swimming out there, by the cave . . .' Her voice sounded flat and low, her eyes looked straight through him. 'I dived a couple of times. As I was coming up, I saw . . .' She gnawed her hand. 'It was terrible . . . such teeth, such *jaws*. I could *feel* it catching up.'

172

Kleist chafed her hands, spoke meaningless things.

'What *was* that?'

'I think . . . I'm sure, it was a moray eel. They don't normally attack unless . . . A freak . . .'

She hugged him tightly, still trembling. Kleist laid her down on a towel and began to massage her shoulders with deep, firm strokes. His hands ranged to and fro along her back until he was tired.

At first Anna fidgeted, unable to relax. It wasn't only the encounter with the eel that troubled her. Before the attack, she and Gerhard had been proximate. Now, suddenly, they were intimate.

'It's been ages since I massaged you,' he murmured. 'Do you remember the first time?'

She said nothing.

'It was after one of your first dates with David . . .'

His words triggered a memory and she smiled in spite of herself. 'The opera.'

'When you spent all evening wondering what this dry old civil servant would be like in bed.'

'And I told him . . . I was staying with friends while my flat was being redecorated . . . and I got him to drop me off in — '

'Hampstead.'

'And I came in . . .'

'And I grabbed you.' He laughed softly. 'You told me that all evening you'd been making love to David, in your mind . . . his body, but with my face.'

'Yes,' she whispered. 'Oh yes. Was that when you massaged me the first time?'

'Um-hm.' His voice was caressing, scarcely louder than her own. When Anna raised her head to smile at him, Kleist loosened the strap of her bikini top.

She tensed. 'No.'

He began to massage her inner thighs. She pulled herself away, out of range of temptation, and sat up.

'Really no?' His smile was teasing. *'Really?'*

'That was over, long ago. When I said I'd marry David. You know that.'

Her face told him how angry she was. 'But it wouldn't be important if we made love. Bodies, that's all. Bodies.' He laughed again, in his typical, easy way.

'And the minds? The emotions, what about them?'

He shrugged.

'You don't believe people can change, do you?' She gave him a look he could not fathom. 'You – a psychotherapist.'

'You've changed.'

'Good.'

'Changed enough to come and spend a few days here, on the island. Not many people are privileged to be invited.'

'Really? What about the other women? What about . . . ?'

When she had not spoken for a long time he completed the sentence for her in a whisper. 'Robyn.'

'My best friend!' Anna wailed. Then, almost immediately – 'God! As if that mattered!'

'Of course it didn't matter. When you married David you made it clear that you didn't want our affair to continue. Friends, you said: let's just stay good friends. So we did, very successfully, I always thought. My life was my own to do as I liked with, after that. And Robyn was recent – 1987.'

'There were others in between, you mean?'

'Is that your business? Isn't that almost as presumptuous as my asking if you love David?' He yawned extravagantly, embracing their idyllic surroundings with a long, slow look before once more turning to face her. 'Do you, by the way?'

She understood that look of Kleist's; and his question outraged her to the point where words ceased to flow. 'Are you implying,' she said at last, 'that I set this up? This . . . crude little seaside seduction, you think it was my idea?'

His laugh had degenerated into an uncertain smile. 'All I'm saying is that you've changed.'

174

'Yes. I've grown. I've got some self-respect.'

'And don't I get any credit for that?'

'You know what you did.'

Her expression, somehow defiant and sad at the same time, did not exactly reinforce the meaning he'd sought. 'Certainly, I showed you how to – '

'Make love.' She dashed something from the corner of one eye with the back of her hand. *'Fuck.'*

Anna snatched up her towel and marched off down the beach, not once looking back.

When they left for home the sun had already begun to sink towards a basket of purple and orange clouds that seemed to float across the surface of the darkening sea. Back at the villa Anna, utterly exhausted, fell asleep at once, with Juliet's corn dolly hugged to her breast. She slept for twelve hours.

She awoke to find herself lying in her low, whitewashed room, now suffused with the warm savour of a Mediterranean morning. Sleepily she moved her head and looked around. Her bed stood opposite the only window. Someone had put a vase of fresh bluebells on the sill.

She saw the flowers, knew who had picked them, and suddenly remembered all that had happened the day before. She sat up. What was she doing here?

Suddenly all that mattered was flight. She jumped out of bed, hastily pulling on her clothes. As she emerged into the hallway a few moments later, she became aware of odd sounds coming from Gerhard's bedroom. She felt curious. She slipped out of her sandals and padded across the breakfast area, along the corridor leading to the front of the villa. His door was ajar.

Anna sidled along the wall until she could look through the gap. As she did so, Gerhard straightened up from kneeling by the bed. He had his back to the door, unaware of her presence. He put something into his pocket. She retreated

175

the way she had come, not daring to stop until she had regained the relative safety of the living room.

She was a prisoner here. Kleist had no intention of letting her go. If forced to it, he would even use the gun which now made such an ugly bulge in his pocket.

SEVENTEEN

David had an easy journey to Cornwall; it was a Wednesday, and too early in the year for holiday traffic jams. He turned off the A30 five miles short of Bodmin, keeping Hawk's Tor on his right. Almost immediately he stopped at a pub for an early lunch. As he drove out of the car park afterwards he checked his rearview mirror and saw a black Audi coming up fast. David thought the driver wanted to overtake, but then the Audi slowed and settled down a couple of hundred yards behind.

He felt his pulse quicken. Wasn't it an Audi that had followed him off the A30? Imagination . . . but as he drove he kept remembering glimpses, or half-glimpses, of big black saloons, perhaps the same vehicle each time, in his mirror.

David tightened his grip on the wheel and on himself. *That way madness lies* . . .

The roughly turfed, unfenced moor stretched out in every direction. Occasionally he caught sight of dirty sheep grazing by the side of the road, or sheltering in the lee of crude but strong stone walls. Ahead of him, a pale blue sky descended to meet the black moor in a hem of pink and yellow. Puffy clouds danced along, their fat fleeces thinned by the breeze, like balls of cotton wool being teased into strips. Here the sun was in his eyes, but he did not mind. After the gloom of London, it was bliss by comparison.

The Audi stayed a constant distance behind him, neither slowing nor accelerating. David experimented. He pushed the Rover up to seventy, and the Audi followed suit. David

177

reduced speed to a crawl, inviting the other driver to pass. This time his shadow – David by now definitely thought of him in such terms – pulled off the road and stopped. David accelerated again, concentrating on his mirror. Sure enough, after he had driven about a quarter of a mile, the black Audi resumed progress in his wake.

The Audi's windscreen was made of tinted glass. David could not see the driver's face.

Once he reached the village of St Breward the signs ceased to be helpful. David consulted his map, only to be buried in a mass of 'Tre's: Tregarrick, Treveighan, Treburgett, Trenewth, the list seemed endless. He asked directions at the Post Office stores and was subjected to a woefully complex saga of 'left by the big farm gate' and 'first turning after you see Devil's Ditch drop away to the bridge', interlarded with 'you can't miss it, m'dear's. But he could. He had to ask twice more before he found the road to St Mary Abbott.

The HVA took him when he was just half a mile from his destination, New Pendoggett Farm.

He was driving down a twisting, narrow hill, careful to protect his paintwork from the sheer stone walls, thick with moss, that bounded what was little wider than a single-track lane. Suddenly the black Audi filled his mirror, causing him to jam on his brakes. As it overtook, David was forced into the offside wall and stone shrieked against metal, but he felt too shocked to worry about the cost of a respray – for the Audi had parked diagonally across the lane a few yards ahead of him, and now the driver's door was opening.

A man got out, doing up the jacket of his single-breasted suit. He was wearing sunglasses. Then the passenger door opened to allow another man into the road; he, too, wore a suit and had on a pair of gloves. The two men began to walk back towards David's Rover. They did not hurry, but they gave the impression of being completely in charge.

David wound down his window. 'What do you want?'

The men continued to approach in silence. Suddenly David had had enough. The Rover's engine was still running. He

178

looked in his mirror: all clear. He engaged reverse and let off the handbrake. When the car began to move backwards, David turned away from the oncoming pair and rested his left arm across the top of the passenger seat, so as to fix his entire attention on the view through the rear windscreen. It wasn't easy manoeuvring the car up that hill, especially since every moment he dreaded to see another vehicle hurtle around the next blind corner, closing what he now felt sure was a trap. As long as he kept his speed low, he could manage. But then he made the mistake of revving the engine and the car jumped against the wall with another expensive-sounding crunch.

David slammed on the brakes. His hands were shaking and sweaty, making the gear-change difficult, and his mouth tasted of iron. He wrenched the shift too hard, putting the Rover into third instead of first. The car lurched forwards, came within an ace of stalling. *Keep calm!*

He let out the clutch, allowing his Rover to slide forward out of contact with the wall. As he raised his eyes from the gear-lever he saw the Audi's driver still walking towards the Rover. But the other man was in the road facing him with his legs apart and arms outstretched. The arms culminated in a point. A black, stubby point, with a barrel and a sight . . .

For a millisecond David stared through his windscreen at the gunman, certain that he could not buy his way out of this: they were not giving him orders, or inviting him to do anything, except perhaps to stay still for long enough to allow an assassin to blow his head into shards of bone. Extreme muscular pain racked the length of his spine: all his body seemed to shrink in upon itself in one huge, spasmodic clench.

The Audi's driver came alongside him. 'Get out.' His voice sounded clipped: David did not think he was English.

'Who the hell are you to tell me to – '

The stranger yanked open the door and reached in with both hands to haul David out by the lapels. David found himself being manhandled as easily as if he was a straw

179

dummy, instead of a fit, forty-two-year-old man. The driver spun him around and hurled him against the side of the Rover.

'Do what I tell you,' he heard the same voice say. 'If you do anything except what I tell you to do, you will be shot. Understand?'

David, still trying to catch his breath, nodded.

'You will stand upright — *wait!* I will tell you when you move. Stand upright, place your hands on top of your head, walk towards the Audi. Do not look at me. Do not look at the other man. Look straight ahead until you reach the Audi. Then stop. Got it?'

'Yes.'

'Move!'

David put his hands on top of his head and turned. 'Do not look at me,' the driver cautioned him again; his voice had risen in pitch, he sounded edgy.

David began to walk towards the other car. He had to negotiate a path around the gunman, who swivelled in such a way as to keep him permanently within range. Ten yards to the Audi. Now he could not see either of the two men and his heart gave a thump: *what was happening?* Five yards . . .

'Stop. Place your hands on the lid of the boot. Keep them well apart.'

David complied. He heard footsteps approaching swiftly and clenched his eyes shut, certain that any second now something would thud into his skull, that there would be pain . . .

Behind him, a horn hooted. As if through ear-muffs, David heard yet a third crunch, but this one sounded different: metal on glass, rather than on stone. Then the footsteps he had heard a moment ago resumed, only now they were running, running *past* him. He opened his eyes in time to see the two assailants diving into the front of their Audi. Smoke appeared at the exhaust, tyres squealed, and suddenly the saloon was away; David just had time to stand up before it vanished around the next tight corner.

David could not move. He felt full of toxins and aches and pains. There was this voice, but he couldn't focus on it; then there was also an arm, clad in dark blue, attached to a hand on his sleeve, and the hand was tugging him.

'Would 'ee mine tellin' me what the hell's goin' orn?'

David turned his head. Standing beside him was a rotund policeman. Sweat trickled from underneath his cap down a broken-veined face dominated by a bulbous nose and a mouth compressed in anger. His enormous pores and vermilion complexion combined to make him look like an irate, fat, strawberry.

'Oos goin' to pay for that, then?' The podgy hand tugged his sleeve again. David looked back. The smallest police car he'd ever seen had run into the Rover's rear fender; he could just make out shards of orange plastic in the road where the indicator light had broken.

David mumbled something.

'What?'

'Emergency stop. Car in front jammed on his brakes. We were having a bit of an argy-bargy.'

He opened his mouth to say more. He wanted to tell this policeman that somebody had tried to kill him, but he couldn't make himself believe it yet and if he didn't believe it, who else would? Besides . . . David was coming to himself now . . . this bumpkin was incapable of taking it all in. There would be delays, formalities; he'd be asked to make a statement.

'In an 'urry, baint they?' The PC looked down the hill with a frown, but only for a moment: there was easier prey to hand. 'I'll be takin' your name, zir,' he said, unbuttoning his top pocket.

David gave his name and address, handed over his licence for inspection, along with his insurance certificate. But all the while his mind was on something else. He had to get to the farm, see Juliet. Suppose they were waiting for him, around the next bend: those men in the Audi, and their stubby black something that might be a gun?

The policeman had finished with David. 'Best be more careful where y'stop, in future.'

The injustice of it filled David with bile — why couldn't this oaf drive more carefully around his own country lanes? — but he managed to control himself. He needed police cooperation, not harassment. 'Sorry, officer. Can you direct me to New Pendoggett Farm?'

'Straight up this road. 'Undred yards on th' left.'

'Are you going that way?' The PC nodded. 'Could I follow you, perhaps?'

The man gave him a scornful look, but nodded again. There was just room in the narrow lane for the police car to squeeze past. David drove slowly. No sign of the black Audi. He began to feel confidence return. The other car's occupants would almost certainly believe that this policeman had noted their licence-plate. Assuming they were up to no good, they must have fled as far and as fast as possible, surely . . . ?

Then he saw the painted sign-board, fifty yards away: New Pendoggett Farm. The police car was still ahead of him. What should he do: seek the protection of the law, or go on?

Go on.

He realized he was taking one almighty risk. But the knowledge that somebody was out to stop him made David more determined. When the police car accelerated, he did not follow; instead, he turned onto the track that led to the farm.

He parked in the yard, got out and stretched. His heartbeat had returned to normal, his body no longer ached. The wind was blustery here, it smelled of the sea. Gulls hovered overhead, calling to one another in penetrating, repetitive cries. A rich smell of horse dung arose from a pile of steaming straw in one corner of the yard, next to the entrance to a corrugated iron barn, piled high with straw. Two cats, one marmalade, one clerical grey, basked in the sunshine on the farmhouse step, ostentatiously taking not the slightest notice of the visitor.

David made his way over to the house and raised the front

door's cast-iron knocker. The 'bang' seemed to lose itself at once inside the grey, stone walls. No one answered.

Directly opposite, across the yard, stood a low two-storey building which might once have been a generous sized cow shed. A steady hammering was coming from inside. David advanced to the only visible entrance, a door split horizontally, and pushed on the top half. It swung open to reveal what looked like an old stable, the rusty manger on the opposite wall still containing wisps of hay.

He stepped inside. A hole had been knocked in the left-hand wall. Through that he could see a large room, barely lit by two windows overlooking fields at the back. A man in a leather apron was sitting astride a bench, still hammering away. He was young, with a faint ginger stubble coating cheeks and chin. Under his apron he wore a vest and a pair of old white jeans, and moccasins on his feet. David looked down to see he was mending a shoe, upended on a last.

'Hello?'

The man went right on working. David took another step forward. When his shadow fell across the shoe the man looked up sharply, but without any sign of alarm.

'Hello,' David repeated cautiously.

The cobbler's face was ugly. Acne had left its traces on a skin already disfigured by birthmarks. The pallor of his complexion was heightened by red eyelids and lips, the latter dotted with small blood scabs. His arms looked thick and muscular; and even though he wore a vest, David could see how his chest rippled whenever he moved.

'I'm sorry to disturb you. I just wondered if . . .'

But the man started to utter noises: groans and little clicking grunts which made no sense. He pointed inside his mouth, then, using both forefingers, at his ears; all this accompanied by an empty grin.

A deaf mute.

David forced his face into an inane smile and tried to work out what to do. But he was distracted by the thought that Juliet had to live here, with this handicapped man, and God

183

knows who else. Automatically he took a backwards step, like an animal skirting a zone that was unmarked on any map but which smelled wrong.

The cobbler went across to one of the windows, leaned out and made a succession of hoots. Shortly afterwards, a quiet step fell on the threshold and a female voice said, 'Who are you?'

David was not sure what to expect. She's living in a commune, Anna had said. They're doing arts and crafts. Someone's given them a grant. Her tone had sounded utterly despairing when she told him that, and he sympathized. Lesbian feminists smoking pot and chucking out the aspirins; or maybe not lesbian, maybe she'd get pregnant . . .

Here, now, was the reality: a bright-eyed, attractive young woman, whose hair had evidently been washed in the recent past, who wore simple earrings and a wooden cross around her neck on a leather thong; whose Indian shawl nearly came down over a tartan skirt as far as soft leather boots, whose accent identified her at once, with ease and composure, as *all right*.

Her eyebrows struck the only discordant note. They were thick and slanted upward at a sharp angle. She had plucked them until they occupied only a short mid-section above each eye. The effect was brutal.

David, relieved despite the eyebrows, said, 'I'd like to speak to Juliet.'

'Why?'

'I'm her stepfather.'

'I asked for a reason, not an ancestry.'

The feeling of relief was wearing off. 'I have things I want to discuss with her.'

'Two "I's" in one sentence.'

'I asked for Juliet, not an English lesson.'

'Everyone who lives here does so for a reason.' Her voice turned aggressive. 'We came to escape from people like you.'

'And what am I like?' His voice had started to echo hers.

'One of those who make demands we're not prepared to

184

meet. Not obliged to meet.' She spoke the word 'obliged' with her chin thrust forward to challenge him.

'I have news for Juliet.'

'You can leave a note, if you want.'

'Or I can come back with a policeman.'

'Oh yes?' The girl leaned against the door jamb, letting her contempt show. 'There's no crime in not wanting to see someone. Not yet.'

'She's still under age.'

'So buy a court order. Access. *Then* come back.'

'To find her gone, I suppose.'

'You're starting to get the idea.'

David counted his options, found them remarkably few. He worked in a well ordered world, one bolstered with rules and regulations which people obeyed not because they had to but because they knew things would grind to a halt if they didn't. Once you stepped outside that world, every move involved a major battle.

'All right,' he said. 'I won't bother with a note. Just give her a message, will you?'

'I don't write blank cheques. Tell me what you want to say. If it isn't racist, sexist or abusive I'll probably pass it on.'

'Say: Anna's disappeared, the police are looking for her, I'm worried about her. I'll go back to my car, now. I'll wait a quarter of an hour, then I'll leave and I shan't come back. That's the message. The whole of it.'

He walked towards the door and the girl made way for him. He did not look back until he was sitting in the Rover, quaking with rage and frustration.

'Hello.'

He jerked his head around to the left. All he could see through the passenger window was a black-clad torso and an arm. The arm was attached to a hand that was trying to open the nearside door. David released the lock. 'Hello, Juliet,' he said. 'How are you?'

'All right.' The torso bent, acquired a head. 'Would you like to come for a walk?'

David got out. 'Where shall we go?'

'The sea.'

She sounded anaemic; her voice came trickling out of her skinny body without conviction. Despite the spring warmth around them she must have been cold, for she wore a black roll-neck sweater with a zip-up front and thick black woollen stockings. Around each leg was an eye-blinding turquoise muff: not a leg-warmer, too short for that, but perhaps a knee-warmer. Ankle-length boots with pointed toes heightened her resemblance to an undernourished elf.

'We'll go through the fields. The farmer doesn't mind.'

She led the way down the side of the old cow shed to a stile. Half a dozen fencing posts were stacked against it, and Juliet somehow managed to dislodge one of them. David, driven by his innate sense of tidiness, stood the post back up again before following her.

Once over the stile the wind came cold off the sea. Juliet folded her arms across her flattish chest, tucking the hands under her armpits in an effort to keep them from turning red. She stumbled awkwardly between the cow pats, as if her boots hurt her.

'I got your message,' she said at last. Her flat, piping voice dissolved away any emotion she might have been feeling inside.

'Good. Who was that other girl I saw?'

'Fergie? Did she scare you? She's Sarah, really. But we call her Fergie. Or the Duchess. Not to her face, though.'

'I felt she didn't have much of a sense of humour.'

'No.' Juliet sighed. 'You wouldn't, if you'd been through what she has. What's Mum up to, then?'

'I don't know. You haven't seen her?'

'Not since Christmas.'

They had reached the stone wall that bounded this field and the girl prepared to climb over another stile leading to the next. Once astride it she stopped and said, 'Joe keeps a bull here. He's not supposed to, because there's a right of way, but he does. You bothered?'

186

'Are you?'

'No.'

David followed her over. What seemed like a long way away, a huge animal raised its head in his direction and treated him to a long, thoughtful stare.

'That's the bull?'

'Yes. He's all right. He keeps people away from our beach.' But she was moving faster now, and he noticed how she carefully avoided looking in the bull's direction.

It looked as though they were making for the end of the world, like lemmings: ahead of him David could see only blue sky and a black line where the land stopped. At last they came to a wooden staircase, sturdy and painted.

'Mind out here, the rocks are sharp,' Juliet said as they reached the bottom. David took off his shoes and socks without a word.

Huge boulders, two or three times higher than a man, lay scattered over a long, narrow expanse of sand the colour of wheat. Rollers creamed in to lose themselves in a mess of suds, leaving the beach washed and shining. David had forgotten how loud, how insistent an interrupter the sea could be. Halfway down the sands lay a round, flat rock. Juliet sat down on it, facing the horizon, and waited until David had settled beside her before she spoke again.

'You made it, then.' She kept her face to the front, but he was aware of her eyeing him surreptitiously. 'Not very civil servant-ish.'

'Oh, you'd be surprised.'

'Would I?' Translation: No I wouldn't, not by you.

David knew better than to rush it. For five minutes he just sat staring out to sea, relishing the feel of salt drying on his face and the deep sough of the sea's constant movement, like the masses preparing for revolution. An angry, impatient sound. He thought of his Nicholson 38 and wondered when next he would sail. He could not imagine it without Anna, and she wasn't coming back . . .

Why did he think that?

187

'I'm not what you wanted, am I?' Juliet continued to stare into space, her little-girl voice competing bravely with wind and sea. 'Sorry.'

He turned and looked at Juliet then, wondering what he did want and how she knew it wasn't her. The girl's red hair hung almost to her waist; it caught the late afternoon sun in myriad tints, ranging from burnished copper to fine old gold. Her complexion remained pale, despite the healthy outdoor life she mentioned in her rare postcards. Her thin, nervous face still betrayed all the old sensitivity it had shown at five, which was her age when their destinies had first crossed.

'I thought we got on pretty well,' he said lightly.

'You didn't chase me, when I left that bloody school.'

'Did you want us to?'

Juliet merely shrugged.

'We discussed it,' he said, 'for weeks on end.'

'I'm sure.'

'Anna wanted to come after you.'

'And you talked her out of it, is that what you're going to say?'

'I talked us *both* out of it. We thought you were making a mistake. But we decided to leave you to it for a bit.'

'Hoping I'd grow up. Grow out of it.'

'Grow into whatever's right for you. How are things, anyway?'

'Oh . . . we live. It's okay in the summer, Sarah says. People buy our stuff. The weaving. Timmy's shoes. Pottery.' She hesitated. 'There's hardly any money.'

'Does that worry you, love?'

'I'm not your love. I don't love anyone.' She jumped off the rock and trotted down to the sea's edge, but not before David had heard her say what sounded like, 'Nobody loves me.'

He made himself sit there, watching her dodge the waves, until at last she tired of the lonely game and came back to stand a few yards away from his perch, not quite looking at him, not quite ignoring him either, just hovering, in case there was something to be said, after all.

'Anna hasn't visited you, then?' David had to raise his voice against the sea.

Juliet shook her head.

'Or phoned?'

'No. Why, d'you expect her to?'

'I just thought she might. Nobody knows where she is.'

'Run away at last, has she?' There was satisfaction in Juliet's voice. Told you so . . .

'Or been kidnapped.' David thought about the men in the black Audi and shivered. 'Driven away, maybe. You said "at last" . . .'

'Sorry. Can't help.'

'Don't you care?'

Juliet, hearing the tightness in his voice, looked at him for the first time since her spell down by the sea. 'No more than she cares about me.'

'She cares about you a lot. She loves you.'

'That's why she's run away, is it, without a word to me – because she loves me? God, thanks!' She came back to the rock, haughtily tossing her long hair. 'Does she love you?'

David said nothing.

'See? You can't answer, can you? Because you don't know.' Another pause. 'She doesn't love you. She wouldn't have left you otherwise, would she?'

David bit his tongue, managed to stay silent.

'Who knows, with Mum? She was always . . .'

'Say it.'

Juliet shrugged. 'I heard her talking to herself, once. At night. After she met you.'

'What did she say?'

'She was wondering what to do with the body, that kind of crap.'

'Body?'

'She had this thing about her body. She didn't want anyone to find it. If she killed herself.'

189

Silence. Stillness. No sea. No wind. No breathing. Nothing.

Slowly the world came back to him. First the insistent sound of the waves crashing down to pulverize the sand, then a gull's shriek, malevolent and dark against the sunny sky, finally the wind.

'Anna talked of killing herself?'

'Once.'

'You're sure you didn't get muddled up with something else. I mean, it is a long time ago . . .'

'It's not the sort of thing you forget, is it? I'm sure, all right.'

'Tell me.' And when she looked at him, superciliously, without friendship, 'Please.'

'She just wanted to . . . disappear. She didn't rate herself, Mum didn't.'

'No.' He remembered. 'Not when I first met her.'

'You think you changed anything?'

'I think so. I loved her.' He paused. Then he said, almost humbly, 'I love her.'

'Maybe. I was never there. Perhaps she . . . I don't know. She was always loopy.' She eyed him as if struggling to work out a complicated piece of mental arithmetic in which he figured somewhere as a cipher. 'Have you seen her shrink?'

'Her what?'

'Shrink. Psycho-whatsit.'

David swallowed. 'Anna was seeing a psychiatrist? Before we met?'

'Yes.'

'But . . . why?'

Juliet shrugged. 'Don't know.'

For the second time that afternoon wind and waves receded, to be replaced by the cotton-wool deadness of shock. When he came to himself, Juliet was saying, ' . . . look through her diaries, in the hols. She never knew. She always had these dates with "G", always on a Thursday evening. I just thought it was a friend. But then it bugged me, not knowing. One day there was this phone number against the

190

G, I think he must have changed houses or something.'

He waited, but Juliet seemed to think she had communicated everything of importance. 'And?'

'I rang the number. This woman answered. "Mr Somebody's consulting rooms," that's what she said.'

'You don't remember the name?'

She shook her head. 'The receptionist said it so fast. "Who is this?" she asked. And I said, I want a consultation. And she said, who is your GP and do you have a referral? And I said, not yet. And she said, to see a psycho-something you need a referral, but I just heard "psycho", see, that was enough, I put the phone down. Mum's barmy, I thought.' She sighed, a great long shudder that rose from the depths.

David slipped off the rock and marched down to the sea.

He rejected all that Juliet had said. His wife was a barrister, sane and successful in a mad world. She had control. Her grip on things was total. And they had no secrets from each other, none whatsoever; the openness of their shared existence was almost tedious. If Anna had consulted a psychiatrist before they met he would have known about it. Surely?

Yes, but it would explain a lot. Suppose Anna wasn't a traitor? What if she was very sick . . . hence the vodka bottle in her desk, the writ . . .

Why had she never told him?

David swung around to find that the rock he and Juliet had occupied now was empty.

'Juliet!' he cried. The wind took his voice, nullifying it. Then he caught sight of her at the cliff stairway, and he began to run. But he had to detour in order to collect his shoes and socks, so that by the time he caught up with her she was already striding across the field.

The bull seemed closer, this time.

'Juliet, listen to me. I need to talk to you. Oh, for Christ's sake, can't you slow down?'

She shook her head and ploughed on.

'Juliet, you have to hear what I've got to say. Your

191

mother . . .' Suddenly his ankle turned awkwardly, making him stumble. 'Your mother took something when she left. Something of mine. A file . . .'

Juliet was running. For an instant David did not understand her sudden urgency. Then he heard the beat of hooves and, ignoring the pain in his ankle, started to sprint.

The girl side-vaulted the stile, landed in a crouch and tumbled over, clutching her knee. David, still twenty or so yards from the wall, dared not look around. His throat was dry with terror. His chest hurt. He tried desperately to listen for hooves but the blood coursing through his eardrums blotted out all other sounds. Ten yards. Five. Then he was clutching the top bar of the stile, his stomach pressed against it. As he brought up the left foot to complete the crossing, his toe caught in a rung and he fell down beside Juliet, banging his forehead on the ground.

Only by screwing up every muscle in his face did he manage to keep himself from blubbing like a kid. He had wrenched a muscle in his right thigh and his arm hurt where he had landed on it.

He sat up. Through the stile he could see nothing. There was no bull. Not without difficulty, David managed to haul himself back to the vertical. The bull had changed position, but now he was unconcernedly plucking at a patch of long grass, as if the only thing capable of arousing his interest was afternoon tea. David realized that for most of his sprint he had been chased by a phantom.

He wheeled around to catch sight of Juliet's face contorted into a scowl. She backed away, fists clenching and unclenching by her sides.

'You say Mum took a file. Stole it, you mean?'

'Look – '

'You're accusing her of being a thief, stealing government papers.' Her eyes blinked, two tears jetted down her cheeks. 'How can you do that, David? You . . . *shit!*'

She broke into a run, sobbing. When David tried to follow, a shaft of fire sprang up his leg, crippling him. Purple patches floated before his eyes. He swore, then limped after her in the direction of the farm.

By the time he got there the sun had mellowed to an orange disk, bathing the yard in flame. As he made his way around the gate he found himself confronted by a wrathful trio: Juliet, the girl called Fergie, and Timmy the deaf-mute.

'Get in.' Fergie jerked a thumb towards his car. 'Don't stop till you hit the road.' She was seething with rage. 'If you come back, we'll call the police.'

'I want to talk to my stepdaughter,' he grated.

Sarah tapped Timmy on the arm and when he looked at her she pointed towards David. The cobbler advanced slowly, still carrying his hammer.

'Are you threatening me?'

'We're exercising the right to have you off our premises.'

'*Your* premises? Don't make me laugh!'

'We've had enough of you. And your German friends. Tell them to stay away, d'you hear?'

'David . . .' Juliet's voice sounded fearful. 'Just . . . *go*.'

'Not until we've talked. Talked properly.'

Timmy was within a foot of David now. He stopped and uttered a selection of horrid grunts, culminating in a drawn-out moan. His eyes were fish-like, cold. He looked brutish.

'I want to talk to Juliet,' David said quietly, but with great force; and Timmy hit him.

He did not use the hammer, which was as well or David would have been killed. Instead, he dropped the tool on the cobbles and punched David's jaw. David saw the blow coming and ducked, but Timmy's fist landed on his fore-head, setting off a fresh round of explosions in his already damaged skull. He swayed groggily, once more unable to see straight.

Timmy came at him again, butting into his stomach. David doubled up with an 'ouf!' of pain and fell to his knees. While he fought to regain control he found himself looking up at

Timmy, silhouetted against the sky. The deaf-mute clasped his hands and raised them above his head.

Before the blow could connect, however, it was intercepted.

Another black figure had come to stand behind the first, with something long in his hands. This object swung through a horizontal plane into the small of Timmy's back. The shape dissolved, reorganized itself, and the shaft came down vertically to land on Timmy's left shoulder. David heard a crack. Timmy knelt on the cobbles, both hands to his neck, rocking to and fro. Above him . . .

Above him, Albert was practising off-drives with considerable *élan*, using for a bat the fence post that had just broken Timmy's collarbone. 'Evening,' he said, catching David's eye. 'Get in the car, will you, be a good chap.'

As David staggered away he heard Albert ask engagingly, 'Any more for any more? Come on, don't be shy.' But the two girls backed off, numbed by the controlled, precisely directed violence radiating from this stranger. Albert threw away the stake and came around the front of the car to let himself in. 'Right,' he said as he slid into the passenger seat. 'Off sharpish, yes, mm?'

David put the Rover into gear. The last thing he saw through the rearview mirror was Juliet running forward to help Timmy up while Sarah continued to stand rooted to the spot, and the sight gave him a perverse sense of pride. He could not have said why.

'You do get yourself into some scrapes. Ouch! As indeed . . . do I. What on earth . . . ?'

Albert felt underneath him. His hand emerged holding a white paper bag. 'Chocolates?'

'Juliet's favourites.' David sighed. 'I didn't even get a chance . . .'

'Never mind.'

Until this moment David had been driving on automatic pilot. Now he started to come to himself. 'Er . . . do you have a car?'

'Yes, I left it at the gate. There it is, beside the pillar box.'

David pulled over next to Albert's Morgan and switched off the engine. 'Lucky you arrived when you did.'

'Coincidence, wasn't it?'

'You were sent to interview Juliet?'

'Mm-hm. Doesn't seem much point now, does there?' Albert sighed. 'David, David, David, what are we going to do with you?'

David looked at him. He was wearing cavalry twill trousers, a check shirt, knitted tie and a hacking jacket, while a tweed cap was pulled well forward over his eyes, its brim almost resting on the tops of his flattened sycamore-seed spectacles. It occurred to David that it would be difficult for the communards to describe Albert's face to the police.

'Do with me? I don't understand. We agreed I ought to try and find out as much as I could.'

'Yes, but not by using the third degree.'

'*They* attacked *me*! And it wasn't the first time today, either.'

'What?'

David told him about his encounter with the Audi. Albert sucked his teeth for a while. 'Aren't you the popular one?' he said at last.

'What are you going to do about it?'

'I'll make a report.'

'And then?'

'Then we'll see.'

'Is that all you can find to say about it?'

'Yes. What did you manage to extract from Juliet, before the fracas?'

David stared at him. It was obvious that Albert did not want to talk about the men in the Audi. 'Very little,' he said at last. 'She hasn't seen Anna, nor heard from her.'

'Was she telling the truth, do you think?'

'Yes.' He opened his mouth to tell Albert what Juliet had said about the mysterious doctor, but to his surprise heard

195

himself say instead, 'Why did that girl mention German friends?'

'I wondered if you'd taken that on board. Mean anything to you?'

'No.' David knew he ought to tell Albert about the 'psycho-whatsit', as Juliet had called him. It was important. But because it was so important he wanted to think about it first. To package it. Construct some way of passing on the information that wouldn't make him out a complete idiot for not having known. 'I don't have any German friends.'

But Anna did! The chairman of the Krysalis vetting Committee had said so.

'Did Juliet say if anybody else had been snooping around asking questions?'

'No.'

'They did have other visitors this morning, very early.'

'How do you know?'

Albert merely laughed. 'They left in a hurry. The other girl, the butch number, got very stroppy, she did. *German* friends, now. Wonder if they were the same as your Audi mob? Could they have been German?'

David shrugged.

'Anna Lescombe, whatever are you up to?'

David wanted to ask what was going through Albert's mind but the other man forestalled him by abruptly getting out of the car. 'Be seeing you, then,' he said through the window.

As David watched him start the Morgan he suddenly resolved not to tell anyone about Anna's psychiatrist.

Thursday

EIGHTEEN

Albert knew a great deal about butchery. He had been studying it, on and off, for years.

Knives, they were the important thing: buy a good one and keep it sharp. His knife had saved him and the squadron more than once on ops. Such delightful games their masters loved to play: drop a handful of bods into Libya, single ticket, find your own ways home, last one in's a sissy . . . 'Fortnight of sun and sand, gentlemen, there's them as would give their right hands . . .' Oh yes, it was a man's life in the army. As long as you had a tempered steel blade, however, you need not starve. Albert's Sabatier had lived with him since Oxford days, although it was much thinner than of yore. Now it resembled a bodkin rather than a kitchen knife. He kept the blade keen enough to kill, skin and chop a snake, but today *ossi buchi* were on the menu and veal required less of an edge. Albert had cultivated the same butcher for years. He could be assured of getting meat from a calf under three months old. Later he would use the same knife to chop parsley for the *gremolata*, which strictly speaking was against the rules, but a well-honed knife would always forgive.

He had just poured the remains of a bottle of Soave around the browned meat and was turning his attention to chicken broth for the *risotto alla Milanese* when the entry-phone buzzed.

Fox raised his eyebrows at the sight of Albert wearing a plastic apron. 'Do Lea & Perrins pay people to advertise their sauce like that?'

'You live in a fantasy world. I can see you've never bought an apron.'

'Never worn one, either. Did I interrupt anything?' Fox sounded arch, as if he suspected Albert might be wearing lacy underwear beneath the laminate.

'No. Wait . . .' Albert went back into the kitchen, where he put a lid over the dish and stuck it in the fridge, refusing to rush a recipe merely to accommodate an unexpected visitor.

'Entertain a lot, do you?' Fox had followed him and was watching with scarcely disguised admiration.

'No.' Albert took off his apron. 'But I like food and I don't have the necessary physical coordination to manage a tin-opener.'

They went back to the living room. 'Nice place,' Fox said, letting his eyes roam. 'Watercolours . . . nice. What's that one?'

'It's a Callow. John, unfortunately; not William. Nineteenth-century seascape.'

'And the one next to it? *Very* striking.'

'I did that. Hobby. Have you read my Cornish notes?'

Fox was wearing a two-piece suit today, but habit still sent his hands to non-existent waistcoat points. Albert monitored the nervous tic with detached professional interest. A man who could not change his ways was a marked man.

'We've all read them.'

'What, the Yanks as well?'

'Oh yes. There's a daily copy command out. They're not best pleased with our failure to recover the file.'

'Oh, *that.*'

'You sound sceptical.'

'Krysalis?' Albert grimaced. 'It's genuine, I suppose.'

'Which is more than can be said for this man Lescombe.'

'He's well-meaning.'

'Well-meaning . . .' Fox gave the word some thought. 'I gather you trust him, from that. Do I?'

200

Dots of fat, products of the recent frying, had settled on Albert's spectacles. Now he took a square of wafer-thin lens tissue from a booklet on the dresser and cleaned them. 'It's unlikely he's a traitor, or involved with his wife in this. She's rotten to the core, of course. But the problem with him's different: he can't be trusted not to get in the way.'

'Do you want us to clear you a path?'

'Not necessary. Yet. Anyway, it looks as though the opposition may save us the trouble.'

'Mm? Oh, the men in the Audi, you mean?'

'Assuming Lescombe didn't make the whole thing up,' Albert said. 'Which I don't believe he did.'

'Five don't think so either. We're providing him with discreet cover from now on. Just in case.'

'Good idea. I approve.'

'I had a session with the lady's GP,' Fox said.

'And?'

'He prescribed the pills in the bottle. He said she'd only asked for sleeping tablets once, more than a year ago.'

'Before that?'

'Nothing. Anna Lescombe's been his patient for approximately nine years, since she moved to the Islington address. She changed doctors when she married.'

'But this new doctor must have her previous records?'

'He doesn't. He filled in the forms, but somehow they never turned up. Happens all the time, apparently. At least, that's his version.' Fox sniffed. 'Did you know doctors come high on the list of alcoholics?'

'That kind of doctor?'

Fox nodded. 'You don't look surprised.'

'I'm not.' Albert's voice was cold. 'We used to be able to rely on professionals in this country. Now they're just like everyone else.'

'The "going to the dogs" syndrome? Funny, I thought you took a more positive view of things.'

'What are you doing about this sot of a doctor?'

'We'll catch up with the records eventually.' Fox heaved

a sigh. 'But it won't be tomorrow or the next day. Match-ups with national insurance numbers, that kind of thing.'

'I can stand down, then?'

'No. You're working well. Apparently Mr Hayes likes your literary style.' Fox's expression was withering. 'On the ball, that's how he described you.'

'On *what* ball? Lescombe screwed up any prospect we might ever have had of learning something from his step-daughter; the lady pulled the wool over the eyes of her lawyerly colleagues . . . this case is C-O-L-D, cold. She's gone. Over the wall. Face it.'

'Not Paris, you don't think?'

Albert glanced at Fox's hopeful expression and pityingly shook his head.

'There's always the Athens lead.'

'You actually think that's worth following up, do you?'

'Yes, why not?'

'Because Hayes was right about that one. Same as Paris: a blind. Disinfo. What brief have Six sent to Athens station?'

'Find out who's going in to ask about faxes every day, follow him, get us a name.'

'Look, don't touch?'

'Right. *Strictly* don't touch.'

'Because you think Anna Lescombe's in danger? *Really?*'

'We have to treat it as a possibility, for the moment.'

'What a waste of time.'

'So how fortunate it is that we have something much more important for you to do.'

'Which is?'

'Lunch.'

'What?'

'Sorry to spoil your culinary arrangements' – Fox nodded in the direction of the kitchen – 'but the department would like you to eat lunch today. It being Thursday. Oh, and whatever you may have heard, there is such a thing as a free one.'

NINETEEN

Kleist had a gun; he meant to keep her prisoner. For a moment Anna could not face the reality of what she had seen. Then acceptance of the truth flooded through her, and she knew there was only one thing for it. She had to escape, *now*.

She retreated to the bedroom to collect her handbag. Cautiously she peered into the passage. Still no sign of Gerhard. She tiptoed to the front door, silently turned the handle and eased her way out. If he caught her now, she could pretend she was just going for a walk. Down the path . . . careful with the gate . . .

She was on the track, running.

Which way?

Left at the road, through the village. Don't look back.

Although the sun scorched down from a cloudless sky Anna scarcely felt it. What she did feel were the first stirrings of nausea. She only fell ill when she resolved to go away from Gerhard; the same thing had happened the day before yesterday. He had implanted something evil inside her brain.

She wiped her face. The back of her hand came away wet, sweat or tears, she could not tell. Where was David? No matter what Gerhard said, her husband did not know where she was.

She was her own last resource: beyond help.

When the sound of a car distracted her she looked back hopefully. But she soon realized that the engine noise came from a section of road above and parallel to the one she was on. Anna caught a glimpse of red paintwork. The Fiat belonging to Yorgos was that colour. Gerhard, already on his way in search of her . . .

She ran down the bank and hid behind the tree, gulping in deep breaths. She heard a noisy gear change; then the car was on the strip of road she had just left, passing over her head before disappearing towards the harbour. Anna slid further down the slope to rejoin the road. She continued to descend through the olive groves, traversing the road twice more before it became straight and ran through the outskirts of the port. She could see the quay; beyond that, a thin line of choppy cobalt-blue water and, in the distance, a green and mauve hill.

But Gerhard was ahead of her.

Anna sank down at the side of the road, afraid she might faint. When he failed to find her, what would he do?

The answer to her question came almost at once. She heard a car's engine start. Anna ran off the road, hugging a boundary wall, to conceal herself behind someone's house. She peered around the wall in time to catch sight of the Fiat as it roared along the road and disappeared up the hill. She waited until silence had resumed sway before emerging from her hiding place.

Dimly she began to perceive the beginnings of a strategy. The ferry left at five, Gerhard had told her that earlier. Wait under cover until ten-to, then make a dash for it.

You can meet the ferry, but so will he.

He can't use his gun in front of other people.

Anna wanted to get well away from the road. As she looked around anxiously, three old Greek women came down the hill. They wore what Anna had come to think of as 'the uniform': two all in black, right down to their stockings, the other in dark blue. They did not walk so much as hump, or limp; each had her own distinctive way of moving, but there was nothing fluid about any of them.

These women carried plastic shopping bags; from the tops of one of them peeped a towel. They were going for a swim!

204

One of the trio treated Anna to a sharp-eyed, inquisitive glance from gleaming black eyes, and nodded. *'Kalimera!'* she rasped in a throaty voice.

'Kalimera.'

The other two women sang out the word, but not in unison, each treating it differently, *'Kal-ee-mai-rah! . . . Kalim'ra.'* Then the first woman beckoned her. 'Swim,' she declared throatily. 'You! Come!' She beckoned again, this time with a smile, but as imperiously as ever. Anna took a step forward. 'Thank you,' she said. *'Efharisto.'*

The Greek women walked on. They knew of a side-road that skirted the main square. Before very long, to Anna's unspeakable relief she found herself following a winding footpath up the side of the hill opposite the port, protected from curious eyes by the ubiquitous olive trees which seemed to cover every square inch of this island. After a while the path petered out, so that by herself she would have had not the faintest idea which direction to take, although fortunately her three guides seemed quite unperturbed. The going was rough, but just when she thought she couldn't manage another step, they breasted the top of the hill and started to slip and slide their way down the seaward slope. The port had been left well behind them. For the first time since leaving the villa, Anna felt almost safe.

At the bottom of the hill they came upon a shingly beach. The three old ladies found a patch of shade for their things, then disappeared, each behind a separate olive tree, only to emerge a moment later clad in surprisingly garish bathing-suits and sunhats. One by one they ploughed into the sea, still wearing their floral bonnets. The eldest waved vigorously at Anna, who shook her head, indicating with the help of sign language that she had no swim-things. She sat under a tree and watched them wallow: three genteel Greek hippos.

Despite her anxiety, Anna found herself fantasizing about what it was like to be old on this island, without ever having known an alternative world: born here, courted, married, and one day buried, all within the same enclosed society.

Maybe their husbands had given them fine, lusty sons to look after them when they were old; they looked like mothers.

Somewhere, perhaps, her own mother was still alive. Now, as she watched the three old ladies, Anna felt stir within her the familiar longing: to seek her out, take her by the hands, ask her: Why? Why did you abandon me, you whose task it was to love me most? What had I done?

The law would help her do it. But there was something the law could not do: provide the necessary courage, and that was lacking.

The ladies floated inshore, where they finally beached. They offered Anna fruit, which she declined, accepting only a drink of water. There was much chaffer directed at her, which she bore in good part, not understanding a word of it. After a while, however, the trio fell silent and, as if at a prearranged signal, dropped off to sleep.

Anna stayed awake, too frightened to relax. Sometimes the day seemed to pass slowly, sometimes fast. She both yearned for the ferry to come and dreaded its arrival. She had to escape; but Gerhard would be waiting . . .

Who *was* Gerhard? What did he intend to do with her? Why had he brought her to this place – to seduce her, as he had tried to do the day before? To rape her; was that the purpose of the gun? Gerhard the psychotherapist, suddenly transformed into the rapist . . .

No. All that could have been stage-managed in London. She was on the wrong track. But *why* . . . ?

Suddenly one of the women stretched, yawned and rolled up into a sitting position. She murmured a few words, looking out to sea. Anna scanned the horizon. A dark smudge had appeared far out on the strait, a smudge trailing smoke.

She looked at her watch. Four-fifteen.

The ladies were packing up, thank God! That meant she would be able to stay with them until the last moment. Anna followed them homeward. At the brow of the hill she paused, surveying the port that lay spread out below her like a model village. No sign of the red Fiat.

She walked quickly, soon outstripping her companions, who clucked and muttered pleasant-sounding goodbyes as she passed. Anna arrived back in the port to find it coming to life after the siesta. Two noisy motorbikes, driven by youthful, unshaven Zorbas, dusted the quay. The owner of the one small boutique was setting out her wares. Earlier that day Anna had noticed an office located in the same building that housed this boutique; on a blackboard outside were chalked fares to the mainland and other tit-bits of information designed to appeal to seemingly non-existent tourists.

Anna slowly made her way around the boutique's scarf-rack and past a revolving stand for paperbacks, until she was on the threshold of the travel agent's office. The agent himself, one of those middle-aged men who like to keep themselves fit, pulled in his gut at the sight of her and smiled.

'Do you speak English?'

'Off coss.'

'I have to get back to England. Today. Can you help?'

'Cer-tin-lee. Yiss.' He stood aside, extending his right arm in what was meant to be a gesture of welcome, but he overdid it and succeeded only in looking like a policeman on point duty. He started to say something about ferries and flights, how they didn't connect. Anna tried hard to make sense of his fractured English. 'So what I want is a . . . a boat ticket to Corfu, then a taxi to the airport, right?'

'Yiss. Plin tick-ay you muss' buy at airpore.'

'Do you take plastic? American Express?'

When he shook his head, Anna gazed at him in terror. She had no local currency. Panic came flooding back. *She could not get off the island.*

Seeing the look on her face, the Greek smiled. 'You haff poun'? Ingliss poun'?'

'Yes!' She burrowed in her purse. 'Here, take them! Is it enough?'

He counted the notes, pursed his lips and sold her a ferry

voucher with enough reluctance to suggest that he was doing her a favour, instead of awarding himself a three-hundred-per cent mark-up. Anna almost ran out into the square, now alive with many voices. Where to go?

The concrete pier was merely an extension of the road, which itself shaded into being the square. At the end nearest the sea was a wedge-shaped hump, used for loading and unloading vehicles when the ferry docked. Several other passengers were already sitting on it, ready to embark as soon as the boat arrived. Now the motorbikes she had seen earlier roared back and the Zorbas began preparing them for embarkation; *good!* People, machines, there was a three-wheel cart stacked high with cardboard boxes, the more cover the merrier . . .

Anna looked at her watch. A quarter of an hour still to go. Ah, the boutique! She would stay in the shop until the ferry had actually tied up, wait until they were ready to lift the gangplank, then make a dash for it. Now, where had that ferry got to? Anna swivelled and saw the bow of a ship, its white paintwork flecked with rust, clear the cape. *Wonderful!*

As she reached the boutique's doorway, however, she heard a car and out of the corner of her eye caught sight of a red flash. Gerhard was here! She began to pick her way along the centre table, nervously turning over key rings and shells. After a moment she became aware of someone watching her.

Anna jerked her head up. The owner of the shop, a woman in her mid-thirties, wore large round spectacles. Their rims intersected above her nose, lending her an owly look. She continued to stare at Anna in dignified silence, occasionally moving her head as if to give her great round lenses a better shot at their target.

A car door slammed. Anna jumped. The lenses shifted slightly, taking note. By manoeuvring herself through the narrow gap between the Greek woman and the far end of the table, Anna was able to look through the window without seeming to. What she saw made her legs start to tremble. The ferry was reversing up to the pier. But between her and salvation Gerhard stood with arms folded across the car's roof while he surveyed the crowd.

Anna heard the woman stir and thought, Christ, she knows Gerhard.

The woman eased past her, obviously intending to go outside.

'Excuse me . . .'

Anna had spoken in a servile whisper which the boutique's owner did not hear. 'Excuse me!'

This time her voice was a shout. The shopkeeper turned back, the glasses magnifying her eyes as they widened in surprise until the owlish effect was almost comical.

'Excuse me, this smock, do you call it a smock only I've never seen one before . . . ?'

Anna held the garment up between her and the window, lest Gerhard chose to turn around. She could not stop grinning like a manic guide in pursuit of a tip. The owner hesitated, then came back with evident reluctance.

A movement on the other side of the window tore at Anna's gaze. Gerhard stood upright before striding off to the left, in the direction of the biggest *taverna*. She dropped the smock and rushed for the exit, stepping on the shopkeeper's foot. She didn't stop until she was safely behind the concrete hump. There she squatted down, trying to locate Gerhard through the forest of legs that sprouted above her head. No sign of him.

The ferry's back-plate banged open; the forest swayed as if in a gale. Anna rose to the crouch, ready to run. There was a delay while two cars reversed out of the hold. She fretted that such a patently *simple* manoeuvre could be made to take so long by stupid men; then she was thrusting her way to the front of the crowd.

The inside of the hold stank alarmingly of diesel oil and car exhaust fumes. People aimed for the left-hand side, where a metal ladder led upwards to the light. She set foot on the bottom step. The strap of her handbag caught in the rail. She tugged it. Behind her, passengers were starting to become impatient. She gave her bag a final wrench and clutched it to her chest.

The stairs were almost vertical; the only way to negotiate them safely was to keep staring straight ahead, which is why when she bumped into someone coming down all she could see was first his two-tone brogues with little holes in them, white and brown, then his cream flannels; and inconsequentially she thought, how funny, cricket, nobody wears shoes like that these days, why is he wearing cricket flannels over them . . . ? Then her eyes were hard up against his shirt, more creamy flannel, how hot, he should give way . . . the hand closing over her wrist, brown, like the shoes, thin fingers with bony knuckles . . .

'Sprechen Sie Deutsch?'

The sibilant whisper came from somewhere over her head. She looked up and found its source in a fat-lipped mouth. Her eyes ranged over a pointed Adam's apple; a moustache of brown and black hairs matching those that splayed out from each wide nostril; and, crowning all, a faded Panama hat, its black band besmirched with what looked like talcum powder.

She could feel nothing around her, there was no longer a world, a context.

'Anna!' Gerhard, it must be. But it was not Gerhard's voice. 'How wonderful to see you! What a coincidence, *ja*?'

She shook her head, wanting to deny him with words, but her tongue was caught up in the general revolt.

'We'll go, have a beer.' Now he was pushing her down the stairs, using her body as a ram to batter the disconsolate passengers below. The newcomer, she perceived, was extremely tall, well over six feet, and thin enough to raise doubts whether his torso could possibly hold all his vital organs. He dominated the ship's hold and Anna, forced to look into his eyes across her handbag, understood that this power derived not from the clothes, with their overtones of merchant marine uniform, but from the depths of his pale grey eyes.

'No,' she managed to get out. 'I have to go! I have a plane to catch. I don't know you.'

When the stranger continued to force her back down the stairway, Anna saw that the time for observing conventions was past. She opened her mouth to shout 'Rape!', meaning it to be heard in Athens. But even as she was drawing breath, another hand tapped her on the shoulder and a familiar voice said, 'Anna, my dear, where do you think you're going?'

She whipped around to find Gerhard standing there, a policeman at his elbow, and for an absurd moment her heart soared while she pretended to herself that the officer had come to arrest him. But then Gerhard spoke some words of Greek, and the policeman translated as if for her benefit: 'You are ill, your doctor says. You are a danger to yourself.'

'And to others,' Kleist added with a commiserating smile.

TWENTY

Fox had identified the restaurant by reference to the transcript of David's interview before the Krysalis vetting committee. Situated on the boundary between financial and legal Londons, it nevertheless managed to attract its share of media folk; and the conservatory-style decor had good associations for Albert. As he sat down, preparing to study the large, but not inconveniently large, *carte*, he wondered who you had to be to rate one of the three best tables, each spaced a generous distance from its fellows and located up some steps inside a semi-circular recess overlooking a garden. The restaurant was well patronized, but that alcove stayed empty. One of the tables it contained was laid for two; and whichever couple sat there would be able to observe all the other lunchers while at the same time preserving their own privacy.

He settled down to the menu with feelings of unalloyed pleasure. This, he knew instinctively, was a dead end as far as the Lescombe case went. No skeins led out of such enjoyable ambience into the heart of darkness.

He ordered a smoked fish pâté to start with and went on to plainly grilled steak, that Becher's Brook of a test for any restaurant. The man who came over carrying the wine list wore a red tie which clashed with his grey suit; that, coupled with his polite yet unservile manner, persuaded Albert that here must be the owner.

'Do you by any chance have an '85 Barolo?'

'I'm afraid not. We do have some of the 1986.'

'Even despite the hail?'

'Ah! I'll tell you what . . . it's not on the list yet, because I've yet to try it myself, but out the back I do have some other Piedmont. A Carema DOC. The last shipment was really rather exciting.'

'Luigi Ferrando?'

'Indeed, yes.' The man's preoccupied expression had mellowed into one of enthusiasm.

'I'll take a chance, then.'

Albert's eyes kept straying to the alcove, where the table for two remained untaken. There was a 'Reserved' plaque on the cloth, half hidden behind a vase of spring flowers, but even when one-thirty came and went, no one removed it. Some well respected patron, who could be relied on to be late . . .

Who never came at all, in the event. Albert drank a cognac, then had another, sipping the second more slowly. By two twenty-five he was the last remaining customer and, as he had hoped, the proprietor came around to pass the time with him.

'Did you enjoy your meal?'

'Excellent. You were spot on about the Carema.'

'This is your first visit?'

'Though I hope it won't be my last. Have you been open long?'

'Thirteen years.'

'Ah. I'm obviously not as in touch with London as I like to imagine.'

'We changed our name a while back. That often confuses people.'

Albert toyed with the idea of abandoning further inquiries, but then remembered that, contrary to Fox's assertion, this lunch was not entirely free. 'Would you join me in a *digestif*?'

The man glanced around to see what still needed doing. 'You're very kind. Perhaps a malt . . . ?'

He served himself from the bar and came back, pulling a chair from one of the other tables to sit down opposite Albert.

213

'My name's Seppy Lamont. Not too many people around called Septimus these days.'

'Mother had a sense of humour, like mine?'

'Father, actually. What's your millstone?'

'Albert.'

'Not so bad. At least Victoria loves you.'

Albert chuckled. 'Army?'

'Guessed, did you? Scots Guards. Got hells bored, actually. Then my wife's father died, left us a bit. She's a fantastic cook, though I say it myself.' He treated Albert to a long, cool stare. 'Which is your outfit?'

'Shows, does it?'

'Um-hm.'

'Paras.'

'Still?'

'No.' Albert took out his wallet and Seppy Lamont, misunderstanding, said, 'I'll get your bill.'

'In a minute. Have a look at this, first, would you?'

Seppy glanced at the plastic-protected card, matched up its photograph with the man opposite and said, 'Pull the other one, old chap. Special Branch you ain't. Look, it's a bit exposed out here, let's go into the office. I'd like you to meet my wife.'

Albert rose and followed him through a door at the back of the bar to find himself inside an unaccommodating office; it was long, but scarcely wider than a single bed, and if you wanted to get to the desk at the far end you had to squeeze around a filing cabinet.

Seated at the desk was a woman, in her mid-forties. She had her legs crossed, giving Albert a good view of fish-net nylons and patent leather shoes, very French; but then she swivelled around from the accounts she'd been working on and he saw that above the waist she became something else: red lips the same lurid colour as Seppy's tie, masses of mascara, medium-length hair that was obviously dark by nature but had been dyed blonde, unskilfully and a long time ago. Hungarian, perhaps. Something Eastern Bloc.

214

'This is Albert, darling. One of the firm. Albert, meet my wife, Racine.'

'Charmed to know you.' Racine uncoiled herself from the chair in which she'd been sitting. She held out a hand with the same studied slowness that characterized everything she did, including the way she spoke: her voice was soft and she chose her words only after deliberation.

'Thanks for a splendid meal. Do you do the cooking yourself?'

'I do. I have help, of course, but one must have a hand in everything. I cook. I shop. I lay the tables. I choose the flowers.'

He could not place the accent, but by now he was moving slowly west. Austria, maybe . . .

'Where did you train?'

She threw back her head and laughed, too theatrically for Albert's simple taste. 'I did not train. I had a father, who liked to eat only the best.' Her head came back to horizontal. 'And a mother who died when I was young. Before we got out, my father owned an establishment in Brno. He taught me . . . *everything*!'

'You're Czechoslovakian?'

'I am.'

'Your name fazed me. Racine.'

'I changed it when I came here. I disliked the one my father gave me. It is something I have in common with Septimus. But fathers are . . . You've been to Czechoslovakia, perhaps?'

'Passing through.'

Seppy grunted. He meant it to be a laugh, but it turned into something less funny. Albert was starting to dislike this man, who understood rather more than was convenient.

'Albert wants some help, darling.'

'And how may we help you, Mr Albert?'

'Do you recognize this woman?' Albert handed over a photograph of Anna, one they had taken from her album;

215

and then, acting on an impulse, he asked, 'Did she have a reservation for today? For two, by any chance?'

Racine shrieked 'Oh my God!' and burst out laughing, a hand held to her throat. Her fingernails, Albert noticed, were painted an unattractive shade of green. 'I thought she was dead, that one! He ran her for so long! And then when suddenly she didn't come I thought she must be dead, at least.'

Albert briefly wondered what was more than death, in this context, but he had no time for whimsy. 'Do you know her name?'

Seppy took a good look at the photo before settling back against the filing cabinet, hands in pockets. 'That's Mrs Lescombe.' Suddenly he seemed less assured, a man apprehensively waiting to see whether the squib will be damp or dry.

'She used to come here often?'

'At one time.' The Lamonts exchanged faintly mocking glances that excluded Albert. 'It's been more than two years now.'

'That empty table, it wasn't for her?'

'No,' Racine said. 'It wasn't for her.'

'But you're close. You see, that reservation was made – '

'Septimus, excuse me, but . . . who is Mr Albert?'

'Ah, sorry. Would you mind . . . ?' Seppy raised his eyebrows and this time the mockery excluded Racine. Albert showed his identification card.

'Police?' She sounded afraid. Albert remembered where she had grown up. He knew he would have to ask the Czecho desk about Racine, which bothered him, because the Czecho desk would then get all excited and start opening files where there was nothing to be filed.

'Sort of police.'

Husband and wife looked at each other for a few moments, sending messages back and forth. When Seppy at last said, 'Of course, we'll do whatever we can,' Albert mentally tipped his hat to Fox, who had counselled the approach oblique,

216

rather than the attack direct. Aggression would not have dented these people. They put on their clothes each morning, but their armour they never took off.

'Tell me all you can about this customer of yours, please. About Anna.'

'I always liked her,' said Seppy. 'She was the best of the lot. And she lasted the longest, too.'

'I never understood,' Racine said. 'She was so dull. All those black clothes, black stockings.'

'She's a barrister,' Albert explained.

'I guessed she was a lawyer of some kind,' Seppy said. 'Very precise. Lovely manners, though.'

'And from the way you talk, she had a companion. A regular companion?'

'Yes.'

'His name?'

Septimus did not answer at once. Albert knew he was missing something and it irked him. Something so obvious, it would stand up and bite him in a moment . . . 'His name?' he repeated curtly.

Racine answered. 'Gerhard Kleist.'

'Kleist.' Albert, remembering one further detail picked out of Lescombe's vetting file by Fox, was startled. 'German?'

'Yes.'

'And he used to eat here with Anna?'

The atmosphere was icing its way towards absolute zero.

'Look, Septimus, darling, I really ought to be seeing Vanessa about those cloths, perhaps you could deal with Mr Albert . . .'

'I'd rather you stayed.' Albert's smile only produced itself after a pause. 'Mr Kleist, he's a lawyer?'

'No,' said Seppy. 'He's a psychotherapist.'

Albert stood very still. 'Say again?'

'A psychotherapist. He became a regular customer. Then he turned into a friend.'

Albert thought of the empty table, its prize location. 'He was supposed to be lunching here today?'

217

'Yes.'

'But he didn't keep the reservation . . . did he telephone?'

'No.'

'Is that usual?'

'Sometimes he gets held up with a patient.' Racine was whispering now. 'He doesn't always . . .'

'He doesn't always bother to let us know.' Seppy finished his wife's sentence.

'He used to dine here with other women, would I be right in thinking that?'

'Lunch. He didn't used to dine here,' Seppy said; and Albert realized it was a kind of answer to his question.

'I suppose you don't, by any chance, have an address for Mr Kleist?'

Septimus stared at the floor. At last Racine said, 'I'll look it up for you.' She opened a drawer. 'My diary . . . an old one. Here we are . . .'

Albert wrote down the address.

'Is there anything else you need?'

'I'd like to look at your bookings, over the past five years. No, that's unreasonable, isn't it? Over a period going back as far as you can and ending with the last time Mrs Lescombe ate here.'

The diaries were produced, after a search. Albert skimmed through them, looking to see if Kleist's reservations married up with the dates in Anna's chambers diary, and was not surprised to find that they did.

'Is it all right if I take these away for a while?'

Seppy nodded. 'Of course.'

'We'll have to analyze them in detail, but perhaps you could help me . . . Was there a pattern?'

'Pattern?'

'What I mean is, did they lunch here, twice a year, something like that? Or three times a week for six months, followed by a break . . . know the sort of thing I mean?'

Seppy thought. 'At the beginning, years ago, they were a couple. Then it changed. There was a long break, as I recall.'

'A row of some kind?'

'I wouldn't know. After two or three years, suddenly there she was again. But by then it had become more like you said earlier: lunch twice a year. Birthday, perhaps. Catching up on the news.'

'And it went on like that, until . . .'

'Two years ago. Or so.'

'And then it stopped. But Kleist continued to be a regular customer?'

'Oh yes. Look, this is all a bit . . . Is there anything else?'

Albert thought hard. 'Only my bill, please.'

Seppy produced it very quickly. Albert paid in cash, Fox's cash, adding a reasonable but not lavish tip.

'I'll show you out,' said Seppy. At the door he said, 'If you do have to get in touch again, perhaps you'd make a point of coming through me?'

'Understood.'

'You see, my wife . . . she was a patient of Kleist's. When her father died.' Seppy made a face. 'Two years. Cost us an absolute bloody bomb.'

'I'm sorry.' Albert knocked his forehead with a knuckle. 'I was being thick.'

'Anna Lescombe wasn't the only one, you know. Kleist had lots of women.'

'Lovers, you mean?'

'I would think so.'

'Anna and Kleist, they – '

'Screwed? I was never there, so I can't say. But I'd guess yes, at the start. You get a nose for what people are up to in this business.'

'And later?'

Seppy shrugged.

'Did you ever hear them talk about . . . about anything, really?'

'Nope. Inflexible rule: no eavesdropping. It's their business and none of yours.'

'Racine, would she have heard them discussing anything?'

Seppy guffawed, then subjected Albert to a look of pity not unmixed with scorn. 'Understood,' he said quietly, putting obvious quotation marks around the word. 'That's what you said, old bean. Understood . . .'

Then, yes, it did dawn, and Albert realized what he had been missing earlier, that obvious 'something'. 'He became a friend,' those were Racine's words; what kind of friend, thought Albert, how close, on a scale of one to a million, just how *intimate*, would you say . . . ? The sudden vision was disturbingly real: Racine Lamont standing in the doorway of her long, narrow office, watching the table overlooking the garden, week in, week out, one face always different, the other ever the same, monotonously the same, with eyes for *l'amie du jour*, not for her. Never again for her . . .

'Correction,' Albert said lightly. 'Under orders. Sorry.'

TWENTY-ONE

Anna tried to struggle, but they bundled her into the car, Gerhard and the stranger off the ferry, yes, and the policeman, too. For her own good. For the sake of her health. When she cried out, at first the onlookers frowned; then they noticed the police uniform and their indignation gave way to smiles. She found herself sitting in the back of the Fiat. Someone had bandaged her wrists together, she was helpless. A prisoner of the man she had once trusted more than any other, apart from her husband David.

'So, Kleist, it's good to find you still alive.'

Those were the last English words she heard for a long time. She remembered nothing of the journey back to the house except lengthy exchanges in an ugly, guttural language she didn't understand but assumed must be German. Then she was sitting at the kitchen table, watching Kleist take beers from the fridge.

'Untie me,' she demanded.

'Will you promise to be quiet?'

'Go to hell.'

Kleist shrugged and moved away. 'Suit yourself.'

Anna fought the bandages but they were expertly knotted; all she succeeded in doing was chafe her wrists.

'I'll be quiet,' she said in a low voice. 'Just untie me, will you?'

Kleist cut the knots with a kitchen knife. He sat down opposite her, next to the stranger, and for a while the two of them drank their *Hellas* without speaking. The man in cream had a habit of sucking both lips after he'd taken a swig, first the lower one, then the upper, his tongue always careful to milk the ends of his moustache of their last vestiges of sustenance.

'Aren't you going to introduce me?' she asked Kleist defiantly.

He looked at the other man first, as if seeking permission, and that really shook Anna. In their world, the one she'd shared with Gerhard up until now, he doled out the permissions. He'd given his consent to her practising as a barrister, sleeping with him, marrying David. She remembered the day her father sold his shops to the chain and invited the buyers home to dinner; that night, for the first time, she had realized he now no longer was the boss, he had a boss.

'This is Jürgen Barzel.'

'You know him?'

'I know him.'

'Who is he? What's he doing here?'

Kleist stared at her. It was as if a sheep had miraculously asked its shepherd what butchers did for a living.

'He's a kind of . . . troubleshooter.'

'Why do you say it like that? As if you were enemies.'

Why? thought Kleist. Because HVA have found out about this villa and I don't know how. I don't know what *they* know, don't know anything except that I'm terrified. That's why my throat constricts and my saliva dries up, Anna.

'Mrs Lescombe . . . have I pronounced it rightly?' Anna found herself being drawn into Barzel's eyes as they inflated to fill her own vision.

'Yes.'

'It's a pleasure meeting you. You have stimulated us! We have been working late nights on your account, Anna . . . I wish to call you Anna. Do I have permission?'

Authority changed hands yet again, muddling her. 'I suppose so.'

'And I am Jürgen. Tell me about yourself, Anna.'

She stared at him, not understanding what he required.

222

Barzel must have sensed what was in her mind, for he smiled and said, 'Don't be nervous, I pray you. I am your friend. That is why I'm here – to help you and Gerhard.'

Not so, thought Kleist.

'What should I tell you, then?'

'About yourself. David. And your daughter, Juliet.'

'You . . . know a lot about me.'

As Anna began to speak, Kleist mentally begged her to be careful. If HVA had discovered the fax he'd sent to London, they would kill him. Execution, that's what they'd call it, because that's what you did with traitors; no good planning a new life in South America, too late for that . . . And since Anna would be a witness, then she too must die.

When did things start to go wrong? The plan he had put together looked so foolproof. For a long time now he'd wanted out; some grand finale on which to bring down the curtain of his nerve-shredding career as psychotherapist-cum-spymaster. He'd been cultivating his contacts in Lima and Asunción, knowing he must flee. Even if it meant the end of his own sister and her family, he could do that. He could do it because each new job for HVA had come to represent a fresh episode in a serial nightmare that would one day destroy him, and when the chips were down it looked absurdly simple: he was more important than Ilsa.

Fear of detection, of prison, had all but disabled Gerhard Kleist. The Krysalis débâcle was the last straw; he knew he would never forget that moment of dread when he had made himself enter the Lescombes' house, only to discover that David might return at any moment. Even his cultured life in England could not compensate for such horrors.

Things had been all right when he was younger, and the tension affected him less. In those days he could lose himself in work, in drink, in a woman picked at random from the hat. But then, too suddenly, and although not yet fifty, he was growing old. The slack skin at the temples. Face no longer quite smooth, more the texture of an orange. Waking at three, most mornings and not only after a night out, to urinate; then unable to sleep again before dawn. Then sleeping like unto death until the alarum clock slugged him with its dreadful, heavy burden of consciousness. An address book full of names and numbers: some of the pages were falling out, as if the loose-leaf binder could no longer contain such hordes. But no one permanent. No one to answer the phone, should the hordes call, and say, 'He's busy, he's my husband, he's mine, you fuck off . . .'

Recently he'd begun to dream about the woman sitting opposite. In those dreams her face was bright, alive with intelligence, ever youthful. After marrying David she had forgotten Gerhard Kleist; or so he'd believed, until the day before, when as she lay on the beach her body had told his massaging hands an altogether different story. Yesterday, for the first time, he had started to toy with a fantasy, oh, it was madness, of course, but still . . . if she would go with him, forget the past, live only for the present . . .

Yes. Madness.

Gerhard came back to reality to hear Barzel say, 'So now tell me – ' he smiled, a beau soliciting some naughty confidence ' – I am a convert. Having talked to you, I understand everything. But why must everyone else in Europe fall in love with you at the same time as me? Mm? Tell me!'

Anna's nervous laugh alarmed Kleist. Be careful, Anna. Keep it bottled up, as always; don't choose this of all moments to change. As long as you have a secret, no matter how trivial, your life is safe.

'Everywhere I go, I find my dear colleagues ahead of me. At the station. At the airport. Everywhere it's the same. The English. The French. The *other* Germans. The – dear God help us all! – Italians.'

Anna's eyes flickered, but she could not look away.

'Even at Corfu airport there were old-time spies standing around, trying to look like touts. You'd think they could afford at least one bottle of fake suntan lotion between them. Fortunately they didn't see me, or I would have been obliged to nod my head, at least. One cannot be rude to colleagues. But Anna . . . in *Corfu*!'

By now Anna was shrinking, or so it seemed to Gerhard.

'What have we here? I will tell you. A major security alert in NATO. You are "hot", Anna, that is how we say it. Scalding. I could cook a nice steak on you, and it would be overdone. Why? Perhaps you have something these people want very badly, *ja*?'

Anna swallowed. There was a long silence, which Barzel broke by saying, 'Do you have the Krysalis file here, perhaps?'

'No,' Anna said. Then, incredulously – 'You *know* about that?'

'I know.' When Barzel turned towards him, Gerhard noted with relief that he was smiling. 'Where is it?'

Gerhard rapidly listed the possibilities. Lie, pretend the file was still in London? Hopeless. Either Barzel would tear the place apart and find Krysalis, in which case he would kill them; or he would use the HVA machine to run checks in London that must come up with the truth eventually. In which case also he would kill them. Tell the truth now, and have done with it? Once Barzel had Krysalis, there was no incentive for him to leave either Kleist or Anna alive . . .

'The file's in my bedroom,' he said. 'I'll get it.'

'*What?*' Anna was on her feet, her face white. 'But you said . . . you told me you'd leave it . . .'

Then Gerhard's expression completed the tale and her legs gave way beneath her. At first she covered her face with her hands, but suddenly she seemed to lose all strength, for her head drooped forward onto the table where she cradled it in her arms, defeated.

Gerhard stood up, telling Barzel with a look that he should guard her; only when the other man nodded his assent did he leave the room.

He closed the bedroom door behind him and ran to the bed. Seconds later, he was pocketing his Luger. He wiped the sweat from his forehead with the back of a hand that shook, only to find that the beads of moisture broke through again at once. This was no time for cowardice. You have a weapon, he told himself. *Use it!*

As he rose from beside the bed, the phone rang. Gerhard stared at it. Who on earth . . . ?

Then he remembered. Iannis.

While in the very act of reaching out for the receiver, he heard footsteps in the passage. Torn between the needs to silence the phone and conceal the gun, Gerhard gritted his teeth, powerless to act. Next second he had thrust the Luger under the bed and was clamping the phone to his ear so hard that it hurt.

'*Ne?*' he snapped, as Barzel entered the bedroom.

'I went again today,' the boy said. 'Nothing.' Then Gerhard heard only the purr of a severed contact.

'Who was that?' Barzel asked.

'No one. Where's Anna, you shouldn't have — '

'What the hell do you mean, "no one"? *Who?*'

'Wrong number. Happens all the time, the phones here are crap.'

Barzel stared at him in silence, as if weighing the truth of his words. 'Where's this file?' he said at last.

Gerhard once more pushed the bed aside and rummaged in the hole. 'Here . . .'

The two men returned to the kitchen. Gerhard poured himself another beer, knowing he'd lost more than a golden opportunity to dispose of his unwelcome visitor; he'd lost vital ground. Whatever Barzel thought when he arrived, he definitely mistrusted him now. Damn Iannis . . .

The boy had sounded odd. As if he wasn't alone, someone was listening in. A girl? Gerhard hoped not; the last thing he wanted was Iannis messing around with strangers.

Strangers. What if Barzel had somehow managed to trace Iannis and . . . no, it was impossible. In that event Barzel would have come to the island with reinforcements and enough hardware to fight a war. Keep your head, he told himself firmly; don't panic now.

Barzel breezed through the file before beginning to study it more carefully. After he had finished he sat for a long time staring into space. At last he turned to Gerhard and said, in English, 'I think, if Anna will excuse us, we must be talking quite seriously . . .'

'Will she run away?' he asked, as they reached the terrace.

'I doubt it. Even if she does, she won't get far.'

'Unlike you. You, Kleist, appear to have got very far, without telling us. Surprised to see me here, *was*? You thought we didn't know about your little love nest?'

'How the devil did you – '

'Oh, a little bird, you know? Many, many years ago. People used to have a good laugh about it. "The look on his face!" that's what we used to say. "When Kleist finds out that we know!" '

'What made you think I'd be here?'

'Vogel initiated an alert when you and the woman went missing. Different people are searching for you in different places: I drew Greece.' Barzel glanced back towards the house. 'Does she understand German?'

'No.'

'All right, we speak German then.' Barzel looked at his watch: a busy man with a plane to catch who had allowed himself to be sidetracked by a snake-oil salesman. 'You're an idiot.'

'Why?' Kleist fell into the sofa-swing. 'I bring you the biggest prize you've – '

'Point one: you brought us *nothing*! You have sat here quietly, keeping us guessing. We shall discuss that, I promise you. Point two: the file is *too* big! Files like that don't come our way, Kleist.'

'But – '

'On my way here, I thought, "Yes; for all this fuss, for such a massive security operation, whatever Kleist is sitting on, it's real." But now I've read it, I think, "No. Definitely not." '

'How can you be sure, on the strength of one reading?'

227

'Suppose you were the President of the United States. Imagine someone came to you, just before a major super-power summit, and told you that he had papers, a microfiche, setting out the entire Warsaw Pact military dispositions and strategy. Would you believe him? Of course not. Why? First, because one of the ways you defeat spies is by keeping information in tiny gobbets; secondly, because in the run-up to a conference you don't believe anything you're told any-way.'

'England doesn't work like that.'

'*Everybody* works like that, comrade!'

'Then how – '

'Because this is a plant. We're meant to read this rubbish, shuffle a dozen divisions in and out of Poland and I don't know what else. It's a trick, you've fallen for it. I'm telling you, Kleist, you're a dead man. Dead.'

'But Vogel himself told me to do this! "Anna's your patient, she's married to a top civil servant who's interesting to us, get the file!" '

'Exactly.' Barzel swung around to face Kleist. 'That's the point. Someone in MI5 discovered what was going on. This is pre-summit counter-intelligence. It means your cover's gone; Vogel's too, probably. We have no further use for either of you.' He paused. Then, amazingly, he smiled. 'Ah . . . if only I could believe what I'm saying.'

Kleist stared at him, incomprehension written all over his face, and Barzel chuckled. 'Either the British are being very clever, or . . .' He came to sit beside Kleist on the swing, one arm stretched along the back of the cushion. 'Some prizes are so valuable, they lure with such power . . . You can't see Krysalis lying in the ditch and pass by without even a glance. The wolf cannot ignore this lamb, not with Vancouver mere weeks away.'

'The wolf . . .'

'Oh yes. It's being run from Normannenstrasse.'

Kleist felt a seed of hope begin to sprout. General Markus Wolf, HVA's commander, did not take a personal interest in silly tricks. If he could only manage to persuade HVA to see this as a coup, rather than a betrayal . . . But then Barzel asked, 'What about the woman? Who's side is she on?'

'No one's. She hasn't a clue what's happening.'

'Maybe that's so, maybe it isn't. We've been rooting around, but so far without success. The people we sent to interview her daughter and husband got nowhere. We can't make a clear picture of your Mrs Anna Lescombe. She's hazy. We need focus.'

'Well, don't ask me.'

'Does she realize you were responsible for introducing her to her husband?'

'No. As far as she's concerned, we went sailing together, Lescombe happened to be in the next berth.'

'Coincidence?'

'Yes.'

'Then she must be very naïve.' Barzel shook his head, laughing. 'How come people never seem to see through you, Kleist? Why have you dragged her here, anyway?'

'Because she screwed up.'

'Explain.'

'I knew her husband was away for the weekend, so I programmed her to open the safe, bring me the file, wait while I copied it, take it back, put it in the safe, and forget everything.'

'So what happened?'

'She had a kind of breakdown. She'd built up inner resistance to my suggestions.'

'Didn't you realize that at the time?'

'No, she seemed normal enough.'

'Aach, I don't understand.' Barzel stood up and began to pace the terrace. 'You were attempting the impossible. Everyone knows you can't force a person to do things they don't want to do under hypnosis.'

'*Do* they?' Kleist scoffed. 'Then "everyone", comrade, is about twenty years out of date.'

229

'Are you telling me that if you put that woman into a trance and ordered her to sleep with me, she would?'

'No, not like that. But there are other ways.'

'Such as?'

'Given time, and a deep enough trance, I could persuade her that you were a doctor, and that it was necessary for you to examine her intimately. I could arouse her sexually by feeding erotica into her mind.'

'That would work?' Barzel sounded incredulous.

'How do you think I got the combination out of her in the first place?'

Barzel rejoined him on the swing. 'Tell me.'

'I persuaded her that her husband's career was in danger, because he couldn't open the safe and needed help remembering the combination.'

'And she accepted that?'

'Of course.' Seeing the scepticism on his colleague's face, Kleist continued, 'Remember, that woman has been my patient, with breaks, for sixteen years. She trusts me. She loved me, once.'

Barzel thought this over. 'Why did she have that breakdown, then?' he snapped. 'How come she failed?'

'I'm not sure.' Kleist looked away. 'I went too far too fast. We hadn't seen each other for two years, my . . . my influence, if you like, must have faded.'

'You were lucky to get out.'

'Yes. What do you intend doing with her?'

'What do you think?'

For the first time Kleist turned to look directly at Barzel. 'You'll kill her.'

The other man's hand strayed along the cushion to grasp Kleist's shoulder. Suddenly he smiled. 'No.'

'What?'

'Without the woman, we can't begin to assess Krysalis' importance. That file is like a beautiful painting: perhaps it's an old master, perhaps it is by a gifted pupil, maybe it's a fake, after all. We need to know its *provenance*. We must

230

interview the *dealer*. Besides, by holding onto her, how can we lose?'

'I don't follow.'

'Well, isn't it obvious? Either she's the source of disinformation, stealing a hoax file at your behest, or she's the possessor of the real thing. We'll take her back to Berlin. There she can be interrogated properly and at length. If she's a phoney, we shall learn a lot about British methods. If she's real, we'll learn whatever it is that she knows about her husband's affairs; not just this file, but perhaps many other files as well. Now do you see?'

Kleist was almost starting to feel reassured. When he first clapped eyes on Barzel coming off the ferry he'd turned numb. Yet HVA did not know about the fax he had sent to London, that was obvious. And now they were suggesting that Anna be brought to Berlin, where he would no doubt be called upon to play a major role in her interrogation. The power he had acquired over her as hypnotist and therapist was beyond any coherent form of valuation. But when they had finished with her . . .

She will stay with me, Kleist told himself. She already loves me, deep down. I can make her forget David. I am growing old; there is a woman in this world for me to love.

'How do you intend to move her?' he asked.

'Ah, yes, difficult. So many observers, on the look out . . . There can be no question of doing it openly. A boat, maybe. Submarine, even . . . It can be arranged, but it'll take a day or two. I need to report back, then we'll see.'

'What do you want me to do?'

'Stay put, protect our "art dealer" in there. Above all, maintain control.'

'I can do that.'

'Good. I'll find a room close by. From now on, you'll be watched, all the time. Don't try to be clever again. Before, I told you you were dead. Maybe I was a little too pessimistic. But there'll be no second chance. Do you understand?'

The light was behind Barzel, rendering his expression a

231

dark mask. Only when Kleist stood up could he read his eyes. They were not cruel, they were not even particularly cold, just *uninterested*; and Kleist the psychologist knew this man could do any necessary killing.

Barzel was on the point of departure when he turned back from the door and said, 'I'm still worried about the woman. What if she tries to escape again?'

'I intend to hypnotize her. I'll use drugs, too.'

'What kind of drugs?'

'A mixture of sodium pentothal and desoxyn. That will totally eliminate any remaining resistance to hypnosis.'

'Inject her now, while I'm here.'

'If you insist. But I warn you: she's much more likely to put up a fight with you around.'

'Don't worry about that, Kleist.' A dreamy smile played about the corners of Barzel's mouth. 'I believe I'm big enough to take care of Mrs Lescombe. Just about, *ja*?'

TWENTY-TWO

The front door opened and there it was, that smell, that overpowering, all-pervasive scented air bottled up like incense inside a *chedi*, only David knew it wasn't incense because Anna's parents would not have countenanced such a thing. It was Ronuk.

Ronuk had never been part of his childhood, he reflected as he followed Mrs Elwell down the hall and into what she called the lounge. There had been nothing worth polishing, and even if there had been, no one could have spared the time to do it. His mother was always somewhere else, often as not Ronuk-ing other people's furniture. But as soon as he met Anna – no, say rather, as soon as he met her *parents*, for by then Anna herself was already in flight from the hijack that had been perpetrated on her when only six weeks old – Ronuk had become part of his existence, a keyword to be used whenever they wanted to summon up that complete and perfect vision of a tight-arsed world.

There was another odour today, he thought, trying to identify it. Old cooking . . . more than that. Old age.

'So nice to see you again, David. Would you like a cup of coffee, to refresh you after your journey?'

In her mouth the drive to the south coast became a Himalayan trek.

'I'd love one. Thank you.' When Mrs Elwell stayed put for a few seconds longer, 'Only if it's no trouble, Lydia.' This, evidently, was the formula that worked, for she at once rose and went out to the kitchen. David knew better than to follow. Kitchens, in middle-class homes like this one, were on a par with bedrooms and 'toilets': inviolable. Non-existent.

He looked around him, re-absorbing the stage set upon which the Elwells lived out their lives. The house stood at the far end of a *cul-de-sac* leading off a road, which itself led off a slightly larger road running due south to the promenade of a small town called Ferring. The dwelling was substantial and detached, too large to be kept up by a couple in their seventies, but there was such a thing as pride. As long as you had your own detached house, you were not old. David understood that without quite being able to admire it.

Mr Elwell had made a little money out of supplying the needs of amateur painters and decorators at a time when the breed had begun to sprout, but not yet proliferate. On his fiftieth birthday he received, out of the blue, an offer that looked too good to be true. It was. The newly-formed chain that took over his four shops employed him as a regional manager; that came with the deal. But his region occupied only two squares on a large-scale Ordnance Survey map and before long Mr Elwell – 'Chappy' Elwell people called him, David couldn't remember why – realized he had been shunted into one of life's duller backwaters. Now he did not even have the financial and emotional advantages of self-employment to bolster him up in his own eyes and those of his family. He found out what it was like to live on a salary, the whole salary and nothing but the salary; no longer were there 'good' months from which to finance a holiday in Jersey (this was prior to the time when profit-sharing and incentive bonuses became a necessary part of every well drawn job advertisement) and 'bad' months, rainy days against which you saved. Now there were just months. The months began to pile up. In the end they buried Mr Elwell under a mountain of dead time.

His wife survived.

'Do you take it black?'

'Mm?' David, lost in a mixture of memories and contemplation of the shiny horse brasses on leather thongs that flanked the brick fireplace, was nonplussed. 'Uh, a little milk, please.'

As usual, he did not know what was expected of him. Where he came from, where he worked, you did not have coffee served from a silver pot into bone china, accompanied by an ivory-handled spoon for brown sugar that was free of congealed, crunchy lumps. He found himself sitting on the edge of his chair. Why? Was he worried that his trousers might soil her furniture, recently dusted, 'Ronuked', as it had been every morning for the past, what, fifty years? Half a century, half a ton of polish . . . how many sunlit days had been passed thus?

He remembered Anna's face as she told him of the summer evenings when she had been forced to lie upstairs in her room, watching the light through the shade, because it was after seven and seven was bedtime for little girls . . .

'Is Chappy well?'

Mrs Elwell picked up her knitting and for a moment did not reply. She had a Madame Defarge style with the needles, shoving them through the wool with the same vigorous determination that she had used to shove Anna through life. Today, as far as David could interpret her bony fingers, they seemed to be saying, 'Chappy, yes, there are things that would shock you, if I had a mind to confide . . .' But what she actually said was, '*Very* well, thank you, David. He's sorry to have missed you. Thursday is his bowls morning.'

'Not to worry.'

'He's become a little set in his ways, I'm afraid.'

'Do give him my best.'

'I will.' Mrs Elwell paused in her knitting for long enough to push her pebble-lensed spectacles on to the bridge of her nose. She puffed a sharp sigh out through her nostrils and said, 'We only ever see you here when there's trouble. I was saying to Chappy over breakfast.'

We, I . . . Chappy drifted in and out of the house like old smoke from one of his Players, intangible but somehow real.

235

'Yes. I'm sorry. We just don't seem to have a lot of time for visits and entertaining.'

'I'm sure. Two busy professional people.'

Strange, he thought; I have been here, in her house, for twenty minutes now, her son-in-law, and she has yet to smile.

'Well, Lydia, I told you the worst of it on the phone. I confess I was half-expecting to find Anna here.'

Mrs Elwell lowered her knitting into her lap without releasing it and said, 'Fat chance.'

David almost gasped.

'You don't think she'd come to us, do you?' Her bright, chatty viciousness was in sudden, complete contrast to the rectitude of the welcoming rites. 'No, David, when Anna married you, she severed connections here.' She resumed knitting, at the same time flashing him a receptionist's smile. 'Time for a straight talk, isn't it?'

'That's what I hoped.'

'She never used to be like this.'

'Like . . . ?'

'Secretive. She used to confide in Chappy and me. Particularly me, I don't think she and her father ever quite shared the same wavelength.'

Straight talking? Should he tell her, then, that Anna had of necessity been lying about things to her parents since she was old enough to understand that she had a secret, inner self? Or remind Mrs Elwell of how she had always criticized Anna for *not* confiding, when she was a teenager, long before he, David 'Wrecker' Lescombe, had come on the scene? Or Anna's confessing to Juliet's imminent birth only when she became too 'fat' for Lydia to go on ignoring her daughter's condition any longer . . . shall we have some 'straight talking' about these and other matters that your daughter revealed to me quite early in our marriage, madam?

No. He repressed the anger seething inside him and moulded his face into the expression of polite deference that represented his only hope of obtaining results.

'Lydia, look, I am really awfully sorry about what's happened, but — '

'What has happened? That's what I'd like to know, David.'

'She's vanished into thin air, taking one of my files with her.' He paused. 'You'd better know that there are some very unpleasant accusations flying around.'

'I'm sure. When a file goes missing . . .'

'The accusations are utterly without foundation. Baseless as well as base. Anna's not a traitor and no one's ever going to convince me of the contrary.'

'Well, at least we can agree on that. Have you heard nothing from her, since she disappeared?'

'Not a word. You?'

Lydia Elwell shook her immaculately-permed head. 'We find we don't have so much contact as we used to.'

'Before she married me, you mean.'

'I suppose you could say that. She was such a lovely child, so obedient . . .' The woman's eyes lighted on a framed photograph of Anna which adorned the mantelpiece. It showed a tense, bespectacled face, with black gown just visible and mortarboard held self-consciously where the studio photographer had instructed her to hold it. 'So obedient . . . and so *fresh*. Her eyes used to light up whenever you did something for her. Childlike. Innocent . . .'

'You did a lot for her, didn't you?'

'Only what any parents would have done for their daughter. It was a drain, I don't mind admitting. When Juliet was still a baby and Anna was working . . . everything was spend, spend, spend, in those days. Nannies. Train fares up to London for Chappy and me. We didn't begrudge any of it, although when I *think* of what we had to go without — '

'Has anything unusual happened?' David interrupted.

'Unusual?' She gave him a calculating look over the tops of her glasses.

'I mean . . . strangers, odd phone calls. Anything.'

'This is Ferring.'

'Did Juliet contact you?'

237

'Never.' Mrs Elwell rounded her lips into a circle of unforgiving disapproval. 'Never. We send her cards and presents at Christmas and on her birthday. She doesn't so much as acknowledge them.'

Poor Anna, David thought. Caught in the generation gap, the meat in the sandwich, with two such difficult females hemming her in. Trapping her.

'Where do you think she is?' he asked.

'I haven't the faintest idea.'

'What do you think she's up to?'

'How would I know?'

'Well, she lived with you all those years, you might just have some idea what goes on inside . . . Sorry. I'm extremely sorry, that was unforgivable.'

Click, click, click went the needles.

'It's just that I'm under strain. You must be, too.'

'If your nerves are bad, David, perhaps you ought to visit the doctor.'

It was clear from the way she spoke that 'nerves' and 'doctors' alike were due to be relegated to one of Dante's less pleasant outer circles.

'Did Anna ever see a doctor when she was young?'

'She had the usual coughs and colds.'

'No, I mean a mind doctor. A psychiatrist.'

Lydia Elwell's hands fell into her lap again, still clutching the needles, and she stared at him speechlessly, as if he had just said something obscene.

'She didn't?'

'Anna had a brilliant career at school and after that at Oxford. She is a very successful barrister. People like that don't require the services of a psychiatrist.'

David realized that she had avoided giving him a direct answer. 'Juliet said her mother did see one,' he persisted.

Mrs Elwell screwed up her mouth to one side, taking her wide nostrils with it. 'Juliet is artistic. Children like that frequently have overheated imaginations. I shouldn't pay *too* much attention to that quarter.'

238

'You certainly had no reason to suspect she was seeing a psychiatrist, anyway?'

'Anna was happy and well adjusted and lacked for nothing. She was an only child so she had all the love Chappy and I had to give.' She coloured a little, the broken veins in the dry skin of her cheeks becoming angry and raw. 'You know we couldn't . . .'

Conceive, is what she meant to say; but David, who had met Chappy Elwell any number of times and still had trouble remembering his face, wondered if there was a hint of some deeper, darker meaning. We couldn't do it. Procreate. *Fuck*.

Which of them couldn't?

'We gave her a model childhood. Except for that business at St Clare's, which I still believe Anna brought on herself, there was never the slightest need for her to be counselled, or consoled, or whatever it is people call it.'

Somehow David knew she was lying. But Lydia Elwell's evasions weren't in the forefront of his mind. *That business at St Clare's* . . . Although he had no idea what she was referring to, he decided not to tell Lydia that. Like the Elwells, he had his pride. 'Oh, the St Clare's thing,' he said casually. 'She got over it, didn't she?'

'Yes, but we had to move her. The *expense* . . .'

'Ah, that's right, she changed schools . . .' David, blundering around in the dark, was beginning to run out of improvisations. 'Let me see, she'd have been . . . how old?'

'Seven.'

'I thought it was eight . . . no, silly of me, seven, of course it was. I never quite knew what to make of all that.'

'Really? Isn't it notorious that convent schools can be difficult? Anna didn't know she'd been adopted, of course, so when those dreadful Catholic girls started to call her illegitimate . . .' She raised her needles and let them fall again, staring at David with something approaching appeal in her eyes. 'How could she have borne that for a year without telling us, her own parents?'

'Perhaps she was . . . afraid.'

239

'Afraid? *Of us?*'

David cleared his throat. 'How did you find out what had been going on?'

'Anna never told you?'

'Not that particular detail, actually, no.'

'She started crying in games one day and couldn't stop. She cried for four hours. The doctor had to give her an injection. At the hospital . . . they called us to the hospital. That's when we first found out . . .' Lydia suddenly covered her eyes. 'I'm sorry,' she said after a pause. 'Children can be such vicious animals.'

'Yes.'

'Before that day, we never knew, Chappy and I. She didn't tell us. She thought she was being brave.'

'I see.'

'They expelled three girls. The ring-leaders, the mother superior called them.'

'Did Anna know that they were expelled?'

'Oh, yes.' Mrs Elwell drew in a deep breath. 'We received these foul letters, from the parents of one of the girls who had to go. If that's what religion . . . Anna found the letters, of course.'

'She read them?'

Mrs Elwell nodded. 'It was naughty of her, but . . . But it's nonsense to talk of psychiatrists, there was never any question of that, our GP gave her a good talking-to, that's all. Psychiatrists, indeed!'

This was the first time David had heard the story. He could see, however, that Mrs Elwell knew it all too well, *and that she was lying*. She was not the sort of woman who lied easily. What secret seemed so terrible to her that it must be covered up at all costs, even if that meant deceiving Anna's own husband?

'She got over the change of school,' he said uneasily; and was it not true, for Anna had never mentioned the episode to him . . .

'Of course she did.'

'But perhaps it affected her . . . changed her in some way, do you think?'

'Not at all. Marriage to you changed her, if anything did.'

The watery eyes remained glued to her needles, determined to avoid David's gaze.

'Changed? In what way?'

'Made her less communicative. Except right at the start. She used to phone us a lot then.' Mrs Elwell resumed her knitting. Click, click, click. 'When you were away. Or late back from the office.' Click. 'When Anna was unhappy.'

He stared at her; she could not see the intensity of his look but she must have felt it, for she went on, 'Her attitudes and yours were very different. She needed pushing, if she was to get anywhere. I told her not to be so silly. I pointed out that when young people are recently married they often want to give in.'

'*Give in?*'

'She used to say she couldn't stand it. Life with you.'

'She actually said that?'

'She implied it, let's say.'

For a long time he was aware only of the clack-clack-clack of her knitting needles as they created some seemly garment in a delicate shade of green.

'What was wrong with me?' It sounded so lame!

Mrs Elwell breathed in and ejected the air through her nose with unrestrained force. 'A lot of things, I imagine.'

'Like what?'

'She wanted a child. Desperately.'

'She told you that?'

'A mother always knows.'

'I wanted one too.'

'Not at the beginning, I believe.'

'Well . . . we both had our careers.'

'Didn't you understand how much it meant to her? With her background? She'd been adopted, although of course she got over that, but . . . anyway. She'd been adopted. Juliet was always a . . . well, I suppose you'd call her a problem

241

child. Anna wanted to make everything right. Didn't you *see* that?'

She continued to gaze at her son-in-law, until it became obvious he wasn't going to answer. 'Having a child of her own, by you, born into a secure home, that would have made such a . . . well, you won't take it from me, I'm sure.'

'She never said anything. Never.'

'Anna found it hard to talk to you, about certain things. I could see that easily enough. You didn't know?'

David shook his head. But then suddenly his mind jumped back to the meeting with Duncan Broadway, and even beyond that, to the summer of 1987, the year of the quarrel. Their disagreement had simmered, with neither of them able to find an honourable compromise. On the surface, they had been fighting over Juliet's future. Now he allowed himself to admit, for the first time, that they had fallen out over something quite different.

It would have been ridiculous for Anna to conceive again, at her age. And her career! She could kiss goodbye to the silk gown, the judgeship . . . Yet in his bones, David knew that this was no lie. Anna wanted another chance at mother-hood, to compensate for her failure with Juliet. No, not wanted. *Needed.*

'Your backgrounds were so different,' Mrs Elwell said. 'Not at all the same outlooks on life. Quite a shock for her, I should imagine.'

'I'm common, is that what you mean? The wrong accent?'

She smiled and raised her eyes, just for a second, as if to say: 'You see?'

'Sorry, didn't mean to shout. I know you think I went to a rotten university. I know you think civil servants are beneath contempt.' Like DIY suppliers, he wanted to add, only thank God he didn't. 'But I fell in love with your daughter and she happened to love me.'

'What do young girls know about love?'

'When Anna married me she was almost *thirty*!'

242

'She thought she loved that odious man Eddy. Love! You want to grow up, my girl, I told her that at the time.'

Anna had been twenty-one when she met Eddy.

'Shared attitudes. Common assumptions. They're more important to a marriage than any amount of love, as you call it.'

'Why, what would you call it?' He stared at her, unable to cross the divide, until it occurred to him that this was becoming too absurd for words. Mrs Elwell, faced with an uncommunicative daughter who'd betrayed her by marrying not once but twice, had constructed this ridiculous figment of the imagination as a means of covering up the hurt. He almost felt sorry for her. 'Opposites attract,' he said, with an attempt at humour. 'Isn't that what people say?'

'Being a man and a woman is opposite enough.'

'So.' David sat back in his chair for the first time, no longer caring whether he spoiled the props. 'She's left me because she's unhappy, is that what you're saying?'

Click-clack-click.

'Yet I notice she hasn't come running home to mother.'

'You sound very pleased about that.'

'Ecstatic.'

'You're a bitter person, David. Chappy was saying so only last night.'

'Is that why she left me? She's got her share of bitterness too, you know.'

'She had nothing to be bitter about. She was a sweet child.'

'A sweet child who unfortunately got herself pregnant and had to marry Eddy – '

'That's an appalling – '

'On *your say-so*.'

Mrs Elwell laid aside the knitting and sat with hands clasped on her lap. She might have been fighting for self-control or she might have been silently praying. 'What a monstrous, wicked thing to say.' Her voice was hardly a whisper.

'She never felt loved. Never. That was her trouble. You

243

gave her things, you forked out, pushed her, but somehow in all of that love got over the wall.'

'Strange she never complained.'

'How could she, when you managed every waking thought? And even if she did assert herself, on those rare occasions, you moved the goal posts, pretending that that was what you wanted, all along.'

When Mrs Elwell spoke again her voice contained a hardly audible demisemiquaver of doubt. 'You make it sound as though everything's our fault.'

'She came out of this house, into the world . . . feeling she was bad.'

'She told you that?'

'Often. I didn't realize why, but now I'm beginning to. She felt it was her fault those girls were expelled, didn't she? If she'd been stronger, kept her mouth shut, there wouldn't have been any problem. All her fault, for being a bastard.'

Another lengthy silence followed. Mrs Elwell broke it by picking up her needles and getting back to work. Now, however, she knitted less stridently. 'I'm glad you came,' she said.

David heard how the demisemiquaver had ceased to taint her voice and felt his heart sink. 'Why?'

'I understand things better now.' She sounded satisfied with her judgement of men and affairs. 'Things between the two of you, I mean. If you spoke to her . . . as you've spoken to me . . .'

David considered this in silence. He had never liked the woman sitting opposite; the momentary flash of sympathy he had felt scarcely survived its birth; now he detested her with a passion. But he would not come down to her level. So he rose and walked out of the room, without saying goodbye, and he closed the front door behind him with all the respectful, lower-class deference that his despicable, lower-class soul could command.

This was a tidy neighbourhood, where people owned

garages and used them for their intended purpose. Apart from David's Rover, only one other car stood in the roadway. He heard its engine start the moment he left the house, and remembered that MI5, like the poor, were always with him.

Friday

TWENTY-THREE

Albert knew things were getting really tiresome as soon as he clapped eyes on the ait.

'Ait' was just a fancy word for island and in his world it did not necessarily mean anything to do with the sea, it signified a position surrounded by space with good lines of sight in every direction and adequate defence mechanisms; they called it 'ait' rather than plain old island because the former encoded comfortably as '8' and the latter did not, one of those things.

There was, he discovered, no easy route between MI6's London station in Vauxhall Bridge Road and Cubitt Town on the Isle of Dogs. As he crawled along the Commercial Road, each set of traffic lights another station of the cross, he listened to Kate Bush lecturing Peter Gabriel, 'Don't give up,' but remained unconvinced. Fox's deputy had told him to look out for a cardboard sign outside a pub . . . ah, there it was: 'Strippers Thursday and Friday Lunchtimes.' What a benighted, bloody country England had become.

And now the target turned out to be an ait.

A house, standing all alone off Manchester Road, with a view across the Thames to Delta Wharf and an empty gas holder, its silhouette like a huge confectioner's basket of spun sugar. The house was Victorian, with gables and attics; a lot of clay-red brick and a slate roof that looked new, also, a wall topped with broken glass in the shadow of which Albert now sat parked.

Double gates stood open, although after dark they would

form a high barrier, doubtless wired up to the kind of sophisticated alarm system that went with the notice outside: 'Warning! These premises are patrolled day and night,' and the silhouette of a dog (wolf?) above the security company's logo.

Inside the gates, a brief stretch of lawn, but mostly gravel. Crunchy gravel, Albert thought to himself, you could market breakfast cereal under that name, people would buy it, there's one born every minute ... up to the front door comes a visitor, crunch, crunch, crunch. An ait. A bloody ait. 'Don't give up,' Kate Bush advised him, and 'Oh, *shut* up!' said Albert, ejecting the tape with untoward malice.

He had a little bet as to what he would find round the side of the house: an alley with a Porsche 944 parked half on and half off the pavement, the driver's door conveniently placed opposite a steel shutter capped with a closed-circuit TV camera. A camera not unlike the one that would be mounted in the front porch.

As he drew near he saw that things had happened to this property. Typical of these renovations was the entry phone: one of those brand new jobs that came with hasty conversions, along with white paint which did not properly conceal the imperfections of the young timber beneath, and putty fingermarks on windows. The entry phone buttons were made of some cheap metal dressed up to look like brass. There were no labels in the slots beside them.

Albert glanced up to see that, as expected, a camera was regarding him with apparent unconcern. He arranged his body between the lens and the bank of buttons. An American Express card materialized in his right hand. The front door was on an ordinary night-latch; it yielded within seconds.

The hallway sported modern reproductions in wafer-thin but colourful frames that did their best to cover the bare walls. Somewhere close by a typewriter clacked intermittently and, as Albert listened, a phone began to chirrup. The stairs were at the back of the house. He climbed three floors in swift silence, noting how anonymously the tenants kept themselves to themselves, and paused on the last landing.

His instincts had suddenly started to become very edgy. It wasn't just standard professionalism, it was a premonition of genuine danger. Albert went up the next flight on tiptoe, craning his head to see the corridor now coming into view on his left on the other side of the bannister.

He stopped while still five steps short of the top. Three doors: one to the right of the top of the stairs, one opposite him, another down the far end, towards the front of the building. Albert completed the climb and stood still, head on one side, listening. Here there were no typewriters, no phones rang. On the door opposite the stairwell was fixed a minute ebony plaque bearing the words 'Asiatica Limited'.

Bingo.

Albert leaned against the door panel above the plaque. His fingers brushed the handle, dithered an inch or so above it, withdrew. Because he was concentrating on the door in front of him he was almost too late.

As the right hand door swiftly opened, he felt the draught of air and turned, one hand already groping for an inside jacket pocket. A blur of browns and blacks. Something long and to his left coming down fast. Human, male, beard, tall, tough. Without thinking, Albert jabbed his left hand up to intercept whatever might be about to land on his skull. A shock ran the length of his arm, nothing smashed, tendons okay, back off, *mind the bloody stairs*!

His assailant looked Arabic. As Albert retreated a couple of steps he saw that the man was holding a blackjack, no wonder his arm hurt like hell . . .

The Arab went into a crouch, jumped upright, feinted left. Albert read the series of movements correctly and spun around to put his back against the wall, minimizing the target. His attacker's rush brought him opposite Albert instead of sending him headlong into him, as he'd intended. Albert stuck out his foot. The Arab saw it, tried to jump aside but succeeded only in entangling one hand in the rails of the bannister. He cried out at the pain, then had the sense to follow through, swinging his whole body around in a semi-circle so that he was facing Albert, who still had his back against the wall.

This time, however, there was a difference. The Arab was starting forward, off the bannister, when he caught sight of the gun in Albert's hand and froze.

The door bearing the plaque opened first a fraction, then some more. Another Middle Eastern type, fatter than his colleague, cautiously emerged, nodding his head to right and left like a bird searching out worms. He, too, saw Albert, registered the gun, and did a comical double-take. Collapse of stout party.

'Oh, God!' drawled an English voice from inside the room just vacated by the fat man. 'Not *again*.'

Albert waved the gun, indicating that the Arabs should lead the way. He was careful to keep a distance between him and his attacker, who had taken a silk handkerchief from his breast pocket and was dabbing at the knuckles of one hand, scraped raw on the bannisters.

Albert had not believed that such offices existed outside the world of advertising. The room was about fifteen feet wide and twice as long. Here the white paint really came into its own, acting as both reflector of the cold northern light which filtered through the huge window, and enhancer of the black furniture littering — really, that was the only word for it — the available space. Stark, cushionless chairs on either side of the glass conference table were offset, slightly, by semi-stuffed leather sacks dotted around, presumably for sitting on. The enormous television set at one end was wholly black, as was the video beneath it. A single white lily arched out of a long-stemmed black glass vase on the blackwood desk opposite the door, behind which sat a man wearing a dark suit, almost fluorescently white shirt and burgundy silk tie.

'Oh . . . *God*,' he said again, as if weary of life's incessant demands upon his patience. 'Not the Browning version.'

252

Albert knew a second's surprise. His gun was, in fact, a Browning.

'I suppose you're going to tell me you've come to read the meter.' The man's voice essayed Oxbridge arrogance, although Albert already knew he wasn't out of the top drawer. Now he sighed, a long, stagey job, and said, 'You are trespassing, you do know that.'

The harder he tried, the more his voice turned into a queeny bleat. He sat with his hands folded in his lap, where Albert couldn't see them. Albert didn't like that. 'Hands on the desk, please.'

Another theatrical sigh. First fingers appeared over the lip of the desk, then two hands scurried along the surface to rest, palms down, a couple of feet apart.

Albert gestured the two Arabs over to the far end of the room while he focused on the face behind the desk. It was pale, clean-shaven, with a thin mouth too long for the narrow cheeks above. His hair was brushed straight back from the forehead in furrows. Age, about forty, which would be right.

'Mr Eddy Clapham? Or is it some other name now?'

Sigh, sigh, sigh. The right hand raised itself an inch off the desk, flapped and fell back. Eddy turned, showing a profile of which he was proud. 'Edward Clapham, at your service. What *can* we do for you, Mr . . . ?'

'Albert.'

'*Really?*' Eddy seemed to have trouble accepting it. 'You don't look like an Albert. I had a shot at a novel, once. Do you know why I stopped?'

Albert said nothing.

'I stopped because it was the damnedest thing, but I couldn't get the characters' names right. I'd be writing about a John, say, and I'd realize he didn't look like a John at all. Not a comfortable, *conforming* John. My characters were never at ease with themselves, somehow. Are you sure you're an Albert?'

A black phone tremoloed. Eddy picked it up, said 'Fuck

off,' and replaced it. Then he picked it up again for long enough to say, 'That's an entire morning's fuck off, you understand.'

Silence fell. There was a general air of resignation in the room that this kind of incident was to be expected in their line of business, whatever that might happen to be.

'I would like,' Albert said, 'to ask you a few questions.'

Sigh. 'Look . . .' *Sigh*. 'If it's about income tax . . . no, they don't carry guns, you must be Customs and Excise. If it's about the VAT . . .'

'It's about Anna Elwell. Your first wife.'

'Oh.' For the first time, Eddy looked less than sure of himself. 'You what?'

Albert noted the descent from Oxbridge to Redbrick. 'You're rather elusive. No one answers the phone and we don't have the facilities to interview you in . . .' He raised his eyes to the ceiling. 'Teheran, Damascus, Beirut, Sana, Baghdad — '

'Yes, all right, all right, so I'm on the computer, I get the message.'

'And Tel Aviv. How ever do you manage the visas, by the way?'

Eddy's already long mouth unzipped even further. 'Pull the other one, it's got balls on.'

The fat Arab giggled. Eddy must suddenly have found the two bodyguards as distasteful as Albert did, for he said 'Oh, do shut up. Get out, both of you, go on, get out.'

The attacker led the way, haughty and lithe, while the fat Arab waddled in his wake, struggling to keep up like a tug they'd forgotten to unhitch from the cruiser.

Albert, watching their departure, was struck by a sudden, recent memory. 'Do you own a Porsche 944?'

'Now look, I paid for that . . . Can we do a deal?'

'Deal?'

'If it's about the Singapore gold — '

'It's not about the gold. Or the arms. Or even the cocaine. Not this time.'

'Okay, then. You tell me where you're coming from.'

'I've told you, I want to ask you – '

'What's wrong with Anna? I don't have to pay her anything. I pay for Juliet, every month, bang, on the nail.'

'Anna's missing. Disappeared.'

The ensuing silence was a long one. 'Who are you, exactly?' Eddy asked.

Albert put away his Browning and produced a card. Eddy held it up to the light, as if suspecting a forgery, before handing it back with the comment, 'You're not Special Branch.' He was neither disturbed nor angry; just certain, in the same way that Seppy Lamont had been certain. 'Let's go over to the window. I don't like a desk between me and my guests. It's a real no-no, where I operate.'

The two men moved into the light. Eddy pulled one of the austere, high-backed black chairs away from the conference table and sat sideways on it. Albert stood in his favourite position, right elbow on left palm and the back of his free hand covering his mouth.

'What do you want to know about Anna, then?'

'When did you last see her?'

'Light years back.'

'Has she written to you since, or have you written to her?'

'No.'

'Phone calls?'

'Never. Clean break. *Finito*. Not *au revoir*, strictly *adieu*.'

'What about Juliet?'

Eddy's face softened a fraction. 'I still see her sometimes. She's in Cornwall, rotten set-up if you ask me.'

'You last saw her when?'

'Couple of months ago. I can check the diary . . .'

'Not necessary. Did you talk about Anna?'

'A bit. Just chit-chat, nothing important.'

Albert began to walk slowly up and down. Eddy watched him for a while, then said, 'What's she done? Has David left her?'

Albert continued his same, even pace. 'Would that surprise you?'

'Not really. She had her neurotic side.'

'Is that why you broke up?'

'Is that relevant?'

'We want to know where she is, what she might be doing, who she might be meeting.' He rounded on Eddy. 'What she's . . . capable of.'

'Nothing bad, if that's what you're implying. Anna's strictly one of the good girls.'

Another long silence.

'Why did we break up?' Eddy said suddenly. 'Oh, all kinds of reasons. Blonde kinds. Brunette kinds. Redheads.'

'You were a womanizer and she was jealous.'

'You could say that. It wasn't my fault she was frigid, now was it? You can blame that on her bloody mother. That and a whole lot of other things.'

'Mrs Elwell. And Mr?'

'No. He was never there. I mean, "there" in the sense of a force, a presence, you know?'

'He was a weak man?'

'Had to be, to live with Mrs. She wasn't the kind of woman to tolerate opposition, believe you me.'

'I've met Mrs Elwell.'

'Then you're halfway to understanding Anna. You know she's adopted?'

Albert nodded.

'The Elwells couldn't have children of their own. So they adopted Anna and smothered her with love. The wonder is how she survived. It puzzled me, she could be so strong.'

'Why is that puzzling? Isn't a loving home supposed to be the best preparation for life?'

'Don't you believe it. The best preparation for anything is hardship. Opposition. Everything else is just cotton wool.'

'Why did you marry her in the first place?'

'Why did you marry your wife?'

Albert ignored the question. 'Anna was pregnant.'

'So?'

'She was pregnant, you'd both just come down from Oxford, she with a first in Law, you with a third in PPE. You got her knocked up, her mother found out, pressure was brought to bear.'

'Pressure! Good God, more like the Spanish Inquisition.' Eddy perhaps realized he had given away more than he intended, for he went on irritably, 'What does it matter why we got married? It was legal, we tied the knot in church.'

'How long did it last?'

'What, the marriage? A year, say.'

'Then you were divorced.'

'She divorced me.' He sounded hurt, even a touch surprised.

'But that year wasn't all bad.' Albert stood staring out of the window at the river. Sometimes it was possible to see for extraordinary distances, even on a day as grey as this one. 'And you didn't marry her just because she was pregnant, did you, you married her because she was a good woman, and fun to be with, and she had prospects, am I right, mm?'

Sigh, sigh, *sigh*!

'So now tell me . . . that year you spent together. What was she like' – Albert turned away from the glass – 'then?'

Eddy rested one elbow on the table and the other on the arm of his chair, interlacing his hands in front of him. 'Like?' he said after a long pause. 'She was like . . .'

Albert idly filled in the gap with possible descriptions. She was fun. Cold. Jolly. A real bitch.

'She was like a goddess, then,' Eddy said; and Albert, hearing his voice, hearing what lurked behind it, was catapulted out of his speculative reverie into an immediacy for which he had not bargained.

'Explain, if you will, what you mean by that.'

'When we were in Oxford, I thought of her as beyond my reach. I was nothing, came from nowhere. She . . .'

'Go on.'

257

'She . . . gave off light. Always a little joke, soothing away troubles. I've seen people stand up when Anna came in. As if she was royalty, you know? And they wanted to get a better view, get close to her. She excited people. Was interested in them. She brought out the best in you, by listening.'

Albert remembered the photograph of Anna that he'd seen in the Lescombes' drawing room. 'I see.'

'She was innocent,' Eddy went on. 'A woman's body wrapped around a child's mind. I thought . . .'

'Yes?'

'Oh, I don't know. When she said she'd sleep with me, I thought this was it, y'know, let's do it and die, there isn't any more to be had, not here, not in this life.' He grunted. 'Talk about a let-down.'

'And on her side . . . what was it about you that Anna found attractive, I wonder?'

Eddy laughed, an artificially elegant sound. 'That's easy.'

'So enlighten me.'

'It was such a fabulous time to be at Oxford – well, all right, every generation says that. But for us it was real wake-up-Sleeping-Beauty stuff: suddenly there was pot, and women, and sod all to do in the way of work if you didn't feel like it. I used to wear these flashy clothes, and played the hard man, and I grew a beard. Anna was just . . . goggle-eyed. She'd never had any contact with someone like me before. Never been *allowed* any, in case she caught fleas, you know?'

'She was infatuated by someone radically different?'

'And dangerous. Somebody *alive*. Someone who cared about things – you'll never believe this, but I had a social conscience then. Demos. Love-ins, I was into all that.'

'Was she?'

'Only for my sake. Not that she didn't have a conscience; hers was even better developed than mine. She didn't care for the, how shall I put it, the stagecraft.'

'But in the end she found you . . . irresistible?'

258

Eddy shrugged. 'We were both young, the genes with a "G" were singing and the jeans with a "J" were too tight, y'know the kind of thing.'

A thought struck Albert. 'Did you *want* her to get pregnant?'

Eddy laughed self-consciously. 'I've even asked myself that. Maybe I did, yes.'

'You were happy enough to get married, anyway?'

'Yeah. Except . . .'

'Except for what?'

When Eddy shook his head and continued to stare at the floor, Albert prompted him. 'She was working too hard because she wanted to get to the bar . . .'

'The exams were tough.'

'And then there was the kid . . . what were you doing, then?'

'Nothing much. I thought I might qualify as an accountant, but – '

'Those exams also were tough.'

Eddy shrugged.

'And then someone told you about the gold. A world where every so often, just two or three times a year, people need to buy the physical stuff, in bars. And because there's so little about, and because hardly anybody knows where to find it, there's this exclusive club, isn't there, which can fix that, mm? Everything from chartering the plane to bribing customs to working out how many Heckler and Koch submachine-guns the guards will need when they land in Benin. Or Belize.'

'It's a dicey world, friend.'

'I don't doubt it. But profitable, very.'

'If you get it right.'

'And did you get it right, you with your contacts and your drinking in night clubs, while Anna was feeding the baby before staying up half the night to study, mm, did you?'

'What's with all this moralizing? Have you got something going with Anna, or what?'

259

But Albert only smiled. 'Let's move on,' he said eventually. 'Anna passed her exams, didn't she?'

'Yes.'

'And wanted support, someone to look after the kid while she practised. She divorced you. You hated that, perhaps?'

Eddy shrugged again, refusing to meet Albert's eyes.

'Because you loved her, and it was only when you lost her that you realized just how much you loved her.'

Eddy started to speak, gave up.

'And the child was special.'

'The child was a pain. She's stayed that way ever since.'

'Ah. The devoted father.'

'Look – '

'I'm looking.'

'It wasn't my fault Anna got frightened she might kill herself. I didn't give her PND, now did I?'

Albert slipped into overdrive, don't think, don't pause, act your heart out, make him think you knew that. 'PND meaning post-natal depression?'

'Yeah. By the time Juliet was born I wasn't having much to do with Anna. So it wasn't my fault.'

'Wasn't it? She blamed you at the time.'

'She was over the edge. Way over, and that's before I came along. She'd got all ripped up over the adoption, changing schools and that. Then after the kid was born, she got this, you know, this terrible downer some women get. Kept on saying, "I'm going to kill Juliet, I'm going to kill myself, if somebody doesn't help me." '

'Would she have done it, d'you think?'

'No. Definitely not. She had too much guts for that. But she wasn't responsible, according to the doctor.'

'Not responsible . . . and so you chose to leave her?'

To Albert's surprise, Eddy made no attempt to dodge his gaze. 'You try living with it for a while,' he said quietly. 'Then come back and we'll talk again.'

'What happened to Anna after that?'

Eddy was looking at Albert now, really looking at him, making assessments. 'I heard she was seeing a shrink.'

'Who did you hear this from?'

'Mrs Elwell told me. Meant to rub it in. Blame me.' He slipped into a silly voice: ' "Edward, I felt you had a right to know, Chappy didn't want me to say anything, but . . ." Christ all-bleeding-mighty.' *Sigh!*

'Do you know which psychiatrist Anna saw at that time?' Albert asked.

'No. I mean, Lydia Elwell may have mentioned the name, but I can't remember now, off hand.'

'Would it surprise you to know that when I interviewed her she didn't mention this episode at all? Even though I asked her a number of questions relating to it?'

'Wouldn't surprise me in the least. Lydia wouldn't go showing the family skeletons to . . . what was it, remind me again, Special Branch . . . ?'

'This psychiatrist. Was his name Kleist, by any chance?'

Eddy pursed his lips. 'Doesn't ring a bell.'

'If you should remember, give me a ring.' Albert started searching through his pockets for a piece of paper but Eddy forestalled him.

'Here, use this. Appropriate.'

'This' was a photograph extracted from Eddy's wallet. Albert flipped it over to see a colour print of Anna's upper half. She was holding a baby, smiling away from the camera at the child. The snapshot had faded a kind of rusty colour and there was a crack across its top left-hand corner.

Albert scribbled a number and handed the photo back to Eddy. 'The only other thing I need to know is how I get out of here without your sidekicks taking their revenge on the way.'

'I'll call 'em in.'

Eddy picked up the phone and spoke soft words of Arabic. The door opened to admit the bodyguards. Albert put his hand on the Browning in his pocket, but the newcomers concentrated on their master, two dogs awaiting a command or a biscuit, there was no way of telling which.

As Albert reached the door Eddy said, 'If you find her . . .' He uttered a high-pitched laugh, mocking himself. ' . . . You might . . . give her my love. Or something like that, yeah.'

TWENTY-FOUR

Anna awoke late on Friday with a blinding headache, doubt-less caused by the foul stuff Kleist had injected her with the night before. The house seemed unnaturally quiet. As soon as she had dressed she went to the kitchen. Barzel was there, by the sink, drying a glass — he'd evidently been drinking vodka, for the half-empty bottle still stood on the table. Anna gazed at it, her nerves writhing with need for the clean white spirit. A shot, just one . . .

No. That wouldn't help. If she was ever going to get out of this alive, it wouldn't be through the neck of a bottle.

Barzel held the glass up to the light to check that he hadn't left any smears; and there was something about this fussy, almost effeminate neatness which chilled Anna. When he put the glass down on the sideboard her eyes followed it, to be ensnared by another object lying there.

Anna stared at it, fascinated. The weapon's surface bore a faint sheen, as if greasy. It was so obviously *metal*, serious. On television, at the cinema, the guns might as well be bits of wood, for all the sense of realism they conveyed. This was different. This had a function.

She looked away to find Barzel examining her with detach-ment, rather like an attendant in the better class of Ladies' standing ready to hand you a towel: aware of what you'd been doing behind the locked door but wholly impassive.

Anna sensed he expected her to ask permission before doing anything. She marched across to the stove and snatched up the kettle. When Barzel moved aside to let her

263

fill it she felt as much exultation as if she had scored a point against some particularly unpleasant professional adversary in court.

She waited for the kettle to boil and made herself a cup of tea without speaking, without even looking at Barzel. She drank it in silence. Just when Anna realized she couldn't stay there forever, she had to do something, Gerhard entered the kitchen.

'Good morning.'

He spoke in English, so presumably this salutation was directed at her. Anna nodded curtly. 'I need some air,' she said, standing up.

'How about the terrace? I'd like to talk to you.'

'We'll go for a walk.' She nodded at Barzel. 'And I think we'll leave the dog at home. He's house-trained. He can do washing-up, I've seen him.'

'Don't do that,' Kleist whispered warningly as they left the house. 'You can't play games with him, Anna.'

'He's a swine and you're another. Take me to the church on the other side of the bay, the one you can see from my room. I want to explore.'

'It's too far.'

'So what are you going to do?' She stopped dead, causing Kleist to cannon into her, and swung around. 'Shoot me?'

He stared at her. 'No,' he said at last. 'I wouldn't do that. I couldn't. But . . .'

'But Barzel could, yes, I know. Don't worry, I can guess the rules. We'll walk to the church. If we meet anyone, I won't try to speak to them. I won't try to escape. I give you my word. There! Does that satisfy you?'

It satisfied *her*, she discovered, to make a promise she had no intention of keeping, because by doing that she entered his world on his terms and thereby secured her only chance of victory. When Kleist reluctantly nodded, she walked away from him without a backward glance.

The approach to the church lay along one of those paths with myriad branches always splitting off and then coming together again to make islands. The church itself stood in a cypress grove. Two or three goats were tearing at the thin grass which sprouted between its damp walls and the surrounding earth; at first Anna wasn't sure how to deal with them, fearing from their impatient expressions that they might trample her; but after standing still for a while they went back to their lunch.

Between the church and side of the hill she found a graveyard sheltered by cypresses and one large, shady birch. Anna could see only five graves. Two of them were old, mere grass-covered mounds, but the others looked recent. The biggest was marble. Stone chips of a lurid and, Anna thought, singularly inappropriate shiny green colour overlaid its large, flat top. The stele, surmounted by an Orthodox cross, bore a faded photograph of the deceased: an old woman whose grey hair was drawn back tightly enough to be painful. Her cheeks were not so much sunken as collapsed, making her appear already dead, but the eyes were wide open and unmistakably quick. They contained a hint of challenge, not unmixed with humour. Her own mother's mother had looked just like that, sometimes.

She sat down on the marble tomb, suddenly overcome by memories. When Kleist finally caught up with her he hung around sheepishly for a while, as if uncertain what to do next. 'You seem very far away,' he ventured at last.

She jerked her head up and looked at him, resentful of the intrusion. 'I was thinking of Nan. Remember her?'

'Of course.'

'How she helped me. After that awful business at school.'

'Yes.'

'Only she died soon afterwards.'

'Oh, Anna . . .'

'Leave me alone. I want to think.'

Nan had taken some of the sting out of being an Elwell only child. She always resolutely sided with Anna, infuriating her mother. Then one day Lydia had come to the new school, the one Anna had been sent to after the débâcle at the convent. It was lunchtime; Anna found herself dragged from the table, into the headmistress' study, wondering what fresh misdemeanour was to be laid at her door. There was no crime, however; only punishment. Nan had died in the early hours of the morning, of a heart attack. Anna could go home now.

From her seat in the shade of the cypresses, a cool sea breeze ruffling her hair, she could not quite recapture the flavour of that day, no matter how hard she tried. She had been dreading afternoon school, because it was netball and she hated netball. As she ate her lunch she was thinking she would do anything to get out of it. Anything . . . but not kill Nan. She felt confused now, as she had done then. She knew in her brain, because Kleist had shown her, that Nan's death preceded her desire to be let off netball, knew also that she must have realized it at the time, but something more powerful than any brain would insist on muddying the waters. If it had not been for her desire to escape the day's sport at any cost, Nan would still be alive.

The man standing with his back to her, hands in pockets, had patiently explained, many times, that this was a normal reaction. But also he had, she felt, ever so gently derided her feelings about the incident, breaking his pattern of treating what she said with serious concern.

She had only one priority now: to escape from this island, and its accursed Prospero. Nothing else mattered a damn.

'We're going to straighten a few things out,' Anna said abruptly; and Gerhard turned towards her.

'Of course,' he said. 'That's what I'm here – '

'No. You're here to do the opposite. That's been your function all along.'

'I don't – '

'When I first met you, I was suffering from post-natal depression, right? A bad case.'

'Yes.'

'And you said all my problems went back to guilt, and you

266

were going to cleanse me of guilt. I felt guilty because I'd been given away at birth and I saw it as my fault.'

'Yes,' he agreed again. 'You felt, quite literally, guilty for having been born. Born sub-standard.'

'And guilt, for me, had become a habit. I was all screwed up because I saw myself as responsible for having had those girls expelled; and for killing Nan, do you remember that?'

'Certainly. You may recall I told you so, at the time.'

He had told her so many things, at different times. She would have to examine them all again, to see which were valid and which formed part of the web of deception with which he'd ensnared her. But that could wait. A specific memory was struggling for mastery in her head.

After Nan's death there had been a funeral where she was present without being present. She had been kept outside the crematorium chapel, in the car, with her father, unable to say goodbye properly, stuck for life with an overweening impression of death as something sinful from which children ought to be protected. She was nine: old enough, she felt, to mourn. Perhaps being made to stay outside was part of the punishment for having murdered Nan.

When the service was over, she had walked with her parents in the garden of remembrance. The park seemed full of people; some of them were upset but she could see that others were relaxed and contented; they, she intelligently supposed, had lost someone in the past and were marking the anniversary. Happy or sad, all the people wandering around seemed part of something, a ritual of social importance which brought them together. It was, she realized later, one of England's rare examples of the family at work. Only she, Anna, was excluded from this family, as from every other. She had never cried for her grandmother's death. Even now, she could not cry.

The cold marble hurt the undersides of her calves. As she shifted physically, so her perspective changed also, enabling her to see a hitherto concealed link between Nan's passing and one of Gerhard Kleist's more poignant insights.

267

'I want to ask you something,' she said. 'To check something, if you like.'

'Yes?'

'Do you remember telling me about the most difficult problem a therapist has to face?'

'Not off hand. Remind me.'

'Death without a corpse.'

'Oh. *That.*'

'Someone disappears, for good. Is he dead? Suffering from amnesia? Or has he just abandoned his family, crushed by pressures they couldn't understand. Yes?'

'Yes. There's nothing for the therapist to seize on, you see.'

'The survivors always feel *guilty*, don't they? They think they're to blame, they drove the missing person away, by not measuring up.'

'What's prompted all this?' He was genuinely at sea.

It was the not knowing that brought them to Kleist, these hapless souls bereaved by a fate colder than death. Anna was beginning to perceive something until now kept at bay: just as Nan had gone with no goodbyes on either side, so, by giving her for adoption, her mother too had 'died' without affording her daughter an opportunity to mourn.

But how, then, Anna wondered, could she have failed her real mother: a child too young to know evil, let alone do it . . . ?

There was only one answer possible. She hadn't failed at all.

Being adopted was not her fault, any more than it had been her mother's!

She studied this revelation for a long time. 'You didn't even try to erase my guilt over Nan's death, did you?' she said suddenly. 'You *nurtured* it.'

'You really mustn't let things distress you to the point where — '

'You wrecked me.'

'*Wrecked* you?'

Gerhard had come to stand in front of her and was reaching

out to grasp her shoulders, but on hearing her words his body became as immobile as if she were the Gorgon incarnate.

'You took my guilt and stood it on its head, until it wasn't *my* guilt any more, it was my mother's.'

'You're talking utter rubbish, and you know it.'

'No, I'm learning. Waking up at last. My mother gave me away when I was born, and that was her betrayal of me, you said: not *my* fault, but *hers*. And all my life's been dedicated to ensuring that the betrayal never happened again.'

'For God's – '

'Be a better traitor, you said.' Anna smiled a brittle smile. 'Quote: "If you're worried about being betrayed, do it yourself. Do it fast, do it first." End . . . of . . . *quote*. God, what a fool I've been. To make it so *easy* for you!'

'Anna!'

But she had jumped off the tombstone and was striding away from him, back towards the house. She knew in her heart that he was her enemy. If she was to have any chance of saving herself, she must fight him as he had fought her: deceitfully, with evil intent, to the last gasp of breath in her body.

She could afford to take no prisoners in her war with Gerhard Kleist.

TWENTY-FIVE

David did not know what had woken him. It was still dark outside. He felt around for the alarum clock and pressed the button to illuminate its face. One o'clock, just after. His heartbeat steadied. He sat up in bed, listening. Silence. Yet he felt sure that a noise had startled him from oblivion, that he was no longer alone in the house.

He knew a wild moment of hope, coupled with utter relief. Anna! He had always known she would come back. Soon she would be explaining four whole days' absence, the only possible story, credible, eminently forgivable, and he would curse himself for not having thought of it before . . .

But the notion scarcely had time to cross his mind before he dismissed it. Anna would have come straight up to the bedroom. The sense of let-down was almost too great to be borne, but somehow he mastered it. There was danger below. The men from the black Audi. Oh God, he whispered; oh my God . . .

Call the police.

David slid out of bed, donning his dressing gown, and padded across to the door. He opened it a crack to listen. The house remained in total silence. But the darkness here seemed diluted. Being in his own domain, he realized what that meant. A light was on in his study at the back of the house, one floor below.

He knew his way around the bedroom by touch. The telephone stood on the table by his side of the bed. He groped his way back to where he'd started. Lamp . . . clock . . . his hand went instinctively to where he thought the phone would be.

Nothing.

David's mouth was dry now. His command of the situation began to falter. *Keep calm.* He'd had a nightmare, struggled without waking, the phone had fallen to the floor. He went down on his hands and knees. Not under the table; try the bed. He was clutching at straws, but still he made himself feel around in the dust where carpet met skirting board.

Light. He must have light. David teetered on the brink of panic. He got up too quickly, knocking against the table. It wobbled, making the objects on it rattle. He heard a moan of apprehension and only a second later did he register that it must have come from him.

David found the bedside light at last. He switched it on. The telephone was nowhere to be seen.

Someone had stolen the phone. He sat down on the edge of the bed, trying to make sense of what he saw. Or rather, did not see. The phone had definitely been in its usual place the night before, when he went to sleep. Which meant that somebody had come into his room while he slept and taken the instrument away, without awakening him.

He forced himself to think coherently. He was alone in the house, without the means to call for help. No, not quite alone: the light still burned downstairs . . .

Under the bed on Anna's side, apart from the dust, was a cricket bat. She kept it there for those nights when David had to sleep away from home. Curious how roles could sometimes be reversed.

As he descended the stairs, bat in hand, he saw that someone had left the study door open – not him, he was conscientious about such things – and that a light indeed was burning there. He had almost reached the doorway when he heard a noise. Voices, speaking softly. He sidled along the wall until he could take a lightning look through the gap.

Two men, one of them black. The latter sat in David's

chair, holding a sheet of paper up to the desk lamp. In his other hand was a portable recorder. His lips moved, so David knew he must be committing the paper's contents to tape. Another man walked about the room, also quietly dictating. The only other thing David had time to notice was the odd circumstance of their wearing dark grey business suits.

The clothes told him the truth. This wasn't burglary, this was espionage. He began to back away, intending to leave the house by any means, just get out, find refuge with a neighbour, then phone . . . phone who?

The question proved academic. Suddenly hands met around his waist, pinioning his arms to his sides. All the breath was squeezed from David's lungs. 'Hey, Bill,' a soft voice said behind his left ear. 'Landlord's come calling.'

Then David found himself manhandled into his own study, to find the black man, evidently Bill, on his feet and wearing a frown. For a long moment nothing else happened. 'Okay,' the black said at last. 'Let him go.'

'Who are you?' David said.

'Bill' produced a perspex-wrapped card and held it up for David to see. 'CIA.'

'What?'

'Surprised?'

'Surpri – you sneak in here like thieves in the night, you read my papers, steal my phone and you want to know if I'm *surprised*! What kind of moron are you, anyway?'

The black man sat down again in David's chair and switched on his dictating machine. 'Keep talking,' he said. 'You're doing fine. Outrage. Indignation. Hey, where'd you learn all that crap? Moscow? Nice line, nice delivery.'

'Now, you listen to me!'

'I'm listening.' Bill lazily lifted a hand in the direction of his two colleagues. 'We can all hear you.'

'You're CIA?'

'You said it.'

'Right. Where's your warrant?'

Bill's face reflected puzzlement. 'Warrant?' he said, looking as if for help between the faces of his henchmen. 'Either of you guys know anything about any warrant?' When no answer was forthcoming, Bill turned back to David. 'Sorry. But this is business. Warrants are for games players. What we want to know is where exactly your wife has gone, who she's with, who are you working for, what are they paying you, how long have you been spying, what have you told them. For starters. We can get onto the secondary stuff later. Oh, and the only "warrant" we're interested in is one for your extradition. We find the British penal system *deeply* unimpressive.'

David stared at him. Then he said, 'Get out of my house. In the morning I'm going to make such a stink – '

'Nobody is about to pay any attention to you, Lescombe. Because you are number one suspect. We've always known that the Krysalis Committee is a potential source of leakage. For a long time, nothing happened. Then *you* join the committee and the New Testament goes missing. How good are your schools? Do two and two add up to four here, like in the States, or is it different? Come on, tell us, we're interested.'

'I've got nothing to say to you. If you want to interview me, apply to my employers. While we're at it – how dare you go through my papers?' David gestured at the pile on top of his desk, *his own bloody desk, by God*! 'Put them back.'

'But papers are our business, Lescombe.' Bill's chuckle was almost apologetic, as if he had trouble locating the source of David's difficulty. 'Tell me, did you study classical mythology at the second-rate school your parents sent you to? Yes, of course you did: you majored in Latin and Greek. Remember King Midas and the asses' ears? D'you understand the moral there? Information is public property, that's the moral. If you don't want 'em to know, don't say it. Certainly don't write, and I quote . . .' He reached out to pick up a sheet of paper at random. ' . . . *I miss having your arms around me so much, my darling, it's as if the whole world emptied itself when you went away this morning* – '

273

'Give me that!' All the blood rushed into David's cheeks, his stomach contracted; but when he launched himself forward to snatch Anna's letter Bill was too quick for him and he once again found himself pinioned. *'Give it to me!'* he shouted.

'When we leave,' Bill said equably. 'Which will be soon. We prefer to go about our work uninterrupted, so we'll come back when you're not at home.' His smile was ugly. 'Might even bring a warrant with us next time, who knows?'

He stood up, straightening his jacket, and made for the door. Then he paused. 'One last thought I would like to share with you, Lescombe. Your wife. She's a courier, right? Well, couriers sometimes double-cross their masters. You want to know what I think? I think Anna may have discovered that life with you is frankly *very* boring. Unless of course you have good friends from way back living in Athens, and she's decided to spend the weekend with them.'

'You're talking nonsense.'

'Yeah?'

'I love my wife. She loves me. She is not, repeat *not* a traitor or a thief. Why can't I make you people understand?' David's voice was almost a wail. 'She's been kidnapped! She's in trouble.' Memories of his conversations with Juliet and Lydia Elwell crept into his mind, *what kind of trouble?*, only to be violently ejected: *don't let them know she may be unstable* . . . 'She's under threat and nobody gives a damn.'

'Oh, about the Lescombes, Mr and Mrs, we care.' The black man made no secret of the contempt he felt. 'Passionately. But let me share with you yet another thought. The evidence against your wife is all one way and you are flying in the face of it. Suppose, however, for one incredible moment, that *you* are innocent. Isn't it time you began to devote a little attention to your career? For when this is all over?'

'What's that supposed to mean?'

'You've been showing a lot of concern for your wife. Phoning her friends – we monitored eighteen calls yesterday.

274

That's eighteen people, plus their wives, husbands, lovers, who now know that she's missing. It doesn't help us, Lescombe. Even if you manage to squeeze yourself out of the frame, people are still going to remember that. Wise up. Forget her. Start doing yourself some good, why don't you?'

He went out. His two assistants followed him. For a second David stood motionless. Bill reached the head of the stairs. Then David came to life. Without thinking what he was doing, he charged forward, hands held out in front of him. The heavies heard David's approach, but only had time to make half turns before he cannoned into Bill's back, punching outwards with all his force.

The CIA man tumbled down fourteen steps in a whirl of arms and legs. David looked and was rewarded with a moment of clean satisfaction comprising many elements: a cracked spectacle lens, blood, groans of pain . . . then a fist travelling with the force and speed of a steam hammer thudded into his solar plexus and he went down retching.

By the time he felt fit enough to stand, the house was once again empty. The last thing he did before crawling back to bed was fold up Anna's desecrated letter and put it in the top pocket of his pyjamas.

TWENTY-SIX

At about the time that Hayes was removing the telephone from David's bedside, Albert waylaid Fox and Shorrocks in the paddock at Crowborough while they were on their way from the helicopter up to the house.

'Progress.' He had to shout to make himself heard above the noise of the Bell Jet Ranger's rotors.

'You'll have to be quick,' Shorrocks brayed. 'Half Europe's waiting for us in there and they're dancing up and down.'

'Hold the chopper, I'm due back soonest.'

Fox showed the pilot two downturned thumbs and the engine died.

'Have you got Redman with you?' Albert asked.

'In Washington, thank God. "For consultations." '

'What about that other — '

'Hayes has gone coy, all of a sudden. Can't raise him. Let's try the stables . . .'

The farm had once housed a livery, there was plenty of space for a crash conference.

'Can you just tell me why our glorious allies have been assembled here tonight?' Albert asked, plonking himself down on a bale of straw.

It was Fox who answered. 'They're hopping mad. Word's leaked out about what Krysalis might contain. We asked them to trace a woman, but we didn't tell them the file enabled the Warsaw Pact to switch off its tactical computers and save electricity.'

'So you're soothing?'

'Trying to. There's a new deadline.'

'What?'

'Redman was forced to bring in the State Department. State are giving the Company another four days to sort out the mess, failing which, they intend to call off the Vancouver summit. A rumour of that got out, but the rest of NATO don't know the reasoning behind it, and *we* aren't allowed to tell them the whole story.'

'I see.' Albert looked down at the straw. 'Rats,' he sighed, apropos of nothing in particular; and then — 'Krysalis . . . damn silly name for a damn silly file. Why do the Yanks always insist on writing everything down?'

Shorrocks glanced at his watch impatiently. 'What's your news?'

'It shapes up like this. There's a psycho guy called Kleist. Anna Lescombe was seeing him for ages, but she seems to have stopped about two years before going walkabout. Social, query sexual affair.' Albert outlined what he had learned at the Lamonts' restaurant. 'Ex-husband told me this morning that she's always had problems. Her old medical records turned up after lunch. And sure enough, she had been referred to one Gerhard Kleist.'

'How long ago?'

'1973.'

'Christ!' Shorrocks made a face. 'Sixteen years. And none of that showed up on her husband's vet?'

'No, you're wrong: indirectly it *did* show up.'

'Explain.'

'Remember that note in the file, about Anna Lescombe having lunch with a German? Same restaurant. Kleist was the German.'

'Why the *hell* didn't Five pick that up?'

Shorrocks had put the question to Fox, but it was Albert who answered. 'Either it was too long ago to be caught in the net, or her earlier medical records had already gone missing by that time, or I don't know what. It happens often enough. My guess is that Kleist cured her of whatever was bugging her and that afterwards they became friends, lovers, something other than doctor-patient.'

'Agent-control, for example?'

'It's starting to look that way.'

'Why was she referred to him?' Fox asked.

'According to her ex, post-natal depression.'

'Really?' Fox was frowning. 'A lot of women get that. They don't all end up on the couch.'

'No, you're right.' Albert tossed his head, impatient with his own lack of perception. 'I hadn't thought of that. So next we need to see Kleist's case notes on the lady.'

'Can you arrange that?' Shorrocks asked.

'Should be possible. Might even be easy: Kleist's vanished. I've checked. He was supposed to have lunch at their usual restaurant yesterday, when I was there. No show. Can you check the computers, see where he's gone?'

'What, airlines, you mean?' Fox asked. 'May take a while.'

'We haven't got a while. Anna Lescombe's with Kleist, I'd bet my life on it.'

'She's somewhere in Greece,' Shorrocks said.

Albert looked at him. 'Tell.'

'Greek immigration came up with the goods. Private plane, chartered in France, landed at a flying club outside Igoumi-nitsa. That's on the west of the Greek mainland, opposite Corfu. Pilot and two passengers, one male, one female. The flight plan showed them on their way to Athens, but the pilot reported engine trouble and requested an emergency landing. Then it turned out that the female passenger was sick, so they got special permission to clear immigration then and there.'

'Anna Lescombe being the sick party?'

'Right,' Shorrocks confirmed. 'The other passenger was travelling on confetti: passport issued in the name of a dead man.'

'That's Kleist.'

'Could well be. He claimed he was a doctor and had the lingo off pat.'

'He said he was taking her to hospital, I suppose?'

'Got it in one,' Shorrocks agreed. 'But we know he didn't, because the Greeks have checked.'

'God damn.'

'One lead: someone *may* have seen them boarding a speed-boat and haring off west.'

'Where would that take them?'

'Corfu, or any one of half a dozen smaller islands. Of course, they could have doubled back. The Greeks are combing the place now, but . . .' Shorrocks shrugged.

'If you've nothing else for us . . .' Fox had been fidgeting with his watch for the past few minutes. His eyes were hooded with tired folds of flesh that Albert had not noticed before.

'One more thing. David Lescombe.'

'Ah.' Shorrocks folded his arms and leaned back against a beam. 'The Americans still reckon he was in this from the start.'

'I don't. Is Five's report on him in yet?'

'This afternoon,' Fox answered. 'Sweet sod all. The neighbours know nothing. He isn't close to his family and it seems he never discussed his work with them. Colleagues describe him as a very persistent man who lets fly occasionally; doesn't suffer fools. Drives himself a little too relentlessly for his own good, perhaps. Not a belonger. Reticent. A bit mean – that's his own mother talking. She doesn't know the price of butter in Safeway, he does, that kind of thing. He sails, but as far as C & E are concerned he's never taken his boat outside territorial waters. That's about it.'

'And the Americans regard this man as a *threat*?'

'They want him, as they chillingly put it, neutralized.' Shorrocks jerked his head towards the house. 'Some of that lot are bound to take the same line.'

'Neutralized . . . you don't think the CIA were behind that attack on Lescombe in Cornwall, do you?'

'No,' said Fox. 'You're assuming there was an attack?'

'He was very convincing.'

'Lovely cover, though. Innocent party terrorized by thugs, oh yes.'

'Don't lose faith in Lescombe yet.'

'We've only got four days,' Fox reminded Albert. 'You still want him to run?'

Albert nodded. 'If he's guilty and makes a break for it, we've got him cold. If not he may, just may, lead us to *la femme* whom we are so busily *cherch*-ing. How can we lose?'

'I'll tell you how,' Fox said, again looking at his watch. 'We can bloody well lose *him* when he runs, that's how.'

'Oh surely not,' Albert said. 'He is only a civil servant, after all.'

'But possibly a treacherous civil servant who's been betrayed by his partner-in-crime-stroke-wife.' Fox shook his head doubtfully. 'In which case he might do something silly. And if he does, the way things are going, that could spell NATO kiss-your-arse-goodnight.'

They were outside now, on their way up to the house.

'Let the other side worry about the Lescombes,' Albert said. 'If he is their man, the chums could be panicking just as much as us, wondering where the hell they both are. Succulent, no?'

'Actually . . . no.' Shorrocks pursed his lips, then let them shape a smile. 'The East Germans know exactly where they are, I fear.'

'Meaning?'

'You remember the fax that arrived when we were down here last?'

'Of course.'

'It caused rather a panic. MI6 Liaison's generic blue fax number known to the enemy, you can imagine the kind of thing.'

'So?'

'The word went out from Number Ten, no less, to find out how that particular trick had been pulled. Amid all the subsequent jumping through hoops, it turned out that Athens station had been rather spectacularly efficient, for a change. The minute we circulated news of that fax, they'd mounted watch on the office of origin.'

'When are we talking about?'

'The afternoon of the day on which it was transmitted.'

'*Athens* station? Good God.'

'They overheard this young Greek ask about a reply that same evening. They put tabs on him and next thing they know he's been snatched off the street.'

'Does that mean our one and only contact's been severed?'

'Yes. Word is, HVA ran the op.'

They had reached the front door; a military policeman was already holding it open for them, but now Albert stopped dead.

'Are you *seriously* telling me,' he began slowly, 'that East Berlin actually does now know where Anna Lescombe is and who she's with?'

'If the Greek boy talked, yes, it looks like it,' Shorrocks confirmed. 'We have to proceed on the assumption that he received his orders from Kleist, face to face, and that he knows how to get in touch with him to report back. So unless HVA have lost their notoriously heavy touch – '

'The boy will have talked.'

'You can bet on it.'

Albert's mind raced ahead. 'And that means HVA could want to talk to *David* Lescombe, find out what *he* knows – so those men in Cornwall – '

'Could have been HVA, yes, it's possible.'

The last words Albert heard Shorrocks say as he entered the house were: 'It follows that the East Germans will know all about that bloody fax, too, of course. What it said, and so on. Which doesn't exactly help, does it?'

The Second Weekend

TWENTY-SEVEN

Robyn Melkiovicz. Strange name: the kind that existed only in the fantasy land of films, among those credits at the end, the ones that strained your eyesight: Best Boys, Gaffers, they were the Melkioviczs of this world. They, and New York lady lawyers . . .

For the hundredth time David looked at the photograph he had taken from Anna's desk in chambers, willing its subject to assume life enough to talk. Was this Robyn? Did those Greek letters on the sign, *The Little House*, connect her with Athens? Bill, the black CIA man, had mentioned Athens as if David knew about that. But he didn't.

Anna's head of chambers had supplied Robyn's missing surname, along with her New York address. David wanted to talk to her. Not on the phone, because people would be listening, Bill had left him in no doubt about that; face to face was essential. But . . . ever the same nagging question. Would they let him go?

His phone was tapped. He was being followed. He had given up trying to trace Anna through their shared network of friends, afraid he might contaminate them. For the Lescombes, it seemed, had begun to stink. The nocturnal visitors from the CIA had brought this into vivid, brutal focus. They suspected he was in league with Anna, that here was a plot to betray the western alliance in which both of them were participants.

He had tried to make a complaint about Bill and his two henchmen. It outraged him to discover that no one was interested. That meant the CIA's suspicions were shared by his own people, MI5 and the rest. This knowledge generated a knot of hard, bilious rage just below David's stomach. For the first time he understood the true meaning of the word 'depressed'. You were pushed down, hard, against a rock. Crushed.

He had to do something or go under. But if he tried to see Robyn, *would they let him*?

He had a plan. Once he was in the States he could make it work. But leaving England, that was the problem. At Heathrow and all the other UK airports, the authorities kept a list of those who were not allowed out. Was his name on it? If so, he could not flee the country, for, like most people, he possessed only one passport. Perhaps they would arrest him at the gate, with hundreds of curious travellers looking on and a press photographer ready to immortalize his downfall. Or perhaps the men in the black Audi would get to him first . . .

He wanted to telephone, or even visit, his mother, but that might mean trouble for her and David couldn't risk it. She was not a well woman, emphysema . . . father had died some years before, he could have taken this to him. Or Natalie, but she was in Australia, with Bob; she hadn't done so badly for herself, not with that latest photo of the pool, and the kids, the eldest was nine now . . .

David realized he'd allowed his thoughts to stray as a means of putting off what had to be done. His bag was packed, one of those fold-over suit carriers you took away for a weekend: nothing elaborate that might signal long-term absence to the watchers. He had spent the best part of a day in the local library's reference section, mapping his route. Then a single purchase at Dixon's and he was ready.

He looked at his watch. Time to go.

He was locking the front door when a voice behind him said, 'David Lescombe?'

He made himself straighten slowly, so they wouldn't think

he had anything to hide. So the gloved passenger from the Audi would have no excuse to open fire. Did Special Branch need a warrant, or could they –

'We haven't met. I'm Eddy. Anna's ex. How d'ye do?'

For a moment David stared at him while his brain caught up. 'I'm in a hurry,' was all he could think of to say.

'Going somewhere? Give you a lift?'

Over his shoulder David could see a black Porsche double-parked. 'This isn't really – '

'A quiet word in your shell-like and you might, as they say, learn something to your advantage.'

'We've got nothing to say to each other.'

'We've got Albert.'

David had been pushing past, on his way down the steps to the pavement, but Eddy's words brought him up short. 'Who?'

'In his thirties. Glasses he doesn't really need. Intense type. Taut.'

'You've met him?'

'Oh, yes. Not from choice. Give you a lift, can I?'

David hesitated. 'I'm catching a plane, I – '

'Thiefrow?'

David nodded.

'Come on, then.'

He drove the car in much the same way, David suspected, as he powered through life: at great speed, with reckless disregard for the safety and interests of other people. 'Look,' Eddy said. 'I know this isn't the greatest introduction in the world.'

'It isn't,' David agreed bitterly.

'But she's in trouble, and I mean a lot of trouble. You don't have to talk to me. But it would help.'

'Help who?'

'Anna.' Eddy took his eyes off the road and gazed at David for what seemed like a perilously long time. 'We got divorced. But we're still married here.' He tapped first his forehead, then his chest.

'You think she feels the same way, is that it?'

'No. Oh no.'

'Then I don't – '

'Albert's visit set me thinking. I want to help. I told him a few things.' Again that unroadworthy glance at David, supercilious and a trifle mocking. 'But not all the things he needs to know if he's to function.'

'Did he tell you what his job was?' David hadn't meant to sound so eager, but the words were out.

'No. He didn't have to.'

'What is it?'

Eddy drove in silence for a long way. When he spoke again he did not address himself to David's question at all.

'Juliet and I meet up, now and again.'

'I know. What – '

'It was she who told me about Kleist.'

'Who?' Then he guessed: 'The psychoanalyst?'

'Psycho-whatever, yeah. Him. She'd got his address and phone number.'

Juliet had said she did not know the name of Anna's mind doctor, and that was a lie. She did not trust her stepfather but she trusted Eddy; a powerful enough demonstration that blood was thicker than water, thought David, eyeing his chauffeur.

'Did you tell Albert about Anna seeing a shrink?' Eddy asked.

'No.'

'Great. Don't.'

'Why not?'

When Eddy did not answer, David's resentment boiled over. *'Why?'*

'Because he's not all there. Not quite out to lunch, but not exactly eating his sandwiches at the desk either, know what I mean?'

'What's wrong with him?'

'Which terminal do you want?'

'I'm asking you a question!'

288

'So am I. Do you want to fly today or not? Which bloody terminal?'

David spat out air through his teeth. 'Four.'

'Right. No need to get ratty. You mustn't tell Albert any more about Anna, understand?'

'I'm damned if I'm taking orders from you.'

'Your privilege, David. But I'm assuming you care about Anna.' He hesitated, suddenly less sure of himself. 'Care more than I ever did.'

'I love her, yes.' David looked down at his hands. His eyes prickled, he felt a bit of a fool . . . but then the momentary embarrassment passed and he said in a firm voice, meaning it: 'I love her more than I ever realized.'

'I understand that. If things had been different . . .' Eddy shrugged. 'All I gave a toss for in those days was bed. I never had any truck with frigid women, until Anna came along. I'm more tolerant now. I'd have given her more time . . .'

'Now *look*. If all you've got for me is maudlin sentimentality about your failure as a lover – '

'All right, keep your hair on.'

'Just tell me what Albert's job is. Just that.'

'You really don't know? Here we are . . . which entrance?'

Eddy was slowing for the last turn, David felt desperate, *he had no time*. 'What does Albert do?'

'If you don't already know . . .' Eddy squealed to a halt. 'I'm in no position to tell you, old man. Too scared. Sorry.'

'*Scared?*'

While David was still struggling to find words, Eddy leaned across him to open the nearside door. David looked at his watch: he could stay and argue or he could miss his plane. He hesitated a second longer, then raced into the terminal.

He drew a lot of money out of a cash dispenser before buying himself a standby ticket to Washington, grateful that the department had obliged him to keep his American visa up to date. They let him through into the departures area, although that didn't even amount to the first hurdle; it was what happened next that mattered. Pick a line, the shortest, get it over with, know the worst. One step, two steps. Pause. His passport officer was a middle-aged woman wearing thick glasses. Did she know this passenger had deliberately chosen her? Was it part of their training to detect such things?

Three steps. His heart was beating at a furious rate, his breath came and went, his stomach tied itself in that familiar knot. 'Good morning.' The woman nodded unconcernedly. *Great!* She glanced at something beneath the lip of her desk. Then she closed his passport with a snap and handed it back, her near-sighted eyes already focusing on the person behind him. David Lescombe did not interest her.

He made himself walk on, don't look back, bag onto the rollers, pass through the arch, *beep!* 'Turn out your pockets, would you sir? . . . Thank you . . .' Then he was in the huge neon-lit hangar of Terminal Four airside. By now his legs were wobbling so that he half walked, half ran to the nearest bank of seats and flopped just before his knees gave way, and he was still in England, this was the easy bit.

On the plane he felt a great desire to drink. The harder he fought the worse it became, but he managed to content himself with two Scotches. If they did little to raise his spirits, at least they took away some of the anger he felt towards Juliet. In the end he convinced himself that by not revealing Kleist's name she had been trying to protect Anna.

Something else that Eddy had said worried him a whole lot more. 'A frigid woman', were those the words he'd used? Something like that. Yet David could not come up with a less appropriate adjective to describe Anna. So what had changed between the divorce and her meeting David? *Who had brought about the change?*

Kleist?

What sort of therapist was he?

David turned to look out of the window. It was a sunny day; he could see the polar snows, only another couple of hours to go . . .

Entering the States proved as easy as leaving England. David told the cab driver to take him to an hotel on Dupont

Circle in the north-west of the city. He knew nothing about this place except that, according to the street map, it was right by a subway station. As the cab pulled into the kerb David caught sight of the brown four-sided pylon with an 'M' for Metro on top, and he felt a tickle of excitement. He could make this work.

He was pleased when they asked for an imprint of his credit card before they would give him a key. It salved his conscience.

The moment the door closed behind him he placed an order with room service, then opened his bag and scattered its contents over one of the two double beds. The waiter arrived with hamburger and french fries to see a guest who plainly intended to stay a while; he was on the phone, inquiring about a tour of the Hillwood Museum in two days' time. The waiter, who had received certain instructions unconnected with room service, did not think this looked like someone with a deep-seated interest in Russian art; but maybe, as he told the two CIA agents who were waiting for him downstairs, the guy just wanted to take in the gardens.

David counted to fifty after the man had taken his tip and left. He went to his bag, pulled out the tape recorder he had bought at Dixon's and switched it on. Then he grabbed a pale green cagoule very different from the grey suit in which he'd arrived, before silently letting himself out.

As he ran down the fire exit stairs two at a time he went over the calculations again, persuading himself that it would work: contrary to popular belief, fuelled by contemporary fiction, the CIA and FBI do not have limitless resources or manpower; they had no idea where you intended to stay in Washington, because you didn't make an advance reservation; it will take time to put men in place; you have been in this hotel for less than twenty minutes; *run!*

At the bottom of the flight he paused for long enough to throw the cagoule around his shoulders and put on a pair of sunglasses. He raced through the shopping mall to Connecticut Avenue; then he was in the Circle and pounding down the subway steps.

He bought a farecard and boarded the first Red Line train to come along. He played all the tricks he'd absorbed in cinemas over the years: waiting for the last moment before the doors closed, then jumping in; retracing steps; crossing from one set of tracks to another. At the interchange station on 12 and G Streets he took the Blue Line out to Arlington Cemetery. There he let several cabs go by before hailing one.

'Are you available for a long trip?'

A pair of suspicious eyes materialized in the driver's mirror. 'How long is long?'

'Baltimore?'

'*Balt*-imore? Shit, man, d'you know how far that is?'

'No. How far is it?'

'Two hun'nud dollars from here.'

'A hundred, says my map.'

'Well, I dunno . . . you got the cash?'

'Yes.'

'Lemme see it.'

David held up a clutch of bills.

'Yeah, yeah. Okay.'

The driver became taciturn after that, much to David's relief. He was hungry, he wanted to sleep, but he dared not relax until he was in Baltimore, on the Amtrak train, heading for New York. Then he could rest.

Is this how Anna did it when she fled, he wondered, as the landscape unwound across his tired vision? Was she alone then? Now? Or was she with Kleist?

How did he measure up against his wife's, his apparently *frigid* (God, how he hated Eddy!) wife's performance, when it came to deception? To flight?

It was going to work.

TWENTY-EIGHT

On Saturday afternoon, Anna visited the church again, only this time she went alone. She passed through the kitchen where Barzel and Kleist were at lunch. 'I'm going for a walk,' she said off-handedly, without so much as a glance at either of them. After she had gone about a hundred yards she looked back and to her surprise found that no one was following her. Anna frowned. What did that mean?

This time she did not pause at the tombs, but straightaway entered the church. Its door swung open with a rusty squeal of welcome. Dried leaves, stirred by the breeze, drifted around the floor with a desiccated scratching sound. At the far end stood the altar, a simple cross and two candlesticks; above them Anna could just make out traces of once colourful paintings of the apostles, done directly onto the wall. The only face she felt confident about identifying was John, reasoning that as Jesus loved him and he was seated next to the central figure in the fresco, he must be John.

There was a box of votive candles, and a brass stand to receive them. But the faithful stayed away, so no flame enlivened the interior, apart from a red spark in the lantern suspended from the ceiling which, she supposed, was God.

Anna placed a candle in the holder before realizing she had no means of lighting it. To one side hung a curtain, which half concealed a hole in the wall leading to the vestry. Inside this cubicle she found a rickety cupboard containing nothing save, oh miracle of miracles, a box of matches.

She sat cross-legged on the floor, watching her candle dissolve into the firmament, with only the red, red eye of God for company. Be vigilant, she warned herself. Use the time to think, before *he* comes . . .

At the beginning, Kleist had tried to help her find real answers. He'd failed. Anna would have liked to be able to say that was his fault. She was a lawyer, dollops of fault came easily to her, one for you, two for you, an infinity of fault for me . . . but here, surrounded by dead leaves, she said goodbye to it for the last time and without regret. She had built a professional existence on the basis that blame both could and should be apportioned; this was, she now saw, a false nostrum. Blame, responsibility, fault . . . these were drugs mankind took to inure themselves against the most painful knowledge: that each event anyway bore its own dread burden of significance. A child died. You could identify its murderer and drop him through a hole in the floor with a rope knotted around his neck. Another child died. The autopsy showed cancer and the parents cursed God. The child, in either case, remained dead.

As a barrister she had failed not because she was blind to this but because she had seen it daily and refused to give it credence.

It was the same with Juliet. Yes, she must face that memory now. Perhaps it would be easier here in the church, with God's help . . .

When the door crashed open she spun around to find Kleist framed against the hot brightness outside.

'I'm sorry, I startled you.'

She nodded token remission. It was not . . . after all . . . his fault. But when he tried to touch her, she stood up, pushing his hands away, and went to close the door. As she reached it, something made her raise her eyes above the level of the path. A man she had never seen before stood a dozen or so paces up the hill, one hand resting on the bole of a eucalyptus tree, the other in his pocket. Now she understood why they had let her leave the house: a guard was already in position, waiting. She slammed the door shut and leaned against it.

'Another Barzel?' she inquired.

'Anna.' He sat down on the floor, inviting her with a gesture to do the same. 'We have to talk.'

'I'm listening.' But she did not sit down.

'You've had the bad luck to fall in with someone who isn't what he appears to be.' He paused. 'Anna, this is very difficult to say.'

'Go on.'

'I work for an organization called *Hauptverwaltung Aufklä-rung*. HVA. It is the East German secret service.'

'They ordered you to steal David's file. Using me.'

'Anna, listen — '

'Just tell me one thing,' she said, ignoring him; and the resolution in her voice surprised her. 'Why did you do it, Gerhard?'

'Why?'

'Is that such a difficult question? Sixteen years we've known each other, we've been lovers, and now suddenly you're a spy. So yes, I'm asking why, what possessed you?'

He hesitated. 'I have a sister. Her name is Ilsa.'

Whatever Anna had been expecting, it wasn't this. First a spy, now a spy with a hitherto unsuspected sister. 'You never mentioned that. Not once.'

'There are lots of things I never mentioned.'

People were shut off. Anna thought she knew Gerhard, just as she thought she knew David and Juliet; she had lived her life in a certain way on the strength of such assumed knowledge. But she did not know them. She did not, in fact, know anyone — least of all herself. Gerhard had seen to that.

'For instance,' Gerhard went on, 'I told you I was born in Germany, and you believed I meant West Germany, but it wasn't so. My father was a high-up in the communist party. He got me out, to the west.'

'Why should he want to do that?'

'I was his . . . favourite. I could do no wrong in his eyes.

Ilsa, you see . . . our mother died in labour, when she was born. Father couldn't forgive Ilsa. He spoiled me.' He laughed, without humour. 'I longed to study in the west, have a good time as well. And although I didn't know it then, that suited some important people who wanted a tame therapist in London, or maybe Paris or New York.'

'These HVA people?'

'Yes. But when they stitch together such deals, there's always an insurance. Someone has to stay behind, to act as a magnet. A guarantee that you will come home, and a security for good behaviour while you are away.'

'And Ilsa was your magnet?'

He nodded again. 'She's younger than me. We were always as close as blood to the vein. When father died, it left just the two of us. She's a paediatrician. A good doctor. Dedicated.' He spoke the last word with a curious mixture of resentment and admiration. 'Before you and I met, HVA came to me one day. One of my patients was a typist in the cabinet office. She was terrified of her employers finding out she was in therapy. HVA told me to go to work on her, play on her fears.' He laughed, a hateful sound. ' "Make her fall in love with you, why don't you?" – that's what they said.'

'And you said yes.'

'I said no.'

'But – '

'I was . . . encouraged to think again. If I wanted Ilsa and her family to go on working. Eating. Walking about the streets. Don't you see the irony, Anna? If I bought this deal, I'd be prostituting everything I'd trained for. Whereas if I refused, the only effect would be to destroy my sister's career, and she's no prostitute, she's the real thing.'

'What happened?' Anna asked coldly.

'This wretched girl, this secretary, told me a few things that I passed on. Enough to satisfy HVA.'

'And when I married David, they came to you again.'

'Yes.' A long pause followed. 'You see, Ilsa and I, we . . . we had a sort of conspiracy. Against my father. Even before

296

I opened my first text-book I knew how wrong he was to blame Ilsa for our mother's death. It made us even closer, somehow. Now she's married, she has children, she's even more vulnerable. Anna, can't you find it in yourself to understand how I felt?'

'What do you want?' She was genuinely curious. 'Sympathy? Forgiveness?' She could have told him: you get used to the guilt, after a while. After a lifetime. But somehow that would have sounded cheap, and have brought her down to his level. So instead, 'I understand,' she said at last.

His expression told her that he found this hard to accept; but Anna found it equally difficult to elaborate. She imagined the HVA holding Juliet, or David; 'Behave or else,' that's what they would say, and she would behave, oh yes . . .

Kleist started to apologize, God knew what for, for everything perhaps, but she cut him off. 'No, don't say you're sorry, you don't have to, families can be so awfully bloody. Is there anything else, Gerhard?'

For a long time he continued to gaze down at the floor as if the secrets of his motivation lay concealed beneath the flagstones. He was wondering how to tell Anna that he had, after all, decided to sacrifice Ilsa; that in the end she had proved as expendable as every other woman in his life. Her or me; it had seemed the right thing to do at the time. Now . . .

'They are sending a submarine to take us off the island,' he said at last. 'That's what I came here to tell you. A Russian submarine.'

She fixed him with one of her level stares, the kind he most abhorred because she could use it to veil herself from him. 'Of course.'

'Why do you say of course?'

'They'll want to interrogate me, won't they? See what else I know about David's work. But why a submarine? Has everything else rusted away?'

'Berlin believes it would not be safe to move you by ship. You would be at sea too many days, visible, exposed.'

297

'You'll have to hypnotize me again, won't you? To remove whatever it was you put in my head at the beginning, to stop me leaving.'

'You knew about that?'

'Oh, I've worked out a lot of things. When does this happen?'

He did not answer immediately. Anna felt like a condemned prisoner who hears that her appeal for clemency has been rejected, that it remains only to pencil a date in the diary. *'When?'*

'Monday.'

'But that's the day after tomorrow!'

'Anna, what you said was right: I did implant a suggestion that you shouldn't try to leave here. So now we really must try and prepare you for the journey, sort you out.'

'But you've been doing that for years! That's why we're here, isn't it?' The bitterness was breaking through now. 'Because you sorted me, and shuffled me, like a deck of cards, and now I've come up trumps.'

'Anna . . . Therapists don't mould other people. They show their patients choices. You can influence someone else's choice. You can't make it for them.'

'You're trying to say that this is all *my* fault! What crap. What utter crap.'

'Unless you start to make an effort – '

'You'll *what*? Go on, tell me, you bastard! Twist me and bend me and make suggestions in the hope I'll believe I thought of them first . . . Come on, you can do it! After all, you made me into a *traitor*!'

She raised her hands to her eyes, wanting more than anything to sleep, perhaps faint; it didn't matter what form oblivion took as long as it came. But then she remembered: this man she had relied on for help over the past fifteen years and more had in fact been working against her. He'd cocooned her in layer over layer of lies and now she must somehow bludgeon her way into the real world, because if she did not save herself, nobody else could.

298

She had one solid, useful piece of information: she knew how he had smashed her. She understood his methods.

'Gerhard,' she said, wiping her eyes.

'Yes?'

'I'm all right now.' She lowered herself down beside him, in such a way that he could not easily see her face.

'I'm glad.'

'But there's something else I'd like to ask you.'

'What is it?'

'When they've finished with me in Berlin, or wherever it is, assuming I cooperate . . .'

'Well?'

'Can I go home then? To David?'

Kleist said nothing.

'Only, that's the one success you did have. He's all I ever prayed for, dreamed of, and I love him.' She looked down at her hands, folded in her lap. 'I love him,' she repeated, 'and he must be feeling desolate beyond belief.'

'He's a sensible man. He'll come to terms with it.'

'But he can't, you see. Don't you realize what he must be *feeling*? He thinks that I've abandoned him, that I don't love him.' She paused. 'Another death without a corpse. You remember, we were talking yesterday: the worst thing in the world?'

When Kleist remained silent she raised her head and looked at him beseechingly. 'If you promise me I can go back to David, I'll do anything you want. I won't try to escape.'

He was almost convinced. 'You promise?'

'Yes. You can hypnotize me, if you like. If that will make you feel more . . . more secure. Only please don't use the drugs again, they're so dreadful. Just put me into a trance. Relax me. Do it now.'

'Here?'

'Yes. It's peaceful here.'

But before he could decide, the church door opened and they heard Barzel say: 'Kleist!'

'What is it?' Kleist made no attempt to hide his anger.

Barzel looked between him and Anna for a long time, appraising the situation. At last he said, 'I have to talk to you.'

Kleist followed him into the sunlight, closing the church door behind him. 'Well?'

'I spoke to Berlin half an hour ago. The woman's husband is starting to make a nuisance of himself.'

'But I thought our people in England were going to warn him off?'

'Warn him off, talk to him, find out how much he knew.'

'Then why – '

'Because they botched it! Lescombe alerted MI5 and he's been doubly careful since then. He doesn't scare easily. Now he's on his way to America. Can you guess why?'

Robyn Melkiovicz, Anna's best friend. Kleist saw the danger at once; but how much did Barzel see? 'No,' he snapped. 'And you worry too much. He'll never trace me here.'

'You're right. It's being taken care of.'

'What does that mean?'

Barzel ignored the question. Instead he nodded in the direction of the church and said, 'You're losing control. This isn't a good time to lose control. Get me?'

Kleist stared at him. 'Yes,' he said at last. 'I understand.'

Barzel sloped off down the path. Kleist waited a few moments, long enough to pull himself together, before returning to the church. 'Anna?' he called softly. 'Time to go home, now.'

'What did Barzel want?'

'Nothing. Nothing to worry about at all.'

TWENTY-NINE

It was night, the streets of New York were jammed with cars and pedestrians. David made his initial pass quickly, first examining the façade of Robyn's apartment building from the opposite side of Park Avenue, then walking by close enough to get a good look at the doorman, wearing his peaked hat, with a pair of white gloves tucked into the left epaulette of his overcoat. He turned off the avenue and ducked into the first bar he found. He ordered a Scotch, straight up, found the last empty table, and wrote a note. Then he went straight back into Park, walking fast, and accosted the doorman, who had just escorted a mink-clad lady from a Mercedes to the door.

'For Robyn Melkiovicz,' he said, handing the note to the man. 'You might be good enough to inform her that it's somewhat urgent.' David did not know he had such reserves of true-grit Brit accent to call upon. 'And I hope you will have a drink on me later this evening. Good day.' Wrapped around the envelope was a twenty dollar bill.

David walked away without looking back, turned right at the next intersection and broke into a jog. He loped all the way around the block, glad to be jostled by passers-by, because they afforded him what he most needed: cover.

The FBI would be closing in now. Perhaps they had already intercepted the note. David pushed through the door of the same bar he'd visited earlier and ordered another Scotch.

Fifteen minutes, he had written in his note. Such and such a bar in fifteen minutes' time; don't phone anyone, don't

301

tell a neighbour, you're being watched, your phone is tapped, you may be in great danger. He had signed himself 'Anna Lescombe's husband, David' and he had included the photograph found in Anna's desk, not knowing if that would work, but praying, praying . . .

He looked at his watch. The CIA and FBI might be finite organizations, but their capacities were great. He had been on the run now for six hours. People would be looking for him, a lot of people. She was late. She wasn't coming. She had not received his note, she was out of town. He should have called, *no, you couldn't call, her phone may be tapped.*

From where he was sitting he had a view of the door. Every so often it swung open to admit a wave of cold air from the street into the bar's overheated fug, and David tensed, sure it would be the police. Feeling another blast of cold he raised his head in time to see a boisterous trio of men come in. The door swung shut.

He half rose in his seat. A second before the door closed he had caught sight of a figure outside. Female. Hands thrust deeply into the pockets of a short jacket, spoiling its shape. Not walking, not talking to anyone, just standing there.

It was her, he knew it had to be her. Suppose she had called the police, 'Officer, there's a man trying to molest me . . .'; what if she had shown his note to someone, 'Go to the bar,' they might have told her, 'persuade him to come outside in the street, we can overpower him there . . .'

What should he do?

A man was sitting at the bar alongside a woman who looked considerably younger than her companion. Now they stood up and bade noisy goodbyes to the barman. They seemed to be in the middle of a good-natured argument.

'Look,' the man was saying. 'Look, on Monday, you just . . . you just *tell* them, right?'

'Oh, you know, you can't just tell those guys . . .'

'No. Listen. Wait. You just, you know, you go in, and you say, "Look, fellahs . . ." '

They had reached the door. As the man opened it, David

caught another glimpse of the person on the pavement. She hadn't moved. He stood up and manoeuvred himself behind the couple who were leaving, did it in such a way that to anyone outside he must look like a member of their party. *Don't scare her. Do not, whatever happens, scare this woman* . . .

As the three of them went out David peeled away from the couple, who had not noticed his existence, and stopped while still a few feet short of the lone figure.

'Don't come any closer,' she cried warningly, holding up both hands. 'Stay where you are.'

David froze. His world began to fall apart. She'd tricked him! Now passers-by would rescue her, maybe somebody had a gun, to come so close and now this!

'Look, I'm telling ya . . .'

'You know, look, will you please listen . . . ?'

The sound of the departing couple's altercation died away. David realized that none of the pedestrians on the street had stopped, or so much as looked in his direction. People went right on hurrying by.

'Robyn Melkiovicz?'

'Stay away from me!'

'I wrote you a note.'

This time the woman said nothing. David took a step forward and she at once retreated, but silently.

'I'm David Lescombe.' He spoke fast, knowing he had seconds left. 'Anna's husband. She's in danger. I don't know where she is. I'm trying to help her.' He stopped, awaiting a reaction, any reaction, from the woman in front of him. 'You're my last chance.'

'Oh, my God,' he heard her say softly. Did her voice have an impediment . . . ? 'Oh, my God,' she repeated and suddenly he knew what was wrong with her, she was crying, at the end of her rope . . .

'Come and have a drink,' he said gently. 'Please.'

Robyn held her fists to her eyes. 'Give me a minute.' At last she lowered her hands and whispered, 'Let's get off the sidewalk. I feel . . .' A violent shake of the head completed the sentence.

He took her inside. There were fewer customers now, it was getting late. They found a place flanked by two other empty tables, right at the back. David ordered a third Scotch for himself and turned to Robyn.

'Perrier . . . no, Canadian Club. On the rocks.'

She sat with both hands cupped around the glass, staring at him across the table. He tried to form an impression of her but she was such a mixture of things. Medium height, slim, with no bust to speak of. She wore a baggy black jacket over dark pants and looked as if she might be going out on an evening date, except that her auburn hair had been coiled on top of her head in braids: a tight, formal style more appropriate to women lawyers at work than at play. Her features were small, delicate, with shadows around the deep eye sockets. Her nose had an upturned tilt, which would have given her an appealing childlike quality, were it not offset by the mouth, which was hard to start with and made harder by dark lipstick applied in a thick layer. Her face was oval-shaped, the eyes beautiful, having a misty quality of all-knowing intuition.

She was the woman in the photograph. She was lovely. She was also very frightened.

'I've been warned not to have anything to do with you,' Robyn said. 'With anybody.'

He stared, trying to make sense of what she'd said. How could they think he posed a threat? 'Warned? Who by?'

'They said they were CIA.'

'So why are you meeting me now?'

'Because . . .' Her voice shook, as did her hands when she tried to drink; David heard the click of glass against her teeth. 'Because I'm just worried to death about Anna . . .'

The last word was swallowed up in a marsh of unshed tears.

'That makes two of us.'

'These men who came to see me . . .' Robyn swallowed a

couple of times and went on, 'They didn't . . . smell American. I have a friend who works for the FBI. I asked him to find out if they were levelling with me.'

'When?'

'This afternoon. Not long before I got your note. He's going to check it out and stop by for a drink later, at my apartment.'

David sat back. He mustn't be around when the FBI man came. By now his would be the hottest name on the entire Atlantic seaboard.

'I want to come to sit next to you,' he said softly. 'I'm unhappy not being able to see the door. Okay?'

She hesitated, searching his face. 'All right.'

He changed seats. 'Those men you described,' he said, 'may be dangerous to me.' Albert lurched into his mind. 'Was one of them young, with pink-tinted glasses?'

'No. Nothing like that. Middle-aged. Slav faces. Or German, maybe. Russian. Kind of rough, anyway.'

German. Russian.

'Did they mention me by name?'

'No. Just . . . if anyone came around asking questions about Anna Lescombe, say nothing.'

'Did they tell you to telephone them if anyone did come snooping around?'

She shook her head.

'Didn't that strike you as odd?'

'The whole thing was odd. That's what I'm telling you, I'm so scared.'

'Me too.'

That was the truth. If Anna had gone over to the other side, 'they,' the mysterious hunters-and-watchers who lived on the borders of his imagination, could consist of more than just Albert and his cohorts. 'They' could have been sent to guard and protect their latest acquisition. 'They', these new ones, intended to keep Anna. 'They' did not intend to let a mere husband devalue their investment.

He remembered the men from the Audi, in that narrow Cornish lane. That pair, too, had seemed 'kind of rough'.

'I don't think there's any need for you to be frightened,' he said at last. 'Nobody wants to hurt you.'

'You don't understand! It's Anna I'm worried about. She's in trouble, I just know, that's all. David, we were that *close*! If something happens to Anna I feel it, here, inside, like somebody is playing a musical instrument in my chest.'

'I had no idea,' he said, sounding foolish in his own ears. 'I mean . . . no idea.'

The bar was hot and stuffy, but David felt cold right through to the marrow of his bones. He was shivering.

'Are you okay?' Robyn was regarding him strangely.

'No. I'm not.'

He signalled for more drinks, and all the while his mind circled round and around the same old territory: he was being hunted, he was probably being watched, right now, and he was in danger of losing his life.

He examined the other tables, one by one. Those yuppie types over by the bar, were they CIA? KGB? The two women sitting in a window alcove, talking with their hands, did they have pistols in their bags?

Robyn jumped when David brought his fists down on the table top. He was breathing quickly. His eyes were clenched shut.

'What's the matter?'

He shook his head.

'Are you in some kind of trouble?'

David nodded three emphatic times.

'Is it to do with Anna? It is.'

Again the three forceful nods.

'You have to tell me! She's my best friend.'

David had not been entrusted with that knowledge. Now, looking across the table at Robyn hugging a glass as if it were clay and she could mould it to her will, he felt an echo of the old, familiar rage; but only for an instant. All that mattered was finding Anna. So he swallowed the anger and said: 'This is going to sound crazy.'

'Try me.'

306

'Anna's gone away. It looks as though she may have taken some papers of mine; they're missing, anyhow. Important papers. The sort of papers that men with German or maybe Russian faces would like to read.'

'Oh God.' It was hardly even a whisper.

'I've been looking for her. But if I look too hard, maybe, just maybe, they'll try to stop me looking any harder.' He burst into a cackle, making Robyn start. 'God, I told you it was crazy!'

'It's not. David, do you understand? I want to help.'

He told her about the last few days: the visits to Anna's chambers, her daughter and mother, Albert, Eddy, the flight to America, the simple tricks that had allowed him to stay one step ahead of 'them'.

'And now I don't know what to believe,' he concluded. 'Broadway said she was being sued for this huge amount of money, her career was in the rough; did you know she drank?'

'She could handle it.'

'Oh, yes! She could handle keeping it from me, anyway. Then Juliet told me Anna had been seeing some kind of shrink. Eddy would have me believe my wife was frigid.'

'Take it easy.'

'You say that, but I didn't know *any* of those things! Can you imagine what it's like, realizing you've been married for nine years to someone you can't recognize, not even *from her own family's description* of her?'

Robyn shook her head.

'Then take this man Albert. Now, him I did trust. Do you know why? It's because when I came out of my chief's office that day, he was waiting in the corridor. It never occurred to me *not* to trust him! He was there. He belonged.'

'I would have done the same.'

'But if he's not what he seemed, and Eddy said as much . . . who is he?' He rubbed a hand over his forehead. 'Robyn, can you tell me anything at all that might help me find Anna?'

'It's not easy. Oh, Jesus, I don't know. I have to go back to the start . . . I came to London. It was a routine sabbatical. My firm wanted me to go, gain first-hand experience of the London commercial court.'

'Yes.'

'She . . . Anna was so . . . so damn *kind* to me. She knew I had no friends in England, so she was always suggesting things for me to do. We shared an office.'

'What beats me is why she never brought you home.'

She took a deep breath and sighed it out with great force. 'This is where it gets tacky.'

'Robyn. *Please . . .*'

'We had something in common. I'd been going through a hard time here in New York. I was in therapy. That's the connection.'

'I don't get it.'

'That's how I met Gerhard. But then she told me you didn't know about him. And . . . well, she thought you and I wouldn't relate, anyway. She saw us as two very different kinds of people, and she was afraid I might blurt out something about Gerhard without thinking – I tend to do that. So we figured we had to kind of make a choice, you know? I could be part of Anna's home scene, or part of Gerhard. And . . .' Another sigh. 'We chose the latter. I'm sorry, I guess this must be very hard for you.'

David wanted to shout with frustration. 'I don't follow anything you're saying. Who's Gerhard?'

'Gerhard Kleist. Anna's therapist.'

'Kleist . . . Eddy talked about a Kleist.'

'She'd been seeing him on and off for nearly thirteen years, when I first met her. That was 1986.'

'Thirteen. Years.'

Robyn nodded. When she put a hand over his, David scarcely noticed. 'She wanted to protect you. She didn't think she deserved you. She believed that if you knew she'd ever needed therapy, you'd abandon her, maybe. She couldn't take that chance.'

He pulled his hand away.

'But it made life hard for her. There was no one she could discuss her treatment with. Not even you, especially not you. So when I came into her life, it was like springtime for Anna. Suddenly she could talk about experiences with someone who'd been there too.'

'I want you to tell me something straight. Why did Anna need therapy in the first place? What brought her to Kleist?'

'I can't tell you that.'

'You've got to.'

'No. It was her secret. She dreaded it ever coming out. She knew it could ruin her career and break up her marriage: her words, not mine.'

'You've told me all this, and now we get to the really important part you're refusing to help me.'

Robyn shrugged. Her hard mouth had set in a straight line; he could detect no sign of give in her. 'This man Kleist,' he said at last. 'Have you any idea where — '

'Yes. I know where he might be.'

'You do! But that's wonderful.'

'No, it's not. David, there's more you have to know. Anna and I had a fight. I don't know if the fight is ended yet.'

His mouth was dry. There must be some limit to the horrors this woman could describe, *surely*?

'I didn't realize how . . . how she felt about Gerhard. So I became friends with him. We got along fine. He's very attractive to women.'

Now David's heart was pumping blood too fast for his system to cope with. A lot of things seemed to be going on inside his body, none of them pleasant.

'We had an affair,' Robyn said. 'He took me to his villa, in the Mediterranean. On an island. Anna was . . . mad.'

David gazed at her, at first refusing to follow where she led. 'You mean . . . it's possible that she and Gerhard are . . .'

'Together. Yes.'

'She . . . felt something for this man?'

Robyn said nothing.

'She loved him? Was crazy about him?' His voice rose. 'Had the hots for him?'

'David, please!'

'Well, *which*?'

Robyn drew a deep breath. 'Years ago, long before she met you, Anna had an affair with Kleist. And although the affair stopped, she remained fixated with him.'

David had been expecting it, but the hard reality still knocked him cold. Long minutes passed before he spoke again.

'The affair stopped?' he managed to say at last.

'Yes. Anna told me that, so did Gerhard, and I believed them. David, she loves you very much. You're the best thing that ever happened to her.'

'But you think she may have run to him?'

'It's possible.'

'Why?' he said, and his voice was savage. 'Why would she do that, if the affair was over?'

'Because whenever she found herself in anything deep, any bad time, she would go back to him for therapy.'

'You mean, she went on seeing him for . . . how long did you say?'

'She first met him in about 1973, I think. He cured her of her problem and afterwards they became lovers.'

'How long did that last?'

'I'm not sure. All I know is that it was over when she met you.'

'But she was still seeing him?'

'As a doctor, yes. And only when she needed help, not on a regular basis.'

David tried to do sums in his head. 'After you came back to New York . . . which was when?'

'Two years back.'

'Two years . . . 1987. After 1987, do you know if she consulted Kleist again?'

'She never mentioned him in her letters. I guess she would have done if she'd seen him. She wanted to wean herself

310

from her dependency on Gerhard. She felt it was bad for her.'

'Yet now you're saying she may have gone to him again?'

'From what you tell me, I think she may be having some kind of breakdown. If so, Gerhard's the one she'll go to.'

He was silent for a while, trying to come to terms with the knowledge that Anna could not take her problems to her husband, only to another man whom he had never met. A man who had been to bed with his wife. Who whilst in bed had taught her . . .

'You told me that you quarrelled,' he said at last. 'What was that about?'

'Gerhard and Anna managed to find a way through their affair to a kind of equilibrium. But when she found out that he and I had . . . she was wild. I mean, truly wild. She knew she was being irrational, she admitted that. Still, if I'd foreseen the trouble it would cause, I'd never have gone with Gerhard.'

'But you did go. To the island.' Suddenly his brain completed the circuit. 'That's where the photograph was taken!'

'Yes. The photograph is what started the fight. It was the first she knew that I'd gone away with Gerhard.'

'Have you heard from Kleist lately – is that how you know where he is?'

'I don't *know*. A hunch, that's all. And no, I haven't heard from him.'

While speaking she had brought the photograph out of her handbag, David's note still wrapped around it. Now he took it from her and read the name on the board yet again. 'Do you speak Greek?' he asked.

'No.'

'You don't know what this sign says?'

'Gerhard told me it's the name of the place. "The Little House." Just that.'

'Would you know how to get there again?'

'Yes.'

'Can you tell me?'

'I don't know, David.' She was facing him now, her gaze coolly analytical. 'I'm worried what you might do, frankly.'

His eyes could not meet hers. There was no answer to her doubts.

'David, listen to me. Please. I feel like Anna and I are . . . well, hewn from the same stone. She's still my dearest friend in all the world. We quarrelled, yes, but we went some way to making up and you know something? Every day I curse myself for my mistake in angering her. And if anything bad happened to her because of something I did, or said . . .'

'I understand. But *you* must understand this: I love Anna. I'm her husband. I'm learning things about her that shock me, and, yes, anger me as well. But I know she's in trouble and she needs help. That's all I want to do: help her.'

He gazed at Robyn, putting every ounce of feeling he possessed into it, until she wavered.

'You promise me you won't harm her?'

'I promise you I'll help her all I can. And if when I've talked to her I'm convinced she's doing this because she genuinely wants to, if she'd rather be with Kleist than with me, then . . .' He drew a deep breath ' . . . I'll let her go.'

He had been putting off the moment for too long; but as soon as he spoke the words aloud he knew that this decision was the right one.

'You mean that? You love her that much?'

'I do.'

For a long moment she sat motionless. Then she reached for her bag and took out a pen. 'Do you have paper?'

'I don't want anything written down, in case I'm stopped. Just tell me; I'll remember.'

Falteringly she began to recite directions. 'You start by going to Corfu. Then you have to get to the other island. There's a man with a speedboat, it's quicker than the ferry. His name's Amos, I think. Yes – Konstantine Amos, with a K. . . . He'll take you to the west coast, this really small place called Avlaki, just a landing pier . . .'

When at last she had finished, and David had repeated

each leg of the journey several times to impress it on his memory, they knew it was time for them to part. 'There's one more thing,' he said as he stood up. 'Your FBI contact. What will you tell him – about me, I mean? This talk . . . and about Gerhard?'

'Tell him . . . ?'

'I need a start. Maybe I won't make it as far as the airport, but I want at least to *try* and get to Anna before anyone else does. Please don't say anything about the villa.'

'I don't know how long I can hold out. I'll do my best.'

'Thank you.'

The door opened, admitting a breath of air from the street, and David looked up fearfully. But it was only a middle-aged man who went to sit at the bar, where he ordered a beer and proceeded to lose himself in his newspaper.

Robyn tensed. She could not take her eyes off the newcomer. David stared at her. 'What's the matter?'

'David. Oh, David . . .' He saw with amazement that tears were coursing down her cheeks. 'I am so . . . so very sorry.'

Still he did not understand.

'I didn't level with you. I told my FBI friend I was coming to meet you, and where. I was so scared. You have no idea. I was so scared.'

The man sitting at the bar folded his newspaper neatly. He took a first, appreciative sip from his glass. Only then did he turn to raise ironical eyebrows in David's direction.

THIRTY

Shorrocks leaned back to rest his elbows on the arms of his chair, hands steepled in front of him. 'Run that past me again,' he said softly.

Hayes coughed in the way a person does when he's nervous and wants to conceal it. 'Lescombe, ah, checked in Saturday around three o'clock and left a tape recorder in his room. It made noises like a guy eating, knives and forks, you know, and then taking a long, long shower. Fancy editing, acoustics.'

'Fancy my arse,' Albert said. 'Anyone could do it. How long before you registered?'

'Say one hour.'

'An *hour*?'

'Tape lasted forty-five minutes. Then there was nothing for a while and our guys got suspicious.'

'And then,' Shorrocks said, 'you lost him. This civil servant, this . . . amateur.'

Hayes said nothing.

It was just after dawn on Sunday morning, six days since Anna Lescombe had disappeared. Hayes, Redman, Shorrocks and Albert occupied a barely decorated cubbyhole without a window on the top floor of the American Embassy in London. A background hum was supposedly guaranteed to frustrate would-be eavesdroppers but Shorrocks mistrusted modern technology. He had seen it fall apart too often.

Redman and his two English guests sat in easy chairs placed around a coffee table. Each held a copy of Hayes'

314

report; they might have been actors at a read-in. Hayes alone occupied a stark metal and plastic chair. He was higher than the others and this should have given him an edge but did not. Perched up there he looked more like a schoolboy on trial before his betters; prefects in the day-room, perhaps, conducting an informal inquiry into misdemeanours with the fags.

'I am sorry, Jeremy.' Redman's voice was rich with melancholy. 'No one's infallible.'

'Funny.' Shorrocks was enjoying this. 'Funny, I thought that was the point of your people, Louis. Infallibility. Or so we were given to believe.'

'Where is he now?' Albert did not expect a concrete answer, but he wanted the question written into the record.

'We'll pick him up, sure thing.' Hayes looked straight ahead as he spoke, not meeting anyone's eye. 'Just a matter of time. He must know people in the US, we can trace them.'

'Then you'll have better luck than we did,' Shorrocks said in a tone that undercut his polite smile.

'At least we know where we stand,' said Redman. 'By running away, Lescombe proves he was in it from the start.' His face brightened. 'As we did suggest to you earlier, I seem to remember.'

'You did,' Shorrocks acknowledged. 'Although if men attacked me in a Cornish backwater and Hayes broke into my house a couple of nights later, I might be tempted to run, too.'

'Yes, well . . . At least you'd agree it's unlikely Lescombe couldn't have known his wife was consulting a psychiatrist over a long period?'

'He's not a psychiatrist,' Albert put in, with tendentious appeal to accuracy. 'He's a psychotherapist and hypnotherapist, as well as being a qualified psychologist.'

'Thank you, Albert.' Louis Redman's most ambassadorial smile was Albert's sole reward. 'To resume, however: what we have to concentrate on now is, who's he going to meet

315

and where does he intend to meet them? His wife seems the logical supposition on the first point.'

'Don't *think* so, Louis,' Shorrocks ventured. 'She went east, he's gone west. Ne'er the twain shall meet, I fear. Kipling, and so on. Looks like a marital double-cross, after all.'

'Well, okay, Jeremy.' Redman dusted an invisible piece of fluff from his right knee. He did it several times, peering closer with each sweep of the palm, but the fluff was evidently a resistant strain. 'Do you have any suggestions, maybe?'

Shorrocks and Albert exchanged glances before simultaneously focusing on Hayes' hunched figure. It was obvious that they could think of at least one.

'Kleist,' Shorrocks said, 'appears to be the key. Albert, you're a little more up on this . . . ?'

'I went back to the restaurant with a photograph we dug out of his permanent-residence application: rather old, but they recognized him at once. So there's an obvious, long-standing connection between him and Anna Lescombe. He's disappeared, too. We're wiring our photo to Athens, so that they can show it to the airfield people at that place, what was it called . . . ?'

'Igouminitsa.'

'Igouminitsa, right. We've also got our consul working on it, but we don't expect much from him.'

'Why not?' Redman asked.

'First, because our consulate on Corfu isn't geared to this kind of thing; secondly because the holiday season's just starting to build and the place is full of tourists. Greek organization isn't the greatest, of course. Trying to interest the KYP in tracing what looks like an unhappily married woman running away with her lover requires more ingenuity than we possess. Sorry.'

'Even if the woman in question has a NATO file stashed away in her luggage?'

'An *American* file, Louis.' Albert paused to let the message sink in. 'I'm sure it won't come as any surprise to learn that you're not terribly popular in Athens at the best of times. In any event, you don't want us to be too specific, remember? Keep the lid on, and all that?'

'Okay, okay.' Redman sighed. 'Didn't this man Kleist leave a forwarding address? Contact phone number?'

'We have a problem there. We don't want to ask too many questions up front.'

'Why?'

Shorrocks cleared his throat, determined to take the heat off Albert. 'Policy, Louis. We don't know what we're dealing with. Kleist could be heading up a cell. If, for the sake of example, his housekeeper – he has a housekeeper, by the way – is in cahoots with him, it would be bad tactics to march up to the front door with a warrant.'

Redman essayed another of his famously diplomatic smiles. Somebody, perhaps a CIA charm expert, had schooled him in the need to reveal all the teeth back as far as the molars when you smiled; since his teeth were big and he suffered from receding gums, the effect could be disturbingly sharklike, the opposite of what he intended. 'Therefore?'

'Therefore, we intend to enter by the, ah, back door. Which takes a little time to organize. As you know.'

Or should do by now, Albert mentally added. Except that you CIA people all seem to possess the two-second memories associated with particularly slow-witted goldfish.

'Time is something we do not have.'

'I know, Louis, but – '

'Excuse me, Jeremy, but I'd like to give you the one piece of good news. As far as our detectors on the ground can tell, the Soviets haven't yet taken a single step that might be consistent with their knowing about Krysalis. State now accepts that the risk of their obtaining the file outweighs any short term inconvenience factor in Europe from disclosing the Krysalis directives and options to our allies. If it will help obtain their cooperation, tell them what the file contains. As of now nothing, repeat nothing, is barred.'

'Thank you, Louis.' Shorrocks toyed briefly with the idea of telling Redman that this permission had already been anticipated, and thought better of it. 'Albert, I'd like you to liaise – '

An electric bell set just below the ceiling in one corner of the airless little room suddenly sprang to life. Redman grunted in annoyance and jerked his thumb at Hayes, who went to open the door and returned carrying a sheet of paper. Redman looked at it, then handed the sheet back to Hayes with a lift of the eyebrows, but the other man shook his head.

'Jeremy, does this name mean anything to you?'

Shorrocks took the paper and shared it with Albert. 'Russian?' queried the latter. 'Polish, perhaps?'

'I mean, for Christ's sake . . .' Hayes sounded relieved to have at last been presented with an outlet for his feelings. 'What kind of a name is Melkiovicz?'

THIRTY-ONE

Tom Burroughs bought his own ticket first, careful not to look at David, before going to rejoin Robyn in the cafeteria. When David gave the British Airways clerk his American Express card and her phone call verified his status as meriting a ticket for the morning Concorde to London, he wondered if life would ever again revert to a semblance of normality.

Tom saw him coming a long way off and was on his feet by the time David arrived back at their table. 'Take it easy,' he said softly, guiding him into a chair.

'I'm broke now, I suppose. More than broke.'

'Me too.' Tom glumly waved his own boarding card. 'But look at it this way. Do you want to find your wife or not? If so, how much is she worth to you?'

David made the effort to smile. 'I really can't thank you enough for offering to come with me. It makes me feel a whole lot safer.'

'Good. Now drink some orange juice and relax.'

But as David looked from Robyn's concerned face to the genial countenance of her FBI friend, he felt only the tension of the past few hours. The grey and white boarding pass in his top pocket, evidence of a freedom that for the moment was being allowed to continue, merely heightened his feeling of foreboding.

Last night, the FBI man introduced himself as Tom Burroughs before shepherding him and Robyn to a Pontiac Sunbird parked in an alley near the bar where they'd been drinking. David, supposing this was the end of the line, had got into the back without a protest. The first hint that he might still have a chance came when Tom parked the car under one of the approaches to Brooklyn Bridge and switched licence plates, a tactic he was to repeat twice more before dawn.

'Shouldn't really be doing this,' he confided as he got back into the driver's seat, next to Robyn. 'But seems like Robyn okays you . . . is that right, hon . . . ?' (She nodded.) ' . . . And I don't want anyone to know where you are for the time being. David – I'm going to call you David, if I may?'

'Yes.'

'We have some serious things to discuss.' He shifted into first gear and pulled away from the kerb, taking great care over his lane discipline. 'Depending on how it goes, I may make a report, I don't know yet. The thing is, I feel I ought to have some instructions concerning you, and yet I don't. It bugs me. I tingle right down my backbone – you ever have that sensation?'

'Sometimes.'

'Okay. You listen to your tingling?'

'Sometimes.'

Tom laughed: a relaxed, country-club sound that David found reassuring. 'For the record, you are officially clean as far as my office is concerned. We have no interest in you. Now you tell me: should I be interested in you?'

David had hesitated. He felt drawn to this man: a handsome, middle-aged, just the right side of fat American with a pleasing manner and homely voice that reminded him of the actor James Stewart. But the thought of confiding in a stranger, even though he was a friend of Robyn's, gave him pause.

Robyn, sensing his doubts, turned around and said, 'You'd better tell him. The harder you make it for him, the harder he'll have to be on you.'

David, still prevaricating, had replied lightly, 'He can be hard?'

'Don't be fooled. He's hard.'

They'd driven around New York while David, haltingly at

first, and then with greater fluency, explained the situation. At one point Tom stopped in Chinatown to stock up with spare ribs and Coke, but mostly he just drove without speaking. When David at last had finished he kept his thoughts to himself for a good few miles.

'One thing occurs to me,' he said at last, 'and it's this. We aren't stopping off any place until we get to the airport tomorrow morning.' He checked his watch. 'Correction: this morning.'

'You're letting me go back to England?'

'I've no reason to hold you. But I sure as hell know one thing, my English friend: I *ought* to have a reason. If all you say is true, and I don't doubt a word of it, the CIA should be breaking every back in Langley to finger you. There's a procedure for that: well-worn and true. It involves briefing the FBI for what we call cooperative action. Yet you don't show up in that frame.'

'You've made inquiries about me?'

'Sure. Where the FBI and the CIA interface, there's grey areas. Give and take, you know? We hack their computer, they hack ours, nobody sweats. But sometimes the grey area turns into a *big* black hole. So much nothingness you can't believe.'

'What does that tell you?'

Tom shrugged. 'I just don't know. I plug in my computer and tap a few keys, and what my screen notifies me is that David Emmanuel Lescombe exists and is of relevance to the United States of America, but that at the same time he does not exist and is of no relevance to the United States of America. With me?'

'Enough to feel pretty sick.'

'Yeah. I need gas; you guys watch out for some place open, will you?'

They found an all-night gas station. While Tom went inside to pay and buy candy, David leaned forward across the front seat and said, 'What am I to do? Trust him?'

'Emphatically yes.'

321

'But why should he help me? Isn't he double-crossing his own side?'

'I should let him worry about that. He's coming over; ask him yourself.'

David waited until Tom had again settled himself in his seat. Then he said: 'Why are you doing this?'

'Helping you, you mean?' Tom eased his Sunbird into the scant, small hours traffic before he replied. 'Robyn's a part of it,' he said at last. 'That's a big plus. But the real answer to your question is that the CIA have been trashing us for too long. I think you're a straight guy and they're using you. I've seen it before and it makes me want to puke. Call it idealism, if you like.' He gave one of his relaxed laughs. 'In fact, I really wouldn't mind if you accused me of being an idealist: no one ever has before.'

'That's it? The reason, I mean.'

'I could tell you a lot of things about the politics of inter-agency infighting, David, but they wouldn't help you. Just accept that you're kind of useful to me and a few of my friends, right now. You . . . well, let's say you represent an interesting opportunity to do good in the world.'

'I'm grateful. But I can't make it up to you.'

'Yes, you can.'

'How?'

'By pretending we've never met.' When David laughed, Tom's voice sharpened into hostility. 'I'm serious. If this goes wrong, and someone asks you how you spent tonight – lie.' He glanced over his shoulder. 'You too, hon.'

David heard the tension in his voice and knew he wasn't faking it. 'I will,' he said quietly. 'That's a promise.'

'Thanks. Now. I've been doing some thinking. Seems to me, your worst problem is with the goons who called on Robyn.'

'The Eastern Bloc?'

'The whatever, yes. I'm guessing they're from the same outfit that attacked you in Cornwall. They've tried to speak to your daughter: no joy – we know that from your conver-

322

sation with Albert. They've tried to neutralize Robyn: no joy. But what's clear from all of this is that they want to break off any line of inquiry that might lead you to Anna.'

David swallowed. 'Break . . . ?'

'Oh, let's not get over-dramatic. Nobody's died yet, and if they wanted to kill you, believe me, they could. Something else to remember: there's other, very powerful agencies who don't want you stopped at all. Your people, MI6 and the rest. If I read the signs right, they're praying you'll find your wife and anyway, they think you know where she is. So they'll help you run wherever, no problem there; not until you either find her, or give up the hunt. Then they'll move in on you.'

'Which leaves?'

'The good old Company. The CIA: US of A Unlimited, incorporated in the state of nowhere, without liability or responsibility. And I'll tell you: after the Eastern Bloc, as you call it, that's what's worrying me most.'

'So what am I to do?'

'Keep running. Run fast. If you can beg or steal enough money for Concorde, do it. And count cents.'

'What?'

'It's a saying we have. It means, oh . . . be suspicious of your own mother, heck, *especially* your own mother. Don't take anything at face value. Don't trust anyone, assume everything put in front of you is rotten through and through. Check the small change. Count cents.'

'I will.'

'You know what? The more I think about this, the more I wish we were in England right now. There's people there who'd talk to me.'

'About what?'

'The CIA's true motivation in all this. You see, David – ' Even though they were in the car and isolated from the street, he lowered his voice ' – an increasingly important task of my department is to monitor the law-breaking activities of other US intelligence agencies. Unfortunately, there's more to monitor all the time.'

'Then why not go with David?' Robyn's tone was urgent. 'If you say there are people in England who'd help . . .'

'You can't ask him that.' David meant his voice to sound final, but the yearning showed through nonetheless. 'He can't just leave his job and spend a fortune on air fares.'

'But this *is* his job – he just said so.' Robyn grasped Tom's shoulder. 'Please go with David. You can do it, the Bureau will pay your fare.'

Tom sighed, shook his head. 'It's tempting, but . . .'

'You've done enough already,' David put in. 'I don't need any more help.'

'But you *do*!' Robyn had grown desperate. 'Why won't you see the danger you're in? Tom, please!'

'It would mean slipping away without a word to anyone,' Tom said after a long pause. 'Or there'd be no point. So I wouldn't need to worry about the Bureau.'

In the nerve-wracking silence that followed, David found himself inwardly beseeching Tom Burroughs to say yes.

'Hell, I'm coming with you.'

'I really can't ask that.'

'Then don't. Just take it.'

Now, sitting in the cafeteria of the British Airways terminal at Kennedy, David felt mortally relieved that he would not be going back to England alone. Seeing Tom in the light for the first time, he discovered a face dark with stubble and lines, blue eyes remarkable for their absence of movement, a heavy-framed torso on which to hang so many cares of state. If anyone could help him, this man could.

'They're calling BA 002,' Tom said. 'That's us.'

David stood up to shake hands with Robyn. After he had walked a few steps away from the table he stopped, turned, and said, 'I won't forget you. Thank you.'

Robyn's smile was wan. 'Count cents,' she murmured. 'Please . . .'

THIRTY-TWO

On Sunday, Anna awoke at the crack of dawn. Her head felt muzzy, which was strange, because she had drunk no alcohol the night before. Was Kleist putting sedatives in her food now? Still half asleep, she went to the kitchen, where she found Barzel sitting at the table, a paperback propped up in front of him. They ignored each other, as had become their custom.

A cup of coffee revived her. As soon as she'd drunk it she set off for the church. Sunrise had begun to enrich the landscape but the air stayed cool and she thrust her hands into the pockets of her jeans. She'd brought Juliet's corn dolly with her. Miss Cuppidge seemed to be the only link she had with the world outside, with normality. Although nothing about her relationship with Juliet was normal, she reflected sadly as she picked her way along the path. It made no sense to say she was losing Juliet, when her daughter had never really been there.

In the old days, Kleist would ask: 'Why on earth do you want David's child so much? After all you've gone through with Juliet . . . ?' 'That's why,' Anna used to say. 'Because of Juliet.' Now she found herself wishing she'd replied: 'Because I'm brave.' That would have been nearer the truth.

Once at the church she looked behind her, expecting to see either Barzel or the other, nameless guard; but the path was empty. Should she make a run for it? No. Even if she could not see them, they were there, waiting for her to do just that; and her only hope lay in building up their trust.

325

Anna entered the church to find the remains of yesterday's candle burned away to a sozzled heap. She cleaned out the holder, and was about to light a fresh one when she remembered having seen huge altar candles standing in a corner of the vestry the day before. She carried one into the church and, not without difficulty, mounted it on a huge brass candlestick to the right of the altar, before sitting down with her back against the wall and her legs folded, a hand on each knee. The red eye of God continued to suss her out, malevolently, benevolently, Anna didn't know. She found herself wondering who tended the lamp and kept it burning through the dark ages which had come again. Yorgos, perhaps.

Although she lacked all religious belief, was faithless in a most fundamental sense, the red eye in the Greek church seemed to vibrate something inside her, like a glass that is struck.

A quarter of an hour ticked away while Anna listened for the sound of Kleist's footsteps on the path. She did not doubt he would come. He wanted to hypnotize her, as a way of consolidating his control. Since she had deliberately implanted that very idea in his mind the day before, the prospect did not daunt her. For the first time, hypnosis would become not a therapy but a weapon. A two-edged weapon.

Long ago, Kleist had told her of a famous mind doctor who once said something profound about hypnotherapy: 'When a physician employs hypnosis with a patient it is wise always to be aware of who may be hypnotizing whom.'

At last the footsteps came. 'Good morning,' he said, radiating confidence. He spoke as if he had some inkling of what lay before them.

Anna put Miss Cuppidge down on the floor beside her. 'I hope you slept well?' Her voice was as formal as the sentiment it expressed.

'Very well, thank you. You?'

She nodded.

'Yesterday you said something about wanting a trance. Do you still feel that way?'

No preliminaries. She had him hooked. 'What do you think?'

'It can do no harm. As you pointed out, I need to erase the instructions I gave you, to prevent you leaving.'

'Up to you,' Anna said, with a shrug; but at the same time she was arranging herself on the floor as comfortably as she could. She closed her eyes. Her heart was beating fast enough to make her afraid for her own well-being.

'It is very peaceful here in the church,' he began, 'very quiet, very safe . . .'

She thought he must realize that it wasn't right. He used to be susceptible to all her vibrations. But when he said nothing to indicate awareness, she remained silent.

'I want you to relax every muscle in your body . . .'

This morning he took his time over the introduction. Anna knew he was preparing her for something special and made a supreme effort not to tense. Part of her wanted to run away: how dare she enter the lions' den, fight him on his own territory? But she knew the answer. Only by doing this could she prevent him from injecting those terrible drugs. Use the lesser evil to ward off the greater . . .

At last he was counting her down to extinction of self with his customary slick skill. But she closed her mind against him and did not go under. It was a sort of under, without ever becoming the real thing. Although she knew the euphoria, the lightness of soul and of body, which accompanied a true trance state, she was conscious of all that she did and said. So she lay quietly, not daring to open her eyes, no longer irked by the hardness of the stone floor but afloat on an ocean thousands of fathoms deep. Her business was to stay there, on the surface; his was to drag her down.

'I'd like us to go back in time,' Kleist murmured. 'You are growing younger now, further and further back, year by year. You have been my patient for about four months. We

327

are talking. And then, for the first time, the very first time, I call you by your Christian name. I call you Anna.'

'Yes. I remember.' She was struggling to articulate her thoughts; but they came easier today, because the trance seemed light and she still had control. 'Why?'

'Because I was proud of you. Do you remember?'

'I'd stopped swearing. I had agreed to work with you, not against you.'

'You, the patient, had begun to take me seriously. At last.'

Anna laughed. It was easy to laugh in a trance, even in a half-trance, surrounded by all that light and lightness of being. 'You told me my self-esteem had come back.'

'Yes, you had self-esteem, then, and we built on it.' He paused. 'Why have you regressed?'

The fringes of the light canopy shivered, just for an instant. Anna struggled to act in character, not knowing how she usually behaved when in a deep trance. Should she deny that she had regressed? No, he was testing her. *Say something!*

'I . . . I felt so . . . hopeless.'

'Why?'

'Losing . . . David.'

'Why would that be so terrible?'

Anna did not know how to answer. But then she forced herself to remember that she had acquired a new weapon, her only source of resistance: as long as Kleist believed that she was in a trance, he would reveal himself to her, and he would not use those drugs.

'He . . . made me worthy. In my own eyes.'

'Why?'

Why, why why? she wanted to scream; don't you know any other words? 'David . . . he . . . made everything all right.'

'How?'

'How?'

'What did he do, to make everything all right?'

'He . . . liked me.'

'Why?'

328

Anna swallowed her resentment and said, 'I suppose . . . he liked me because I'd put up a front, as usual. And he couldn't see through it.'

'Front?'

'Successful, calm, no hang-ups.'

'Ah, yes.' Kleist allowed a long pause to develop. Anna would have given anything to be able to open her eyes, find out what he was doing. Had she fooled him? *Had she?*

She could smell danger, without being able to identify the source; knew how witnesses felt in court when she was still two questions away from springing her trap.

After what seemed an interminable time, Kleist spoke again. 'But of course this man David, this very nice man liked and respected you for the image you tried to project, not the reality beneath, which would have shocked him.'

A long silence.

'It would have shocked him,' Kleist repeated, with studied emphasis. 'Wouldn't it?'

Anna's chest was heaving. Her head rocked from side to side. The waves of that fathomless ocean were sucking at her now, drawing her into its depths.

'I'm going to tell you the time now, Anna. I need to look at my watch. It's my best watch, the gold one. The Omega . . .'

A lead shutter came down between her eyelids and her brain, bang! Suddenly she was no longer afloat on the surface of an ocean, she was in a fog without metes or bounds. She did not know who she was or where she might be, not even the dimension of time and space she occupied. Everything was nothing. And yet part of her brain still registered that this was familiar, although she had never consciously experienced any of it before.

Somewhere in the distance a child was calling her.

There were other voices in the greyness, several of them, all speaking at once. There was something wrong with her ears, as when you have a cold and wake at night with aural catarrh soldering you into a landlocked world.

Wake up, cried the child.

Kleist's voice asserted itself over the rest, but even so it echoed inside her head, as if from a whispering gallery.

'There were mitigating circumstances,' she heard him say. 'Adoption and a repressed childhood had conspired to damage your personality, long ago. You were exhausted, without money, husband or hope. On the day of the crime, life held nothing for you.'

'Nothing.'

Had she said that? It sounded like her. And it was true. That day, she had nothing . . .

Wake up. Wake up. Wake up.

No, that wasn't true: she had a daughter. A bundle of joy. A screaming, sleepless, vomit-and-shit-dispensing, smelly, ugly, bad-tempered . . .

Kleist again: 'You had no one . . . except Juliet. Your own child. And here we have the nub of the problem, don't we, mm?'

Anna wanted to speak. Alive inside her was this vast, comprehensive explanation that would make everything right if only she could manage to articulate it. But the words remained trapped inside her, like a still-born infant.

'Because if there are points to be raised in your defence, there are aggravating factors as well.'

Anna opened her mouth and discovered she could speak; but the words that came out were different from those she intended to utter. 'I don't understand.'

'Well, let me help you, then.' Kleist no longer whispered; his voice sounded in her left ear as if he were lying down next to her. But she could not feel him. She could not feel anything, not even the floor.

'Your life at that time was, when viewed objectively, "good". People envied you for your education, your looks, your comfortable, secure, middle-class home. You had been blessed with a healthy child. Your first husband, Eddy, was a mistake, you were well shot of him. You had no *excuse* to be unhappy, there was no reason for it. Yet you despaired.'

Anna's head felt as though it would explode. She wanted to scream: *'That's what I always told you! And you said I was wrong, wrong, wrong! You said I was suffering from post-natal depression!'* But no words came out. When two tears trickled down her cheeks she was powerless to wipe them away.

'So now we will go back, together, to that day, just before you and I first met.'

'No. I don't want . . .'

'It is evening. You are at your parents' house.'

She was dimly aware of a sensation in her hands. As they clenched and unclenched, the nails were grinding into her palms. 'Don't . . .'

'Yes? What did you say, Anna?'

'Don't . . . do . . . this . . . *please*!'

'But we must. You are there, at the house in Ferring. Your parents have gone to bed. You are in your room, with Juliet. Just the two of you. Alone.'

'Don't . . .'

'You can see what you saw then. Feel what you felt then. Hear what happened then.'

'No.'

'*Yes*, Anna.'

Her heart was beating uncontrollably now. Tears flowed down her cheeks, a poisonous migraine throbbed inside her skull.

'Juliet is lying in the bed, beside you. She is helpless, utterly dependent on you. She has been crying; you have been nursing her.'

'Nursing her . . .'

'Tell me what you feel, Anna.'

'Nursing her . . .'

'*Tell me what you feel.*'

'I . . . can't reject her.'

'No, you can't.' His voice had a new note in it now, telling her he'd scented victory. 'But you want to, don't you?'

'Can't do what my mother did to me. Can't . . . give her away.'

'So what *do* you do?'

'No!'

'What do you do?'

'You *promised*! Gerhard! Never again, you needn't go back to it ever again . . .'

'What do you do?'

'I . . .'

'Yes?'

'Put my hands . . . desperate . . . oh Christ, I'm so un-happy, so depressed. She won't take my milk . . . won't feed.'

'What . . . do . . . you . . . *do?*'

'I put my hands . . .'

'Where do you put your hands?'

Anna cried out, but Kleist was remorseless. *'Where?'*

'Around . . . Juliet's . . . throat.'

She began to keen, beating her clenched fists against the floor, but still unable either to rise or to open her eyes.

'And then your mother came in, didn't she? *Didn't she?'*

'Yes.'

'And your baby was saved. Your innocent, beautiful child, who'd never done anything wrong, was saved. So that David need never know who you really were, what kind of woman you were.'

She saw him then, quite suddenly, even though her eyes stayed closed. She could see every lineament of his twisted face, each of the hundred tiny details that betrayed his need to destroy her before she did the same to him.

He wanted to render her harmless. In order to achieve that, he was prepared to do anything, and he had chosen the weapons with which he was most familiar.

No. There was more to it than that. He wanted *her*; and so he was going to have to eradicate David.

Anna's hands pounded the floor as if she were having a fit. Suddenly one of them made contact with the roughness of the corn-stook doll and — *Wake up,* the child's voice screamed. Juliet. Her daughter.

'Anna? Anna, why don't you answer?'

Silence.

'Anna.' Gerhard's voice was low, coaxing. 'Anna, can you still hear me? If you can, raise the middle finger of your right hand . . .'

But she did nothing of the kind. Instead, she slowly opened her eyes. She emerged into the light. 'You can't do that to me.' Her voice, astonishingly, was perfectly calm. 'You can't say it. I love David. And he loves me. In spite of what you've done.'

Kleist looked at her, his face expressionless. Anna understood what he could see: not a tired, frightened woman on the edge of forty, but a threat to all his hopes, of everything he'd worked for: the Krysalis file, the protection of his masters and the hope of the good life to come. Anna saw these things through his eyes and braced herself.

He pounced with a clumsiness born of his own awkward leap from the floor, wrenching her shoulder muscles. At first, all she could think about was the pain: she closed her eyes against it and tried to raise a hand to protect the spot from further damage. But Kleist, intent on achieving his twin goals of revenge and punishment, dashed her hand aside, twisting two of the fingers until she screamed.

She fought back. 'Gerhard,' she cried, 'don't . . .' But the next thing she knew he was rolling her over, using his body weight to keep her pinned down. Her right hand threshed wildly, sending Juliet's corn dolly scudding across the floor into the curtained-off vestry. She clenched her fist and swung it against the side of his head with all the force she could muster. He howled with surprise and pain; it did her good to hear that. But when he continued to pummel her with his head, his torso, his legs, she knew she had to change if she wanted to survive.

Anna extended all her fingers. Go for his eyes.

He saw it coming and arched upwards. His body was off hers, she was free. Anna tried to rise, slipped and found herself face down on the floor. She began to wriggle away

333

from him. The altar: some muddled, atavistic instinct made her turn east for sanctuary. But then her strength deserted her and she lay spread-eagled with her head towards the red eye of God, helplessly waiting, aware that losers must pay, in life as in law.

When Anna heard his footsteps it took her a moment to realize that they were retreating. Then the door banged shut and a blessed silence filled the church. Kleist had gone.

Slowly she raised her head. Through a mist of tears it seemed to her that now the red eye beside the altar glistened like freshly spilled blood.

THIRTY-THREE

Albert was clipping recipes from one of the Sunday colour supplements and enjoying his pre-prandial glass of *Punt e Mes* when the phone rang. 'It's a nice morning,' he heard Louis Redman say. 'Come for a drive. I'll be outside.'

Albert had just finished locking up when Redman's Granada pulled into the kerb alongside him.

'Are we going anywhere special, Louis?'

'Uh-uh. I was thinking of taking a walk in the park.'

'Sounds good.'

'That meeting was a mess,' Redman said as he drove off. 'Although enlivened by your contributions, if you don't mind me saying. Do you have any appointments, by the way?'

'I might pop up to Hampstead later on.'

'Hampstead . . . ah, time to take a look at Anna Lescombe's case notes, right?'

'Time to prepare the ground, anyway.' Albert yawned and stretched. 'What's all this about?'

'I told you, a walk – '

When Albert sighed theatrically, Redman laughed and swung left out of Queensway. 'Look,' he said, becoming serious. 'First of all, this conversation is none of my idea, right?'

'If you say so.'

'Only someone called me from Washington this morning and . . . well, the situation has definitely not improved.'

'Oh?'

335

'We managed to locate Lescombe in New York only because his contact, this Melkiovicz person, called a friend in the FBI. His name is Thomas Burroughs. She tried to notify him about some foreign hoodlums who'd come to lean on her.'

'Tried?'

'Luckily for us he was out, so Melkiovicz got his assistant and left a message for him. The assistant automatically did what she was supposed to do, incredible how people sometimes do that, and even before checking it out with her boss she phoned *her* friend in the CIA; we ran a watch on Melkiovicz . . . and Lescombe showed up in the frame.'

'Do I gather that if Burroughs had got the message direct, the CIA still wouldn't know about it?'

'Damn right. Burroughs is *not* a friend of ours. Anyway, David Lescombe spent last night driving around New York with this Melkiovicz woman and Burroughs.'

'That's bad?'

'It complicates things if Lescombe's changed sides, yes. Burroughs has a big, wide-open mouth: a Freedom of Information man at heart.'

'In the FBI?'

'Unbelievable, isn't it? Anyway, if Lescombe's going to defect, the thought of him taking anything from Burroughs with him causes us deep concern.'

'This does rather presuppose that Lescombe will defect.'

'We're convinced of it.'

'We're not.'

'Albert, I will be very frank with you: the loss of Krysalis represented some kind of low point in Anglo-US relations. But what's made things worse is the way you Brits are handling it.'

Albert kept quiet.

'The call I took this morning originated from the Executive Building at the White House. My caller was taking a break from what I think you call a "full and frank exchange of views", have I got that right?'

'If you mean he was getting his "ass" – have *I* got *that* right? – kicked, then yes.'

'When the Vice President demands to see the Director of the CIA at eight o'clock Sunday morning, you may assume that more than one ass is going to be kicked.' Redman shook his head, patently angry. 'Unless we can manage to save Vancouver, seems I'll be going back to live in the States.'

'And you'd like to prevent that?'

Redman laughed. 'Is what you've just said meant to stand as an example of ironical British understatement?' When he spoke again he appeared to be changing the subject. 'How would you feel about undertaking a one-off assignment for the United States government?'

'You have plenty of your own unskilled labour.'

'But none of them in place, or easily put in place. The reason I'm talking to you is that you're exactly where we need someone to be if he's to do the job I'm talking about.'

'Tell me something quickly,' Albert said, 'tell me now: does Hayes know about this contact?'

'Not Hayes, not anyone.'

'This, what we're doing, is principal to principal?'

'Correct. It would be part of any deal that you kept it that way too, on your side, as we would on ours.'

'Go on.'

'I'm backing a hunch that I know exactly what orders you've received, and I don't want you to give me any confirmations.'

Albert smiled, but held his peace.

'David Lescombe is likely to lead us right up the wire to his wife within the next forty-eight hours. What's that famous line . . . "Where the bee sucks, there suck I"? Or, in this case, you.'

'I catch your drift.'

Redman stopped for a red light and swivelled so that he could look squarely at Albert. 'What I mean is, an opportunity will have opened up for you to do your job.' Sensing that Albert was about to speak, Redman took his left hand

337

off the wheel and held it up warningly. 'Please! Remember – no confirmations. You are listening to a long-in-the-tooth American fantasist and because you're a gentleman you're politely allowing him to ramble to his conclusion.'

Albert laughed. The lights changed; Redman drove into Hyde Park and sped along the Ring, down to the Serpentine. 'What do you say we take that walk now?'

'Fine with me. Got any bread?'

'You mean money?'

'I mean bread, Louis. For the ducks.'

Now it was Redman's turn to laugh. 'I love London,' he said, suddenly turning serious. 'Spring, like now, is okay, but fall is the greatest time. Come September, October, I wouldn't be any place else in the world.'

They got out of the car and began to saunter along. There were crowds of people about doing Sunday-ish things; it would be hard, Albert reflected, to beat this location for what they had to negotiate.

'Let's take it a stage further,' Redman said. 'Some time within the next two days, you will be presented with the opportunity you've been seeking. In the heat of such moments, mistakes sometimes get made.'

'You would like to purchase a mistake?'

'That's more or less the sense of my call from Washington, yes.'

'Why have your people waited until now to make this proposition?'

'We didn't rate Lescombe. Until he managed to shake surveillance, we didn't realize that he was a pro. He's going to get to Anna and he's going to manage to go over the wall with her.'

'Mistakes,' Albert said after a pause, 'can be costly.'

'Funds are available.'

'Something left over from the Contras? Or would you have to sell a missile to Iran?'

'Now Albert, that's not funny.' Redman smiled, nevertheless. 'Funds are available, let's leave it like that, shall we?'

338

When his companion made no reply, the American prompted him: 'Care to give me an initial reaction?'

Albert made a long face. 'Difficult.'

'Is that another word for impossible?'

Albert stopped for long enough to pick up a discarded can and drop it in the nearest litter bin. 'I'd want proof of total, watertight, absolute deniability,' he said.

'No problem.'

'After all, and forgive me for doubting what you said earlier, the task you have in mind could perfectly well be done by an American. You're just keen to avoid the fall-out.'

They walked in silence for a long way after that. 'What made Langley think I'd be interested?' Albert said at last.

'You're in place, as I say. But also I guess . . . because they believe you share a certain view of what is wrong with the world. That you hold to your convictions every bit as passionately as they do to theirs.'

'Not a word about your own convictions, I notice. My word, Louis, you *are* distancing yourself from this, aren't you?'

'Am I?' Redman's smile was wry. 'Ideologically, I'm not so far away from the man who called me this morning. We are lurching to the left, we lack control; the talk is all of rights and none of obligations, duties.'

'The centre cannot hold,' Albert murmured absently. 'I see. Yet I hear a "but" somewhere, do I?'

'It's the methods I quarrel with.'

'Ah.'

'Are Langley right in what they think about you?'

'No confirmations, Louis. Your words.'

They walked on. To Albert's irritation the cafeteria was shut; he would dearly have liked a hot drink. But this was an English Sunday in April and the sign outside said 'Owing to staff shortages . . .'; they must not expect too much. Work, for example. Service.

'Would you be interested in the proposition?'

'Perhaps,' Albert said. 'But there's one thing I'd like to

339

know. I don't need to know it, but it's a seller's market and if you want me to do this job you have to tell me simply because I'm curious, all right?'

Redman looked at him. 'Ask.'

'Is Krysalis or is it not . . . kosher?'

Redman didn't even hesitate. 'Not.'

'Thank you. Why, then, all this pretended fuss about the Vancouver summit?'

'Because not everybody knows Krysalis isn't what it seems to be.'

'The Russians, you mean?'

'I mean *us*! Our side. Krysalis is part of an operation that didn't need Presidential approval. It's been floating around for years, waiting for someone to bite. But once it got entangled with Vancouver, we had to play straight.'

'Surely all you have to do is brief the State Department and everyone can relax?'

'We can't just . . . *do* that, Albert.'

'I don't see — '

'Krysalis did not originate with State, it never received State's blessing.' Redman scowled at the Serpentine. 'It's directed against a major European ally.'

Albert took a moment to digest this. 'Against . . . Britain, you mean.'

'Look, I said a major European — '

'All right, all right. Keep your hair on.'

'So. Now you've done that bit of homework, I guess that's it, then.'

But Albert pursed his lips. 'I don't see why, as long as the assignment has some intrinsic worth, which it does. Incidentally, concerning your . . . sorry, your *superiors'* proposition . . . there'd be no question of payment. I'd do it because it needed to be done.'

'That's very fine of you, Albert.' Redman paused. 'You understand our requirement?'

Not far from where they stood, a brace of magpies was pecking ferociously at some morsel of food, flung down,

340

Albert supposed, by one of the oiks who populated England nowadays. He nodded his head at them and said, 'Do you know the old saw? One for sorrow, two for joy, know it, do you?'

Redman had to think about that. 'Right,' he said at last, relief sounding in his voice. 'Two for joy. Right.'

'Okay,' Albert said. 'Don't know about you, but I could really murder a cup of tea.'

THIRTY-FOUR

David Lescombe knew he was eight miles high over the Atlantic, but beyond that he could perceive only the dazzle which enveloped the British Airways Concorde. Supersonic flight, he'd soon discovered, held no allure for him. Everything aboard seemed to be the same drear grey colour, even down to the menus and the headsets – the latter being useless, in David's case, because he was sitting so far back that the noise of the engines drowned out everything else. The famed curvature of the earth lay concealed behind a yellow-white glow and anyway he found it impossible to see out of the ridiculously modest portholes that passed for windows. The cabin seemed stiflingly hot. He took little pleasure in travelling at – he glanced up at the green fluorescent screen – twice the speed of sound, in the equivalent of an Aga.

David and Tom sat close but apart, wanting to avoid giving the impression that they knew each other. Awareness of his companion sitting behind him brought David great comfort.

This morning, a Sunday, the plane was nearly empty: a dozen or so passengers were scattered around the two double banks of leather-covered seats. For the most part they sat quietly, all except for a couple in the row across the aisle and immediately behind David's, opposite Tom. Young, American and, it would seem, on their honeymoon. They had spent the entire flight so far swilling champagne, cuddling, kissing and exchanging some of the most ridiculous dialogue David had ever endured. He felt that if he heard the word 'Smoochums' again, once this flight was over, he would throw something at the speaker. But when he tried to change seats the chief purser demurred, making unctuous noises about payload distribution which sounded important without making sense to the uninitiated.

David was half-aware that Tom kept looking at this ridiculous couple. Did that mean he suspected them? Surely not . . . but then why did the FBI agent spend so much time keeping them under surveillance?

David pushed his feeling of unease to the back of his mind and tried to plan. He loved just one thing about Concorde: its speed. His only complaint on that score was that it couldn't fly fast enough.

He didn't want to eat. He tried to sleep and could not. He realized that somewhere aboard, perhaps in the cockpit, it was a certain time; this plane, supersonic or not, could no more divorce itself from the world of which it formed part than it could travel back through the centuries. But in his seat there was no time. They were chasing the day's end. So far it had eluded them.

David sought truth. It was as elusive as the sunset.

He tried to remember why he had gone to New York in the first place, to understand the nature of his pursuit.

He had wanted to find his wife, knowing in his heart that she would not be there, which seemed in retrospect an odd thing to do. Perhaps he had merely gone to find out about her. So what had he learned?

She'd once had an affair with her analyst. She might be with him now. He couldn't avoid it any longer: she might have betrayed both him and her country. A lot of evidence suggested that this conclusion was the right one.

But David had learned something definite about himself: that he was more in love with Anna than on the day he had married her. He did not believe that she was a traitor. He wanted to save her from whatever peril threatened her, and then, because he loved this woman, he would help her to become whole again. Become what she once had been.

343

Which was what?

A businessman in the row of seats opposite stood up, adjusted his shirt-cuffs and walked back along the aisle in search of the lavatory. David eyed him warily, conscious of Tom Burroughs doing the same. But the man passed by without so much as a glance in their direction. Moments later he returned. As he drew level, the plane gave a lurch and he fell awkwardly against David's seat, putting out a hand to steady himself. David flinched as if the man had tried to stab him.

'Sorry, old boy. Sorry about that . . . can be a bit rough, the last hour. Do this often, do you?'

'No.' David heard Tom's restless movements in the seat behind him and resolved to be extra careful.

'Wish I didn't have to. Ninth time this year and it's still only April. What line are you in, old boy?'

Fortunately, at that moment the plane gave another leap across the sky, flinging his tormentor back into his seat, and the 'fasten seatbelt' sign came on, once again enabling David to pursue his thoughts.

Why had Anna sought therapy in the first place? That was a question which Robyn had ducked. What had been her last straw? *Why did she never discuss any of it with him?*

David raised the blind and stared into a seamlessly domed sky, one lacking the familiar demarcation of hours and minutes. Beneath him, a little to one side, he could make out the beginnings of a white blade, and he shook his head. A wing but no prayer . . .

Did he still love her? *Of course.* Even though she may be with Kleist, may be in love with him . . . ?

It was not too late. He could get back to London, seek out Fox, say, 'Look, I realize I've been pig-headed about this one. Anna's a bitch, I see that now. How can I help? Let me tell you what I've managed to discover about her so far. She's a lush. She's been in therapy for years – bet there's a few red faces about that with you MI5 chaps, eh? – and she had an affair with the therapist, and by the way, can I have my

344

career back, still not too late to hitch a ride to Vancouver, is it . . . ?'

The businessman across the aisle looked up in surprise to see what had made David laugh out loud; but his fellow-traveller was sitting bolt upright with both hands clenched, staring at the seat in front of him.

David glanced over his shoulder to find Tom still intent on the honeymooners, lips slightly parted. The FBI man's forehead creased in a frown, he looked tense, edgy.

David tried to ignore the implications of his companion's behaviour, but felt his heartbeat quicken nonetheless. Surely the sozzled couple couldn't represent genuine danger? *Surely?*

Everyone was dangerous. Everyone. No, don't think about that, plan ahead, use the time . . .

When he'd gone down to Yarmouth, that first day of life with Anna, he had been in search of a bracing weekend and had found love instead. It came late, unlooked for, and was rich. He could choose, if he wanted, to put it all behind him. It would require a supreme act of will, but he could do that. He could turn his back on love, preferring not to know.

Perhaps that blindness was genetic; for there was, he realized, a precedent.

His grandfather had been a mean, cold-spirited man, a hospital porter who hoarded money in tobacco tins and stuck them under the mattress of the bed he shared with Gran. They possessed only a thin mattress, Gran was bony; she did not have to be the princess in the fairy tale about the pea to suffer from those tins. She was a gifted woman, artistic before the lower classes had been allowed to think of themselves in such terms, so the neighbours were reduced to calling her 'clever with her needle', or someone 'who's got a real way with painting a room, you should see it . . .'

She died on that bed, with the tins grinding her wasted body into eternity, one February, the bedroom grate without a fire because Gramps didn't believe in throwing money away needlessly. She died insane.

After her death, grandfather had changed. In addition to being cold and mean, he began to suffer from a profound, cancer-of-the-bone style remorse. He missed his dead wife. For the first time he realized that she had been a treasure, a woman beyond all price, who had loved him fiercely. The pangs of this horror began to wear him down, just as his tins with their rounded, hard edges and corners had ground her into nothing. In the end it killed him. The doctors called his disease cancer too, but David knew that for a lie. Remorse had killed his grandfather, as surely and as slowly as arsenic self-administrated over a long period. David felt glad when he died. Mentally he consigned him to a hell of his own mind, for the sin of choosing not to know.

Later today he would be in London and, all being well, in Corfu by the following afternoon. Then, with Tom's help, he could go to the island, following Robyn's directions. By the time the sun went down on Monday, he could know.

If he wanted to.

David dozed for a while. He was wakened by the chief purser walking down the centre aisle, checking seatbelts and chair positions for landing. By peering out of the porthole he could see the ground, obscured by low cloud. Almost before he knew what was happening they had hit the runway and begun to hurtle along it without any sign of slowing. The engines reversed thrust, the brakes went on, David was thrown violently against his belt. The noise level inside the stuffy cabin became intolerable. Somewhere behind him, female 'Smoochums' was uttering whoops of delight.

Then, beyond all hope, they were decelerating. As the plane turned off the runway, David saw that the pilot had ten yards to spare, and he wiped the sweat from his face with a handkerchief that came away soaked.

The honeymoon couple were keen to disembark. David sat in his seat gathering his wits while they and the boorish businessman who had pestered him earlier busied themselves with hand luggage. Male 'Smoochums' escaped first, leaving the female of the species to wrestle with her Gucci bag. She could not stop giggling. 'I can't get the strap right,' David heard her say. 'I can't fix it . . . you go on ahead.'

'I won't leave you,' the man said, throwing his arms around her.

'Lissenname . . . we wanna trolley, right?'

'Righ . . .'

'Go get one, then. Go on.' She shoved his shoulder. 'Go on!'

Her husband reeled away towards the front of the plane. David rose to the half-crouch and slid sideways, preparatory to stepping into the aisle, when he felt a discreet tap on the shoulder. He looked back to find Tom on his feet, lips tightly compressed as he tried to keep both members of the young pair firmly in view. David hesitated, unsure what Tom wanted him to do. There were very few passengers left now: just him, Tom, the businessman opposite, and the vile couple.

Something about their grouping spelt danger. David, feeling the first brush of panic, instinctively took a pace backwards.

When her husband was already some yards away, Lady Smoochums managed to disentangle her bag. She tripped, still giggling. As she did so, Tom made his move, coming smoothly out of his seat to take her by the arm, manoeuvring himself between the woman and David. His jacket-sleeve brushed David's own. In his right hand he held what looked like a leather wallet.

The boorish businessman chose that moment to stand up, reaching for the overhead locker. Because he had been sitting in an aisle seat, the effect was to bring him into the line of the drunken woman's awkward stumble, throwing Tom Burroughs off balance.

David saw the look on the FBI agent's face and for a second could not understand his rage. Then Tom's own words came back to him, *count cents!* and he knew why he was angry, just as he knew why the businessman's face had turned blue and he was now staggering back into his seat, fighting for breath . . . So David grabbed the businessman's briefcase

347

and, holding it in front of him like a shield, yelled at the top of his voice, *'Steward! Emergency! There's a dead man back here! He's been murdered! Help! . . .'*

Disjointed realizations flooded through his brain. Burroughs had been working for the enemy all along. He'd come to the bar, intending to go to London right from the start. But before David could analyse the knowledge he remembered, just in time, that he was still hemmed into the row of seats. Now he retreated as far as he could, until his back came up against the hull. *'Murder, murder!'* he shouted again. Tom Burroughs turned on the balls of his feet and lunged at him, holding out his wallet. After a second of disbelief, David's brain alerted him to the truth: somewhere in the leather there had to be a poisoned pin, maybe a blade; his only chance was to stay out of range.

'Stop!' he heard a voice shout from the front of the plane, but he dared not look forward. 'Security!' the same voice shouted. 'Stop or I shoot.'

David parried Burroughs' next thrust with the briefcase, pushing him aside. Burroughs lowered his right hand; David caught a flash of something metal as the American prepared to lunge up, beneath his guard; but as he did so, from somewhere near the front of the cabin came a loud 'plop!' The woman screamed in pain and fell across Burroughs, bearing him down, and he sank to the floor, where he stayed, pinned by her weight, until stewards dragged him away, leaving David with a drunk and a corpse for company in the world's most prestigious aircraft.

David could not move. There was this voice, but he couldn't focus on it. At last he managed to haul himself into the aisle. There he was met by a man he vaguely recognized as a fellow-passenger, who'd been sitting up front throughout the flight, in the act of holstering his pistol. 'You've killed her,' David muttered. Even as he spoke he was angered by the knowledge of how feeble he must sound.

'I doubt it. The bullet's a tiny bag, containing sand, you see. Safe to fire even while we're flying.' The speaker bent

348

down to check. 'Yes, just stunned.' He stood up again. 'What was all that about, anyway?'

David, still too shocked to speak, merely shook his head.

'From where I stood, it looked as if someone was trying to kill you.'

Yes, that was right. They meant to stop him, and Burroughs had been part of it. *Who was he working for, really?*

The security guard turned his attention to the business-man, who now sat white-faced with his eyes closed. 'Got the wrong chap, by the look of it. Now he *is* dead, if you like. Can I have your name and address, please sir?'

David complied. *They'll do anything to stop you. Anything at all. Your faith, against their force.*

'Occupation?'

'Uh . . . civil servant. Actually . . .'

Faith? Do you have faith in Anna?

The security guard had been writing details in a notebook. Now, hearing hesitation in David's voice, he paused. 'Yes?'

They will do whatever they have to, to prevent you from reaching the woman you love.

David realized why he felt so uncomfortable: he had been holding his breath. 'I'm about to resign,' he said.

THIRTY-FIVE

'Of course, whoever goes in will have to remember to steal something.' Fox looked more than ever like an operator of risqué night-clubs. 'Make it look like a real burglary, and so forth.'

'You'd better let me do it, then,' said Albert. 'At least I know what I'm looking for.'

But now that the time to prepare had arrive . . . did he? Albert asked himself. Was it not the case that he actually knew less about Anna Lescombe than when he'd started?

He spent the afternoon idling his way around Hampstead, guidebook in hand, eventually closing in on Keats' house, which was near where Gerhard Kleist lived. He took it slowly, absorbing patterns through his pores until he had the feel of the place. There were few cars parked on the street. Luckily for Albert it was a Sunday; he guessed that four o'clock on a weekday, when the schools came out, would be a noisy time, with mothers of fashionably sluttish appearance emerging from these large, isolated houses to collect offspring in middle-range BMWs or Volvo estates. But this was not an area where kids played in the road or teenagers gathered to loll on its leafy pavements at weekends. Albert might have been a ghost for all the attention he attracted.

Kleist's house was halfway up a short hill. Albert's saunter slowed to a crawl. What a nice place to live, he thought. Trees, grass, big imposing houses set well back. Tiresome about the red boxes: each residence (he had somehow stopped thinking of them as mere houses) had a burglar alarm prominently displayed. However.

Trees in the street. Trees in the small front garden. More of them visible over a first-floor gable, around the back. An Edwardian pile, all bricks and red tiles, with fresh-looking white paint; privet hedge, a mixture of healthy yellows and greens, to the left; close boarded fence to the right, no gravel to worry about, unlike Eddy Clapham's ait.

In an emergency, what help would the back garden be? Where did it lead? Albert strolled on, determined to make a circuit of the property. But it was harder than he'd imagined, for these oh-so-desirable residences had a tendency to sprawl in many directions, and it was a while before he knew where he ought to park his car, later that evening. Only of course it would not be his car; nothing traceable.

With every step he took, Albert became more convinced that no one from the opposition was watching Kleist's house.

What did that mean? Nil surveillance was consistent with Kleist's having chosen this moment to implement a long agreed plan, for then his people would have been expecting him to go. But what if he'd done a bunk — in that case, surely you'd find the street crawling with spooks? Ah, not necessarily; Albert remembered the disappearance of the Greek post-boy in Athens. HVA would know about Kleist's fax, offering MI6 a deal. They wouldn't need to watch his London base if they'd already found him. Him and his lady companion . . .

Albert took a last, affectionate look down the hill. Five o'clock, and there was no one about. Strip the street of its twentieth-century accessories and Dr Manette's Soho Square home in one of Dickens' Two Cities must have looked something like this: quiet, clean prosperity and order, leafy stillness, how did it go . . . ? 'A cool spot, staid but cheerful, a wonderful place for echoes, and a very harbour from the raging streets.' Albert would have liked to live in those days. England had been a better place, then.

Back home, he chopped steak for *boeuf bourgignon*,

351

wondering how best to play the night's programme. He would check with Fox to ensure he had a clear run from the police, at the same time querying the truth of his assumption about absence of surveillance and what it meant. Then dinner.

Albert liked dealing with raw meat: its sogginess, its wetness, above all, the smell, which lingered on the skin long afterwards. He was mixing the steak with seasoned flour, taking his time over it, relishing the way the blood supped up gluten to make his fingers sticky, when the phone rang. He gave his hands a cursory wipe with a piece of paper towel and lifted the receiver from its wall-mounted rest.

'Go now, right this minute.'

Fox, in a phone booth, urgent, panicking.

'What's happened?'

'M Centre's gone berserk. Their cipher traffic's splitting our machines apart. Redland's on the warpath.'

A long breath escaped Albert's lips. 'When?'

'Eight o'clock. There's a connection. Tell you what it is later. And for the love of God, *be careful*.'

'Don't forget to warn off your Leadbetter friends.'

'Sorry, can't. Security overload.'

'Shit!'

He had showered and dressed for the occasion earlier, so he did not even have to think; just lights off, car keys, out.

He drove carefully but fast, avoiding the main arteries and making every effort to keep his anger reined in, but that was hard. When they sent a man to do this kind of job, they always tipped off the police first. Routine. High on the 'To Do' checklist. But this time Albert was on his own.

The phrase Fox had used, 'Security overload', meant they had reason to be afraid of leaks. Albert was disclaimable.

While still some yards short of his destination he switched off the engine along with the lights, allowing his car to roll until at last he was parked in the spot he had marked down earlier. No more planning, no hesitations, just get in, target, penetrate.

Albert slipped through the darkness, a liquid, elemental part of it, flowing in utter silence around to the front of Kleist's house. The front garden was long: no other part of London offered such priceless facilities to nocturnal intruders, and that of course was why he now had to deal with a professionally installed alarm system.

He did not pause for breath until he had skirted the side of the house and reached an area of shadow at the back. Albert looked up. No lights. Perhaps the housekeeper had gone out for the evening, it wasn't yet ten o'clock. Recce.

He found a terrace, onto which opened a pair of French windows. Albert risked a burst of light from his torch and made a face: metal shutter gates on the inside. But almost certainly there weren't any pressure pads. Another flash showed him only black rectangles, unmarred by the tell-tale white rubber circles. Risk it. No choice, anyway. Risk it.

He had passed the regiment's 'advanced lock neutralization' course and he came better equipped than most burglars, but this part of the job was child's play. Mushroom-shaped blob of putty on the outside of the pane, a glazier's blade for the circle, one smart intake of breath, a tap . . . and there was a hole large enough to admit his hand.

No alarm went off. Albert smiled. People always thought they had done enough. They did not know it, but they had never done enough. It was only a matter of time before someone finally got away with the Mona Lisa.

Instinct made him turn his head. Behind him, the back garden — dark and peaceful. Beyond that, another house framed against the dim lighting in the street where he had parked. Upstairs, a single window showed lit. Albert knew himself to be horribly exposed. What if the night-owl behind the window chanced to look out . . . don't think about that. *No time*.

The hole he had made was above the lock of the metal shutter gates but he couldn't see a keyhole on the outside. Fortunately Albert's hands were small; he managed to insert two fingers through one of the diamond-shaped gaps between the struts. The shutter lock yielded at his third attempt with the skeleton key and the fastening of the French doors themselves was a doddle.

He had started to sweat and he did not know why. He looked over his shoulder. Nothing. Only the house beyond the wall, where that light still burned. That ominous light.

Albert stepped back, wiping beads of perspiration from his face. What kind of alarm was this? He increased the odds in his favour by removing one entire pane of glass from the right-hand door, enabling him to pass through easily when the time came. That left the metal gates, unlocked but still shut, to circumvent.

Now he was tingling all over. He jerked his head around. Everything seemed the same. No, it didn't. Someone stood at the illuminated first-floor window in the house behind. Seconds ticked by, but the silhouette remained motionless. Was the person looking out, or did he have his back to the window?

Ignore him.

Since when have you ever ignored your instincts? The police don't know about this. Yet! Stay alive!

He had hunches but no choices, and Albert found himself cursing Fox. He lacked an alibi, resources, time . . . A minute passed. Too long. Use the shadows, just *penetrate*!

He made himself get on with the job. There were the wires! At the top of the gates, two of them, one at each side, which meant more glaziery and the removal of the other pane of glass. Albert took a closer look. The wires ended in square metal contacts, one male, one female, which linked when the gates were closed. Break the contact, and . . .

The wires extended right and left along the gates at the height of a man's mouth. They were attached to the struts by metal brackets. Screwdriver, some fancy double-jointedness on the part of Albert, who caught each bracket as he prised it loose, and the wires, still joined, hung in loops.

354

Now, when he slid the shutters open, the struts moved independently of the wires, leaving the electric contact solid.

Behind him he heard a window open and a voice called, 'Who's there?'

Albert immobilized himself.

'Who is that? I can see you.'

Long pause. The voice belonged to a man but it was high-pitched and quavery. Old? No, not old, but . . . something weird about it.

Albert ground his teeth, eyes flickering between the French doors and the window of the house behind. Now it was open, a shadow leaned out, probing the gloom. Albert did calculations with the speed of light. No alternative.

One last potential obstacle remained: contact pads under the rug beyond the windows.

Acrobatics. *Crash dive!*

He retreated a dozen paces, took a deep breath, and launched himself forward. As he reached the hole where the glass had been he was travelling horizontally, diving beneath the coiled wires, over the rug, to land on his stomach halfway down Gerhard Kleist's living room.

He was into the trap. And now he had bare seconds in which to work his way out of it.

Albert knew all the places where people keep burglar alarm control boxes. They have to be near an entrance, so that when the owner comes back to an empty house he can negate the system within forty-five seconds of entry. Most householders, worried by the thought of arousing neighbours and police unnecessarily, keep them mounted by the front door. Albert sprinted along the hallway and discovered that Kleist was the norm. Another skeleton key, into the control box, *twist*, safe.

He had been in the house for thirteen seconds.

Cut the phone. Junction box on the skirting board, one kick, two kicks, done.

Lounge, kitchen, dining room, study: each room got two seconds and a burst of light, nothing, *up!*

Waiting room, consulting room, *yes*. What was happening outside? Had the watcher called the police? Was he wasting time, trying to phone Kleist's housekeeper?

Filing cabinets. Two seconds, burst the locks. Suppose the late night watcher was making his way around to the front of the house, right this instant, don't think about that, don't meet trouble before it comes, ten seconds, Lescombe, under L . . . no. *Shit!* Five seconds, E for Elwell . . . two thick, dog-eared cardboard folders, one orange, one a faded green. He opened the orange one, glanced through the first half dozen pages, yes, yes, *yes*!

Penetration exactly one minute old, time to go.

He tugged his black polo-neck shirt from out of his waistband and stuck one file up the back, the other up the front, before once again tucking the shirt back in. Not comfortable, not wholly secure, but it left his hands free.

The voice had been pounding inside his head almost ever since his entry. Now it suddenly became a roar, a chorus. Get out. Don't stop to think, don't wait, don't plan. *Out, out, out!*

He was leaving the study when he heard the start of a furious knocking on the front door, accompanied by the bark of a dog, dogs, more than one. Then another sound caught his attention. Above. Second floor. Steps, coming downstairs.

Albert retreated into the study while the fracas below steadily increased in volume. Two voices. Female, shrill, frightened. And a man who seemed to be mad, spitting a mixture of strangely accented English and a sibilant language suddenly identifiable as Japanese.

Albert opened the study door a crack. ' . . . working late, I see this man, he break, he smash, *ka-cha, ka-cha!* I watching, let's go, *pow-eeee!*' He recognized the voice that had challenged him in the garden. Now it was the woman's turn to speak in querulous tones too low for Albert to catch.

'Yes, yes, po'liss, po'liss, you cor, I rook.'

Again the woman; this time Albert got the word 'dangerous'.

356

'No dangel, we have dogs. Hai, *hai*!'

But the woman must have instilled some caution into him, for next the man shouted, 'Oh yes, then I ret the dogs go, dey fine him okay.'

Albert heard the click of claws on polished wood and his throat tightened. He'd known Kleist didn't own a dog, he had come without gas or poison, who would have predicted a mad oriental neighbour?

The dogs wasted no time on the downstairs rooms, but bounded straight up the stairs, pulled inexorably by the intruder's scent. Albert closed the door; no key, *damn!* Then came a heavy thud, and claws began to work against the panels.

Find a weapon, anything. He flashed his torch around. A wood-carving table . . . There must be a knife, a bradawl, something with a point to it. Steel files, they'd do.

But there were two dogs. Even if he managed to neutralize one, the other would get him. Keep the door shut. Which left . . . out the window, jump, run for it.

As Albert tugged the curtains aside, however, he looked down and saw a figure march around the side of the house: human, carrying what looked like a club.

The clawing at the door rose to a crescendo. Albert prepared to open the window, regretting the operational necessity that awaited him beneath. As he did so, however, the door gave under the weight of the dogs and sprang open.

Two black shapes bounded into the room. Albert shone his torch. Alsatians: big, bouncy dogs. Animals with body weight and teeth. Christ Almighty, how could he have failed to shut the door properly . . . ?

He held out the brace of steel files, waiting for the brutes to home in. It took them less than a second. All the while his brain continued to function, as it had been trained to do in any crisis, analysing data, forecasting possible outcomes, percentages, worst scenarios. Whatever happened, this was going to leave marks. If Kleist's housekeeper was in league with him, if Kleist was a villain, if Anna Lescombe had fled with him, they would all know they'd been rumbled after this night's work. Catastrophe, disaster, *obliterate*!

Negotiate the dogs, negotiate the people downstairs, seal the house, run, buy maximum time, *execute*!

All this was processed in the instant it took the leading dog to stop, turn and leap for the motionless person by the window.

He knew what to expect. They would have been trained to go for the throat. He forced himself to stand perfectly still until the first dog was within feet of him and already launched into its spring. Albert, both hands full and without light, judged his thrust as best he could, going low, underneath the beast's belly. He lunged upward, hoping for the stomach, but the point of the file glanced against bone and slipped sideways instead. The dog shrieked. Albert kept pushing, twisting, gouging, until his hand was suddenly showered with invisible wetness and a dead weight bore down on his hand, carrying him with it.

He expected the second dog to jump, so he kept his free arm up to cover his throat. He could sacrifice his forearm. As long as he kept the use of his hands and his legs, he could sacrifice any part of himself.

Things didn't work out like that. Instead, he felt long hard needles drive through his left hand: the agony was a mixture of having his skin doused in scalding oil and the electric shock of a deep cut from a razor. Albert dropped the second steel file. His jaws locked. Grenades were going off inside his head, he couldn't hear, think, move, but he *must not cry out*.

He knew what had happened. This dog could smell meat, best quality steak. Albert had the blood of recent butchery on his hands and the dog wanted it.

He fought to separate himself from the corpse of the first Alsatian, but it was heavy and lay on his forearm. The second animal was tearing at Albert's left hand. He felt something give inside, a tendon; pain took him to the borders of unconsciousness and he knew he had to end this now or go under.

Somehow he managed to yank his right hand free, still holding the file. The other dog growled rabidly; if he hadn't been starving, desperate for the blood left on Albert's hands, he would have torn out the intruder's throat long before. As it was, Albert had mere seconds' respite. He raised his one good hand and drove the steel file down into the back of the dog's neck with all his remaining strength.

Go, go, go!

Albert came upright, still holding the second metal file, and slid over to the window. The French doors through which he had entered were open, allowing light to stream onto the lawn. Through the flashes that tore across his vision he could see a woman, dowdy, middle-aged, her hair in curlers, hugging a lumpy pink dressing gown around her body. She was saying something, but her words were lost in the noisy antics of a second person.

This man stood not more than five feet two in his white socks and trainers, wearing a tee-shirt and blue shorts that extended down past his knees. On his head, pushed far enough back to reveal an almost bald pate, was a fluorescent, orange sun-hat that produced a tiny trail of light whenever he moved, which he did frequently. In other circumstances he might have come across as an eccentric, mildly amusing phenomenon, but he was holding a baseball bat in both hands and, as Albert looked down, he executed a series of Samurai-type sword exercises with it that were anything but funny. 'Oh, God,' Albert muttered. 'Oh, God.'

The Japanese lifted his head. He must have possessed remarkable night vision, for he caught sight of Albert's face at the window and cried: 'Rook!' Next moment he was running into the house.

Albert, too, was running.

He took the corridor in three strides, vaulted onto the bannister and slid all the way to the bottom. The front door was still open. Before he could reach it, however, the frantic figure of the Japanese sped along the parquet floor to land in the opening, baseball bat raised ready to strike.

Albert came to a dead stop. He lifted his hands in the traditional attitude of surrender, and the Japanese grunted with satisfaction.

Albert lowered his hands. As he did so, he allowed the steel file which he had kept concealed inside his sleeve to drop into his palm. The Japanese waved the bat warningly, but Albert made a break for the open door.

His opponent, surprised by the sudden onrush, backed up a pace and found himself against the wall. He brought the bat down, aiming for Albert's head as he skated past him. In the split second before it could land, Albert leapt in the air and spun around through a semicircle. The Japanese, impelled by the force of his own blow, floundered forward and then fell to the right, in a vain attempt to recover. Suddenly he found himself rammed up hard against the bannisters, with Albert's face inches from his own. Then a wet, sticky hand inserted itself under his chin and began to push his head backwards, until Albert had a clean shot at the underside of his jaw. The steel point rose inexorably up, through the man's tongue, through the roof of his mouth, into the brain, and there Albert left it.

As he sped through the front door he caught the first blue flash from a police car's roof-light turning into the street. By now he was opposite the entrance of the house next to Kleist's. He vaulted the wall and hid behind it, flat on his stomach. The car cruised up the street and came to a halt. Albert listened. Doors slamming. Two voices. Footsteps, swiftly entering Kleist's front garden. Any more in the car? Pray God not. He risked one look. All clear.

His sprint might have won him a place on the Olympic hundred metres team. He ran so fast that he was back in his car and rolling before he remembered that he had not stolen some precious object to give himself cover, and in a rage smashed his good hand down on the steering wheel, wishing with his entire soul that it could have been the Japanese man's bald, fluorescent but now dead head.

The Last Day

THIRTY-SIX

Albert's reaction on boarding the plane only to find Hayes in the next seat was one of irritation. 'Babysitting?' he inquired.

'Officially, my role is a PAE one.'

'A *what*?'

' "Provide advice and encouragement." But me, I'm way too old to play word games. I like babysitting just fine.'

Albert stared at him. 'Why should I need advice and encouragement from you?'

'Because last night Bonn issued an ultimatum.' Hayes lowered his voice to a whisper. 'Find Krysalis or we'll blow the whole thing. Tell the world that in the event of nuclear war, the United States intend to sacrifice a West German corridor five hundred miles across, total civilian population three and a — '

'You can't be serious!'

'Better believe it. The West Germans say you British lost the fucking file, which you did, and allies like that they don't need. And the Pentagon doesn't exactly rate your efforts up until now to find it again. I'm deleting some expletives in there, incidentally. What happened to your hand?'

Albert grimaced. 'I caught it in a door.'

'Yeah?' Hayes treated the bandage to critical inspection. 'My sympathy's with the door,' he concluded.

Their plane reached the end of the runway and accelerated to take-off speed. Albert gazed out of the window, seeing only a bleak prospect that owed nothing to Heathrow Airport. If

363

West Germany carried out its threat, it could put an end to NATO; simple as that. Yet he understood the remorseless logic of their position; for Krysalis' principal message was that if war came, they would be expendable; in which case NATO ceased to have relevance for them anyway.

Reluctantly he went back to his study of Anna's case notes, now typed.

'You got the lady there?'

Albert nodded.

'I couldn't understand a quarter of that shit.'

'It gives us a fairly comprehensive picture of who we're dealing with, I'd have thought.'

I know what you're going to do, madam. I know the way you think, feel, love. Now I am *Anna Lescombe,* née *Elwell, oh yes . . .*

'Does it by any chance tell us where she is?'

'We should know that when her husband arrives in Corfu.'

'I thought your police were holding him for questioning.'

'That Concorde business, you mean? He's not a suspect, although he may have been the intended victim. Either way, we arranged for him to be processed very quickly. The last thing we want is to see him kicked into touch.'

'Did the other guy die?'

'Which other guy?'

'The man Burroughs stabbed, or whatever.'

'Yes, he died very quickly. I thought you might mean Burroughs. He's dead, too.'

'What?'

'Hanged himself in his cell last night.'

'Jeesus!' Hayes shook his head. 'Who do you reckon he was working for?'

Albert eyed him suspiciously. 'Not you?'

'Oh, come *on!*'

'Kleist, maybe. HVA.'

'Damn right. It's got HVA scrawled all over it. When does Lescombe get to Corfu?'

364

'If Olympic Airways' reservations computer is to be believed, in about five hours' time.'

'Do you rate this submarine thing?'

The submarine. In the course of his panic-stricken telephone call to Albert on Sunday evening, Fox had let slip that there was some unspecified 'connection' between Moscow's sudden burst of activity and the need for early penetration of Kleist's house; but . . . 'I'm worried by all the coincidences,' said Albert.

'Figure them to me.'

'One. HMS *Danae* is on her way to manoeuvres off Crete when her sonar picks up a sub. Engine signature and wave configurations tell her officer of the watch it's a Russian Tango patrol class – old, noisy, identifiable. Pure chance?'

'Okay, *Danae* was lucky. So?'

'So secondly, Russian submarines do cruise the Med, and they normally manage to do it without causing the Admiralty's officer of the day to have hysterics.'

'Not while Krysalis is off and running, they don't. The course the sub was on would have taken it straight towards Kithiria, ready for a turn into the Ionian.'

'*If* it did not change course. And since we've lost contact with her – '

'Yeah, yeah, I get the picture. But it's all we've got, isn't it? Eastern Europe's one big Yawnsville. Everyone's gone for the summer, *except* the crew of that submarine. Now if she is heading for an r.d. near Corfu, she'll be there tonight. And that gives us maybe twelve hours, maybe less. So what do you plan to do?'

'The Greek navy has agreed – '

'Oh, Jesus, tell me you're kidding.'

'No joke. I am to be the guest of the Greek navy, which is cooperating on the orders of its government. I imagine you're in the same . . . boat.' Albert raised an eyebrow, awaiting a reaction, but none came. 'It would help, of course, if this woman lawyer, this Robyn with the unpronounceable surname, would come clean about Kleist and his villa.'

365

'We tried everything. She genuinely does not know the name of that house.'

'Surely she must remember how to get to it?'

'She says not. Can't even remember the island's name, there are so many around those parts.'

No, that was wrong. There were only very few, as Hayes would have realized if he'd taken the trouble to scan a map. Albert could imagine himself falling in love with a lady psychotherapist and spending an idyllic month or so at her villa on a Greek island. He could not imagine failing to find out the island's name. But the woman whose grandfather had walked off the boat from Poland and run slap into one of the few immigration officers able to spell, she wasn't talking.

So what did David know that he and Hayes did not?

He knew his wife's whereabouts, Albert felt sure. Did it mean that he, too, was a traitor? Or . . . Albert's eyes strayed to the briefcase under the seat in front of him. He had the measure of Anna Lescombe, now; but he felt an uncomfortable absence of certainty about her husband.

Albert liked Corfu on sight: dry sunshine that was truly hot, whiteness that without exaggeration could be called brilliant, scents that he nearly knew, not quite. He had only two items of luggage, the briefcase and a long metal box, but his left hand still stung, his body was full of antibiotics, and he was pleased when somebody came to smooth a path through customs.

Their host was waiting for them in the car park. The vehicle looked like a typical camping trailer, slightly larger than the norm; but as Albert approached he noticed an aerial on the roof and saw that the windows of the back cabin had been blocked with newspaper; although the occupants might have been trying to protect themselves from the heat while they took a siesta, he doubted whether that was really so.

Inside the trailer there seemed to be hordes of people and only one electric fan, which was troublesome, especially since the phalanx of wall-to-wall radio equipment gave out

366

a lot of heat and everybody smoked; but as Albert and Hayes entered, a number of men went out to make room for them. In the end, only one was left. He half rose from his folding-seat behind the table, cluttered with maps, and extended his hand.

'How are you? Vassili. Deputy Director KYP Implementation Group, department two.'

When he offered no surname, Albert began to feel comfortable. As he introduced Hayes he managed to take a good look at the Greek, liking what he saw.

Vassili was in his fifties, with more thick black hair than a man of that age had a right to, and a chubby, smiling face. He wore a khaki short-sleeved shirt and lightweight trousers of the same material, ringed with a gold-buckled belt. The resulting military air was slightly spoiled by the wide holed vest visible at his open collar. He wore a diver's Rolex on a metal strap, which puzzled Albert, because he knew how irritating that would be for someone with so much hair on his arms. Perhaps Vassili had scant regard for life's niggles.

'There's not a lot I can do,' he said in excellent English. 'But you are welcome to what I have. I spoke to Jeremy Shorrocks as you were leaving London, so I am, you might say, "in the picture". Not a pretty one. Smoke?'

Albert and Hayes shook their heads. Vassili took out a black cigarette-holder, inserted a Papastratos and lit up. 'We cannot find your Russian submarine,' he went on. 'And we cannot find your Mr Kleist.'

'Well, shit,' said Hayes. 'He's resident here. Surely the police – '

'Greek law,' Albert broke in, 'prohibits the ownership of land in frontier territories by foreigners. Am I right, Vassili?'

The Greek responded with a massive shrug, lifting his shoulders and hands together. His smile revealed a lot of silver and a lot more nicotine. 'It's so. Many foreigners get around it by using Greek friends, Greek companies, on their certificates of title. Down in Athens, they are hunting. But . . .' Again the theatrical shrug.

367

The fan siphoned smoke from his cigarette, wreathing it around their heads. Occasionally one of the radios would squawk a babble of Greek, which Vassili consistently ignored.

'But what about the police? They must know him. I mean, the guy has to register or something . . . ?'

'Most foreigners never bother. Certainly no one called Kleist ever did.'

'But somewhere some cop has to have seen him, he's been coming here for years.'

'Mr Hayes . . .' Vassili stubbed out his cigarette in a tin lid and removed the filter-tip from his holder. 'There is a great film I once saw. In English, perhaps I should say in American, its name is *Witness*. You saw it too, perhaps? A man loses himself inside the Amish community. The local police can't find him, because it would mean searching maybe thousands of small farms and they don't have the resources, a thing that the city police could not understand. But *I* understood, because the Greek islands are like that. Each summer, thousands of foreigners come and go. Policemen too come and go. Your inquiry was made very late. No doubt you had your reasons for that. And I can assure you, we are looking.'

A long speech; but his shrug said it all.

'I need to ask you a question,' Vassili went on. 'Lescombe will soon apply to enter Greece. What do you want to do about that?'

'Let him in.' Albert spoke decisively; and Vassili nodded.

'I assumed that would be the case,' he said. 'You want to tail him, see which of the ferries he catches.'

'Why a ferry?' Hayes asked. 'Why shouldn't his wife be right here, on Corfu?'

Vassili waved a hand, dismissing the proposition. 'Our resources are limited, yes, but Corfu is a cosmopolitan place and the police are efficient. We can assure you, neither Kleist nor Anna Lescombe are on Corfu.'

'Actually, I'd rather you didn't tail him,' Albert said. 'Because I don't want him scared. You needn't worry, I'll be looking after him. I want to talk to Lescombe.'

368

'You *what*!' Hayes was half out of his seat. 'Now you just listen to me – '

'No,' Albert said. 'You listen. I've made contact with this man. He trusts me – or at least, he did. I think he'll talk to me. If I'm right, we can short-circuit this thing.'

'But the guy isn't stupid! Once he sees you, he'll know there's bound to be others, that he's being followed. Hell, look what happened in Washington!'

'Yes.' Albert flicked something off his knee. 'Oh yes indeed.'

'What's that meant to mean?'

'That you fluffed it, it's our turn, and we're prepared to back our judgement against yours.'

Hayes found himself looking through the palely tinted spectacles into a perfectly still pair of eyes.

'You're wrong. You are as far out of line as it's possible to be and stay in the ball-park. Lescombe is going to lead us straight to his wife, Kleist and Krysalis in one neat bundle. And you – '

'Lescombe gave Washington's finest the slip. So it's time to add another string to the bow.' Seeing Hayes about to speak, Albert raised a hand. 'Sorry.'

Vassili lowered the emotional temperature a few degrees by saying, 'You still have an hour or so. Let's go into town, get some lunch.'

'Thanks,' Albert said, 'but I'd like to catch up on my reading.' He tapped the briefcase with Anna's case notes inside. Then he turned to Hayes. 'You go.'

He was surprised when the American accepted Vassili's invitation, but then no doubt the CIA had posted other pairs of eyes in Corfu airport. Albert bought himself a roll stuffed with cheese and washed it down with a small bottle of *retsina* while he read. Suddenly he could not get enough of Anna Lescombe. She fascinated him.

David's plane was five minutes late. Albert stood on the terrace, enjoying a breeze that might have come from a blowheater, and watched the passengers disembark. The

369

third man down the steps raised his hand as he reached the tarmac, evidently greeting someone who was waiting for him, as indeed Albert was. The signal meant: Our man is right behind me.

Albert drifted downstairs to take up position behind the glass screen facing the customs hall. He watched David pass immigration and then pause, evidently unsure whether to join the crowd of holiday-makers around the baggage carousel or walk straight out.

Then came a hitch.

A telephone was mounted on the wall behind the nearest immigration desk. David went across to it, lifted the handset and dialled. Albert swore. It was almost inconceivable that Vassili would have bugged that line. Who was Lescombe phoning? Did he speak Greek? Yes! He had studied classics at his minor public school, could almost certainly make himself understood. One minute into stress-time, and already a gigantic hole was opening up before Albert's very eyes . . .

The man who had got off the plane just ahead of David now stood behind him, tossing coins from hand to hand, but the quarry concealed what he was doing with his body. He made two calls, one short, one long, staying on the phone for about five minutes altogether. Then he came through customs without waiting for bags. Albert caught the other watcher's eye. The man shook his head, mouthed the one word 'Greek' and shrugged.

Albert smiled at the memory of the Washington hotel room, with possessions scattered around it and a tape recorder playing in the bathroom. No luggage, an empty pair of hands . . . expert, oh yes. Who had taught him that?

He caught up with David as he was turning away from the money-changing kiosk with a wad of drachmae in his hands. 'Hello,' Albert said quietly, and David seemed to shudder.

'What are you doing here?' he asked. No fear, just righteous indignation.

'Waiting for you.'

'Am I going to be arrested?'

'Haven't you had enough of the police for a while? Incidentally, I admire your grit. Not many men would have boarded a plane so soon after what you went through yesterday. Didn't it occur to you that they might try again?'

'Since Cornwall I've had to learn how to look after myself.'

'Indeed.' Albert smiled faintly. 'Although it now seems reasonably clear that all your Cornish friends wanted to do was talk to you. Let's go and get ourselves a glass of wine.'

David stared at his bandage. 'You've hurt yourself.'

'An accident. Nothing serious.'

'I see. Look, I'm late. My travel agent's sending someone to meet me, at the harbour. I suppose I can't stop you riding with me, if you want.'

'That was a nice trick you pulled in Washington,' Albert said as he settled back in the taxi. 'Grosvenor Square had its share of red faces, but your score of brownie points with us increased dramatically.'

'Is that why you've been letting me run?'

'Why on earth shouldn't you be free to go wherever you want?'

'Then tell me the reason you're here. Two weeks' holiday in the sun? Or is the regiment practising beach landings?'

'I've come for one specific purpose: to talk to you about your wife.' Albert unfastened his briefcase. 'These papers are a transcript of the case notes maintained on Anna by a man called Gerhard Kleist . . . you've heard of him.'

He had been intending to frame it as a question, but David's facial reaction to the name rendered that unnecessary.

'Kleist has been treating your wife, on and off, for almost sixteen years now; first for post-natal depression, then, at intervals, for other depressions usually triggered by crises at work. After the first treatment, the two of them became . . .'

'Lovers.'

Albert nodded. 'It's clear from the notes, however, that it didn't last.'

371

'Three years! You call that not lasting?'

'But they stayed friends. On and off. Until the break.'

'*What* break?'

'After Robyn Melkiovicz went back to the States, in 1987. There's no record of Anna and Kleist having been together after that. You must *study* these notes. They may help you to help us find out where your wife is.'

'Don't you know?'

'I wouldn't be talking to you if I did.'

There was a long pause. 'Let me see those notes.'

Albert handed them over and sat back to enjoy the scenery. They were descending a street of attractively colour-washed houses, with balconies, and plants in huge amphorae, and an occasional garden where yellow grass bunched thickly. A wonderful place. His hand was feeling better already . . .

'How did you get hold of these? Make them up, did you?'

Albert regretfully turned away from the street. David's face was white and drawn. 'Judging by these notes, Anna's insane,' he said. 'Good God, how in hell could she have been a barrister all those years with this . . . this muck churning about inside her?'

'We haven't had time to take professional advice about that, but she's emphatically not insane. Not yet, anyway.'

'What does that mean, "not yet"?'

'One theory current in London, on the basis of what I've shown you, is that Anna has been skilfully manipulated by a rogue therapist. He's been moulding her, if you like.'

'I've never heard anything so daft in all my life.'

'It's not daft, David, it's simple fact. The techniques for treating depression are well known. The notes show that he applied them to Anna, but half-heartedly, not following through.'

'Why should he do such a thing?'

'Because each time she left him, "cured" as it were, he planted a hook to draw her back with later. Perhaps he wanted to get their affair back on the rails; maybe he was acting under orders from East Berlin, we just don't know.

372

But he abused Anna, professionally; his own notes prove that much. She's in great danger from this man. It's possible that when she fled she was suffering from something called a fugue.'

'A what?'

'It's a major state of personality dissociation characterized by amnesia and actual physical flight.'

'But why on earth should – '

'Because she is very disturbed.' Albert spoke quietly. 'She's in danger of doing something irreparable or, more probably, being *made* to do something irreparable.'

'She'll go . . . disappear?'

'Yes.'

The taxi drew up on the quay beside an English sign that said, 'Parga, Igouminitsa,' followed by an arrow. As they got out, the sea flashed white fire into Albert's eyes. He breathed deeply, relishing the feel of heat on his skin.

The English-language sign apparently held some deep source of fascination for David. 'I'll have that drink after all,' he said slowly, but without taking his eyes off it.

'Good.' Albert looked around the chock-a-block scene and his expression was wry. 'Two things this place isn't short of are people and places to drink. Over there, look, we can sit outside . . .'

They ordered beer. While they waited, David turned the pages of notes faster and faster until Albert knew he was not really reading, he was hunting for the end in the faint hope it might be a happy one.

'Cheers,' said Albert.

David took a handkerchief from his pocket and used it to wipe his face. Beads of sweat broke out again at once. 'She's a split personality,' he said hoarsely.

'No. She is not. Multiple personality, which is what you are thinking of, is a class of psychoneurosis. Specifically: *grande hystérie*. Anna couldn't have operated under those circumstances, and we know she led an outwardly normal life all the time she was under Kleist's care.'

'Then how – '

'I want you to understand something. It's important. Your wife is an immensely brave woman.'

David's face showed how taken aback he was.

'She had a difficult childhood – she was an only child, remember – following on the trauma of adoption. A lot of people can handle that, others can't; she couldn't. Then came an unhappy marriage which ended in desertion, at a time when she was still suffering from post-natal depression.' He paused. 'She may have tried to kill her child.'

'Oh, rubbish!'

'You've read the notes.'

'Compiled by someone you described as a rogue therapist.'

'Not at the start. He had no motive to mistreat her, then. And you might be surprised to learn how many women come within an ace of damaging either themselves or their baby, in the post-natal state.'

'But she's a barrister, dammit!'

'Isn't the real point that she's a strong, courageous woman? Against all the odds, she made it. Every single day of her life was a long, gruelling, uphill battle with guilt, and feelings of rejection, and the fear of losing you, which is why she never told you about the stew she'd been in. A battle which she won, until right at the end. Until now. And now . . .' He leaned forward, resting on his elbows, until David could no longer avoid his gaze. 'We've got to save her.'

David broke the long silence that followed by saying, 'How do you know all these things? You talk like a – '

'I was trained to know them. It's part of my job.'

'Which is *what*, for Christ's sake?'

'Cleaning up messes.'

'You see only a security "mess". I'm looking at my wife. I love Anna. She's my whole life, all I've got.' David seemed on the verge of panic. 'I've come so close and now I run into you. I don't know your real name, I don't know who you are, what you do . . . you say you're an army officer but you talk like a psychiatrist . . .'

'If you comb the army thoroughly enough you'll always find someone with certain skills.' Albert grimaced. ' "In my father's house are many mansions." And believe me, if I could tell you more about myself, I would. Do you know anything about the vampire legend?'

'What kind of question is that? For Christ's – '

'It goes like this. Once the vampire has tasted your blood, you die. But it takes a long time. You exist in a twilight world, and with each passing day you slip further from the light, while the vampire continues to prey on you. That's how it is with Anna. Kleist's her vampire.'

'Ridiculous.'

'David, there's a possibility, a real possibility, that they're sending a submarine to take her off tonight. That'll be the end of it. No more twilight world. Anna will have gone.' He leaned forward to grasp the other man's wrist. 'Is that what you want?'

When David made no reply Albert sat back, releasing his grip, and waited.

'Can you help her?' David's voice was low. 'She'll go to prison . . .'

'Not in the light of these case notes. I doubt if it would even get as far as a prosecution.'

What, Albert wondered, was the nature of the struggle going on behind those flickering eyes, that moist fore-head?

'Vampires . . . they drove stakes through their hearts, didn't they? Superstitious peasants hounding the village wise woman . . . stakes and silver bullets. All right. All right. I'll trust you, God knows why.'

Albert's sigh of relief seeped through his lips without a sound. 'You said you were going to see a travel agent . . .'

'I lied. There's no one.'

'Who did you phone at the airport?'

David's head jerked up, his stare had become dangerous.

'I see. One-way traffic, is that it? I have to trust you but tails I lose, my God, what kind of man are you?'

'The airport?' Albert said gently.

'I was phoning first the operator, then directory inquiries. I wanted to find out if they had a number for Kleist in Parga. It's a port on the mainland. Kleist's villa is five miles inland and it doesn't seem to have a telephone. That's where I'm going. Where we're going, I guess.'

Albert remembered something about David's calls that had struck him as odd at the time: he didn't appear to have the first number written down anywhere. That tallied. He'd kept his body close to the telephone, so there was no way of knowing how many digits he had dialled. And it sounded like the truth. Or would have done, but for one thing.

'Robyn Melkiovicz told the Americans that Kleist's house was on an island,' he said.

'She lied.'

'Why should she do that?'

'Because I asked her to. I wanted a head start.'

It could be true; Hayes had remarked earlier on how uncooperative Melkiovicz was. 'All right,' Albert said. 'But we're going there together.'

As they got up David pointed to the low, white roll-on roll-off car ferries waiting beside the jetty. 'We get to the mainland that way. I don't know which one, we'll have to ask.'

Albert, keeping a few steps behind David, noticed how as he scanned the busy harbour some object caught his attention. He glanced in the same direction, but nothing stood out: fishing-smacks, a tug, several motorboats, including one fearsome red and white monster with its engine whisking the waters of the harbour into froth.

They were halfway along the pier. David stopped a passing Greek and spoke to him. The man pointed to the furthest ferry. David turned to Albert. 'That one.'

His face looked terrible, all the muscles were working as if any minute he might have a convulsion.

'Are you all right? You look green.'

'Been travelling too much. Jet lag. Feel a bit sick.'

Suddenly he reeled to the side of the pier, holding his stomach. Albert went to help. But the hands clutched to David's stomach turned out to form one big fist. As Albert came alongside him, he stood upright and the fist swung into Albert's abdomen; before the officer could regain his balance one hand took his collar, another landed in the small of his back, there was water rushing up to meet him . . .

The shock of entry, salt in his eyes, forks of agony sparking through his injured hand, all conspired to lose Albert valuable seconds. By the time he had hauled himself back onto the pier and cleared his vision, there was nothing for him to see but the red and white speedboat creaming out of the harbour with David at its stern.

THIRTY-SEVEN

Barzel came to the church, that Sunday morning, soon after Kleist had slunk away; he hauled Anna to her feet and dragged her back to the house. There he had to hold her down while Kleist administered the injection. She tried to bite him but he was savage, rendering her semi-conscious almost before the needle entered her vein. Only when her eyes were shut and she lay still did Barzel release her. 'Make sure she stays that way,' he said.

'You think I have a factory for this stuff?' Kleist's voice was a mixture of anger and fear. 'Look!' He held out the case in which he kept his syringe and ampoules. 'One left!'

'How long will that hold her for?'

'God knows. So much depends on her general health, her resistance.' He remained lost in thought for a moment. 'Now's Sunday . . . tomorrow lunchtime, I think. When are we leaving?'

'Eleven o'clock Monday night. Have you got any rope?'

'Rope?'

'To tie her up if she wakes, idiot!'

'There should be some out the back.'

'Well, *find it*!'

Kleist, Barzel and the third man alternated two hour watches after that, so that Anna was never left alone. She first showed signs of life on Sunday evening, during Kleist's shift. When she was fully conscious but still unable to move, he tried putting her into deep hypnosis, without visible

378

effect. So reluctantly he administered the second and final dose of sedative, praying he had guessed right.

She was still asleep when Kleist again began his shift in the small hours of Monday morning. He waited until Barzel, who'd kept the previous watch, had had time to bed down before creeping out to the kitchen and appropriating a bottle of rum.

Anna awoke as Monday's dawn was beginning to tint the room grey. She turned her head and saw Kleist asleep in a chair beside her bed, an empty bottle on the floor next to him.

She lay still while she analysed the messages her brain was sending out. Her limbs were stiff and useless; a headache tortured the backs of her eyes, blurring vision. She tried counting up to ten, then simple multiplication sums. She functioned; not brilliantly, but well enough to work out the next step.

Her mind was flashing a message, on and off, on and off, like a neon sign. This represented a chance to escape, and it would be her last. So she must not make any mistakes.

What should she do?

Get up. Leave the room. Find a way out of the house. One thing at a time.

Very cautiously, so as to avoid making the slightest sound, she tried to bend one knee. Agonizing pins and needles shot through her leg from ankle to groin. It took her three attempts before the knee was upright. She looked at Kleist. He had not stirred, and his snores continued unabated.

Now the other knee. This time it came easier to Anna, because she was expecting the pain before it could shock her. Both knees bent. *Good!* If she could only get them horizontal again . . .

When she was once again lying flat she slowly drew her hands up the bed until they would go no further. The circulation was coming back, every move she made seemed less of an effort than the previous one. Using her right hand she stuffed the sheet into her mouth, to stifle any cry she might make. Then she pressed down on the mattress and tried to sit up.

The room spun around her, nausea swamped her stomach, she bit on the sheet for all she was worth. Blood throbbed through her temples at a frightening rate; she felt the arteries must surely burst. But no: she was sitting up, both arms at full stretch, and Kleist still slept like a man condemned to spend the rest of his life in oblivion.

Anna silently massaged her legs beneath the sheet until she felt confident of being able to move without falling over. Then she slipped her feet sideways on to the floor and, resting her weight on her hands, struggled upright. For several minutes she stood still, waiting for her body to adjust. She took a tentative step forward, quickly followed by another. She could walk!

Next — to escape from the bedroom . . . ah, and from the house at the same time! Pain had made her forget the terrace outside. From there she could make her way into the garden . . . then where? Did she have enough strength to swim?

It was steadily growing lighter outside. While Anna pondered her best choice of exit, her eyes were drawn to the sliding window overlooking the bay. At first her brain did not register what she saw as anything other than an illusion, a product of the drugged sleep from which she had woken. But the longer she stared, the more convinced she became that this was no mere dream. A small yacht had anchored opposite the house on the other side of the cove, beneath the church.

The sight dazzled her. She swayed a little, then reached out for the dressing table to support herself. Less than a quarter of a mile separated her from freedom and safety. Kleist still slumbered on. There was no sign of the other two men. *All she had to do was reach the yacht.*

No, wait. Were the owners of the yacht likely to be friends or foes? That was the first question — no use killing herself to cross the strait if the only result would be fresh captivity. But nothing had been said about a yacht in her hearing, all the talk was of submarines. And the boat seemed to be one of those small flotilla cruisers built for amateurs, hardly the sort of thing a secret service would send to rescue its agents. Holidaymakers who, God bless them!, had chosen this of all bays in which to rest up for the night . . .

Kleist. What to do about him? He looked out for the count, but suppose he awoke and found her gone? Anna stared through the gloom at his vague, comatose form. He had been drinking and anyway he was a heavy sleeper by nature. She must take a chance. There was no alternative.

Yes, there was. If she could somehow reach the empty bottle by his side, without waking him, and bring it down, hard, on his head . . .

It would increase her chances of success, of survival, tenfold. Anna took one step towards him, and stopped, her breath coming in gasps.

Hold it. Where were Barzel and the other man? Suppose they heard the noise of glass meeting bone, oh God! The breath flowed out of her in a wave of relief. Just pray Kleist would not wake, and go.

But the thought of Barzel and his colleague, once raised, refused to leave her. Suppose they were keeping watch somewhere? Check . . .

The bedroom door stood ajar. She glided through it. Nothing stirred. She padded from room to room, risking one glance into each as she passed. Empty. At last she came to the kitchen. The other man, the one with no name, sat at the table with his back to her. His head rested on his folded arms. He, too, was asleep. No sign of Barzel.

Two enormous, battered suitcases were stashed either side of the man's chair. Anna had never seen them before; she wondered what they contained. But then everything else was drowned in the knowledge that if she kept her head and moved fast, she could get out.

The sun had risen halfway above the horizon. With every second that passed she stood to lose her chance: either her guards would awake, or the yacht would put to sea.

Anna slipped back to the bedroom for long enough to put on a few clothes before stepping out to the terrace. The garden below was empty. She went quickly down the path, making herself ignore the vicious pounding inside her head where the residue of whatever drug Kleist had used was distilling itself into neat poison. Through the gate, that's right, follow the track until it peters out in the sand, so far so good. Don't look back, above all *don't stop*!

She came to the beach, where she flopped down exhausted, suddenly realizing she had no idea what to do next. A stretch of placid water, clad in diamante by the early sunshine, still separated her from refuge. She could not detect any sign of life aboard the boat opposite. So near yet so far; surely she hadn't come this close only to be defeated?

She might swim. But she felt so weak. What if her strength deserted her halfway across? She would cry out, and no one would hear her. The thought of drowning mere yards away from salvation was too much to bear. If she shouted from the beach, without attempting to swim, perhaps the owners of the yacht would come to her rescue? No, long before then her cries would have roused Kleist and the other man.

She wanted to sob. The sight of that small, rather grubby, indescribably beautiful boat lying at anchor almost within hands' reach was too much to be borne.

'Er . . . excuse me. Hello?'

Anna raised her head and looked around. No one was visible. Yet surely she hadn't imagined that voice – male, educated, *English*! 'Who's there?' she called.

'Over here . . . behind the rocks.'

She swung around, jerking her head in all directions. At first she could see nothing, but then she noticed a tousled head and a pair of red, blistered shoulders emerging above some boulders to her right. 'Ah . . .' said the head. 'This is a bit embarrassing. Actually. I'm off that boat over there, see, and I thought I'd go for a skinny-dip . . .'

'You're *English*!'

'Yes. Tony Roberts. I'm a doctor, actually. You look upset.'

382

'Oh my God,' she cried. 'Oh my God, help me! *Help me*!'

'What's the trouble? I mean, I heard you coming so I . . .'

Anna stood up and stumbled towards Doctor Roberts as if to the saviour of her soul. The head eyed her apprehensively. 'Sorry,' it muttered. 'You don't have a towel or something – '

'Oh God, just shut up, please shut up. I'm desperate. My name's Anna Lescombe, I'm being held a prisoner by the East Germans, they're going to kill me, I know they will, you have to help me. Take me on your boat. Please!'

The Englishman came out from behind his rock, no longer embarrassed. His eyes, now not quite so friendly, viewed her with professional detachment. Anna realized he was quite young and a little unsure of himself. 'You're ill,' he said. 'What's the trouble?'

Anna reached out to grasp his arms. 'I'll tell you everything, *everything*! Only please, please just call your friends on the yacht and take me away from here, get me to Corfu, to the British consul.'

'All right, all right.' His face had grown pink to match his shoulders. 'Now, calm down, do. Where have you just come from?'

'Up there.' She pointed. 'They're all still asleep, but they'll wake up soon and then they'll come for me . . .' Part of her acknowledged that he must think her mad, perhaps she was mad, but she must make him see, make him believe her enough to take her away.

'Okay. Okay, now, try to relax.' He disengaged himself and put two fingers to his lips. A long, loud whistle echoed out over the water. 'Pete,' he shouted. 'Show a leg!'

'Not so *loud*! They'll hear you!'

'Sorry. Got to get things moving somehow. Ah, good . . . Pete's an early riser, like me . . .' He waved a hand, beckoning to someone aboard the yacht. Anna heard an engine cough into life. She swivelled around to look up at the house, then gazed across the cove. The boat was moving, but slowly, so slowly! 'Hurry up,' she breathed. 'Hurry up, for God's sake . . .'

383

Footsteps on the path. Kleist's voice: 'Anna! Where are you?'

She raced behind the boulder that until a minute ago had concealed Tony Roberts. 'Help me!' she cried. 'Don't let them take me!'

The yacht was about halfway across the strait. 'What's up, Tone?' she heard a woman's voice shout.

'Got a bit of a problem. Gloria, chuck me a towel, for Christ's sake.'

Kleist had reached the sand, with Barzel a step behind him. Something crunched against stones as the yacht went aground. Anna turned her head. A bikini-clad blonde girl was standing up to her knees in water, towel at the ready; two other people, one man, one woman, were on deck, trying to assess the situation.

Kleist advanced slowly towards the doctor, hand outstretched. 'Morning,' he said easily. 'Gerhard Kleist. I'm so glad you were able to come to our patient's rescue.' He glanced back. 'This is Doctor Barzel, of the Endemann Clinic in Hamburg.'

'Doctor?'

'Yes. I'm a doctor also.' He laughed. 'Sorry I don't have my cards with me. I'm a consultant psychologist. You are . . . ?'

'Doctor Tony Roberts.'

Kleist's eyebrows rose. 'A professional colleague! We don't expect to have such treats in our hideaway.'

'We're all from the London, actually.'

'Whitechapel?'

'Yes.'

'Then you must know Rayner Acheson. Your head of clinical psychology.'

'I've never met him. I know *of* him, of course.'

Anna could not believe her ears. A medical convention had got under way. 'Don't listen to them,' she blurted from behind her rock. 'They're not doctors, they're spies!'

Barzel coughed and turned away, evidently to conceal a smile. Kleist's face, however, remained serious. 'Perhaps if your friends would like to come down from the boat we could discuss this more sensibly on dry land. I make a point of never concealing anything from my patients; there's been too much hole-and-corner psychology. Rayner did a paper on that very topic last year, funnily enough.' He raised his voice. 'Anna, come here, please. I want you to be a part of this. Don't be shy. You've nothing to be afraid of.'

'Doctor Kleist . . .' Roberts' voice had taken on a hard edge and Anna, hearing it, knew a moment's resurgent hope. 'Can we be clear about one thing, please: is this lady free to come and go as she wants?'

'Most certainly.' Kleist frowned. 'Has she suggested otherwise?'

'Somewhat forcibly.'

'Well, we can deal with that straightaway. It's a splendid boat you have there. If you feel you wouldn't be inconvenienced, I can't think of anything more therapeutic than for you to take Mrs Lescombe on a little tour of the island while Dr Barzel and I catch up on our sadly neglected paperwork.'

Anna stared at him. The four young sailors eyed each other uncertainly, not sure what was happening.

'You wouldn't have any objections?' Roberts' voice had lost some of its former harshness.

'None.'

In the ensuing silence Anna said, 'I'd like to come. Thank you.'

'Tone . . .'

It was clear that the blonde in the bikini and Doctor Roberts made up a pair. She was looking at him bleakly, as though she suspected his sexual motives.

'Hold on, Gloria. Dr Kleist, would you mind giving us a quick rundown on what exactly is wrong with Mrs . . . Lescombe?'

'Lescombe, yes. Not in the slightest. She's a successful barrister, married to a senior civil servant. She's been undergoing therapy with me, on and off, for several years.

385

Recently she suffered a series of blackouts, culminating in a serious fugue, personality dissociation and resultant acute depression, necessitating rest and absence of excitement. I invited her to stay with me here, with her husband's permission. He'll be joining us at the weekend, incidentally.'

Roberts turned to Anna. 'Mrs Lescombe, is that true?'

Anna had more than enough courtroom experience to grasp the trap facing her. If she admitted any part of what Kleist had just said, it would be tantamount to admitting the whole: people heard concessions rather than details and that was only human nature. But if she lied, and said none of it was true, Kleist must surely have some way of proving his claims. Her passport was up at the house, so no point in denying her name was Lescombe. How much else could he prove?

She became aware of not having spoken for a long time. That in itself was damning. So – 'My name is Lescombe,' she blurted out. 'I am a barrister. My husband, David, is a civil servant. He will not be joining us at the weekend.'

So far so good. But she had dodged the worst bit. How was she going to deal with –

'Have you been undergoing therapy with this man?'

Anna took a deep breath. 'Many years ago, yes.'

Anna, seeing the expression on Roberts' face, tried to dig herself out of the hole she'd burrowed and only succeeded in bringing down more earth on her head. 'Like he said, I've been working as a barrister since then, do I *look* mad, for God's sake?'

'Why did you embark on therapy with Dr Kleist?'

Anna stared at him. 'Why?'

'Yes.'

Because I tried to kill my child. Go on – say it!

'I don't see what that's got to . . .'

'You won't tell me, in other words?'

'It's not that I *won't* tell you, it's just that . . .'

But he was no longer paying her any attention. As he

386

turned back to Kleist the smile on his face became friendly. 'And Dr Barzel – what role does he play in all this?'

'He is a professional colleague of many years' standing, who some months ago arranged to spend his summer vacation at my villa. It's a happy coincidence that he happens to be the world's foremost expert on the fugue state. The circumstances are from our point of view ideal, as you can appreciate.' Kleist spread his hands. 'None of which need impede a day's cruising in your company, should you be kind enough to agree.'

He had them, they were his. For the first time Anna noticed the second girl: a brunette in a black one-piece bathing costume that looked as if it had been sprayed onto her hourglass figure from a can. She was staring at Kleist with a star-struck kind of gaze that Anna recognized. She had contended with it in restaurants across London; in theatre foyers, opera boxes, concert halls; while walking, while talking, in the act of raising a glass to her lips. Certain kinds of women always adored Gerhard Kleist: particularly the kind that saw how he could wrap them around his little finger, and wanted it.

Anna's attention suddenly divided. Barzel, keeping both hands in his pockets, had begun to saunter along the beach, kicking stones, peering closely at lichens where they sprouted from rocks. He had drawn almost level with Roberts; another few steps would bring him to her side. At the same time, she heard the dark girl say, 'Dr Kleist, I know Rayner Acheson.'

'You do?'

'Mm-hm.' The brunette nodded vigorously, eager, nay desperate, to please. 'He lectures us nurses. I want to get into psychology. It's terribly hard, though.'

'But *so* rewarding.' Kleist had become animated. He started to draw pictures in the air with his hands, bewitching the girl with his love of the job, his dedication.

'Anna,' she heard a low voice say, and she jumped, for now Barzel was standing close by with his back to her and she had not seen him approach. She waited for him to speak

387

again, but he remained silent. Then she lowered her gaze to see that he had removed both hands from his pockets and was holding them clasped loosely behind his back. To the others, it must have looked a natural enough posture: relaxed, unthreatening. Only she could see that the right hand held his gun.

Barzel had left no room for misunderstanding. If she persisted in trying to escape, she would oblige him to liquidate every trace of these people. But on the other hand, she could save them. Her choice.

'Mrs Lescombe . . .'

Roberts had to say it twice more before she realized he was talking to her, that everyone was looking expectantly at her.

'Yes.' Her voice was scarcely audible.

'Would you like to come for a sail with us? We'd be only too pleased to give you a spin around the bay, as it were.'

Anna managed to tear her eyes away from the gun. For a moment she gazed sightlessly into the distance; then she refocused, looking as she did so from face to face. Roberts, amiable, concerned. His girlfriend, Gloria: still glowering, her mouth halfway between a sulky smile and a pout. The other man, Pete . . . no, she could not look at his face for he was stretched out on the deck of the yacht, catching the early morning rays, fashionable sunglasses circumventing his head in a black band. And the brunette: the one person Anna might, just conceivably, have been able to order into extinction if it had been a clean-cut choice, her or me . . .

And finally, Kleist. Smiling his unperturbed smile. Indifferent.

'Mrs Lescombe. We really would be ever so pleased if you wanted to spend a day with us. Really.' Roberts waited a moment. When still she did not speak, he said again, 'Mrs Lescombe . . .'

'I'm sorry,' she heard herself say. 'I'm so sorry to have made such a fool of myself. I think I'll go and lie down. I'm so very, very sorry . . .'

THIRTY-EIGHT

Robyn Melkiovicz's memory proved accurate: there was a place called Avlaki on the west coast, it did have a landing-stage. As David disembarked a thought struck him: if by some remote chance he survived, he was going to need an escape route. He asked Amos, his boatman, 'What will you do now – go back to Corfu?'

'No. Mr Kleist has arranged for me to meet him here later.'

David's pulse quickened. 'You're expecting him tonight?'

'Yes.' The Greek was young, high in his own self-esteem. He did not look inclined to waste time answering importunate questions, but David needed to know.

'Ah, I suppose that means we'll be going for a barbecue. Like last year.'

'Perhaps.' The young man hesitated; then the desire to manifest superior knowledge won out. 'Although Mr Kleist does not keep a barbecue on Antipaxos any more. Not after the fire.'

'Oh, so it's Antipaxos tonight, is it?'

The man nodded. David paid him off and walked inland for a few miles before coming to a hamlet. There he had no trouble in persuading someone to rent him a moped. After that he did not stop until he reached the outskirts of the larger village where Robyn had told him she used to buy bread. He bought a box of matches from the main store, at the same time inquiring the whereabouts of The Little House. David was a friend of Mr Kleist? Indeed yes; was he in residence? He was, together with a few friends. Directions

389

were forthcoming. David thanked the shopkeeper and went on his way.

Who were the 'friends'? Anna, maybe: but the shopkeeper had plainly spoken in the plural: *filoi*. More than one friend. Be careful. *Count cents!*

He stopped, wiping his brow, and looked around him. The village had receded into the distance and the light was going. Olive trees grew sporadically in expanses of dry, yellow grass beside the road. Houses were visible here and there, through the branches; all of them stood well back, secluded from the curiosity of strangers like himself. On the road he was too prominent. In this quiet place the phut-phutting engine of his moped invited attention like an ice-cream van's bell.

David knew that Kleist's villa lay off to the right, down a hill, perhaps a quarter of a mile, not more, from where he was now. He quit the road to the left, deliberately seeking cover in the opposite direction. Before long he came upon a huge pile of rotting straw which someone had hollowed out to form a kind of igloo. It was an isolated spot. Hurriedly he stowed his moped deep inside the cavity, and set off on foot.

He kept the road in view wherever possible, anxious to avoid losing himself, although this meant that sometimes he found himself blundering through nettles or having to climb over barbed wire. At last he felt sure he must have arrived more or less opposite Kleist's house, still on the other side of the road.

David was standing at the top of a slope. Cautiously he began to make his way down, hugging the treeline for as long as he could, until at last he reached the verge.

Damn! Emptiness yawned on either side of him. Not even so much as a gleam of white wall could be seen anywhere: this stretch was utterly deserted. He waited a moment, checking both ways, then ran across to the other side, where he again lost himself in the obscurity of the olive groves. Here he found a narrow path winding along the foot of an embankment: nothing like the stone driveway to the house that the store-keeper had described. David followed it for a few yards before stopping, certain that he had veered off course.

He flopped down beneath a tree and rested his head on his arms, suddenly tired. For the first time since quitting Corfu he let himself dwell on the case notes Albert had shown him. Every assumption he had ever made about his wife, every lesson supposedly learned, was founded on falsehood.

Occasionally Kleist would record in his notes verbatim snatches of dialogue taken from the sessions. One of them had leapt off the page at David when he read it in the taxi.

'My mother always insisted she loved me, but if that was love . . .'

'You didn't want it?'

'And that made me feel evil. Because what good person rejects love?'

'My mother . . .' Mrs Elwell. She must have known about Kleist; and about the chain of events that had led Anna to him in the first place. But when he'd asked her about those things, she had lied. Keeping up the front mattered more than her daughter's happiness, perhaps even more than her life.

David raised his head. Something was wrong.

For the past few minutes he had been half aware of a curious noise, neither close nor remote. Pods snapping in the heat, perhaps, or rats . . . but the evening had turned cool and the noise was too loud to be caused by rats.

He stood up and looked around. What should he do next? He resolved to push on in the direction he'd been taking before his rest. After a while the path sheered away from the wall and began to zigzag down the hill through dense undergrowth. From the breeze that now refreshed his skin he judged he must be near the sea. Ah, yes: a pale shimmer of molten gold cupped in the V made by two hills, off to his right.

He heard the noise again, louder this time, and looked over his shoulder. At first the dusk defeated his town-orientated eyes, but then his sight sharpened and involun-

391

tarily he let out a sharp breath. Twenty yards away, someone stood lighting a cigarette.

Fortunately the stranger was facing in the opposite direction or he could not have failed to see David, who now slowly edged around the nearest tree until its trunk screened him from the other man. He willed his heartbeat into a more regular pattern and tried to think. The person he'd just seen didn't look Greek. He might be a tourist, well off the beaten track, but David didn't think so: this island had yet to be ruined by the summer holiday crowd, tourists were scarce. Kleist, on the other hand, was said to be staying here with *friends*. Bodyguards, maybe. Watchers.

Suddenly a twig broke, David heard a cough. The aroma of smouldering tobacco entered his nostrils, faintly at first, then more strongly. The man was moving towards him. David jerked his head back to its original position. Should he move? Stay put? He looked to the left and right. Trees, nothing but trees . . . Wrong! — up ahead he could see a luminous pallor: a wall, maybe, some kind of building . . . Kleist's villa? No, he was way off course. But perhaps he could hide there?

David began to map out a route. At least a dozen olive trees stood between him and the whiteness. If he dodged from tree to tree, moving quietly and fast, he might make it undetected.

He turned to either side, saw nothing suspicious. Then he pushed himself off the tree trunk and went forward at a brisk walk. He was lucky; the earth stayed silent beneath his feet. A few seconds later he had his back to another tree and was peering around its gnarled bole in an attempt to work out if he'd been spotted.

No one.

He took a deep breath and made for the next tree on his route. Now he could see that the whiteness belonged to a small church, its silhouette broken by two powder-blue blocks of sky framing a black bell. It looked deserted. If only he could get inside . . .

The sunset was dissipating swiftly; it would be no easy task for anyone to catch sight of him through the dusk. The smell of tobacco smoke had faded. Not a sound disturbed the evening stillness. While he stood there, indecisive, a feeling of exposure swept over him. On impulse he ran forward to push against the church door. But as he did so, he heard that cough again, very close this time, and the unmistakable click of a cigarette lighter.

'Hey,' said a voice. 'You!'

David fled into the church, closing the door behind him. He had expected to find the place in darkness, but to his surprise he saw a feeble yellow flame at the far end. He raced down the aisle towards it. The remains of a single large candle stood on the altar, nine-tenths burned away and drooping but still bright enough to show his position to an enemy. David made a lunge. The candle toppled to the floor and went out. As much by luck as judgement the solid brass candlestick was left sitting snugly in his palm.

Outside the church he heard a voice say, 'You! I know you're inside. Come out!'

The speaker used stilted English, but he didn't sound either English or Greek. David let his eyes stray to the windows, now glowing electric blue in the gathering dusk. Soon night would fall, but there was just enough light left to show him an opening, over which hung a curtain. A vestry . . .

'Who's in there?' The church door rattled.

David's throat had sealed up tighter than a fist. He sidled into the vestry, allowing the curtain to fall across the gap after him.

'You cannot hide!'

A prolonged creak, coupled with a warm breath of air, indicated that the outer door had opened. The stranger walked down the centre of the church, disturbing leaves as he approached the altar. *How much could he see?*

'Aah!' The footsteps halted. David's head seemed full of blood, he felt it would explode; surely the newcomer must hear the thudding of his heart? 'Aah, show yourself, why don't you? Nothing to be afraid of. I only want to talk.'

Another pause. David was standing with his back against the wall that partitioned the body of the church from the vestry, as close to the curtained doorway as he dared. He knew the man was mere yards away from him. How well did he know this church? *How much could he see?*

More footsteps, going away this time. Another creak, followed by a slam. David was alone again. But what would the other man do — wait for him to emerge, or muster reinforcements? *Why had he left the church without searching it?*

By now the gloom had become all but impenetrable. The vestry lacked a window; David could scarcely see his own hand in front of his face.

He came off the wall and turned, preparing to twitch aside the curtain that hung across the doorway. Another second and he would have passed through the gap, into the church itself. But then many things happened at once: someone nearby violently scattered leaves across the floor; David caught a glint of metal; in a flash he knew that the stranger hadn't left the church, he'd opened the door and slammed it again to fool David and now was mere feet away, ready to strike.

The man growled in satisfaction; David felt the air move; he leapt backwards. Hands punched his solar plexus, winding him. A head butted into David's chest, slamming him back against the wall. For a second he merely let it happen, powerless to help himself. Then he remembered what he was holding.

His first blow landed across the other man's shoulders, causing him to freeze with a grunt of mingled surprise and pain. Not much of a respite, but enough. David lifted the brass candlestick as high as he could and brought it down in a vertical stab, aiming just beyond the hands that had been pummelling him seconds ago. Someone groaned. David took the candlestick in a double-handed grip and began to flail it around like a sword, slashing the darkness on either side of him. His third swing made contact: another groan, this time near his feet.

David stepped back a pace, raised the candlestick above his head and axed downwards with all his might.

The sound of brass clanging on stone revealed his mistake. Too late: he was already toppling forward, unbalanced by the force of his own blow. A foot lashed out of the darkness, entangling his own, and he fell.

Somewhere close he could hear panting. His opponent was still on the floor: it was a kick that had laid David low, not a punch. *So don't let him get up again.* David rolled as far as he could, hugging the candlestick to his chest. The wall stopped him. He managed to stagger up to the kneeling position before hands met around his throat and began to squeeze.

The enemy was behind him, also kneeling. Not a good position, but he was as strong as an ox and clever, too: anticipating the likely reaction he kept his body arched left, away from David's increasingly weakened blows with the weapon still clutched in his right hand.

David's strength was going. Each breath was a nightmare. Purple blotches marred his vision; from the pain in his throat he felt his head must be coming off. Suddenly the right hand on his windpipe fell away and he sensed that the man had made a grab for the candlestick. He missed. Instead of trying again, he moved his left hand from David's throat to his hair, and started to bang his head against the wall.

David cried out. His adversary immediately let go of David's hair and clamped his left palm across his mouth instead. In the darkness, the move was clumsy; his forefinger landed between David's teeth. With whatever strength he had left, David clenched his jaws together and shook his head from side to side.

Until then, the other man had been fighting in near silence – which made his roar of pain all the more gratifying. David managed a half turn, still keeping his teeth closed around his attacker's finger. Through a blur of weakness he realized that his right hand was free. He stabbed to his left with the candlestick and made soft contact. He thrust again – but this time hands stronger than his own managed to grasp his makeshift club, and next second David was defenceless.

A whoosh of air, frighteningly close, told him that his assailant was trying to duplicate his own move of a moment ago and lay him out cold. He ducked to one side. The next swing caught him on the shoulder, making him howl. That meant the end: his voice would have given away his position.

David fumbled desperately on the floor, seeking purchase. His fingers brushed something spiky and spasmodically closed around it. In the same instant, he heard a clang as the other man threw down the candlestick and launched himself downwards. David found himself crouching with his back against the wall, those terrible hands once more around his throat.

This time his opponent was in front of him. *Light going now, can't breathe. Last chance. Go limp. Sink . . .*

As the other man was pulled forward under the weight of the inert body he was holding, David tightened his grip on the spiky thing and drove it with all his force at the two glittering points of light in front of him.

He missed the eyes; but a squeal reassured David that his thrust had done good work. The vice around his throat relaxed, he was free, he was running. As he hurtled through the church's outer door, something made him look down and see that he was holding Juliet's corn dolly. He raised Miss Cuppidge to the light. His hands were shaking. Anna . . . Don't think of that, don't stop, to the right, trees; ahead, a path leading up the hill; on his left, a short drop, then rocks and the sea. A bay.

For a split second he found himself looking across the cove to a house on the hillside opposite. Light streamed out of its downstairs rooms to illuminate a terrace, where two men were standing with their backs to him. David had eyes only for a third figure, seated just inside, but nevertheless clearly visible through the open doorway. A woman. Her pale green

V-neck dress with short, white-cuffed sleeves stood out boldly in the artificial light. The dress was Italian, made of cotton, and it zipped up at the back. David knew these things, because he had bought it for Anna last year on her thirty-eighth birthday: one of his rare but outrageously extravagant declarations of love.

THIRTY-NINE

They moved fast through the night, Barzel riding next to Yorgos, who drove, with Anna and Kleist in the back seat.

Kleist had been unable to hypnotize Anna. Her resistance to him was at its greatest; his skill had dwindled almost to nothing. The best he could manage was a patient explanation of the arrangements, hoping that would calm her – they were going to a place called Avlaki, there a boat would be waiting to take them on to the small island where they had swum, they would be in the car for so many minutes, on the sea for so many minutes more – but it was useless. Their first night on the island, he had told her that David wanted her to be here, so she must stay; now he could not unscramble those instructions. He was afraid to contemplate what the effect might be.

At the start of their journey Anna lay huddled against the door, as far away from Kleist as she could manage within the confines of the car. They had untied her legs but her hands were still bound. She was shivering, sometimes violently, sometimes a mere murmur of the body, reminding him of a very sick animal.

'The submarine,' she cried suddenly; and seemed on the point of speaking again but was silent.

'What about – '

'Can't face it. Steel trap. Don't let them.' She raised her voice in desperation. 'Don't let them do it!'

Barzel, in the front seat, half turned and muttered a few

words in German. When Kleist snapped at him he tossed his head like a man who doubts, but made no reply.

'Don't deserve this. Leaving Juliet. Everyone. Poor David . . .'

He touched her cheek. In the second before she pulled away, it felt wet beneath his palm.

Anna was silent for a long time; she seemed to be asleep. But suddenly Kleist became aware of her eyes studying him intently. Before he could react, she said, '*Herr* Barzel, you really must come around for dinner when we're all living in Berlin. We'll have a laugh about old times, a few drinks. *Lots* of drinks . . .'

No one said anything. Barzel continued to gaze through the windscreen as if Anna had not spoken. Kleist peered at her, his professional intuition already mapping the catastrophe before him.

'You must bring your gun. I want to see you shoot. Can you knock hearts out of playing cards, and things like that? Bet you can.'

She was sitting up now, taking interest in her surroundings. When Barzel still did not answer she leaned forward to rest her wrists on the back of the driver's seat — 'Sorry, Yorgos, did I bump you, it's this rope' — and say, 'Out of the run jobs like yours can be so fascinating.'

Her giggle was childlike.

'Anna.' Kleist tugged her arm. 'Anna, stop it.'

'Mm?' She glanced back at him.

'*Anna!*'

She swayed. Her eyes, so intent and alert a second ago, unfocused, and in the same instant her face underwent a subtle change. It was a question of millimetres, nothing more: a sagging of the chin, drooping eyelids, slack mouth . . . countless details emerged to change her personality, along with the outward show.

'What? Did you say something?' she asked.

'I . . . you weren't quite yourself.'

'No. No. What . . . was I saying?'

Barzel broke the barbed silence. 'You were inviting me to dinner, Anna; you wanted me to bring my gun and show you tricks.'

Kleist examined her face, what he could see of it in the car's dim interior. He needn't ask if she remembered any of that, because plainly she did not. She was tearing apart, severing, in front of him. His handiwork, brought to its logical conclusion at last . . . two Annas. Two separate people. He turned away from her and stared out of the window, as if darkness held a peculiar fascination for him.

Anna fell back in her seat. The car cornered sharply. When she lurched against Kleist some hard object in his pocket ground against her thigh. She knew what it was. His gun. She had seen him furtively take it while Barzel was still preoccupied with the other man, who had staggered back to the house with blood on his face and a long story to tell; but because he told it in German she did not know what was the matter with him.

A tic started at the side of her mouth. She had a sore throat. All her nerves seemed to be at war with one another, right up against her epidermis, suddenly making it impossible to sit still.

You must not leave this place!

They're taking you away. Can't fight them.

David is here. He's come for you. He wants to rescue you.

No, he can't do that. Can't.

It had been David she'd seen, outside the church, a few hours before. They'd left her facing the cove while they argued across the top of her head, as if she didn't exist. But she did exist, and she had seen her husband.

He isn't real. Couldn't be.

Before they tied her up, she had somehow managed to slip his photograph out of her handbag and leave it under a vase of flowers on the window-sill. If he found it he would know she'd been there.

Her last message of love.

Fight it!

400

I can't.

Can't.

Can't.

Do.

This.

Barzel again half turned his head. 'We are nearly there. Get ready, please.'

FORTY

Albert had told Vassili, 'I don't care what colour it is as long as it's black.' And the Greek replied, 'Black is impossible. Grey.'

Lindos P.269 was grey and against a background of mainland mountains the coastal patrol craft became almost invisible, moving soundlessly through the water at twenty-seven knots. But there was a moon, just three days off full, and more stars than Albert thought the cosmos capable of holding, so he cursed his luck and prayed for rain.

A lot of people now seemed to be involved in the tracking of Anna Lescombe, something else which gave Albert no pleasure. Half a dozen taciturn men clad in black tracksuits had joined the party before the *Lindos* left Corfu. No one introduced them, they simply materialized and stayed. Albert looked at them, raising one eyebrow for Vassili to see, but the Greek merely lifted his shoulders in one of those thespian shrugs.

When they reached the island where Kleist had his villa they found the local policeman waiting on the quay. Albert forced himself to stand with a patient look on his face throughout the involved colloquy that followed. At last Vassili turned to him and said, 'He's sure he knows the person you mean. A doctor who sometimes brings his patients to the island for treatment: always beautiful women, never men.'

'That figures.'

'Something else. A few days ago, the woman he's with

this year made some trouble, here at the port. From the description, it sounds as if it could be Anna Lescombe.'

'Why the devil didn't he report that before?'

'He says no one asked him.'

'I thought you'd issued an alert?'

'He didn't read it until this evening.' Vassili hesitated. 'Pay on the islands is low, and perhaps this man is more friendly with Kleist than he should be. But that can wait for later. Right now, we're wasting time.'

'What about David Lescombe?'

'Nothing.'

'But you did put out an alert on him, too?'

'Of course. As I've told you: a hundred boats go in and out of here every day. Not all of them use the main port. There are beaches, coves . . . Lescombe is maybe here, maybe not.'

Albert knew already that an air search had failed to locate David's speedboat. Three quarters of an hour elapsed between his climbing out of the water and the first chopper taking off, seventy miles away on the mainland. Lescombe could have defected to Albania in that time; he could have *swum* to bloody Albania . . .

'God damn!'

'Do you want to go up to the villa? It's called "The Little House", by the way.'

'How charming. Let's get a move on, shall we?'

But it took a while to organize enough transport for everyone; another quarter of an hour lost farting about, Albert thought savagely. At last he was on his way, sandwiched between Vassili and Hayes in the back seat of a Fiat.

'What are you doing about the coastguard?' he asked.

'They have been told — '

The car swerved violently to avoid a motorcyclist; for a moment all was cursing and confusion. Albert gritted his teeth at the agony that suddenly boiled through his injured hand.

'We've ordered the coastguard to stay on watch, but don't

expect too much. When we first put out a description of that speedboat we got three sightings in the first quarter of an hour. Trouble is, they were all in different places.'

'But one of them indicated a course to this island, you did say that.'

'*En daxi.*'

Got him, thought Albert. Got everyone. Never mind the ifs and the buts, think positive. What idiot drove a motorcycle like that at night? Not a motorcycle, a moped.

'We're almost there.'

The convoy slowed to a halt. Everyone got out. The six black-clad newcomers were already in a huddle when Albert and Hayes came up. Albert looked around for Vassili to do some translating, but he had disappeared.

Suddenly there was just three of them: Hayes, Albert, and the policeman.

'We're being set up,' Hayes muttered.

'What?'

'They're running this thing for themselves. Although it may have passed by your lofty attention, we don't figure any longer.'

'Then we shall wait,' Albert said calmly, 'until they collect us again.' But Hayes' words jarred him.

He moved away, deliberately distancing himself from the other two in order to listen. He had not experienced such stillness since his last foray into the Empty Quarter, and as for the stars! . . . Albert, enveloped in a velvety darkness that seemed neither moist nor dry, gazed up at them in awe.

He would come back here, when this was over, for a holiday. Perhaps he would hire a motorbike . . .

His memory kept looping back to the barely avoided accident on the road as they were coming out of the port. What sort of maniac rode a motorbike in that way on a hot night *while wearing grey flannels and a long-sleeved white shirt?*

The thump might have been anything, except that Albert's instincts were honed to recognize a stun grenade when one went off. As he crashed down he heard five rounds of automatic fire, muffled by distance, something more than distance. Interior, two o'clock, seventy, *go!*

His night vision was superhuman; trees and rocks seemed not to exist for him. Less than twenty seconds after he'd risen to the crouch his back was jammed hard up against an outside wall of The Little House. Listen. Wait. *Go!*

Roll around the corner, down, monkey-crawl to door, Christ, what a stench! Mayhem . . .

Albert stood up silently, raising both hands above his head. These men were as professional as any he'd encountered, but sometimes the best of us make mistakes . . .

Vassili was standing inside the hallway. Hearing the Englishman clear his throat he swung around, holding in both hands a pistol aimed at Albert's stomach.

The next seconds seemed inordinately long.

'Come in,' Vassili said softly, holstering the gun. 'But watch your feet.'

A living room, once cosy, now disordered. On the table by the fireplace, two large, empty suitcases and a radio set, powerful, not plugged in. It looked as if someone had been setting up an aerial. They'd interrupted him before he could complete the job, however; he lay on the floor, his legs entangled with the chair on which he must have been sitting when the five rounds drilled through his chest. Face a mess, too: had he been in a fist fight? Halfway between him and Albert lay a Luger, beside that a holster.

It had been a case of 'No Surrender', then. Whatever official doubts might be expressed in London concerning the Lescombe woman's importance, the people holding her did not share them. Suddenly Albert did not share them either; and in that moment Anna became terrifyingly real to him.

'You okay?' Hayes asked as he came through the front door.

Albert nodded. 'Too late. Birds flown.'

Vassili and his squad were already taking the house apart, aided by the policeman who had entered as soon as Hayes demonstrated by his own example that it was safe to do

405

so. Nothing showed up, except the radio. Albert wandered about, trying to picture what had gone on here.

Only in the last bedroom did anything attract his interest: a vase of bluebells, now somewhat limp, on the window-sill. He went over to look. Then he saw something else. There was a small square of card under the vase: not aligned like a coaster, but skew-whiff, as if someone had put the vase down hurriedly to stop the card from blowing away.

Or to hide it.

Albert lifted the vase to one side and picked up the card, turning it over as he did so. A photograph. David Lescombe, wearing a white, long-sleeved shirt. *You moron, get after him!*

'Vassili,' he yelled. 'The guy on the moped, it was Lescombe, out, out, *out*!'

In the car they tried to make sense of it, paint a picture they could all believe in, but nothing worked. If Lescombe was part of the opposition, why didn't he escape with the Germans? If he was straight up, why did he lie to Albert in Corfu? Where was Anna now? Who had her?

Back in the port Albert and Hayes stayed by the car, watching the Greeks fan out. Albert kept his eyes on Vassili, who was on the point of entering the biggest *taverna* when a woman in the doorway of a nearby boutique said something that made him pause.

Albert, sensing game, drew closer.

Vassili was having an expressive conversation with the boutique lady, who wore large, round spectacles that made her look distinctly owlish. She seemed angry, perhaps a touch scared. Vassili was pushing her too hard. It ended abruptly, with him throwing up his hands in a gesture of despair.

'The man next door,' he said to Albert, 'runs some kind of travel company. He has boats.'

Albert took in the chalked notices. 'Yes?'

'This woman saw a foreigner come up to him. He could speak some Greek. He wanted a boat to go to Antipaxos, right then. The woman got interested, it's forbidden to take

406

a boat to Antipaxos after dark: too dangerous. But the foreigner had a lot of money, seemed really desperate, so in the end they did a deal.'

'How long ago?'

'Maybe half an hour, she's not sure.'

'What is this Anti-place?'

'A smaller island, uninhabited, due south, one mile.'

'Time to go,' said Albert.

FORTY-ONE

David had travelled a long way without knowing real fear. When it hit him it came out of nowhere, hard, like an iron force of nature.

Stiff gusts whipped up the channel between the two islands, sending huge surges of sea against the side of the boat. It was small, powered only by an outboard engine. David sat on the middle thwart, gripping the sides. His hands ached with strain.

He knew he might die out here.

The travel agent had warned him: the strait between the two islands was unpredictable, hazardous even to those with years of experience of Greek inshore waters. Night was worst. At certain times the sea glittered beneath the moon like a millpond, with scarcely an eddy to marble its silver surface; at others it would dissolve into fury at the behest of some whimsical gale or freak tide. If you were caught up in it, there was no going back: all you could do was run before the waves, praying they would not swamp your boat.

In the end, greed overcame caution. The man said he would try a crossing. At £100 for one mile, it made Concorde seem like a cheap-day excursion.

It had not felt too bad at first. The sea looked choppy, rather than rough; David was an experienced sailor, so this did not daunt him. Shortly after they left the lee of the big island, however, the screw began to leave the water with each pitch and toss. The first wave broke over the prow of the boat. Then another, high enough to soak David's shoes and ankles. He tightened his already painful grip on the planking. If the boat shipped too much water it would founder and sink. He was a strong swimmer, but he was realistic, too, and he was sure he would not be able to survive a sea running this high.

He distrusted the boat's owner. Now he understood the man's cupidity: he was terrified. He kept up a low, monotonous litany; its burden seemed to be not so much that what they were doing was dangerous as that it was illegal, for at night the port police closed this strait to traffic. That did not concern David. The most welcome sight in the world, right then, would have been an irate harbour master in his cutter.

They were three quarters of the way across when they started to ship water in alarming quantities.

Cross currents.

The land mass in front of David lurched from side to side, all scrambled up with black sea and grey sky and white horses, like a demented television screen. The wind had risen. When David felt the boat smash against the first 'V' of converging waters, he panicked. He could no longer hear the Greek helmsman's chant against the howl of the wind, but the sound of his own voice echoed inside his head like a ghoul's. He was screaming.

He was going to die.

No conscious thoughts. No prayers. Just the fear, the shit inside him welling up in animal protest at the horror of it. The totality of 'me'. Bottom line: *save me*.

His legs were soaked to the knees; water swished about everywhere, slowing them down, making them unstable. The boat began to rock forward and back, like a swing. Sometimes a wave took her sideways on as well, bringing her to a crazy kind of halt, but then the weight of sea on one side would yield, abandoning them to the mercies of the next watery trench. The Ionian, no longer an azure, picture-postcard lake, was black and chill.

This penetrating cold did more than anything else to keep

David thinking clearly. The small island lay dead ahead, less than a quarter of a mile off. Anna had already landed. He'd found her. Triumph. And he wasn't going to let the sea rob him of it now.

He launched himself forward, feeling in the wintry bath for something to bail with. The boat plunged, banging his head against a thwart and he temporarily lost control, stunned. He was floundering around, soaked to the skin, at the mercy of waves which flung themselves down in a whirl of destruction, of malice concentrated against himself. His fingers made contact with something solid, a bucket . . . no, it was a cork life-saver, *God damn*, there must be a bailer somewhere . . .

He found a plastic pot barely larger than a tooth-mug and frantically hurled water left and right until his arms were ready to drop out of their sockets. Useless. Ten, twenty quarts of water landed in the boat for every one he managed to displace. Suddenly the panic he'd conquered earlier had him by the throat. He couldn't draw breath. He cried out, exhausting the last reserves of oxygen inside his lungs. With that, the sea moved in for the kill. The starboard side of the boat slowly sank down, allowing water to pour over its edge. David had no time to take evasive action. His feet kept in contact with wood for a few seconds longer; he felt the boat sink away from him, kicked against the hull one last time, and then he was fighting for his life.

The sea was a mindless creature, home to other mindless creatures. It slaughtered blindly, like justice. And always the ground, if that were the right word, was of the sea's own choosing. By embarking upon it, you accepted its challenge on its own terms. David could not win this struggle.

He swallowed a lot of water and vomited it up. As he surfaced he realized that what he could see was land. He began to swim towards it, hauling himself through the swell about as effectually as if he were already wrapped in his winding-sheet.

A wave came down on his head, leaving him breathless.

He trod water. The land seemed closer. David struck out once more.

He felt himself weakening. All his effort went into forcing one arm over, left, then right, then left again, but each circle took longer than the last, and cut less of the sea. His legs hardly moved. His clothes hampered him, but it was too late to think about taking them off. Wasted effort. Swim. Left. Right. Left.

David, down to his last breath, opened his mouth, and a wave filled it.

The swell that had overwhelmed David Lescombe made little impression on *Lindos P.269*. By propping himself against the navigator's console Albert was able to read the signal without difficulty.

89/44303/A:SIGINT9 YOUR 56 AND 57 WELL RECEIVED + COMPSEARCH SHOWS SIG CON GERQUARRY PREV A/R CASE CABOFFSEC TREATED + GANDERGOOSE GQEQ + NILCONF + SEETWOENDIT

Albert devoted a lot of thought to deciphering this. The word 'Gandergoose' leapt off the flimsy as if a highlighter pen had been run through it, and he was anxious to guard against any possibility of error.

So what did it mean? He knew even before receiving the signal that the computer had been at work: all of Kleist's patients were being subjected to scrutiny as Albert left London with Hayes. The search had apparently thrown up a 'Sig Con', or significant connection, between his German quarry (Kleist) and another case where action had been required ('A/R'). A cabinet office secretary had been treated, was that right . . . 'Caboffsec treated' . . . ? Albert frowned at the deliberate obscurantism, which, he realized, had been designed to confuse 'trusted allies' like Hayes and Vassili. Anyway, since he could not even confirm safe receipt of Shorrocks' cable ('Nilconf'), Gandergoose was up to him.

He folded the sheet of paper and stuffed it into his pocket. 'How much longer?' he asked Vassili.

'That will depend on whether the commander here obtains clearance from Athens.'

'Can't we cut the red tape?'

'I'm sorry. Somewhere close to where we are now, there may be a Soviet sub, probably containing a highly-trained Special Operations unit. If it comes to a fire-fight, our commander cannot just hope for the best.'

'Is that why we're cruising so slowly?'

'Yes.' Vassili went across to the chart table. 'Let me show you what we think we are up against.'

Albert looked around for Hayes, who a few moments ago had been standing beside him, ostentatiously trying to read London's signal, but the American was nowhere to be seen.

'Here . . .' Vassili ran a finger north-south ' . . . is the Vespuga Deep. A trench, wide and very deep, as you guess from the name. If they are anywhere, that's the place. Put yourself in the Soviets' position. What would you do?'

'Stay down until D minus five, then surface for long enough to ship the boat that'd be waiting for me up top.'

'I don't think so. The sea around here is treacherous, especially at night to those who don't know it. Kleist and the woman would be mad to take such a risk: floating around in a rising swell, with winds and tides against them.'

'What, then?'

'We believe the submarine captain will send a boat to make landfall. Whichever option they choose, there has to be a boat, on the surface, at some point and for some time. There's a good chance we shall pick her up. But . . .'

'But what?'

Vassili unwound hands, arms and shoulders in the finest production Albert had seen yet. 'You won't let us help you. Surprise, you tell us. No helicopters; one ship only. It may be *possible*; easy it isn't.'

Albert moved to the nearest port and stared out into the darkness. 'Kleist and the woman will have gone ahead,' he

412

said to the glass. 'I can't think of any other reason why Lescombe should be so desperate to get to the small island.'

'Unless that was a blind. You have told me already: he's good.'

'Not this time. He's getting close to home now. Starting to panic.' Albert paused. 'I want us to go there too. But quietly. Undetected. Does the captain know where they would have landed?'

Vassili called across to the commander. The man squinted at the ceiling and spoke a few words.

'He says, along the eastern side of the island there are many fine beaches. A man could land there if he didn't mind getting his feet wet.'

What if the enemy's already in place? Albert thought grimly. Suppose the submarine had surfaced, sent a task force. A German-occupied Greek island; how history does repeat itself . . . He became aware of another voice speaking. The signals officer was at work in his cubbyhole behind the bridge. Vassili glanced in that direction, then back at Albert. 'Orders,' he said softly.

Albert nodded. 'Vassili, where did you stow my bags?'

'Aft. There's a rope-locker — '

'I know it. Excuse me.'

The breeze had stiffened while they were talking, but Albert relished the feel of damp salt air on his face as he made his way towards the stern. The locker stood in the centre of the deck. He opened the lid and took out a long rectangular case: the sort of thing professional snooker players use to carry their dismantled cues. Then a voice behind him said, 'Hold it right there.'

Albert obeyed.

'Turn around.'

Albert did so. 'The thing that's been puzzling me,' he said conversationally, 'is why you waited so long, Hayes.'

*

413

David was lying on sand; and still he nearly drowned.

A wave, the same one that had filled his gasping, wide open mouth, met an opponent coming from the other direction. The incoming water proved stronger; it swept him almost as far as the beach. He felt something hard beneath his feet, only to lose it again. Then his heart seemed to explode and he knew nothing more until he came to, spread-eagled face down on relatively solid ground. Every third wave or so sluiced over his shoulders; if he had taken mere seconds longer to recover, he would have died.

He crawled up the slope inch by painful inch, until water no longer deluged his body. When he finally managed to push himself onto all fours he could see great gouges in the sand. He had clung to the beach as if it were a life-raft, trying to become one with the earth, so that he, like it, might become indestructible.

The moon shone brightly, but it provided an ominous, ghostly illumination, one which gave more intensity to the shadows than sunlight ever could. He looked out to sea, still in the throes of upheaval, its white horses prancing wildly. Apart from flicks of foam, nothing showed. The boat had gone. So had the boatman.

David sat down heavily. If it weren't for him, another man would still be alive. No! You can't be sure he's dead yet; suppose another freak wave washed him ashore, further up the coast . . .

To hell with it. Tomorrow. He could adjust then, fiddling the books of conscience until they came out right. Now, status check. Nothing broken. No bleeding. A head that ached where he had bumped it against the side of the boat; bruises left, right and centre; stomach, nauseous. But alive, thank God.

He had lost a shoe. *Better take off the other one, you're on sand, it won't hurt your feet . . .*

The beach was narrow, perhaps a hundred feet long, bounded by rocks at either end. He could not see a light anywhere. Nor could he hear anything above the wind and the pounding of the sea. Which direction . . . ?

He had come down from the north and something told him that Anna was ahead of him. *Go south.*

He kept away from the shoreline, wanting to see if there were any paths leading inland. He knew there were several people involved, because he had concealed himself to watch while they loaded Anna into the car and drove off: even allowing for the fact that not all of them might have come as far as this, the group would be bound to have left traces. But he discovered only a few false trails, little more than trampled undergrowth leading back to piles of picnickers' rubbish or heaps of ashes.

When he came to the furthest limit of this particular beach he began to climb over the rocks. He was at the summit of the outcrop when something made him raise his eyes. And he saw her.

Anna was standing at the end of the next cove with her back to him, head bowed. She was alone.

David resisted the impulse to shout. He did not want to startle his wife; and who else might be within earshot? He slid off the rocks, seeking the shadow of the vines, which here came down almost to the sand. Now he moved slowly, anxious to avoid making the slightest noise. Sixty feet away. Fifty. Forty.

Anna did not move. She seemed to be asleep, suspended upright by invisible puppet-strings.

Closer. Thirty feet. Twenty.

As David opened his mouth to speak, something struck him violently in the small of the back. He fell. Anna started to turn, he caught a glimpse of her ghostly face, stagnant, like that of a long-drowned corpse, with two black wounds where the eyes should be . . . then his mouth was full of sand, his mind full of darkness, and the road he had followed so tenaciously at last ran out.

FORTY-TWO

'Wait so long?' Hayes tilted his head to one side, but the black object in his right hand did not waver. Albert found it impossible to gauge its stopping power by moonlight.

'I've been slow,' he said. 'I admit that.'

The shadows did not permit Albert to see if Hayes smiled, or what expression his face wore. He decided to keep going.

'That awful scene at Crowborough, with fists pounding and cups being thrown. Metaphorically, of course. So unlike you. Unprofessional behaviour from a very professional person.'

'Shove the compliments.'

'Of course. The real question being, what shall we do about it all?'

'Do? Tell me, Major Albert of the SAS regiment, "Who Dares Wins" and suchlike crap: what do you believe is going on here?'

'Me? Nothing. I'm just a simple soldier.'

Hayes shook his head. 'No. You're not. You're a highly complex individual. I've read your Northern Ireland stat sheet. "Cold personality masked by scrupulous politeness, coupled with significant absence of morality," isn't that how it goes?'

'I wouldn't be a bit surprised. You can always rely on Army Intelligence to get it wrong.'

'No commitment to any one government agency, but held ready at all times for secondment. "Special operations," that is to say, state executioner. Freelance.'

Albert made a deprecating *moue*. 'Would that I were. The regiment pockets the fee, I don't see a whisker of it.'

'So what? You don't need money, because you have no life outside your work. Not even a sex life. Relaxations: hunting, painting, long solitary walks. But oh boy, can you cook! And you're a psychologist. Now, that really interested us. Why in heck should MI6 need a psychologist?'

'Thinking man's thug, you know the sort of thing.'

'No, I don't. I don't understand any of it. I'm just here to do one job.'

'Make sure I don't do mine. Yes. Oh, quite.'

'What exactly *is* your job, Major?'

'I'd have thought that was fairly obvious.'

'Pretend I'm stupid.'

Albert smiled; but the question exercising his mind was precisely how stupid Hayes might turn out to be. *Did he know about the deal that Albert had cut with Redman?* Redman said not, but . . . 'My orders are simply to ensure that the Krysalis file doesn't fall into enemy hands.'

'You're to kill the woman, in other words?'

Albert's smile did not waver. Hayes was silent for a long time. No matter how the deck swayed beneath their feet, his stance never changed. Albert's brain was busy with spans, ranges, angles, light. Nothing balanced; the lines steadfastly refused to meet. 'Why are you so determined to stop me?' he asked. 'I'd have thought you'd be rather pleased to let me get on with it.'

'You know why, Major Thinking-Man's-Thug.'

'The Krysalis file is a fake. Disinformation, which your side wanted to see fed to the Russians. How's that?'

'*Very* good, my friend. Go on.'

'That file always was too good to be true. No one keeps data assembled in that way and leaves it lying around London.'

'They do if they're being taken for a ride.'

'What?'

'For an ally of the United States, England is pretty careless. Over the past three years, the Foreign and Commonwealth

Office has been leaking like a sieve, Major. We wanted to find the holes and plug them.'

'Ah, so you were playing *two* games: spreading disinformation, meant to confuse the Warsaw Pact, and flushing out moles at the same time.' Albert sounded admiring. 'That's imaginative. How did it work? You kept close track of every copy of the file, waiting to see who did what with it?'

'More or less.'

'You didn't foresee the Anna Lescombe angle from the start, then?'

Hayes laughed. 'Man, when they told me what had happened, that stuff with the psychoanalyst, you could have slain me with one chop from your upper-class Brit accent.'

'Doesn't it strike you as at all odd that, although the leaks started — three years ago, you say? — David Lescombe only joined the committee a few weeks back?'

'No. Lescombe's had access to lower grade material for years, so we assume he cut his teeth on that. Good practice for when the big chance came along. And he's one of many. We're happy to make an example, any example.'

'But . . . excuse me, I just want to get this straight . . . it isn't Lescombe that's got the file, is it? It's his wife.'

'That doesn't matter.'

'Ah, no, I see . . . we're back to the disinformation angle, aren't we? The exact method of feeding the file to Moscow's immaterial.'

'Right.'

'Apart from tracing your mole, all that concerns you is that the file should fall into Soviet hands, and should be seen as having been lost by London.'

'Close enough.'

'So that when it began to look as if we seriously might prevent that happening, Langley engaged in a considerable rethink, right?'

'To the extent we were prepared to slip a copy of Kleist's fax to the HVA, tipping them off about him, the messenger-boy in Athens, everything. Yes.'

418

'Which explains your presence here. And why you took a free lunch off Vassili, out of my earshot, when you ought to have been staking out the airport with me, if your cover story was true. You wanted to make sure he didn't become *too* efficient at helping me.'

'Unfortunately, I got to him a little late. Like you, I've been slow.'

'Oh, I don't know. Vassili did his stuff: one dead German radio operator meant that nobody could milk him of his codes, send a decoy message, abort the Russian rescue operation.'

'Vassili's one of the good guys, yes. A pity I didn't think to contact him earlier; perhaps he'd have persuaded his government to withhold cooperation from you altogether.'

'But apart from that, all's well that ends well. Except that you still haven't found your mole.'

'We think we have.'

'What, *Lescombe*? Seriously?'

'The evidence is kind of one-sided. It certainly wasn't the CIA pitched you into Corfu harbour, now was it? Anyway, you can relax now, Major. Krysalis will be away shortly, so will the lady and her husband.'

Hayes still thought that Lescombe was going to escape. He didn't know about Albert's deal with Redman!

Why didn't he know?

Albert fought to make sense of the mess. Redman and Hayes were supposed to be on the same side; yet here was Hayes, parroting an out-of-date line as if it were current policy. Redman's change of course seemed logical enough: the Director of the CIA had called him after a meeting with the Vice President, the state department would do anything to salvage the Vancouver summit, now the only priority was sweeping Krysalis under the carpet. Albert followed all that. So what was Hayes playing at? Surely Redman wouldn't have just let him go to Greece believing nothing had changed? Unless . . .

'Tell me,' Albert said. 'Does Redman know you're here?'

Hayes chuckled.

'He *doesn't* know.'

'Oh, come on! I long ago figured he wouldn't want me any place near the real action. So I let him think I had to take a trip to the States. Kind of a misunderstanding, you could say.'

Redman, believing that Hayes would be somewhere else, hadn't bothered to bring him up to date. Albert thought swiftly. Hopeless to try to persuade Hayes to contact London now. So he sighed, and — 'I'm afraid I've got a job to do,' was all he said.

'No chance. Anna Lescombe and Gerhard Kleist are going to stay alive. Sorry.'

'One problem.'

'Namely?'

'I'm still holding this case.'

There was a moment of silence, of immobility. Then Hayes retreated a step, bringing his back against the rail, which was exactly where Albert wanted him. He heard a heavy click and knew that what Hayes held was a revolver, now cocked, not good, not good news at all . . .

'Put down the case, Major.'

'Going to have to make me, old boy.'

Albert's brain was subconsciously counting seconds. The radio officer had been receiving when he left the bridge. So much time to decode. So much time to formulate tactics. So much time to brief. So much time to execute. Now it was D minus nothing. And if the orders said 'No,' if the game had gone against him . . .

With a sudden surge of power the ship leapt forward, going from five to fifteen knots in exactly the flash of time it took Albert to swing his case up and knock the gun from Hayes' hands. Then the case became a battering ram. It thudded into Hayes' left side, below his breast bone, crushing the pancreas and rupturing his spleen, but, before agony could transmit itself through the American's brain, hands grasped his ankles and somersaulted him backwards over the rail. Hayes was bleeding to death, internally. By the time

420

he hit the water he had been immobilized beyond any possibility of salvation. He died slowly, in pain, at a great depth.

As Albert thrust his way onto the bridge Vassili turned to him and said, 'A boat has already landed on the beach. We are late. What have you – '

'Power, please; make what speed you may. And *no light* until the end. Have you got that?'

'Yes.'

'*No light at all!* I'll be up top.'

Only then did Vassili notice what he was holding.

'Get up!'

The voice sounded as if it came from miles away. David instinctively knew Kleist was speaking. Someone kicked him, the same voice commanded, 'Get up, I say,' and at that David levered himself onto his knees. A woman stood in front of him. Because his head was still spinning she seemed to ripple from side to side. 'Anna?' he breathed.

She stared straight ahead of her. He could not tell if she recognized him. Somehow he staggered to his feet. 'Are you all right?' he asked; and on hearing that, she lifted her chin, but still she did not speak.

'Anna, it's me. David.'

For a moment longer she continued to gaze at him in silence; then – 'Go away,' she burst out. 'Please go away. They'll kill you. There's nothing you can do.'

The three people on the beach stood at the points of an invisible, equilateral triangle, facing inwards. David longed to go to Anna, but he felt sure Kleist would have a gun. So he was destined to die here without ever holding his wife in his arms again. He yearned to speak to her, let her know how much he loved her. All that came out was, 'Oh God . . .'

Anna raised her hands and David saw that they were bound with rope. So she had not gone willingly, then. The rope vindicated him. It meant that he'd been right to trust her in spite of everything. She wasn't a traitor.

'Barzel will be back any minute,' Anna said. 'Gerhard, can't you help him hide?'

But then a new voice spoke from the edge of the moonlight, where sand met trees. 'I don't think so,' it said. 'Your husband and I must have a talk, Anna.'

Barzel stepped forward far enough to let David see the weapon he was holding. 'We'll go up the beach,' he murmured. 'Talk in private.'

When David stayed where he was, Barzel gestured with his Luger. 'Please,' he said softly. 'Not here.'

'Gerhard!' Anna's shriek made David start, but its effect on Kleist was remarkable: a shudder seemed to pass the whole length of his frame. 'He's going to kill David,' Anna cried. 'Gerhard, *stop him*!'

At first no one moved, or said anything. Then Kleist put his hands in his pockets and stepped to one side, as if conceding a point. Barzel gripped David's shoulder. 'Walk,' he muttered.

'Jürgen.'

But Barzel paid no heed to Kleist. He continued to march David back along the beach, towards the rocks.

'Jürgen, stay away from him. It's not necessary. We'll be gone in half an hour.'

When Barzel did not so much as break stride, Kleist took his right hand from his pocket. He was holding a pistol. *'Barzel!'*

At that the other man faltered. 'You don't understand,' he said in a weary voice, as he began to turn. 'You're not going anywhere. You shouldn't rely on fax machines.' He was nearly facing Kleist, not quite. Suddenly he clasped his hands, bringing the Luger up to horizontal; and Kleist fired three times.

Barzel stared at him, not accepting that the reality of his fate could ever be death. He dropped onto his knees and fell forward in two distinct movements, as if at exercise. When

David rolled him over his face left an impression in the sand, like a mould for a death-mask.

Something rectangular and white lay on the beach, half-concealed by Barzel's body. David picked it up, scarcely daring to believe what he held. But yes — in the top right hand corner, by the light of the moon, he could make out a handwritten number amongst typescript; and, centred upon the page, a single word in black capitals. He could not decipher that, but nor did he need to.

Krysalis.

Suddenly Anna came to life. 'I'm not dreaming,' she cried. 'Tell me I'm not dreaming, oh *David*!'

As he rushed to take her in his arms, no longer afraid of the consequences for they were going to die anyway, Kleist rapped, 'Listen! Can you hear it?'

At first neither of the Lescombes understood. Then David caught the sound of a muted engine, as yet still far offshore. He could not see the boat yet, only its mother ship, visible as a silhouette still far out to sea but already careering towards them. A coastal patrol craft . . .

He swung around to face Kleist. 'What happens now?'

Kleist allowed the gun to slip from his fingers, and sank down to join it. 'Don't . . . know.'

'Why did you stop that other one from killing me?'

For answer Kleist merely stared at Anna. Then he shook his head and laughed. 'Because I'm dead anyway,' he said; only the curious elation in his voice would have gone better with 'I'm free now', or something like that. 'I'd betrayed them, and they found out. I should have known they would.'

'Betrayed *them*! So why didn't he kill you earlier?'

'Because Barzel had to wait for the submarine, to be sure of getting away, along with Anna. Until he was safe, he needed me to control her.'

'Submarine . . . ?' David struggled to make sense of what Kleist was saying. Suddenly it all came together. 'That boat we just heard . . .' He spun around, only to be faced by the impenetrability of night. 'It's from a sub . . . *Anna! Run!*'

But then from out of the darkness by the water's edge a hoarse voice shouted, *'Barzel!'*

Before Hayes died he had succeeded in opening up a Pandora's box of doubts, so that Albert, like Pandora, was left only with hope. He perfectly understood the chance he was taking, but they did not pay him to duck risks. His course was clear: he had his orders and would obey them.

He also had his agreement with Redman to honour.

Perched on top of the bridge, the sling of the FR-F1 tight around his left arm, he knew that even for this, the greatest sniper rifle ever made, it would be an impossible shot at the best of times, without an injured hand to worry about. But just as he had to take risks, so it was part of his job to put the bullet where it mattered.

Albert hugged the Sopelem nightsight nearer to his eye. Range five hundred, closing. He evaluated the ship's movements, counting seconds between troughs and highs. Four hundred . . . feed it into the computer along with everything else, let the brain do its own calculations, don't disturb it, trust your instincts . . . how long before Vassili switched on the spotlight, speed, range, movements . . .

First the woman, stop the disease from spreading, then the man, that was what 'Gandergoose GQEQ' meant, sauce for German quarry, sauce for English quarry . . .

Closing, closing . . . tight group of three, one of them sitting down, that would be David, a prisoner, of course, he can wait, *what was that beside him, ignore,* what would she do, what would she do next . . . ?

The Soviet landing party had seen the *Lindos* by now. Some were taking cover behind their own boat. Lights dotted the luminous blue circle into which Albert was peering, automatic fire . . . hold it, Vassili, don't panic, hold your fire while Anna works out what to do.

Albert knew. He had lived with this woman until she'd become a part of him and he of her. He was inside Anna

424

Lescombe's head now. Besotted with Kleist, she would accompany him aboard the submarine; but first she would want to kneel down and hold her husband and bid him look after Juliet . . .

Range three hundred . . . no light, not yet, not yet, ignore the bullets, Soviet ping-pong balls, they never hurt anyone . . .

She'd hold David, wait, get it right, get it right, three bursts of two, 'double-tap', first the woman, then the man, last the husband for Redman, 'two for joy', David and Anna, that was the deal . . . hold it, Vassili, *hold it*! Wait for the Greeks to return fire, make it look like a stray round, there mustn't be any witnesses, *no traces*, Shorrocks had said, *accidental death, act of God, no traces, no traces* . . . what's that on the beach, looks like another man, lying down, ignore, ignore, shoot before the light, *take the first pressure*, range two hundred, *fuck those bloody dogs*! Wave trough, rising, rising, wind gust, second pressure . . .

That's not David sitting on the beach!

Freeze!

Albert nursed the trigger home.

The Soviet marines had beached their boat, but even when David pulled Anna's arm she refused to move. She was staring at Kleist who sat resting his head on his forearms. Suddenly all the emotions which had warred inside her for so long coalesced into a single passion, and that was rage.

'You . . . *bastard!*' Her mouth formed the words, but no sound came out. She approached him cautiously, as if afraid he might yet have the power to destroy her. 'They needed you to *control* me, did they? And you betrayed them, you couldn't even keep faith with your own side . . .'

'Anna!' David tugged her sleeve, but she shook him off.

'*You couldn't even play straight with Ilsa!*' So many years of manipulation, and damage, and the uprooting of love before it could grow. '*You sacrificed your own sister!*'

425

'And you,' Kleist said quietly. 'Did you keep faith with your own child?'

Oblivious to danger, she raised her hand to strike him. At that moment the first fusillade of automatic fire rang out, and David flung himself on top of his wife, dragging her to the ground.

As they fell, some hard object ploughed into the sand between Kleist's feet, spattering his face with grains.

A shaft of light burst from the *Lindos*, swiftly raking the beach. David hugged Anna to him and rolled away from Kleist. As the Soviet landing party answered a volley of fire from the Greek patrol craft, David grabbed her hand, leapt up and sped towards the nearest trees.

To the Lescombes, lying in the brushwood, the fight seemed to go on for ever. In truth, the exchange was a short one, lasting less than a minute. The Soviet contingent, six of them, were both outgunned and pinned to the beach by the *Lindos'* searchlight. They made a last stand behind their upturned dinghy but it did not take the Greek machine-gunners more than a few seconds to find the range, and then streams of bullets sliced up the flimsy cover like so many chain saws.

The firing stopped as suddenly as it had begun. From his perch atop the bridge of the *Lindos*, Albert surveyed the deserted beach, now as dazzlingly illuminated as a football stadium ready for an evening fixture, and he sighed. Hearing footsteps on the metal-runged ladder behind him, he turned to see Vassili's head come into view.

'All right?' the Greek inquired.

'Yes, thanks. Any survivors?'

'Unlikely. We're sending men to look.'

'What are you going to do about the bodies?'

'Lose them.' Vassili's smile was friendly, but it did nothing to dilute the quiet authority in his next words. 'You can stand down now. We've won.'

'Yes.' Albert dismantled his rifle and replaced it in its carrying-case, out of sight of curious eyes.

'Where's Hayes?' Vassili asked.

'Haven't seen him for a while. Sorry.'

While they spoke, the crew of the *Lindos* had been unshipping her inflatable rubber dinghy. Albert and Vassili stood together on the roof of the bridge, watching its progress towards the shore.

'So much trouble,' Vassili said, 'for a worthless file.'

'Worthless?' Albert's voice was non-committal.

'Hayes told me many things.' The Greek looked at Albert, and for an instant dropped his mask, letting the other man see his resentment at the way he'd been used. 'Worthless.'

'Ah.'

On the whole, Albert agreed with Vassili. It had turned out a pretty worthless operation, one way and another. Shorrocks' orders were very precise: if there was no other way of preventing Anna Lescombe from going over to the other side with Krysalis, then Albert was to kill her, making it look like an accident. With the *Lindos* now lit up brighter than a floating gin palace there was no longer any scope for an 'accident'; and besides, the lady had not, in the end, gone over. Nor had her husband: one in the eye for Louis Redman, who presumably would now have to look out for another opportunity to 'make an example'. Waste of time all round, really.

Albert found himself looking back along the wedge of moonlight to where Gerhard Kleist still sat on the sand in sepulchral immobility. Not a total waste of time, perhaps . . .

He pointed. 'Here come the Lescombes.'

The dinghy couldn't hold everyone, so Kleist had to stay behind on the beach until David and Anna were aboard the *Lindos*. Albert watched them. As Anna's feet touched the deck David slipped a hand through her elbow and she looked at him. Albert heard her say: 'You must have learned . . .'

'Everything.'

'Even about Juliet . . . at the beginning?'

'Everything,' he said, drawing her close; and Albert suppressed a yawn.

'David,' he called, in his easy, light-hearted way.

The couple at the stern wheeled around, seeking the source of the voice. Albert waited until Anna was looking straight at him. He knew she could not see his face, that to her he was nothing but darkness against a lesser darkness.

'Hullo,' he murmured. 'We haven't met. I'm Albert. Look, have either of you got the file?'

David stared at him. Then, very slowly, he held up Krysalis, which he had somehow managed to keep clasped to his chest throughout, for Albert to see.

'Oh, great. Tell you what . . .' Albert's last words were addressed to Vassili. 'Why don't I go and see about the chaps still on the beach?'

It wasn't until Albert's boat had almost reached the shore that Vassili remembered: only corpses remained on the beach. Apart from Kleist.